"Alexa Riley de...
feel-good roma...
suspense, and ...

"Alexa Riley delivers big time in this first full length scorching romance! Addicting, fun, over the top, and utterly delectable, *Everything for Her* is a guaranteed delight from start to stop. I couldn't put it down!"
—Angie, *Angie and Jessica's Dreamy Reads*

"Alexa Riley has given me everything I want and more. Sizzling passion, a devoted and loyal hero and a safe love story that has me sighing with pleasure at the end."
—Nichole, *Sizzling Pages*

"Just when you think Alexa Riley can't possibly get any better with their over the top romance, they go on and deliver a sizzling romance in their debut full-length novel, *Everything for Her.* Charismatic characters, palpable chemistry, blazing hot sex scenes, and raw emotions make this book an easy one to devour. Alexa Riley packs a one-two punch of entertainment that will have readers begging for their next Alexa Riley fix."
—Michelle, *Four Chicks Flipping Pages*

"Alexa Riley sucks you in like a vortex and grips your heart from the start like only she can do. No one else can give you an insta-love and make it 100% believable. Be prepared to go on a journey of love, uncertainty, devotion, and passion. This is the sexiest book I've read all year. You will be on the edge of your seat trying to figure out what will happen next. Prepare for your heart to pound rapidly in your chest and for Miles and Mallory to steal your soul."
—Tina, *Bookalicious Babes Blog*

ALEXA RILEY

EVERYTHING
for Her

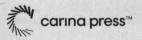
carina press™

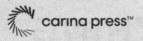

carina press™

ISBN-13: 978-0-373-00452-2

Recycling programs
for this product may
not exist in your area.

Everything for Her

This edition published by arrangement with Harlequin Books S.A.

® and TM are trademarks of the publisher. Trademarks indicated with ® are registered in the United States Patent and Trademark Office, the Canadian Intellectual Property Office and in other countries.

www.CarinaPress.com

Printed in U.S.A.

Author's Note

We wrote *Everything for Her* based on what we admire most in romance. Obsession, seduction, love and lots of steam. We hope you enjoy our first full-length novel and get lost in the story of Mallory and Oz. Bottoms up!

Dedicated to dirty books and friendship. We couldn't imagine our lives, or a world, without both.

EVERYTHING
for *Her*

Coming April 2017 from Alexa Riley and Carina Press

His Alone

PREFACE

Miles

I'VE WATCHED HER since the beginning.

It's funny, but I don't really remember much before her. It's as if I could split my life into two halves. Before her and after. I remember my life with my parents, and I remember getting into college, but it's all gray before her. Until the day I saw her, there was no color. But once my eyes landed on her for the first time, it was like when Dorothy landed in Oz and she opened the door. The world went Technicolor, and she was my very own Glinda the Good Witch.

I was twenty-two years old the first time I saw her. She was seventeen and competing in a state-level high school math competition.

Yale University asked me to represent them as a student judge, and I nearly declined. The state of Connecticut is small but houses one of the greatest Ivy League colleges in the country. One that makes becoming a standout almost impossible. I was among the top 1 percent in my class as a senior at Yale, with a major in statistics.

The only reason I'd accepted the invitation was to play a part. Many expected me to follow in the footsteps of my father, and I wanted them to believe that, but my end goal was a little different than anyone knew. I was on the path of revenge, but playing a part would help me on that path. Rubbing shoulders with the same men my father did, even if it left a bitter taste in my mouth.

Agreeing to judge the competition was life-changing. The bitter taste in my mouth altered that day. A sweetness took over. I wanted it. Needed it.

I'll never forget the way she looked, so confident and sure of herself. I watched her from a distance, like you would a lioness in the wild. I didn't approach her and I didn't disturb her, but I never once took my eyes off her.

I found out later she was being sponsored by her high school so that she could attend the competition. She had no family and was being raised in a group foster home, so her school funded the trip. She was smart, and they wanted to see her succeed, which she did.

I saw so much in her as she competed. She knew all the answers and was absolutely sure each time. She trusted her instincts, and they didn't let her down. There was so much potential in her just waiting to be unleashed. I wanted to sit down and have her tell me everything, anything, as long as she talked to me.

She swept the competition and won first place in her division. I was strangely proud of her.

When she walked out of the hotel ballroom after the competition was over, I let her go. It was the hardest thing I'd ever had to do. But I knew that if I went after her too soon, or too fast, she would run. Not only was she too young for me, but something about her told me she was the kind of woman who came along once in ten thousand lifetimes.

This wasn't to be rushed. It was to be savored.

I may hate my father, but I've learned from his mistakes. I'm going to use those mistakes for my own advantage. He's smart but sloppy at the same time and it's been showing. But I know if you want something, you work hard for it, plan out all the details to make it yours.

From the beginning, I knew that she would be my greatest achievement, so the day I let her go, I set down a path for her.

A path to me.

No one knows it's been me behind the curtain, pulling the strings. I've constructed everything in our lives so that at the perfect moment, I could have her.

The time has come.

ONE

Mallory

"JESUS, THAT THING is hideous." Paige scrunches her face in disgust as she continues to run on the treadmill. She set it up in the living room first thing when we moved in. Her long auburn ponytail bounces behind her with each stride. She's been on it for thirty minutes now and hasn't even broken a sweat.

When we lived together in the dorms, she always went to the gym at the university, which she hated. I'm guessing it was because guys were usually hitting on her. If it's anything like when we go out, I'm sure there were a few trying to talk to her. But this is just a guess because I'd never gone to the gym with her, nor would you ever see me on that treadmill. I don't run, unless I'm running late, which I never am.

"What? It's cute," I protest, pulling the pink fuzzy blanket to my cheek, rubbing it against my skin. "And it's so soft."

She shakes her head at me, and I throw the blanket across the back of the leather sofa.

"This place has no color. It's gray, black or white. It needs a little something." I move the blanket to show her how good it looks. I know nothing is going to get her to love the pink throw, but I know she'll let me keep it here.

Paige doesn't really care about fashion or design. She likes things simple, clean and put where they belong. It's a trait I loved when we got paired up to room together at Yale. Being crammed in a small space with someone else is rough, so it makes things easier if the other person is clean. It's something I came to value after growing up in foster care, where you're often shoved in a room with three to four other girls.

"Leave the stupid pink blanket. What's next? Vases with fake plastic flowers and throw pillows?" This time she smiles as she says it.

"No, not plastic flowers. That's tacky." I turn around, picking up another box we need to unpack. We've been here for a few days but all I've been doing is reading anything and everything I can about Osbourne Corp's financials and investment reports. "But throw pillows might be nice, maybe some pictures on the walls, too," I suggest, making her laugh. I want this place to be homey. I'm starting off on a new adventure, and this is the first part of that.

Paige and I have been together since freshman year at Yale. We were practically attached at the hip when we weren't in classes. We oddly fit together, even though we're so different. I think it's why we work well together. We balance each other out. She's loud, in your face and always seems to be two steps ahead of everyone else. She's petite, but I once saw her take a two-hundred-pound man to his ass when he got a little handsy with me in a bar.

Most of the time she's like an older sister. She's the closest person to me in the world and the only person I can count as family.

"You can do whatever you want, Mal. Just don't paint the walls pink." She pulls the emergency stop chain and jumps off the treadmill. "Please."

"I wouldn't do that," I protest as she grabs a water bottle from the refrigerator in the kitchen. The condo has an open floor plan for the most part. The living room, dining room and kitchen all flow together, and there are two bedrooms down the only hallway, each with their own bathroom.

It's more than I could've ever dreamed of having, and Paige is the only reason I'm standing here to begin with. It's her condo. She bought it when I said I'd gotten an offer to intern at Osbourne Corporation, and she'd insisted we go.

I wasn't going to pass on the opportunity, knowing there was no way I could make it in New York. I didn't have the funds, and to be honest, I was scared shitless. I'd yet to fail at anything in my life, and I wasn't ready to start. I'm not cocky, just determined. Osbourne Corp is no joke. They offer three internships a year, and I'd landed one. I may have had a leg up because I'd also earned one of their top scholarships and they were already aware of my performance. The scholarship paid my way through college and covered everything: board, food, books—you name it. I graduated at the top of my class and first in my major. Osbourne Corp had given me my education, and the internship would give me a chance to show them what I'd become because of them.

I wanted to prove myself, but trying to make it in New York intimidated the shit out of me. Thankfully, Paige was there to offer this place and help me start a new chapter in my life.

At first I was disappointed I didn't get any other offers after graduation, but the job market is tough. I guess I was surprised that I got an Osbourne scholarship and then an internship offer but never any other offers.

"You look like you're thinking awfully hard over there," Paige says, taking another big chug from her water bottle before putting it down on the counter.

"I guess I'm a little nervous about Monday."

"Are you serious right now?" Paige comes over to stand in front of me, taking the moving box from my hands and putting it back down on the ground. I know what's coming, and I crack a smile. It's something she does for me sometimes. "Who busted their ass through high school and got herself a full fucking ride to Yale?"

"I did."

"Who graduated top of her class?"

"I did."

"Who corrected that cocky-ass-dipshit Professor Sitten when he tried to say your answer was wrong, and then broke it down to him like he was in the second grade and made him cry?"

"He didn't cry."

"Oh, he cried on the inside. Trust me. I know the face a man makes when he's crying on the inside."

I can't help but laugh because it's true.

"Who?" Paige pushes.

"I did."

"And who landed one of the best internships in the country?"

"I did."

"Fuck yeah, you. You're going to rock that accounting department. You're going to own those numbers or whatever it is you do with them," she says, like reading numbers is like reading alien code.

"I love you." I pull her in for a hug. I know I'm smart and can do anything I put my mind to. It's easy to be driven when you only have yourself to rely on your whole life. Only you can catch yourself, and that's how it's always been, until Paige pushed herself into my life. Sometimes I still need a little shove, and she has enough confidence to easily hand one out.

"I'm hard not to love." Her freckled nose turns up, and she makes a smug face.

"Except when you're making men cry on the inside," I add.

She shrugs before picking up the box, taking it over to the coffee table and ripping off the tape.

"We should have burned all of this stuff instead of taking it with us. I think I can still smell ramen noodles. I swear the whole floor of our dorm smelled like it."

She waves her hands over the box like she's trying to air it out.

I come around beside her, dropping down on the couch as I watch her pull random things out of the box. This one is mainly filled with framed pictures. I love taking pictures; capturing our memories. Paige hated having her picture taken, but after four years I've worn her down and now she smiles when I tell her to. I never really had much to be happy about, didn't have anything I wanted to capture before college, so I kind of went nuts at first.

"Which of these are mine?" she asks, going through them.

"Oh, now you want one?" I smile, rolling my eyes.

She pulls one out from our freshman year. I'd dragged her to a football game, saying we had to get all the college experiences we could. I was very eager to soak up everything my first year. As much as I rubbed off on Paige, she'd rubbed off on me, too, because by junior year I was much more blasé about college life.

"God, I must love you. I can't believe I went to this with you."

She hands me the picture, and I burst out laughing. I'd taken a picture of us at the same time she was dumping her soda over a guy's head. He'd been talking about loving new freshman pussy for half the game and Paige finally cracked.

"That one's mine." She takes it back from me.

"Oh, I've got copies," I remind her. That was the day I realized Paige wasn't a normal student at Yale. The boy she'd dumped the soda on tried to get her expelled, but he was the one who ended up waist-deep in trouble.

Paige's dad had money and power, but it wasn't something we talked about much. She didn't offer a lot on the subject, and I didn't push. I had things of my own I didn't care to talk about, too.

"I'm over this." She gets up and plops down on the other sofa, throwing her feet up on the coffee table. I cringe a little. This table is probably worth more than I could make in two months, just like the rest of the furniture in here. Most everything was already here before we moved in. Paige acted like it was no big deal.

"You've literally unpacked one frame."

"You need to feed me, or I'm going on strike."

"I'm actually pretty hungry, too. You're from here—

what should we order?" I pull my phone from my pocket and look for local delivery places.

"Forget that. We're going out. It's Friday night, and it's our first night in the city."

"We have a lot to unpack and I need to study more." I pick up one of the books off the coffee table to remind her. The internship had sent over a stack of books and folders I've been combing over. I've read them all at least three times but I still want to go over them again. Maybe make some flash cards. I don't want to be asked a question and not know the answer immediately.

"Nope. We have all weekend. I've decided. Dinner and then out for a few drinks. We can unpack Saturday and Sunday, and you can do all your overthinking and analyzing about your new job then. Tonight let's have some drinks and shake our asses."

She grabs the book from my hand, tossing it back onto the coffee table and knocking the stack of books over as she hops up from the sofa, then holds on to me and pulls me with her.

"We haven't unpacked our clothes or makeup or anything!" I try to reason with her as I think about what I'm going to wear. This is New York. Aren't I supposed to meet, like, a sheikh or something? All I really have are jeans and tops. And a few business clothes I'd picked up for my new internship.

"We can do a little of both. Get some stuff unpacked while we get ready."

"I'm not sure I have anything that will work for whatever it is you have in mind," I tell her, following her to our rooms, dodging random boxes in the hallway.

"Simple and sexy. Wear your tight black pants, and

you can wear my black boots. Then all you have to do is find a cute top."

"That'll work for where we're going?" Before this I'd been to New York twice and was completely lost both times. It's a little overwhelming for me, a step out of my comfort zone. Even after being at Yale for four years, I still sometimes feel out of place, like I don't quite fit in.

"Mal, I'm not taking you anywhere crazy. Just getting a steak down the street and stopping in somewhere we can have a few drinks. Girls' night."

I know she added the last two words to sucker me in.

"Can I do your hair?" I ask, wanting to play with her long auburn locks.

"Will you eat whatever I order?" she fires back. Paige has this thing where she likes to pick up the bill, but she also likes to eat at the most expensive places. No one can rip through a steak like her. I had to stop fighting her on picking up the bill, but I try not to order anything crazy-expensive. She's not having it tonight, it seems.

"Deal."

"No hair spray," she adds quickly.

"No appetizers."

"Fine, hair spray," she grumbles before heading into her room, making me burst into laughter. Maybe I can talk her into a little mascara.

"No makeup!" I hear her yell from her bedroom, making me laugh even harder.

TWO

Mallory

"JAMESON. NEAT," I shout over the music in the club.

After Paige and I finished dinner, we took a cab to the Upper East Side, closer to where our condo is. She said we'd have a couple of drinks before we headed home, and I thought she had something a little tamer in mind. I didn't want this to be a long night. I need to be up early and at it again. I only had days before I started my new job. I should have known better when we pulled up outside a bar and there was a line out the door. Paige wiggled her eyebrows at me as she hopped out of the cab and went straight to the bouncer up front.

I jumped out of the cab behind her and barely heard what she said to the doorman as he unfastened the velvet ropes and waved the two of us in. I didn't get to ask her how she did that before we walked through the double doors and were hit by loud music.

Seven Eight Nine is more of a club than a bar. The place is swanky, but there's a dance floor in the middle of the place and a DJ throwing down like it's New Year's Eve. It's dark around the edges of the dance floor, with big velvet couches huddled up in corners. I rest against the bar, waiting on my drink as I watch Paige talk to a guy on the other side of it.

As if she senses my stare, she looks across at me and winks.

The music is good, and I've already had one drink, so I'm beginning to really like this place. I ended up wearing my black skinny jeans, teamed with Paige's stiletto boots and a black silky tank top. It's June in New York, and the humidity is killer. Cool air blows around the bar, and I close my eyes, enjoying the breeze.

My short brown hair exposes my shoulders, and the slight breeze is nice. But suddenly the hair on the back of my neck stands up, and it's as if someone is watching me.

I open my eyes, and at that moment, the bartender passes me my drink. I lay some cash down, but a hand comes out holding a black American Express card, and the bartender takes it without a second glance.

Turning slightly, I see a man with dark hair and a short dark beard. He's dressed in a suit and tie and is somewhat hidden in the shadows, but he smiles at me, and I can see his full lips spread, showing straight white teeth. His smile is easy and welcoming, and I smile back.

"You didn't ask," I say to him as the bartender brings his card over and hands it to him.

"What would you have said?" he asks as he signs the receipt and pushes it back to her.

I lean back a little, making an exaggerated motion of looking him up and down. It's too dark to see all of him, but what I can see is very nice.

Being a kid in the foster system, I never had nice things. But I was really smart and did well in school, so because of that I was almost always surrounded by privileged kids. I was raised around Manchester, Connecticut, in a lower-middle-class neighborhood. My foster home didn't have a lot, but the people who took care of us were nice and tried to make sure we all had a good education. Being around rich people, I saw what nice things were. I may have never owned them, but I'm not ignorant to what money can buy.

Looking him over, I see the shoes he's wearing cost more than a month's rent in our Lenox Hill condo. My eyes travel over his fitted suit, which can only be custom tailored, and he reaches down, unbuttoning his jacket and opening it slightly as if to let me get a better look. His dress shirt is crisp white, and his tie a deep purple with little white flowers. His hand comes up to smooth it down, and I notice he's wearing cuff links that are the same color as his tie. I also catch a glimpse of his watch, and I'm sure it's something expensive to go with the ensemble.

When I look up, he's come into the light a bit more, and I see that he's got dark blue eyes, like sapphire stones. He watches me watching him, and the area around his eyes crinkles as his smile widens.

"So?" he asks, leaning in a little more and waiting for my answer.

"Definitely not," I say, taking a sip of my whiskey and letting the warm flavor hit my tongue.

I look at him over the rim of my tumbler, and he lets out a small laugh. He looks like the type of man that smiles a lot. Which is very sexy. His dark wavy hair is cut short, but looks long enough to run your fingers through it. There's so much wave on top, I bet if he grew it long, he'd have gorgeous curls. It's not fair for a man to be so pretty.

"Good thing I didn't ask," he says, and his scent travels toward me as he shifts in a little closer.

He smells like warm amber and honey, and I move toward him unconsciously.

Reaching between us, he takes the glass from my hand but doesn't make contact with my fingers. I'm mesmerized by him, and I easily let him take it from me.

I watch as he turns the glass, placing his lips where mine were, and takes a drink of the whiskey. My eyes move to his throat, where his prominent Adam's apple moves and he drinks the liquid down. Once he's finished, he pulls his lips away slightly, then licks the remaining drop left on the rim of the glass.

It's erotic and sexy, and I've never been so weak at the knees from something so simple.

"I thought since I paid for it, I should at least get a taste."

He turns the glass so that the same spot is facing me, and places the glass gently back in my hand. This time, though, his fingers make contact with mine. I don't speak as they linger there, the two of us locked in an invisible embrace as his fingertips travel to my wrist. He holds them there lightly as he smiles at me again.

This man's smile could knock down a building.

Bringing the glass back to my lips, I taste where his mouth was. I don't know what possesses me in this moment, but seeing him do it makes the need to do the same that much greater. I've never behaved like this before, never been this flirtatious with a complete stranger.

I down the whiskey, drinking what's left in the glass, and it burns the back of my throat. His hand moves from my wrist and takes the glass from me. He sets it on the bar, and then looks back at me, smiling.

"Tell me your name."

He's demanding something I'm not sure I want to give. If I tell him, then we're no longer strangers and the spell may be broken. He's ungodly gorgeous and obviously has money, but this isn't the type of guy I want to get tangled up with.

He's the type of man I saw all over Yale. He'd take me out and go on and on about his bank account commas while I tried to talk about Fermat's Last Theorem. He's entirely too charming for my taste, and a man in a place like this isn't the kind of man I'm looking to settle down with.

"Let's not, shall we?" I say, turning away to the bar to order another drink. I look for the bartender again and talk over my shoulder to him. "Let's pretend this is the Emerald City and you're the wizard behind the curtain."

His hand slides to my hip, and I stop my movement, looking back up to his eyes. There's a desperation there now, as if he's pleading for me to give him something. Anything. His smile is gone, and there's a vulnerable fear in its place. I want to comfort it.

"Please."

I see his lips move, unable to hear anything over the sound of the music. I take a step toward him and lean up to his ear, giving him what he wants.

"Mallory."

When I pull back, I'm suddenly shy, like telling him

my name is exposing something rare in me. It's just my name. Why does it seem so intimate?

Looking over across the bar, I see Paige is still there, chatting with the guy from earlier. She hasn't moved from her spot, and as if she senses me watching her, she looks over at me. She looks at the man in front of me, and then looks back at me, raising her eyebrows. I shrug one shoulder a little and the heat of a blush creeps across my cheeks. I'm not doing anything bad. I don't know why I'm embarrassed.

She gives me a nod and taps her watch. It's our signal to wrap it up. She then turns back to her guy.

"Are you leaving?"

Looking up to him, I smile. "It appears so."

"Give me your number."

It's another demand. There's no question about his approach. He's obviously used to getting what he wants. I look around hesitantly, trying to come up with a good excuse not to.

"If I ask your friend over there, will she give it to me?"

My smile is smug when I look over at Paige and back to him. "Not a chance."

Paige is always keeping guys at a distance from me, saying that I need to wait on the right one and not waste time on losers in college. She was right in saying that most of the guys in college were snobs, and maybe this guy is, too. But never giving myself the opportunity to make a mistake when it comes to men has left me sheltered and inexperienced at twenty-three. I want this guy to disappear, but at the same time I don't.

Looking back to him, I see him reaching into his

pocket and taking out his phone. He stands there waiting, and I decide to give in.

Letting out a huff, I ramble off my number, thinking there's no way he can hear it over this noise. I don't even know this guy. Why would he want to call me? Obviously, I'm not trying to go home with him, so I'm not a sure thing, and that's all any guy in this place is looking for.

Paige walks over as he puts his phone away, and she looks between the two of us.

"You ready?"

"Yeah. I'm right behind you," I say as I watch her walk toward the exit.

Looking into his sapphires, I'm lost again. It's like being in the center of a tornado. Only I don't know if he's the wind that's going to wreak havoc, or if he's the calm in the middle that will hold me steady.

He reaches out and runs the edge of his knuckles along my jaw, as if testing the softness of my skin.

"I wanted more." I can barely hear the words, but I catch them.

I don't know what he means, and I'm not sure how to respond. Instead, I'm frozen in place as he touches me. I should tell him to stop, or walk away, but something about him is mesmerizing, and I can't stop myself from leaning into it.

"She's waiting."

I look over to see Paige leaning against the wall, watching us, and I know I should go.

He drops his hand and takes a step away, smiling at me like before. It's an easy smile, but it doesn't reach his eyes. There's something there, something I can't read, but I want to. I have this need to know everything about this stranger.

Taking a deep breath, I walk a few steps away from him, breaking the spell. Once I've cleared away the fog, I'm more like myself. I turn back to see he's watching me, and this time the smile hits his eyes.

Once we get outside, my phone vibrates in my back pocket, and I pull it out to see if it's him. Paige pulls me into a cab and tells the driver the address as I read the text.

You tasted sweeter than I ever imagined.

I'm buzzed with excitement while texting him back.

What do I call the man behind the curtain?

I smile as I wait for his response.

OZ.

THREE
Mallory

SUNDAY NIGHT, I pick up my phone again, checking to see if I have any new messages, and disappointment hits me again. This is worse than waiting for grades to be posted in college.

"Don't chase, Mal," Paige says, not even looking up from her laptop. We'd finally gotten everything unpacked and settled in, and we decided to spend the rest of the night vegging out while studying and ordering Chinese food. Neither of us had the energy to cook because it would mean going to the store, which we still haven't done. You'd think after living in a dorm for four years we'd be excited about having a kitchen, but takeout is too damn easy.

"What? I was checking my emails," I protest, quickly pulling up my emails like she can see my phone or something.

"Sure. And I'm not cruising Tumblr over here."

I roll my eyes because she's right. I *was* checking my text messages. He hasn't texted me since Friday night. I should get back to reading up on Osbourne Corp, learning all I can, but I keep clicking our text messages to see if there's something new, and then reading the last one he sent on Friday.

OZ.

I drop my phone next to me and pick up a textbook and read over the highlights I've made. I've read them so many times I think I can recite them at this point. I last about ten minutes.

"But isn't it my turn to text back?" I pick my phone up and hold it out, showing her that he texted me last. Maybe I was supposed to say something back. I'm not good at this dating thing, seeing as I've never really done it before.

She sets her laptop down next to her on the couch and bends over, looking at my phone screen. She studies it for a long moment, like she's mulling it over.

"If you want to text him, text him," she finally says, leaning back on the sofa and going back to playing around on her laptop. "Not like you can read those books anymore. They look like they are about to fall apart," Paige teases me about my worn books.

"Really?" I ask again. That's not what I thought she'd say. Paige is not about dating. At least, she wasn't when we were in college. I'd thought about doing it a few times, when I'd been asked out, but I ended up siding with her because I wanted to stay focused. School was the most important thing, and I had the rest of my life to date. I must be more excited about the prospect of dating than I thought, because the first guy to show me attention, I'm already pining after. And Oz is definitely not someone I should be chasing. I've seen guys like him in action. I went to school with them. They think money can buy anything, and they burn through girls like I burn through ninety-nine-cent ebook sales.

I hate to judge him before I even know him, but a girl has to be smart. He probably thought when he flashed his American Express card it would have me desperate to crawl all over him. I wasn't impressed. Like being in a museum—look at all the pretty, expensive things, but whatever you do, don't touch.

"Yeah, why not? I mean, don't chase the guy or anything. Make him do the work, but if you want to send him a text, do it. He was cute."

I stare at her. "Is this like the Body Snatchers or something? You said the word *cute* and you're encouraging me to talk to some guy."

"Fine. Whatever. Don't text him," she says defensively.

"Paige, I'm teasing."

"I know. I'm sorry. Just a lot on my mind." Her shoulders drop a little, her auburn hair falling in her face. She scoops it up, pulling it into a ponytail out of her way.

"Want to talk about it?"

"Not really, just going through emails and weighing my options on what I want to do next."

I let it go. Paige will talk when she's ready. She's not someone you make good progress with if you push.

"So," I say, trying to change the subject to something lighter, and her eyes narrow at my tone. "Who was the hunk you were talking to on Friday? Did you get his number?"

"No. I'd be surprised if he even knows how to work a phone," she growls, clearly agitated about the guy.

"That's some serious aggression you got going on for such a short conversation."

"Let's say we have history, something else I really

don't want to talk about." She shuts her laptop and places it on the coffee table before pulling the pink blanket over herself and turning on the TV above the fireplace.

She's been off since Friday night, and maybe that guy has something to do with it. I would kill to know what history they have. I've never seen Paige give a guy the time of day before. She seems more annoyed with men than anything.

Lying down myself, I pull out my phone and debate what to text, but my phone vibrates before I can come up with something to say.

Oz: I've spent the weekend thinking about you.

My heart flutters. I look over at Paige, who quickly looks away from me.

Me: I'm sure you have better things to do than spend your whole weekend thinking about me.

Oz: That's where you're wrong, sweet Mallory.

Me: Such a charmer.

I wonder if these are lines he uses on women. I debate asking Paige to read the messages, but decide against it. *Keep it fun and light*, I remind myself.

Oz: Seems you bring it out in me.

Me: What did you really spend your weekend doing?

Oz: Aside from thinking about you, I worked. Always working.

Me: You found your way out to have a little fun Friday.

Oz: Lucky I did, or I wouldn't have gotten to see you, gotten a taste.

His words make goose bumps break out across my skin. I bite my lip, having no idea what to say to that.

Me: What are you doing right now?

Oz: Sitting in my office. I finally broke. I thought you'd text me. I tried to hold out, but I couldn't last.

Me: Sorry, been busy. Unpacking and all.

Oz: Just move?

Me: Yep! Brand-new to this whole New York thing. It's a little scary but also exciting.

Oz: You have to let me show you around.

I wonder if he's asking to be friendly, or maybe he's suggesting a date... I look over at Paige, who is now sleeping. I remind myself of her words. *Don't chase.*

Me: Are you asking me out on a date?

I send the text and regret it immediately. Maybe I

should have done, like, a winky face or something so it's more of a tease. Grr.

Oz: Call it anything you want as long as you agree to come.

Me: I'll think about it.

I wonder whether I should go out with a random man I met for five minutes at a bar, but that's what dating is, right? Not like I'm agreeing to go to his place or something. We could meet somewhere. Talk a little. Maybe I can try to see how genuine he is. He seems sweet. Too sweet maybe, like maybe it's a game.

Oz: Fair enough. Think about it over something to eat with me.

Me: LOL. When?

Oz: Now.

Wow, that seems really fast. Here I was wanting him to text me and now he wants to do something right this second. *It's all a game*, I tell myself. He's looking to get laid. I decide to be blunt and to the point. I'm sure that's what Paige would want me to do if I showed her the messages.

Me: I'm not going to sleep with you.

Oz: Sweet Mallory, sleeping is the last thing I want to do with you.

I clench my phone in my hand, hating that I was right. The disappointment is too strong for the short time I've known him. Hell, *known* isn't even the right word because I *don't* know him. How can he already be taking up so much of my head space? Head space that I should have somewhere else right now. Tomorrow is one of the biggest days of my life. That's where my mind should be. Not here, flirting on the phone with someone who wants in my panties. His words irritate me, and I don't like the presumption.

Me: Cocky much? I don't like cocky.

Oz: It's not cocky. It's true.

I take a deep breath and think about my next words.

Me: Sorry, Oz, but I don't think this will work. I'm not that kind of girl. You're a hot guy. I'm sure you can dial someone up and get a hookup if you want.

I send the words with confidence. That's that. But I can't stop myself from staring at the phone, waiting for a message to come. Minutes tick by and nothing.

Frustrated with myself, I click the sound off my phone before getting up from the couch and scooping up my books and folders. I make my way to my room, tossing the phone and everything onto the bed before grabbing a pillow and taking it back out to the living room and putting it under Paige's head. I cover her up more with the blanket and turn off the TV.

I go back to my bedroom, strip off my clothes and jump into the shower, running through my nightly routine. Trying to keep myself from checking my phone, I blow-dry my hair, then go and pick out something to wear tomorrow.

I'm worried that what I have won't work. This seems like the one place I'm lacking at the moment and it's driving me a little crazy that I might come up short here. I can study my ass off but do I look like I belong? New York City is so glamorous, and everyone seems to have the nicest things. I got all my work clothes from Macy's, maxing out a credit card because I needed them. And here I stand, still thinking they won't be up to par. Even the price tags at Macy's made me cringe. If only Paige and I wore the same size. I could borrow some of her stuff. But she's pint-size. Luckily, we have the same size feet, so I do get to steal her shoes.

After deciding on a gray pencil skirt and a soft pink blouse, I move to Paige's room to dig through her shoes. I grab a pair of tan shoes with a lower heel, not knowing how much I'll be on my feet tomorrow. Once I've got everything set out, I grab my laptop and take it to bed with me. I want to refresh myself a little more with the Osbourne Corp before tomorrow. I already know a ton about the company since they were the ones that gave me my scholarships, but I just want a quick update in case someone asks me something tomorrow about their current numbers.

Pulling back the covers, I climb into bed and grab my phone. I finally do what I've been wanting to do for the last hour. I unlock the screen and see three text messages and four missed calls. All from Oz. Holy shit.

Oz: So you think I'm hot?

I roll my eyes at the first text.

Oz: I want you because I know you're not that type of girl. This might surprise you, but I'm not that type of guy. Like I told you. All I do is work. Give this a chance. I'll show you.

Oz: Mallory, please answer me.

The calls came shortly after the text messages. I don't know what to make of all this. He's coming on strong. Part of me likes it, but another part of me is scared. Oz could probably steamroll right over me and my heart.

The phone vibrates in my hand, making me jump. Oz's name flashes across the screen, and I debate answering it. After only a millisecond of hesitation, I cave.

"Hello."

"Mallory." He says my name like he's utterly relieved.

"Oz." I seem to only be able to speak in monosyllables. I'm not sure what else to say.

"Don't do that to me."

"Do what?" I ask, having no idea what he is talking about.

"Tell me you're done, and then not respond. You didn't even give me a chance to explain what I meant." His voice is desperate.

"I'm sorry, it's just…"

He cuts me off. "Promise me you'll never do that again. You'll give me a chance to explain."

I laugh. "I didn't say I was giving you a chance."

"You answered the phone."

He's got me there. I did. I could have just ignored him and then blocked his number.

"Is this just about sex?" I push, wanting to know.

"No, Mallory, this is about so much more."

Could he be telling the truth?

"Promise me," he says again, and I give in. I have this need to give him what he wants.

"I promise." For some reason, it's like I'm promising more than what is being said.

I hear him sigh with relief into the phone. "Are you in bed?"

My heart does that stupid flutter thing again. Maybe I should get that checked out.

"Yes." I blush and snuggle down into the blankets.

"My sweet Mallory."

I should tell him that I'm not his, but I kind of like the way it sounds. It makes me feel nice, which is scary because it should probably make me run.

Wanting to break the silence, I try to come up with something that doesn't have the potential for innuendo.

"I start a new job tomorrow. It's my first day working at Osbourne Corp. Have you heard of it?"

"Yeah, I've heard of it."

I expect him to say more, but he doesn't. Normally when I mention Osbourne to people, they just rattle on and on about it.

"I'll let you sleep," he says, not offering up any more

conversation. It's strange. He's already so familiar, yet he's a total stranger. "I'll text you tomorrow."

"Good night, Oz."

"Sweet dreams, baby."

FOUR

Mallory

I WAKE UP before my alarm goes off. I'm excited for the day. I had a weird dream last night about sapphire-blue eyes and being lost in a maze. I don't think I need a psychologist to translate that for me.

Reaching over to my bedside table, I check my phone and see I have a text message.

Oz: Good luck on your first day. You should wear your hair up.

I raise an eyebrow, wondering what kind of request that is. My hair is kind of short, just coming to my shoulders, but I could pin it up if I wanted to. I don't text back, unsure of what to say—*Thanks, but I'll do what I want?*

I get out of bed, put my phone on my dresser and begin getting ready. I pull on a pale pink lace bra and matching panties. I need some confidence today. Paige gave me an outrageous gift card to Victoria's Secret for my birthday this year, and I went crazy in the underwear department. It's weird, but having something sexy on under my clothes gives me the sense of being a superhero.

After I slip on my skirt and blouse, I walk to the vanity in my bathroom and put on some makeup. It's nothing too heavy, but I want to look polished. I've got time, so when I'm done, I decide to pin my hair up. Completely my own decision and nothing to do with Oz's request. At least, that's what I keep chanting over and over in my mind.

When I'm finished, I slip on my heels and pull on the matching suit jacket, standing in the mirror to check myself out. I look so grown-up. Before I can stop myself I go over to my bedside table and grab my phone. I send a quick text to Oz.

Me: Thank you. And I'll consider it.

No sense letting him know I did what he asked. I just agreed with his idea, that's all.

I grab the last of my things and head out of my bedroom to the kitchen. When I walk in, Paige is holding out a to-go thermos of coffee for me.

"I'm like a proud mom on your first day of kindergarten," she says, beaming at me.

I can't help but giggle and shake my head. She's truly adorable. Taking the coffee from her, I give her a hug and give silent thanks that I have her in my life. I don't know what I'd do without her.

Pulling back, she hands me a brown bag, and I laugh. She packed my lunch?

"You did not."

"Oh, I did. Peanut butter and strawberry jelly. Doritos and a banana." She crosses her arms and looks at me with the smuggest face. "I'm the best mom ever."

"Thank you." I take the lunch and slip it into my shoulder bag. It's a designer purse Paige got me for Christmas and wouldn't let me refuse. She said if I didn't keep it, she would never speak to me again. It's nice because it's big enough for lunch and a couple of necessities, but looks stylish.

"Wish me luck," I say, heading out the front door. I hear her say it as the door closes behind me. I take the elevator to the first floor. Our building is around ten stories, and we live on the third floor.

We're three blocks up from Osbourne Corp, and the heat isn't too crazy this morning. Putting in my head-phones, I switch on an audiobook and make the easy walk to work, trying to focus and pump myself up. I'm smart; I'm confident; I can do anything in the world. My superhero underwear cheers me on as I take the final steps toward the building.

I'd timed it once before, just to be on the safe side, but it looks like I'm only about a fifteen-minute walk from work, which is great. The front of the building is a bit intimidating, but I'm about to be a part of this machine, so I try to step through the glass doors with self-assurance.

Once I'm there, I do as instructed in my new-hire email and head to the front security desk. One of the guards at the desk gives me a temporary pass and takes me up to Human Resources, explaining what's on each floor as we go up.

The building is twenty floors, with the top three floors reserved for the executives of Osbourne Corp. Human Resources is located on the fifth floor, with a cafeteria and company gym located on the floor below.

I may have Googled the building just to find this all out. I might have gone a little overboard with studying. I'll be working on the tenth floor in accounting, and interning with their comptroller on statistical trajectory for the company, along with fulfilling everyday duties.

I'm introduced to Agatha, head of HR, and I like her immediately. She's like a grandmother with a wicked sense of style in her blue suit and red heels. She has a soft smile, and I want to give her a big hug, but I think it might be inappropriate. Agatha takes her time going over my new-hire paperwork, insurance benefits and my bank account information.

Once Agatha is finished, she introduces me to the two other interns who were hired with me for this program.

"Mallory, this is Eric and Skyler."

We all say hello, and I stretch out my hand, greeting each of them.

Skyler looks like a cool kid. She's got on a plum pantsuit with hot-pink heels, and her jet-black hair is stick straight and pulled back in a low ponytail. Her almond eyes are warm, her handshake is firm and her smile is genuine when she greets me. I like her, and I like that there's another girl in the program with me.

Eric seems normal enough. Average height, dark blond hair and blue eyes. He looks like an all-American Abercrombie boy. Definitely the kind of guy I've seen before, and avoided. His eyes move down my body when we shake hands, and I pull my hand back quicker than I intended. He flashes his megasmile at me, which I'm sure has some girls swooning, but I just give him a tight-lipped one in return and pretend nothing happened. I want to make a good first impression, especially with Agatha here, so I keep my mouth shut.

We're taken to our floor and introduced to our supervisor and head of accounting, Linda Green. She's short, and well dressed, with a professional smile. She's enthusiastic about us being on board and welcomes us to the company. Afterward, her assistant shows us to our cubicles, and we all settle in. My desk is between Skyler's and Eric's, but thankfully it's not too cramped.

They drop a stack of work for us to do for the day. I dive right in, going over the numbers in the spreadsheet and even finding a way to do them faster if we just reformat the spreadsheets. I show both Skyler and Eric how I have all of mine done before it's even lunchtime so I decide to write up how to do the sheets faster so everyone knows.

ERIC ASKS US OUT to lunch, but Skyler brought hers, too, so we opt for eating in the cafeteria together. I'd rather stay at my desk and keep working while I eat but they don't have any more reports for me to do since I finished mine so quickly.

At lunch, I learn that Skyler was valedictorian at Stanford and turned down a job at the White House to take this internship. We talk a lot about school and what led us to this job, thankfully steering clear of family talk. I never have much to contribute when people ask about my parents, and when I tell them I'm an orphan, they always look so sad. I grew up in a big foster home, and while it wasn't the greatest, I had nice people who took care of me, and I never had anything bad happen. I've heard so many horror stories that I consider myself lucky.

"You got a scholarship? From Osbourne Corporation?" Her tone of voice makes it sound like she thinks I'm joking.

"Yeah. It was a big shock. I didn't even apply for it. I competed in a couple of state-level math competitions, and afterward, it was offered to me."

"Damn, girl, you must be something special. I've never heard of them doing that." She cocks her head to the side, and then smiles like she's happy to be next to someone she considers her equal.

"From what I was told, it's very rare. And I'm pretty sure that's how I landed here. Either way, I've worked hard to get here and I'm excited to see where it takes me."

"Me, too. I've worked my ass off, and I just hope Pretty Boy didn't skate in on his daddy's name," Skyler says, putting away her lunch wrapper.

"Who, Eric?"

"Yeah. Did you not catch his last name? Westmoreland. If I had to guess, he's related to the governor. That's probably how he ended up here. I could be wrong, and I hope I am, but I'm usually not."

I nod, not commenting as she stands up. She takes out her phone and looks down at it. "We've got fifteen minutes left. I'm going to respond to a few emails and play some Candy Crush before I head back to work." She looks up and smiles. "See you up there."

She winks and walks away with such confidence, it's like she's been working here her whole life. She must have on superhero underwear, too.

Reaching in my bag, I pull out my phone thinking I'll send a text to Paige about the first part of my day. When I swipe the screen, I know I'm grinning like a loon when I see that Oz has texted me.

Oz: How's your first day?

Me: Going good. Just had lunch.

Oz: Good. Let me take you to dinner to celebrate.

My cheeks burn from the blush, and a shot of disappointment hits me as I answer.

Me: Sorry. Already promised my roommate dinner out.

Oz: How about a celebratory breakfast before work?

Me: Maybe.

Oz: Maybe? It's better than a no. I'll come pick you up and have you at work on time. Scout's honor. No funny business.

I laugh out loud at the words *funny business*. He's definitely not giving up.

Me: It would have to be really early.

Oz: You name the time and I'll make it happen.

I bite my lip hesitantly but am way too excited to say no.

Me: Okay. Breakfast.

I text him my address, and he agrees to pick me up at seven in the morning. I get up from the table and head back to my cubicle, and my smile stretches from ear to ear. I have a date. A breakfast date, but still a date.

Before I make it back to my desk, I look down at my phone and see I have a new text. I check it quickly before putting it away and see that it's from him.

Oz: I like the hair up.

As I'm about to ask him how he knows I wore it up, Skyler comes around the corner. Not wanting to look like I'm playing on my phone on company time, I slip it back into my bag and let it go. I'm sure Oz was making a joke after I'd said I would consider wearing it up.

The rest of the day is spent with Eric and Skyler as we're taught a few of the programs used in the company, all three I've already practiced using. I'd seen them mentioned in the folders they had sent me and looked into them all. We also go over what's expected of us each day. There's a lot of grunt work that we're expected to do, but that's part of earning our chops here. I notice that, as we work and things are delegated, Skyler and I seem to agree on it, taking notes, while Eric makes irritated noises. I think she may have been right about him.

When I make my way home after the day is over,

I have a bounce in my step and a smile on my face. I impressed a few of the department heads with how quickly I caught on to everything and my knowledge of the programs. Day one down and I'm excited for what's to come. And a little part inside of me is humming with happiness, because in the morning, I have my breakfast date.

FIVE

Miles

ONE WOULD THINK that having Mallory so close to me after all this time would take some of the edge off. To know I can see her at any moment because she's only a few floors away would help. It hasn't. If anything it's gotten worse.

My already-short tolerance for bullshit is at an all-time low. So much time has already been wasted. I don't want to do this right now because it's something that should have been done weeks ago. Before my Mallory even came to New York.

I was sick of this game I was having to play. Sick of pretending she isn't mine, and making her and I together, common knowledge. It was time everyone knew the truth. These final pieces finally coming together so I could have her.

"These are the final terms you're prepared to offer?" The lead attorney in the room, Mr. Ware, looks up to me for confirmation. Something he shouldn't need at this point. We have been after the deal for months. Fuck, it should have been locked up from almost day one. He knows how bad I want this. I shouldn't even have to have this discussion. We should be on to the next thing already. No wonder lawyers get paid by the fucking hour.

"As I've stated several times today and days before, I'm prepared to offer whatever is necessary to purchase this company. This isn't a negotiation, and if you don't understand what that means, then I can find someone else to manage this deal." I toss my pen on the table, giving him a hard look. I don't like repeating myself over and over again and that seems to be what I'm having to do here. What's the point of hiring the best if I have to go behind him? I would call and make the deal myself but I'm trying to keep it hidden that Osbourne Corp is the one after the deal until it's done. "Ask them what they want and give them the fucking money."

"Yes, Mr. Osbourne. We'll present this new deal and let their team know that we are more than happy to entertain any offers they have." He looks sheepish and goes back to the papers in front of him, straightening them. I don't know if I'm impressed I've intimidated one of the best lawyers in New York or annoyed.

"We aren't happy to *entertain*." I clip the last word to get my point through as I stand. "The only deal I want is the one where you ask them how much and give it to them. In fact offer over their asking price."

"But sir, I think we could get it for less, maybe even—"

I slam my hand down on the table making the whole thing rock. All three of the attorneys give a jerk back, surprised at my reaction. My assistant, Jay, doesn't even flinch, the bored look on her face not changing.

"You seem to have no problem wasting my money when it comes to your services, Mr. Ware." I flatten my hand on the wood table, edging forward. My palm still stings from when I hit the table, but that helps dull the pain I've had deep inside me since I saw Mallory Friday night.

"Sir—" he tries again, but I don't let him. He's wasted enough of my time on this, and either it ends right now, or I'll end him.

"Get it done or." I flip my wrist in a tossing gesture not finishing the sentence. He gets it. I can tell by the widening of his eyes he does. Everyone in the room does. He might be a top attorney but if anyone knows that I get my way, it's him. He's been working with me for years. No one stands between me and my end result. Maybe for a moment, but in the end I get what I'm after, and Mr. Ware has witnessed many of those dealings.

Maybe the threat is fucked-up, but when it comes to this, to her, I don't care. I'll do anything including getting my hands dirty if I have to. A trait I clearly got from my father.

"Now, next item on the agenda. Sarah, would you please inform the room about our next potential acquisition. The details are outlined on the PowerPoint."

I click the remote before dropping back down into my chair and the room turns to the screen on the other side of the room. Sarah, our head of purchasing, presents the data I went over and sent her at the end of last week. On what will happen when we acquire the businesses. All the different options available. I told her everything I wanted and that she needed to put it in a presentation for everyone to see, but I'm still toying with the idea of getting what I need from them and burning them to the ground. They'd probably be better off that way.

I think of Mallory and wonder what she would say

about the numbers I came up with. Would she be impressed or offer her own opinion? It's a funny and foreign thought to me, considering someone else's opinion when making a decision. It's not something I've ever done before, because I never cared what people thought of my ideas. But I find myself listening to Sarah go over everything I'd pulled together, and wondering if Mallory would agree.

Then my mind wanders further, and I think about Mallory in my bed after I've thoroughly loved her. Her mouth still swollen from mine, her hair messy from the things I'd done to her. We would lie there and I would talk about work. Share things with her I'd never shared with anyone else. I push the thought away when my body starts to react to the image in my head.

I wait for Sarah to finish the slides so I can answer any questions the room may have. But I'm comfortable there won't be any. Sarah has been with me for years and I've never had to repeat myself with her. Ultimately I make all the final decisions at Osbourne Corp, but I understand what having a team around me can do.

I try not to think about Mallory because she's been consuming my thoughts all day. I run my hands through my hair to calm myself, and try not to rush through this important acquisition meeting because I'm dying to get to her. Even if it's only a glimpse. I look down at my phone to see if I've gotten any messages, but nothing.

The room goes over the proposal, each of them asking questions while I make notes. This is one of the last buyouts I'll make before my plans are fully in place. I acted too soon with Mallory, and now I'm pushing hard and fast to clear everything up. I've had meetings all day to make this go forward, but I think things are finally settling into place. I'm cleaning up the mess I've made by striking quickly, and doing something I told myself I'd never do again. I showed my hand, and that has to be rectified.

WITH THE SUN SETTING, I dismiss the group, which is all too eager to leave. Even I can sense the tension that's coating the room. I let them know I want responses by tomorrow with concrete plans in place. On the way out, my assistant follows behind me taking notes.

"I want the Harford deal closed by the end of the week," I tell her, hitting the down button for the elevator.

"Hmm. How did you know I could move mountains?" she teases but I keep going, certain that she will in fact move one if need be. Jay might come off a little peppy but it's actually her strong suit. She'll annoy and bug anyone and everyone in this office until she gets what she wants, and that works for me because she's getting what I want.

The elevator dings and we both get on. She hits the button for the lobby.

"What about Mr. Carson? This really is a problem. I still haven't got an email back from him about the Stine project." She lets out an annoyed huff. I know it's because he's working away from the office, meaning she can't go knock on his door every five minutes.

"Fire him. Problem solved."

She smirks. "Someone is extra perky today. Oh, and Taylor Campbell called. Again."

I level her with a stare. Taylor Campbell is an up-

and-coming politician and I can smell his shit a mile away. He keeps trying to get me to come to his events. Something I hate doing. All the people trying to get close, wanting to rub elbows with you. Always wanting something you can give them. I think about Mallory and how she would look all dressed up and on my arm for everyone to see. The thought is appealing but I liked the look of her in my bed more. Just the two of us.

The elevator dings, breaking me from the thought, and I exit. Jay doesn't follow me. I turn and grab the door before it can close. "I left a few things in our share box I need you to clear out. If you work late, have one of the guards walk you to your car."

She smiles. "Worried something might happen to me and you'll never find someone to replace me who can deal with you?" I ignore her because she's probably right. I used to burn though assistants every two months before her. A cold insensitive jerk many had said.

"Call Ivy and have her come in. We have a few things to finally tie up."

SIX

Mallory

"How can you eat all that?" I ask Paige as she shoves a giant piece of steak into her mouth before washing it down with a beer.

"What? We're celebrating here." She cuts another piece of her rib eye and sticks it in her mouth. I have no idea where she puts all this food. Her workouts must really work.

"So, dish. Who do we hate and who do we like?"

I laugh and give her a rundown of how my first day went. It was actually a lot easier and smoother than I thought it would be. I enjoyed everyone for the most part. Eric was a little odd and liked to stare a bit too long, but Skyler was cool. I could see myself easily getting along with her. Eric, I would have to keep an eye on. He seems like the type that would try to take credit for your work or throw you under the bus to save his own ass.

"I knew it'd be easy for you. Shit like that always is." She picks up her beer and polishes it off. I play with my pasta, pushing it around the plate, not really that hungry. I'm energized and excited about everything that's happening. Today went better than I could have imagined and I have plans with Oz tomorrow.

"What about you? Anything on the job front?"

A smile breaks across her face. "Actually yes. I was waiting to tell you, but I applied for a job at Osbourne Corp."

"Really?" The surprise is clear in my voice. I honestly had no idea what Paige was going to do. She got a degree in criminal justice and a minor in cybercrime. She'd talked about doing security, but I had no idea what that entailed. For some reason, I kept picturing her in a car parked outside someone's house, taking pictures and turning in cheating spouses. Maybe giving them an ass-kicking afterward. She's incredible, though, so I know she'll be great at whatever she does.

"They had an opening, so I went in and applied. Got the job right on the spot. Obviously," she says, making me snort.

"Obviously," I agree, smiling at her. "What will you be doing?"

"They're going to train me in different areas and see what works best. I'm hoping to guard one of the higher-ups."

"Like a bodyguard? That interests you?"

"I think it's what I'd be best at," she says, beaming. I can tell she's super excited, which makes me excited, too.

Paige is always well aware of her surroundings, and she remembers everything. She has a photographic memory. It's freaky sometimes, the things she remembers, but she doesn't like people to know that either. It wasn't until we were living together for two years that I finally busted her on it.

"Does that mean I'll get to see you around? Have

lunch together sometimes? Even walk to work together?"

I love the idea of us getting to work together. It might not be together-together, but I'll take it. I don't know anyone here, and I'd like having her at work with me, too. Almost like a comfort. We might be becoming codependent.

"That would be pretty kick-ass. I guess we'll find out soon enough."

The waiter stops at our table, dropping off another beer for Paige. I lift my wineglass and hold it out to her.

"To us. Adulting," I say as we clink glasses and take a sip.

"This definitely calls for dessert," she adds, unsurprisingly.

"When doesn't it call for dessert?"

"Touché, but we aren't splitting this time." She says it like we do that all the time.

"We haven't split a dessert since the snack bar incident, freshman year," I shoot back, giving her a hard look.

"You're never going to let that go, are you? It's been almost four years and you're still hanging on to that. I pity the guy who marries you. You'll never let anything go." She shakes her head like she can't believe me, her auburn hair bouncing.

"You bit my finger." I can't even say it without laughing. When it first happened, I wondered who in the world I ended up rooming with and was a little scared. Now it's just funny.

"Well, don't grab things off people's plates without asking and your fingers will be safe." Her tone implies it's common knowledge that people will bite your finger if you come near their plate.

The waiter comes by again, picking up her empty dish, and Paige immediately requests a dessert menu.

"You done with that?" She doesn't wait for an answer, using her fork to pick bites of my pasta. The law of not taking food clearly doesn't apply to her. Knowing Paige, though, she'd risk a finger bite for food.

I reach for my phone, wanting to see if I have any missed messages, but before I can check, I hear his voice.

"Mallory." The sound rolls over my skin, making goose bumps rise on my skin. "I'm going to pretend you were looking to see if I texted you." Turning my head, I stare up at him.

He looks like he came from the office, wearing the same kind of fitted suit he wore the last time I saw him. This time the suit is a deep maroon, almost black in color. His jacket is open, revealing a vest the same color as the suit, with a black tie over a crisp white shirt. It's sexy as hell when a man has style.

The only thing that's out of place is his hair. It looks like he's been running his hands through it; the dark waves are a bit unruly, but it makes him look impossibly sexy. I'd love to see it long enough for some of the curl to come out. The short dark stubble on his face isn't really a beard and isn't really a day-old shave. It's the kind of length that looks yummy and leaves a mark after kissing. Or so I've been told.

He places a hand on my bare shoulder, and the warmth spreads through my body. I changed out of my work clothes when I got home, putting on something more casual before we went to dinner. It's so hot out that I put on a thin tank top and some shorts, leaving as much skin exposed as possible. Now I feel nearly naked as the simple touch turns almost intimate.

He leans down next to my ear as his thumb strokes my skin. "I did."

"Oz. What are you doing here?" I ask, flustered by his presence.

He smiles, and it's then I see he has dimples. I must have missed them in the dark club the other night. They make him look even more attractive, and I didn't think that was possible.

"Sir," I hear someone say, drawing my eyes to a man in a suit. I'm guessing he's the restaurant manager or maybe even the owner. I'd seen him working the room while we ate dinner. "I didn't know you were joining us this evening. I'll get your table right away, Mr.—"

Oz holds out his hand, cutting off the man's words. "I'll sit here." His voice is firm allowing no questions. He pulls out the extra chair at our table, sitting down without even being invited.

"Of course. I'll have a drink brought over," the manager says without even having to ask what he wants. It's clear they know him here. It makes me wonder who he is. He seems to be more than some rich guy. Those kind of men are everywhere in New York. Part of me wants to ask who he is, but the other part doesn't want to burst this bubble we're in. He's on a level I can't compete with, and I don't want to bring that to reality yet. I want to enjoy all the things he's doing to me.

Oz places one hand on mine on top of the table and lazily strokes the inside of my wrist. Once again just doing what he wants. No question. It's an intimate hold, like he's been doing it forever. I stare at him, still shocked. I'm not sure if I'm excited about him being here or not. This wasn't the outfit I had planned for when I'd see him again. I hadn't come up with things to talk about yet. I take a breath, trying to calm myself. *Dating isn't like studying for a test*, I tell myself.

"I'm Miles," he says to Paige, holding out his other hand to her. She shakes it.

"Miles?" I query. I guess I only know his first name, or what I thought was his first name.

"Only you have the pleasure of calling me Oz, Mallory."

His soft smile—along with knowing that something is mine only—makes butterflies take flight in my stomach. It makes it sound like we're a couple and I have my own little nickname for him. It's ridiculous, and I have to bite my lips to keep from smiling.

"The guy from the club and the one who's been texting Mal?" Paige asks, dropping his hand.

"You've been talking about me?" His eyes come back to mine, the smile still lighting up his face. I don't think I've ever really thought about a man's smile before, but his makes me warm inside. And knowing I'm the reason for it makes me all tingly.

"Yeah," is all I can manage to get out. Jesus, I'm terrible at this. "What are you doing here?" I say hurriedly, trying to cover up my awkwardness. I never thought I was shy, but then again, I've never been attracted to someone like I am to him. Something about him is different. Maybe because he doesn't take no for an answer. When I push him he only pushes back and for some reason I like that. Probably more than I should. Maybe it's the sweet way he does it.

"I come here a good bit. It's close to home, so I can pop in for a quick meal from time to time. It's nicer than sitting at my desk or alone at home."

I immediately regret asking what he's doing here. I had assumed maybe he tracked me down or something, but I see that's not the case. If it's close to his home, then that means he lives close to Paige and me. We're only about two blocks from our condo.

The manager appears again, Oz's drink in hand. "Can I get you anything to eat, Mr.—"

"Dessert," he says, interrupting him again. The manager almost seems flustered now.

"I'm down with that," Paige chimes in.

"She doesn't share," I add.

"One of everything then," Oz says, slowly running the tip of his finger over my wrist.

"There are eight desserts," the manager says, like he can't believe Oz is going to order them all.

"Should I order two of everything since she doesn't share?"

I laugh, knowing that comment will definitely win him points with Paige.

"Oh, I like him," Paige says, and I laugh.

"I like that sound." Oz's eyes are on me like no one else is at the table. His gaze is romantically possessive as his fingers continue to slowly caress me.

"Hmm?" I lean in a bit more toward him, moving closer without thinking. I want to see if he still smells like warm amber and honey, a smell I can't seem to stop thinking about now.

"Your laugh. It's lovely. I like it. I like even more that I made you do it."

I'm in way over my head with him. He's too charming, too consuming and already acts like I'm his. I could get lost in him far too easily.

"One of everything should be fine," comes flying out of my mouth. My face heats, knowing everyone heard what he said. He's so bold with his words. Uncaring of anyone hearing what he said. It's a little intimidating. You'd think I'd be used to it living with Paige, but he keeps knocking me off my feet.

My eyes dart over to Paige, who's studying us. She's quiet, which isn't like her. Even less so when a man is hitting on one of us. She's normally quick to shut it down or even poke at something they said, trying to irritate them.

"Perfect." His finger strokes across my cheek, like he's touching my blush. I actually jerk back. He pulls his hand away, and the look on his face is as if I struck him. For a second he looks almost pained.

"Sorry. You caught me off guard," I try to explain, hating my reaction. I'm not used to being touched.

"No, I'm sorry." He gives me a long look, one I can't read, before pushing back his chair. "I'll leave you ladies to it." He extends his hand to Paige once again. "It was a pleasure to meet you." She shakes his hand and nods.

"You don't have to go. Dessert is coming," I protest, guilt growing, like I made him uncomfortable or something. Wow. Maybe I should have tried dating in college, because I'm seriously awkward at this. Then again, I don't think anyone I've ever met would have had me tripping over myself like this. Not to mention no one ever piqued my interest like this either.

As he turns back to me, his sapphire-blue eyes have something hidden in them. He leans down and gives me a kiss on the cheek, and for a moment he lingers there, his soft lips grazing where he touched moments ago, and I finally get that warm amber and honey smell I'd been craving. Desire runs through my body, and a chill races down my back, making my nipples hard. An audible breath leaves my lips, and I close my eyes, completely taken by the slight contact.

"Enjoy your dessert, sweet Mallory. I'm sure it won't be as decadent as you."

With that, he's pulling back and heading across the restaurant. I watch as one of the hostesses steps in front of him as he tries to leave. She looks like a model who moonlights here to make ends meet. She's flawless with her straight blond hair and legs that go on for days in her short black dress. She reaches out to touch his arm, but he sidesteps her, giving her a firm head shake, clearly dismissing her, before exiting out the front of the restaurant. What was that all about?

"That was intense," Paige says, pulling my eyes away from the door.

"Was that a goodbye?" Maybe my awkwardness was too much for him. He shot out of here rather fast.

"Well, yeah, he left." She eyes me like I'm crazy and doesn't get what I mean.

"No, I meant like goodbye-goodbye. No more texting me or whatever." I wave my hands around like that might help explain what I mean.

"No." Her eyebrows rise, and she shakes her head

like I'm crazy. "That man is hooked." She says it with such conviction that I'm almost afraid to doubt her. But yet I still do.

"How do you know?"

"Anyone with eyes could tell, Mal. He's into you. Like really *into* you."

Just then our desserts arrive. Three people drop them off, and the plates and bowls cover the entire table.

"Jesus." Paige's face lights up like it's Christmas morning. "Marry him," she says, picking up a fork and digging in.

"The check has been taken care of, ladies." Without waiting for a response, the waiter scurries from the table.

I pick up my phone and see the text that Oz was talking about.

Oz: I spent an entire meeting not paying attention to anything that was being discussed, nodding along. If I agreed to give my company away, I blame it entirely on you. And if one of the questions my secretary asked me was about attending some charity event, then you're coming with me. It's the least you could do.

The words make me smile.

"Looks like someone is equally hooked."

That's an understatement. I'm far too gone for Oz. I'm already freaking out that I blew things.

My phone buzzes, a new text from Oz. My heart skips a beat.

Oz: I forgot to tell you how stunning you looked. I was too busy staring at you. I couldn't help myself.

Me: You looked pretty handsome yourself.

Oz: I can't wait to see you tomorrow and have you all to myself.

Me: Me neither.

I look up, and Paige is in a dessert fog. It's then I see the hostess who tried to talk to Oz earlier giving me a death glare. I look away. I definitely don't like that. What if this guy has a line of women I'll always have to put up with? It makes me wonder who he is, but dealing with women he's left in his wake isn't something I'll do.

Me: Your hostess is giving me a death look.

Oz: Is Paige still with you?

His text comes fast.

Me: She has eight desserts to get through. We might never leave.

Oz: She isn't my hostess.

Me: Okay. But I think she thinks she is.

Oz: I've never said more than table for one to her, so

I'm not sure how she could be mine. The only thing I want to be mine has me on the chase for her.

His words calm me, and my jealousy dissipates.

Me: I'm not making you chase me.

Oz: Oh, but you are. It's a chase I'll enjoy every moment of, if it gets me you.

SEVEN

Mallory

I HAVE A restless night, the nerves of anticipation keeping me up. I have dreams where I'm on the run and Oz is hunting me. The last dream I remember is being in a grassy field, hiding among flowers. Oz finds me and holds me down while he kisses my body. I wake up covered in sweat and more turned on than I've ever been in my life.

Looking at the clock, I see it's before six in the morning. I give up on trying to go back to sleep after that dream, so I reach over and grab my phone. There's a text from Oz lighting up the screen, and I smile like a lunatic.

Oz: I can't wait to see you today. It's been too long.

Me: Did you forget you saw me last night?

Oz: You're up too early. Go back to sleep, baby. And I would never forget seeing you.

My cheeks burn. Thank God he can't see my violent blush.

Me: Maybe I can't wait to see you today, too.

Oz: You have no idea what hearing you say that does to me.

Biting my bottom lip, I try to think of a sexy response, but he's quicker.

Oz: What color tie should I wear today?

I like the notion of picking out something he's going to wear, that I could be a part of his day in some way.

Me: Blue...like your eyes.

Oz: I prefer yours. Light gray with just a hint of gold.

Me: Someone's been paying close attention.

Oz: My sweet Mallory, if only you knew.

I love how he calls me his. I should be putting up more of a fight, but it's so nice to belong to someone.

Me: Then gray...like my eyes.

Oz: Anything you ask, it's yours.

With that, I throw off the covers, deciding to go ahead and get ready for our breakfast date. I need to cool off after my steamy dream and all the blushing from our texts. I take a cold shower to finish waking me up and to shut my body down. I don't need to be sitting across the table from him all gooey and doe-eyed.

Oz is a man of power, that much is clear from his presence. I'm a smart woman with self-confidence, and I have a lot to bring to any conversation. I don't want to sit there, tongue-tied because I can't control my erratic hormones.

After my shower, I do my makeup and decide to pin up my hair again. It was nice not having it hanging around my face at work, so keeping it up is totally my decision. Not because I'm seeing Oz this morning. Definitely not.

Once I'm finished doing that, I grab some superpower underwear. I need all the sexy confidence I can get. I decide on a gray satin set, thinking that I want something classy yet sharp. And it has nothing to do with the tie Oz will be wearing. It's all completely coincidental.

I pull out a gray pencil dress that fits my curves nicely. I pair it with a wide black belt and black peep-toe heels. I'm suited up, and it's exactly what I need today. Armor to take on my libido and wrestle it to the ground as I have breakfast with that gorgeous man.

Grabbing my phone, I'm anxious, because I've been avoiding it. I didn't want to be rushed as I got ready, and I've tried to keep myself calm.

Sliding my finger across the screen, I see I have a couple of texts from Oz.

Oz: Wear red lipstick.

Oz: Please.

The request is odd, but I guess since I got to pick out his tie, the least I can do is fulfill his wish. Going to the bathroom, I take out the red lip stain I bought a long time ago. I thought I'd wear it to a party or something but ended up never using it. *I guess today is a day for a power color*, I think as I swipe the brush across my lips. This stuff will take a sandblaster to get off, but at least I don't have to worry about reapplying it or having it rub off while we eat.

I send him back a kiss emoji that's got bright red lips, and he sends back a thumbs-up. It's so silly that it makes me giggle.

Grabbing my notepad off my nightstand, with all my notes from the day before, I slip it into my bag before I sling it over my shoulder and make my way out to the living room. Paige is at the kitchen counter with a bowl of cereal. She's dressed in a white button-up shirt and black slacks. She's currently barefoot, but I see a pair of red heels on the floor beside her.

"Breakfast date?" she asks as I walk in and set my bag down. I nod and try not to blush.

I told her about my date last night after we got home, and she seemed excited for me. It's unusual for Paige to be excited for me to be going out with someone, but I guess she sees something in this.

"Ready for your first day?" I ask, looking her over. Her auburn hair is pulled back in a ponytail, but it looks professional. She's so tiny, but she's got an incredible body, and I'm sure she's going to rock those heels all day without complaint.

"Definitely. I want to get there early. Make a good impression."

I nod as my phone vibrates in my hand. I look down to see a text from Oz.

Oz: On my way to you.

I panic for a second, thinking I'm not ready for him to see the place. What if he asks to see my room? I've got shit everywhere.

Me: I'll meet you out front!

I grab my bag and dash out the door, throwing Paige a goodbye over my shoulder. I hear her laugh as the door shuts behind me, and I make my way down the stairs.

Walking out of the stairwell, I open the door to the lobby and see Oz. He's dressed in a black suit with a crisp white shirt and a heather-gray tie. He looks like some kind of sex god advertising cologne with his gorgeous waves brushed back and his smile so big his dimples show. How I'm still standing and not in a pool of melted need at the sight of him is beyond me.

For a split second I'm surprised he got here so quickly, but it's followed by relief that I didn't let him up to our apartment.

"Wow, you got here fast," I say, walking over to him, trying to grasp my confidence with each step.

"'Wow' is right," he whispers, walking to meet me halfway. "You look stunning."

He comes right to me and puts his hands on the exposed skin of my arms. His warm palms send pleasure through my body. The dress I'm wearing is sleeveless, and he's already taking advantage of what's uncovered.

Leaning in, he places a kiss below my ear. I'm assaulted by his scent, the rich fragrance enveloping me. The intimate sensation of his soft, full lips against my skin has a flood of desire pooling in the lower half of my body. Like nothing I've ever felt before. Fucking hell, I think my knees are going weak. How does he do that?

He pulls back, looking at me, licking his lips. It's incredibly sexy seeing his tongue run along his mouth, and I want to lean up and taste him.

"I thought the red lips would keep me from kissing you. But I guess I found a way."

His voice rolls over me, and it's another way in which I'm lost in his presence. Jesus, this man puts his hands on me and I'm gone. Thoughts of anything else leave my mind. It's scary and exciting all jumbled together.

"Lucky for you it's a stain and won't come off." I blush a little, thinking how terrible I am at being sexy.

He gives me a wicked smile while taking my hand in his. "Challenge accepted."

He leads me from the lobby to a waiting limo. I'm a little surprised at how formal this is, but maybe this is the kind of car he rolls around in. Oz opens the back door and helps me in. I'm flummoxed by the sight that greets me.

When the door opens on the other side and Oz slips in, I look at him in shock.

"I thought this would be…" He hesitates for a second, as if trying to think of what to say. "More intimate."

"So you had breakfast brought to the back of a freaking limo?" I look around at all the trays of food as the car pulls away from the curb. "This is crazy. I was thinking some diner close to work."

"We can do that if you'd prefer it."

I look over and see a little look of disappointment on his face, so I reach out, taking his hand. I don't want him to think I'm unhappy or ungrateful for the over-the-top gesture. I love it. It's sweet he took so much effort to do this. At every turn, this man keeps surprising me, showing me he isn't who I pegged him for that first day. A little guilt hits me.

"No!" I say too loudly, and then try to recover. "No. This is perfect. Thank you. This is more than I expected. It's really sweet."

He squeezes my hand back, and the dimples return. Those adorable dimples are going to break me. Even more so when I say something that makes them appear.

"What would you like?" He indicates the trays, and I'm overwhelmed.

"I think I have too many butterflies to eat yet. Coffee?"

He smiles at my words and reaches for a cup beside him. "Lots of cream, lots of sugar and a dash of cinnamon."

"How did you know that?" I ask, gripping the cup. I take a sip. It's perfect. Exactly how I like it.

"I have my ways," is all he says in response. It warms me that he's taken so much effort to find out little things about me, adding to the bubble around us. It's almost like a thrill and I want to hold on to a little bit of that mystery.

He looks down at my coffee cup, and I raise an eyebrow in question.

"Looking to see if you left a mark." He takes the cup from my hand and places it back in the holder next to him. He looks at me with such intensity, I'm about to ask him what's wrong. But suddenly, his hands come up to my face and his mouth is on mine.

His lips are so soft, but in them is a need beyond anything I've ever experienced. My mouth opens, taking a breath, and his warm tongue slips inside. He moans at my taste, and I put my hands on his shoulders, clinging to him. Not wanting the kiss to end, or the sensations that it's causing. I didn't know a simple kiss could do this. Make every part of you come alive. All thoughts of the world dropping away and leaving only this one moment. But that's because this kiss isn't simple at all. This kiss is everything.

I lick him back, wanting to taste him, too, and needing to be as close to him as possible. I run my hands up the back of his neck and into his hair. My body is out of my control as I grip the short length and try to hold on to him.

His huge hands slide down my sides to my waist. He pulls me to him in a possessive hold, and suddenly I find myself sitting on his lap, his erection digging into my hip. It should probably scare me but it doesn't. It makes me feel desired and feminine. The kiss deepens, and the taste of cinnamon goes from my tongue to his. His cologne rubs onto my body as my full breasts push against his suit. For a split second I want to reach down and rip his shirt open so I can touch the skin of his chest, but as he bites my lower lip, all I can think about is the ache between my legs unlike anything I've ever experienced before. I had no idea it could be like this.

He palms my ass and pulls me closer to his hard cock. I'm sideways on his lap, but I want to wiggle my dress up and straddle him to try to relieve this pressure that's building. I want all of my body against his, and I want it now. It's the first time in my life that I've ever lost control, and it's fucking amazing.

When I make a move to straddle him, one of his big hands comes down to gently rest on my thigh. Breaking the kiss, he looks at me, and I see the need in his eyes matches my own.

"Mallory," he whispers, and it sounds like he's begging me.

Doubts of this all being a game to him slip past me in that moment, in the way he says my name. The hunger he has for me. I've never had that from anyone. To look at me with so much want and need. I want it. I might be jumping off the deep end, this being my first relationship, but for once I don't care. I'm not planning and looking at it from every angle. I'm going and it's a little freeing. To let go. Let him catch me even if it's only for this moment and it's all I have. He could break my heart but I'd still remember every second of this. This seems so right. It has to be. I've never felt like this with another person before and I can't let this moment pass me by. I won't let it.

I try and move again, but he holds my legs together so I can't. When I open my mouth to ask him why he's stopping me, he plays with the hem of my dress.

"This." His voice is soft as his fingertips trail up the inside of my thigh.

I keep my eyes locked with his as I let my legs fall open for his touch. His hand slips under my dress and up to my panties, and I nearly moan at the contact. I've never had a man touch me here, and as Oz's big fingers delicately touch the damp spot on my panties, it nearly makes me combust.

"Oz." There is such need in my voice, but a little panic, too. I want this, but I'm terrified. This is absolutely crazy, but I don't want to stop to think about that right now. Later. I will think through all of this much later.

"I'll take care of you, Mallory. Always."

He slowly pulls my panties to the side, and I shiver at the first touch. He rubs my soaked pussy, reminding me of how turned on I am. His breath catches as he touches me, and knowing he likes it turns me on even more.

I cling to him, my fingers in his hair, my legs open for his touch. He rubs my clit, and I tense under him, so close to an orgasm. I've given myself a few, but they're always a lot of work, and never really worth it. This is nothing like that. This is already way better than anything I've given myself, and I'm climbing toward something gigantic.

"Let me have it, baby." His breath hits my lips, and I want to do what he says. Looking over, I see his suit-covered arm working up and down, and it's so fucking erotic. Knowing that arm leads to the hand that's under my dress, the one that's getting me off, is too much for me to handle.

Looking into his sapphires, I bite my lip and give in to the orgasm I've been terrified of.

The wave is intense and so powerful, I see stars. I let out a shout of release as his fingers rub me, drawing out the pleasure. My body is close to breaking into a million pieces, yet I'm held together as Oz's arm comes around my back.

I melt into his hold, gulping in air as my body collapses against him. He pulls his fingers away from my heat and readjusts my panties. The cool damp satin is a balm on my overstimulated pussy right now.

Oz brings his fingers up to his mouth, and I watch as his tongue comes out to taste them. He closes his eyes, moaning at the flavor. His cock twitches under my hip and it turns me on all over again. Knowing he likes it is so dirty, but I can't be bothered to care.

Once he takes his fingers from his mouth he looks at me with the most intense stare. I think he might take me here on the floor of the limo, and to be honest, I don't know that I'd stop him. Instead, his lips come to mine again, but this time it's gentle. It's a sweet kiss of thanks, and I can taste a hint of myself.

He breaks the kiss, putting his forehead to mine and taking a deep breath.

"That was so much more than I expected. Thank you, Mallory."

I redden all the way to my toes. "I think I should be the one thanking you."

He squeezes me to his body and lets out a little laugh. "Have lunch with me today. Then dinner tonight."

"You're so greedy," I say, trying to play off how much I want to do both of those things, but I know I shouldn't because I need to stay at work over lunch.

He pulls back to look at me and gives me those dimples I love so much. "For you? Always."

It's then I realize the limo has stopped. I look over at my watch and see it's almost time for me to be at work. I think about saying yes to both, but I need to keep my wits about me. If lunch turns out anything like breakfast, I won't be able to make it back in. My legs are going to be shaky as it is.

"Dinner," I say, running my hands through his hair. Something about him has taken me over, and I get tunnel vision when he's near me.

He rubs his hands up and down my back, like he can't stop touching me.

"I'll pick you up right here after work." He leans in, giving my lips a kiss, and then sets me on the seat beside him.

Instantly, I miss being close to him, and a slight chill settles into me. But I smile as I watch him pull out a small paper bag and fill it with some of the pastries from the tray in front of us. Once he's finished, he takes my bag and slips the paper bag inside.

I look for a mirror to right my hair and my makeup, which are surely all over the place, but Oz leans over and takes my face in his hands.

"You look perfect. Not a hair out of place." He kisses my lips again, and this time, his tongue is slow and sweet. He's savoring me. When he pulls back, he's beaming again. "That lipstick is no joke. I should buy stock in it."

I redden a little as I grab my bag. Before I can turn back to tell Oz goodbye, he's out of the limo and coming around to open my door. He holds his hand out and I take it as I step out and adjust my dress, smoothing it down. He takes my chin and makes me look up at him.

"I'll be waiting," he says, leaning down and placing a soft kiss on my lips.

With that, I walk away and enter the building. Once I'm past the glass doors, I turn back and see him give me a little wave. It makes me blush all over again, but it's kind of adorable.

I scan my pass and hop on the elevator, standing in the back corner as people enter. I bring my fingers to my lips and wonder if anyone has a clue that I had the greatest morning of my life.

EIGHT

Mallory

I PICK AT the limp lettuce in my bowl. After not eating much at breakfast, I'm starving, but this salad actually looks kind of sad, even with all the ranch and cheese I piled on it.

I pick up my phone to text Oz. We'd texted a few times this morning after I got out of the limo but once I got to my desk I'd put my phone away to make sure I got everything done that needed doing. Even if my mind kept wandering back to him over and over again. At least it was busywork and I could do both things at once.

Me: I hope you have something yummy planned for dinner. I'm starving.

Oz: Did you not get lunch? You have to eat.

I smile at his concern, and it warms me all over.

Me: I'm actually at lunch now, but this cafeteria at work kinda sucks.

Oz: Oh, really?

Me: What'd you do for lunch?

Oz: You tasted like peaches when I sucked you off my finger this morning, and it's all I've wanted since. So I had peach cobbler for lunch.

My cheeks flush. No one has ever talked to me like this. Heat rushes to my core as I think about what he did to me this morning. The look on his face when he tasted me, like I was the best thing he's ever had in his life. It was a look I'll never forget.

Oz: Are you blushing? You have no idea how hard it makes me when you blush.

Feeling sexy and a little bold because of the text messages, I hit the camera app and take a picture, sending it to him. My cheeks are clearly red.

Oz: Fuck, baby. Are you in the cafeteria? I'm not sure I like the idea of others seeing you blush.

Me: Jealous?

Oz: Incredibly.

I smile even bigger at that. Is it messed up to be happy someone's getting jealous over you? Maybe, but I don't care.

Me: There's not a ton of people, and I'm off to the side. Besides, it's pretty lame in here.

Oz: What's wrong with the cafeteria?

Me: I got a salad and the lettuce looks pretty bad. They don't have a ton of choices. Maybe I'll go back to packing my lunch.

I should have done that in the first place but I got a little flustered about my date with Oz and forgot. I'd rather be eating at my desk trying to get the pile of reports done.

Oz: What do you normally like to have for lunch?

Me: A salad or deli sandwich, something not too heavy.

I glance up when I hear the chair at my table move. I see Eric sit down beside me. I give him a soft smile, trying to be nice. I don't like him, but I don't really have a solid reason why.

"Those reports are taking forever." Eric sighs, like he's been worked to the bone. Maybe they wouldn't take so long if Skyler and I didn't have to fix his mistakes, but I keep that comment to myself.

"There are a lot of them," I say, not really agreeing with him. There are a lot of them to get done, and as we're new, they're having us all go over each other's work to make sure we aren't missing anything. It's easy enough. They're redundant. I'd label it more busywork, but it's stuff that has to be done, and being at the bottom of the food chain makes it our job. I'm happy to do it and will do it with a smile on my face because

I'm glad to be here. They could stick me in the mailing room and I'd still be thankful. It takes time to get what you want. That's something I learned early in life, and I have no problem doing the work to get it.

"Well, I got told I'd be working late, and so did Skyler. I'm sure when you get back to your desk, you'll be asked, too."

Well, that sucks. I guess I won't be seeing Oz tonight.

"Thank for the heads-up." I push my chair back, not wanting to hang out, and I'm not eating this salad. Maybe I can grab a bag of chips from the vending machine to hold me over if I'm going to be working late.

"You heading back already? You didn't eat yet." He points at my plate.

"Yeah. I'd rather get back to work and get these reports done. The sooner I get back to them, the sooner I can leave tonight, if we're working late."

"I was hoping to eat with you. Get to know you a little better." His eyes travel over me, making me think he doesn't mean getting to know me on a friendly co-worker level.

"Sorry," is all I can manage in reply, because what else can I say to that? I have no desire to get to know him better. I turn to leave, and I swear I can sense his eyes on me, but I refuse to turn around and see. Dumping my tray, I make my exit from the cafeteria and see Paige talking to a man next to the elevator. She has her hands on her hips, and I can tell by the look on her face that she's agitated by whatever it is they're talking about.

The man makes Paige look smaller than normal, even in her tall heels. Not that it takes much with her tiny size. He's got almost a foot and a half on her. Not only that, but the man is built like a freaking linebacker. He's wearing a button-up white shirt, but the sleeves are rolled up, revealing his muscled forearms and the tattoos that cover them. His black slacks are fitted to his thick thighs, which look to be about the size of Paige's waist. Everything about the man is muscle. He's got short blond hair and bright blue eyes. He kind of reminds me of Captain America, if he had tats.

He has a smirk on his face at whatever Paige is going off about, almost like he finds it adorable. I stand and stare, wondering what's going to happen. The guy probably works in security with her, and after a second I realize he looks familiar. Then it hits me. It's the same guy she was talking to at the club the other night. God, I hope she doesn't get fired on the first day. She was so freaking excited about getting this job.

As if she knows I'm looking at her, her head turns my way and she's surprised. She quickly schools her features into a polite smile. She turns and says something to the man, who shakes his head and hits the elevator button like she dismissed him or something. After that, she walks toward me and he watches her go.

"Everything okay?" I ask when she finally reaches me. She turns to watch the guy get into the elevator, his eyes locked on her as the doors close.

"My boss," she mutters, like she's annoyed.

"Isn't that the guy from the club the other night?" With her photographic memory, no way would she miss that. But I could be wrong. It was dark and she was across the room talking to him that night.

"Ah, yeah."

"Yikes. Did he hit on you that night? Because that would make things awkward for sure. Dating and working together can't work. It would be a mess." It's definitely something I wouldn't want to do. This job is too important to risk.

"Because I date?" she jokes, making me laugh. No, Paige doesn't date. She flirts sometimes, but that's about it.

"How was your breakfast?"

My face warms once again, and her eyebrows rise.

"That good, huh?"

I've really got to get this blushing thing under control.

"It was wonderful. I really like him, Paige. Like scary-like him, and this is happening so fast. It's kind of freaking me out a little."

"Wow, that much?" Her brows furrow a little in concern.

"Yeah. It's too fast, isn't it?"

"You can't help your emotions, Mal. You'll be fine. You're a smart girl, and if something happens I'll be here to help you pick up the pieces." She reaches out, grabbing my hand. "I got you."

It's an odd way to put it, as if the heartbreak is impending. But I shake it off, thinking Paige always looks at things differently than I do.

"I know. I'm so lucky to have gotten to pair up with you." I wonder how things would have turned out if I hadn't had her by my side these last four years. Would I have made it through college? Yeah, but having Paige has made things so much easier. She's the first person in my life I could ever rely on, and I felt like she was there to catch me. She's my only real family.

"Don't get all mushy on me." She pulls me in for a hug. "Get back to work," she says in my ear, making me laugh.

"I'll be home late. I hear I'm working after hours."

"All right. I'll order something in. You can reheat it when you get home."

"Sounds good." We say our goodbyes before I head back to my floor, stopping short when I get to my desk. There are six cubicles in the center of the floor with full offices all around them. I'm between Skyler and Eric.

There is a sub sandwich sitting on my desk, and a coffee that looks to be made the way I like it.

"Did you see someone drop this off?" I ask Skyler, who stands up to look over the low cubicle wall.

"Some delivery boy dropped it off a few seconds ago. I thought you ordered it or something." She shrugs, then leans a little closer. "If I have to fix one more of Eric's reports, I'm going to choke him," she whispers conspiratorially. I nod in agreement.

"I know," I tell her.

She rolls her eyes, taking a deep breath before sitting back down at her own desk. Just then, Linda comes strolling out of her office. Like everyone else in this building, she's dressed to the nines. I'm going to have to spend my first few paychecks on getting some better clothes. Maybe I can find stuff I can mix and match so I won't need as many things. I didn't notice it the first time we met, but she looks extremely young to be my boss. It gives me hope that you can move up fast if you work hard.

"Mallory, I need you to stay with Eric and Skyler until all those reports are done."

"Of course."

She nods and turns, heading back into her office.

I sit down at my desk, pulling out my phone. This sandwich could have only come from one person. I laugh when I see I have three missed texts and a missed phone call, all from Oz. He's clearly not patient.

Oz: You have to eat, baby.

Oz: Is there something else you can get there?

Oz: I'll get it worked out for you.

How he did this so fast blows my mind.

Me: I swear, you really are the Wizard of Oz pulling all the strings. Thank you for the sandwich and coffee.

Clearly, the man can pop out of nowhere and make things happen.

Oz: I don't like when you don't respond to my messages.

This should worry me, but again, the stupid butterflies in my stomach have a mind of their own. This can't be healthy.

Me: I'm at work. Sometimes things come up and I can't text right away.

Oz: I can't wait to see you tonight.

I snort at his change of subject. I love how he doesn't seem to care that he comes on strong and almost sounds a little needy. This isn't a game with him.

Me: About tonight, sorry, I can't make it. Something came up with work and I have to stay late.

I send the text message and wait for a response before I get back to work, but nothing comes. The silence is very un-Oz-like. He's always quick to respond, and when I don't respond to him fast enough, he's sending another message or calling.

I wait a few more moments and think maybe he got caught up with work, so I put my phone into my bag and take a sip of the coffee sitting on my desk. I smile, thinking of this morning. I'm mystified as to how he knew the way I like my coffee.

I let myself fall into my work, wanting to get everything they added to my pile done. Eric was already slowing us down. I tried to show him each time he messed up where the problem was but he seemed more interested in me fixing it.

"Mallory." Linda says my name, and I sit up straight like I've been caught doing something bad. I turn around and see her coming out of her office again, her face a little pinched.

"I won't be needing you after all."

"Oh." I don't understand why she seems upset. Maybe she isn't happy with something I did. "It's quite fine. I'm more than happy to help," I tell her, trying to reassure her. I don't want everyone else working late and I'm not.

"No, no, I'm sure Skyler and Eric can handle it."

I see Skyler looking at us, probably wondering the same thing I am. Why don't I have to help?

"Ma'am, I'd really like to stay and help them." I'm a little panicked, like I did something wrong. Why is she cutting me out?

She doesn't answer me for a second, almost like she's thinking about it. Then she lets out a breath, like she's giving up.

"I'm sorry. I meant I won't need any of you tonight. We can get them finished tomorrow." With that, she turns and leaves.

Skyler and I look at each other as if to say *what was that?* Then Eric comes strolling back from lunch.

"We're not working late now," Skyler informs him.

"Nice," he responds, sitting down in his chair.

I sit back down at my desk, thinking how weird that was, but then I get excited and reach into my bag, picking up my phone to text Oz after letting Paige know my change of plans.

Me: Never mind. I don't have to work late. Can't wait for dinner!

His response is instant this time.

Oz: I'm counting the seconds.

Me: I'll text you when I'm out front. I really need to get back to work. xoxox.

Oz: Eat your lunch first. See you soon, baby. xxx.

NINE

Mallory

THE REST OF my day is spent elbow-deep in reports. We may not have had to stay late, but that doesn't mean there's not a stack of work to be done. I refrain from checking my phone throughout the day as I try to focus on work. I know that the second he sends something, I'll spend an hour melting over it. He's so charming it makes me ache.

I can't believe what I did in the car with him this morning. Every time it crosses my mind, the blush burns my cheeks. I've never done anything like that with a boy before, but Oz most definitely isn't a boy. No, he's all man, head to toe.

Caught up in the moment, I'd let myself be taken away by desire, and it felt completely wonderful. Although Oz and I don't know much about each other, there's something happening between us. He's sweet and intense, but I'm pulled to him like nothing I've ever felt before. He's nearly a stranger on paper, because there's not much I know about him. But the more I get to know, the more I like him. And isn't that what dating is for? To get to know each other while having a good time? I'm sure I should be more worried about the fact that I'm so eager to get to know him, but I'm going with my gut. Although I don't have any frame of reference and no real starting point, all I've ever really wanted in a man is someone who loves me and treats me well. Maybe Oz can be that.

"I'm headed out. See you girls tomorrow."

I lean back out of my cubicle and watch Eric's back retreat from our desks. I look over to see Skyler standing up and watching the same thing.

"That little shit is getting on my last nerve," she says, and I can't hide my smile. She looks down at me and shrugs a shoulder. "I'm finishing this last one up, and then I'm calling it a day. Want to grab a drink afterward?"

"Oh, I'd love to, but I've got plans." I'm disappointed because Skyler seems like fun. And she doesn't seem like the type of girl to ask if she doesn't mean it. "What about Friday?"

I'm unsure what's happening the rest of the week. It's only Tuesday, and I want to hedge my bets with Oz. But I'm sure I can do drinks after work one night with Skyler, and then maybe Oz and I can do dinner after. Or maybe I'm getting ahead of myself. I keep telling myself to play it cool, but here I am, planning days together.

"Oh, that sounds good. I met a couple of the junior associates on the top floor this afternoon when I took those forms up. Maybe I'll invite some of them. I know everyone likes to go to Marie's Yacht Club next door."

"I'll ask my roommate, too. She works in security here." Skyler smiles at me and I'm excited. "It's a plan," I agree, and then we go back to finishing our work.

Skyler and I get ready to leave at the same time, both of us cleaning up and grabbing our bags. Before we get to the elevator, I grab my phone and check for text messages. I'm not disappointed when I slide the screen and see what Oz left for me.

The first is a pic of a grumpy cat that says *I love math. It makes people cry.* Skyler looks at me and raises an eyebrow when I snort. I end up showing her the pic, and she snorts, too. We're obviously easily amused.

He also left me a few texts that I read privately as we wait for the elevator.

Oz: I'm thinking of you too much today. I fear for the future of my company.

Oz: In case I forgot to tell you, you looked gorgeous today.

Oz: How's the red lip stain holding up? Will we test its durability again after dinner?

Oz: I'm outside waiting when you're finished with work.

My cheeks burn, and I bite my lip as I send him a quick response.

Me: All finished and on the way down. Lip stain is doing well...but could be faulty. We should do another case study, just to be sure.

His response is immediate as the elevator doors open and Skyler and I step through.

Oz: If anything, I'm thorough.

"Is that your boyfriend?" Skyler asks as I tuck my phone away.

"Yes," I say, thinking he may be. I don't know how soon into dating you do that, but it's like we are headed in that direction. That's something to bring up with Oz tonight. Are we exclusive? I think I know what his answer would be, but I'd like to put it out there and be sure. "Yes," I say again, this time a bit more confidently. "Do you have a boyfriend?"

"Girlfriend. We've been together since high school." Skyler pulls out her phone and shows me a picture. "This is Jamie." The dark-haired beauty is next to Skyler on a beach, the two of them in bikinis. I'm immediately jealous of their slim bodies.

"Wow, she's hot," I blurt out. Realizing that may have been rude, I follow it up with a hurried, "Sorry."

Skyler laughs and puts her phone away. "I know, right? She's a babe. I'll see if she wants to come out with us on Friday…if it's okay to bring our partners."

"Oh, that sounds like fun. Maybe I'll ask my—" I pause for a quick second, then just say it "—boyfriend. See if he wants to come, too."

"Sure. Sounds like a good time. After we hit Marie's Yacht Club for some food we can go to Seven Eight Nine—it's a club next door if we want to go dancing after."

"Good call." I think about Oz and I meeting there. Maybe he'd like to go back so we could dance.

We exit the elevator and walk through the lobby. I make my way toward the front of the building. Skyler said she was taking a cab to meet Jamie for dinner, so we walk outside together. Looking left, I see Oz's limo, and as I spot it, the door opens.

"I'm this way. See you tomorrow," I toss over my shoulder, making my way over to Oz.

He steps out as I approach, his black suit looking as crisp as it did this morning. The gray tie catches a little of the setting sun, and his smile beams at me, dimples and all. As I approach him, I see his eyes move past me, and then his smile drops.

I turn, looking over my shoulder, and see Skyler staring at us. She has an odd look on her face, but after a second, she walks away in the other direction.

I turn back to Oz, and he looks down at me, but there's something in his eyes. I can't tell what it is. It's almost like he's hesitant. The happy beaming face from before is gone, replaced by worry.

"Hey. Do you know her?"

"No," he says quickly, and then his eyes clear of whatever it was that was bothering him. Letting out a quick sigh, he smiles at me and reaches out, pulling me into his arms. "How was your sandwich?"

When he leans in and places a soft kiss on my neck, all thoughts of Skyler vanish from my brain. The feel of his warm lips on my skin makes everything wonderful and perfect. I want to wrap around his body and soak in his size and strength, but he pulls back, taking my hand and helping me into the back of the limo.

Once we're in, he takes my hand in his and brings it to his mouth. He places a soft kiss on the inside of my wrist, and the heat warms my cheeks. Even the simplest things he does to me are sexual. I love that he can't seem to stop himself from touching me.

"Dinner?" he asks, moving his lips back and forth across my wrist.

"Hmm?" I'm not sure I understand what he's asking because I'm so focused on what he's doing.

The car pulls away from the curb, and he smiles, bringing my hand to his face. He holds my palm there, looking at me, and it's the most intimate thing in the world.

"I missed you," he whispers. I don't know why, although it's only been a few hours since we were together it somehow seems longer. The way he says it makes it sound like it's been years since he's been with me.

After a second of looking at me, he reaches over with both hands, pulling me onto his lap. I laugh, thinking that he can't stand even the smallest distance between us.

"I love that sound," he says, burying his face against my exposed neck.

The heady smell of amber and honey hits me again, and the familiar rush of excitement pools in my lower belly. Being this close to him is dangerous, but I can't seem to find it in me to stop him. His big hands come around my back, holding me to him, and I reach up, running my fingers through his dark waves.

"How was your day, dear?" I joke, holding him to me. It's as if we've done this every day for our whole lives, falling into a well-known embrace.

"It was miserable. You were in it far too little."

I laugh again, and he squeezes me tighter.

"What did you really do? I was deep in reports all

day," I ask, wanting to know. I have no idea what he does on a day-to-day basis.

He lets out a deep sigh, like his day was long. "I mainly had to wrap up some deals and close some things out."

I look up at him. His answer is very vague and I'm sure he can tell what I'm thinking by the look on my face.

"I buy businesses and either dismantle them and sell off the parts or I turn them into something more. I spent a lot of my day looking at numbers."

It makes me smile that we have something in common. "You like the numbers, too?"

"Everything comes down to numbers." He moves in a little closer, like he is going to kiss me. "Except you. You're one formula I can't seem to crack or predict. It's different and I rather enjoy it."

I like that because I'm the same way. Numbers are safe and easy. There's always an answer and the rules don't change. There's no questioning them. They are what they are. It's nice to have someone like Oz. Something that's not an equation.

"Where are you taking me to feed me?"

He pulls back looking up at me excitedly. "It's a surprise," he says, wiggling his eyebrows.

After a moment, the limo stops. "Are we here already?" I ask, trying to look out of the limo windows. They're beyond blacked out, so even seeing what street we're on is nearly impossible.

"Would you like to ride around the block a few more times?"

Oz gives me a wicked grin and I know exactly what

he means by that. But I've told myself that tonight I'm getting to know this gorgeous man who's taken hold of me. I want to get some answers about him and see where he thinks things are headed. I may be new at this, but I want to be honest about what I want and what I expect. I don't want to get a few months in and find out we aren't on the same page.

Setting me off his lap, he opens the car door and steps out. He offers his hand and I take it as he helps me out of the back. When he closes the door behind me, I look around and see we're outside the New York Aquarium.

"Are we in the right place?" I ask, looking for a restaurant on either side of it.

Oz holds out his arm, and I slip mine though it as he leads me to the entrance. He looks down at me, smiling as he leads us up to the door, but doesn't say a word. A short bald man on the other side of the door unlocks it for us and holds it open as we enter. Once we walk through, he closes it behind us, and I hear the lock click back into place.

An older gentleman approaches us and reaches out his hand to Oz. "Welcome, Miles. Good to see you again."

"You too, Eugene. This is my Mallory." Oz shakes the man's hand, and then looks down at me.

I look up to see Oz beaming, as if he's showing me off with pride. It makes me warm and tingly, and I know my cheeks are probably cherry red.

"I've heard a lot about you, young lady. Welcome to the New York Aquarium." He holds out his hand to indicate the room, and I finally look around. There are tanks of tropical fish at the entrance, and I want to go over and look, but I'm still unsure if I can. "If you will both follow me, we've got your table set upstairs."

Oz takes my hand and leads me through the entrance and down a hallway. The walls are lined with glass, and there are colorful fish on either side. It's as if we're underwater, and I'm smiling from ear to ear.

At the end of the hall there's a large spiral staircase, and Oz grips my hand a little tighter as we make our way up. Once we get to the top, I look around and see gigantic cylindrical aquariums throughout a huge room. The only light in the room is coming from them, the softly lit water making a beautiful glow. Oz lets go of my hand as I walk forward in a trance. Once I get to the first aquarium, I see that inside are little pink jellyfish swimming in the water. They float and glide gracefully through the water, delicately dancing with each movement.

I sense Oz behind me, and I turn my head slightly, smiling up at him. "This is incredible. They're so beautiful."

"Not nearly as beautiful as you," he says, and leans down, giving my neck a soft kiss.

He takes my hand again and leads me over to a table that's set up in the middle of the room. It's rectangular in shape, but the two chairs are both on the same side instead of across from each other. I look at the table, and then look back at him quizzically.

"Just wanted you close," he says as he holds out a chair for me to sit on.

Once I'm seated, I look around the room at all the

giant tubes of jellyfish that surround us. It looks magical and it's like we are under the sea.

Oz takes the seat to my left, and I look over at him and smile. "This is wonderful. Thank you so much."

"Anything you want. You need only ask." Reaching out, he takes my hand in his, and it's then that I see the advantage of sitting on the same side of the table.

Eugene appears at our table. "Enjoy your evening, Miles. Tell Vivien we said hello, and that Louise and I look forward to seeing her next weekend."

"I'll be sure and pass along the message."

Once Eugene is gone, a waiter appears and pours us each a glass of red wine. After that he's gone, and Oz and I are alone.

"No menus?" I ask, looking around the table.

"A special favor called in. It's a set menu."

"I see," I say, and he gives me a wink. "Vivien?" Reaching for my wine, I figure I'll put that out there. I don't want to come across as jealous, but it was brought up while I was sitting here.

Oz drapes an arm along the back of my chair as his fingers lazily stroke my exposed neck. There are definitely some advantages to wearing my hair up.

"My mother. Eugene and his wife, Louise, are my godparents."

"What about your dad?" I take a sip of the wine. It's warm and rich.

"I don't care to talk about my father. The day my mother left him he died to me."

"Oh, I'm so sorry—" I try to apologize, but he holds his hand up to stop me. I can't imagine what his father must have done to make him so angry, but I can tell by the tic in his jaw it isn't something he cares to talk about.

"It's fine—it's not something I want to ruin the evening with. Another time."

"How old are you?" I blurt out, thinking I should probably know this. It's also a nice change of subject.

He laughs a little, letting go of my hand and taking a sip of his wine. "I'm twenty-six, but my birthday is next month. So almost twenty-seven."

I nod, thinking that's not too bad.

"Are you going to tell me your real name?"

"It's Miles." He doesn't look at me when he answers, and it's like he's avoiding it.

"What's the rest of it?"

"Henry."

"Miles Henry. It sounds so posh. I think I like Oz better."

He looks at me and gives me a wicked smile. I take another sip of my wine and look at him over the top of my glass.

"I think I like it better, too."

His fingers caress the back of my neck, and the soft touch relaxes me. Maybe it's the wine, too, but it's nice to sit next to him, surrounded by his scent. The warm amber and honey clings to my dress. The scent is now becoming ingrained in my mind.

"What is it you do for fun, Oz? Are you always renting out whole buildings to entertain yourself? Sounds expensive." I pick up my wine and take another sip, noticing that he pays attention to my every move.

He lets out a little laugh. "I'm afraid not. I keep to myself for the most part. I wasn't lying when I said all

I do is work. The closest thing to a friend I have is my head of security."

"I really only have Paige. I seem to get lost in my work, too," I admit. Seeing something else we both have in common.

"Not anymore. Now you have me, too." He sounds so sure that he'll always be around. That whatever this crazy thing is will last forever. The waiter appears again and this time brings us one small plate of antipasti. After he walks away, I look down at it. *I guess we're going to share.*

There are olives and cheeses with a few dried meats and some tomatoes. Oz reaches out, picks up an olive and holds it out for me. I open my mouth slightly, and he places the salty olive on my lips. I bite it, loving the taste. He eats the other half while his eyes stay on my mouth, and the act is so erotic. Something about his feeding me is turning me on, and excitement rushes through my body.

He continues to feed me little bites of everything, always offering it to me first. When the plate is empty, I'm a little sad it's over as the waiter comes and takes it away. But as fast as the empty plate is gone, a new one appears with a single plate of tortellini in a red sauce.

Reaching over, Oz takes his fork and scoops one up, offering it to me. It makes me smile, and I open up and take a bite. The combination of the spicy flavor of sausage and the sweetness of tomato is perfect, and I moan at the taste. Oz's eyes narrow on me, and for a second he looks like he wants to come at me. I take another sip of wine, and after a moment he takes a bite of the pasta, too.

"Are you close with your mother?" I ask between bites. I normally don't like to talk about family because it can be a little awkward for me but I want to share these things with him. To know what makes Oz, Oz.

"I am, yes. We have lunch together every Wednesday. Would you like to come with me tomorrow? I think you'd like her."

My eyes must show some kind of alarm because he smiles gently at me.

"Or not. Another time perhaps," he says, feeding me another bite.

All of this is happening so fast, but meeting the mother might be a bit too hasty. Even if a little part of me wants to jump at it.

"Speaking of this week." There's aggravation clear in his voice, and I see his brows furrow. "I have to go out of town on Thursday, and I won't be back until Saturday. I've tried my best to avoid it, but our London office requires that I physically be there, and I can't put it off another day."

"Oh." I'm suddenly disappointed, but I shake it off, trying to find the positive. "That's okay. It's only for a couple of days. I'll be here when you get back."

He doesn't seem happy with my answer, so I try another tactic.

"I'll miss you while you're gone. Maybe we can talk on the phone while you're away."

This seems to be better, because his smile returns. "You'll miss me?" he asks, leaning forward a little.

"Yes." My answer is a whisper as his lips are a breath away from mine.

When our mouths connect, his tongue sweeps in, and

I give him what he wants. The flavor of the wine and his warm scent turn me into a puddle in his arms. His hands wrap around me as I slide mine along the back of his neck. My fingers grip his hair as his teeth bite down on my bottom lip, and suddenly I have this overwhelming urge for him to take me to the floor.

Potent desire runs through my body, and need pulses between my legs. My nipples ache, and my panties are drenched as his kiss consumes my whole being.

Just as quickly as he begins the kiss, he stops it, placing one final soft peck on my mouth before putting one hand on the back of my chair and wrapping the other around my fingers.

I look around, a little dazed, and see the waiter approach us. Oz must have been more aware of our surroundings than I was. I had completely forgotten we weren't alone.

The waiter takes our empty plate of pasta and leaves a large slice of chocolate cake. With only one fork. I smile at Oz, but he shrugs and picks it up, offering me a bite.

"Do you get to go any other fun places?" I ask before I take a bite of the delicious cake.

"I've been all over but lately I've been trying to keep it stateside. The traveling gets wearing and New York has never been so appealing now with you in it." He reaches out his thumb, wiping some cake from the side of my mouth. He brings it to his own mouth, sucking it clean.

"What is it you want to do at Osbourne Corporation? You said you had an internship."

"It's an internship in their accounting department. I'd like to one day run a department like that. I went to

Yale, and my major was in statistics, which basically means I'm good with numbers. I'd like to put that to good use."

He puts his hand on me again and runs his thumb along the back of my neck as I explain what I did in college and how I ended up working for Osbourne Corp. It's like he always has to be touching me. Every now and then he asks me a question about something specific, but otherwise he lets me talk. I tell him about my time at Yale, and Paige, and what I thought my career path might be. I tell him about my past, about growing up in foster care, but he listens and nods through all of it.

After a while, I realize I've been talking about myself nonstop for probably over an hour.

"I'm sorry," I say, looking away. "I've never done that before."

"What? Why are you sorry?" Oz leans in and wraps his arms around me again. "Don't ever be sorry. For anything. I love hearing you talk. Don't ever apologize for that." He gives me a quick kiss on the lips, but doesn't deepen it. Instead, he stands, holding his hand out to me. "I think they'd like to close this place up."

I take his hand, and he leads me away from the beautiful jellyfish room and out of the aquarium. Once we're outside, the limo is there, waiting on us. He reaches out, opening the door and helping me in before sliding in after me. As soon as the door is closed behind him, he's pulling me onto his lap.

He rests his hands on either side of my neck and looks into my eyes. Something flashes there, but again, I don't know what it is. Longing? There's a need there, but I can't place it.

"Come home with me," he whispers so softly I almost don't catch it.

I hesitate, wanting to give him what he wants, but unsure if this is what I'm ready for.

"I—"

"When I get back," he interrupts, giving me a sweet smile that shows one of his dimples. "Maybe then. We don't have to do anything, Mallory. I want you in my bed."

Before I can answer, he leans up, kissing me softly, but it's not enough. This time, I'm the one sweeping my tongue into his mouth and deepening the kiss. I want more, but it's so fast. Maybe these couple of days apart will give me some time to clear the lust-filled fog from my brain.

Oz runs his hands down my back to my ass, pulling me closer to him. I rub my breasts against his chest, wishing there was nothing between us. Breaking the kiss, I'm about to tell him to take me to his house, when the limo stops. It's then I realize I never felt it start. I was so lost in our kiss that I didn't realize the car was moving, let alone that we'd traveled so far as to reach a destination.

"Can I take you for breakfast in the morning?" he asks, kissing down my neck.

"If it's anything like breakfast this morning, yes." My words are breathy. I love the heat of his lips on me.

He pulls back, smiling, both dimples out in full force. "You need only ask, my sweet Mallory."

With one final kiss, he helps me out of the limo and watches me enter the lobby of my apartment on wobbly legs.

TEN

Mallory

"SOMEONE IS ABOUT to get throat punched!" I hear Paige bellow. The shout is followed by a loud pounding on the front door. I roll over and look at the clock. Five a.m. shows in bright neon blue. I spring from the bed, chasing Paige down the hallway before she ends up arrested for assault. It's way too early to bail her out of jail.

I catch up to her as she flings open the door to reveal Oz with a smile on his face that drops instantly.

"Did you look through the peephole?" he barks at Paige, taking me by surprise.

"Oz," I snap before Paige can say something and an argument sets in. They've only met once and for a very brief moment. I want them to like each other, and this isn't a good start. She's the most important person in my life, and Oz is beginning to mean a lot to me. It's important they get along.

Oz's eyes snap to mine and go soft again. He eats up every inch of me as he looks down my body to where my legs are bare. I'm only wearing a pair of panties and a worn-out Yale T-shirt that drops to midthigh. I've had the thing since my freshman year of college, and I always sleep in it.

"It's 5 a.m.," Paige says, releasing the door. Oz

catches it, stopping it from shutting. "I'm going back to bed." Paige shakes her head, clearly annoyed, but I'm glad she didn't lay into Oz about the peephole comment. She must be tired.

Oz steps in, shutting the door behind him and flipping the lock. Placing a bag and drink holder with coffee down on the table next to the door, he turns to me. Like always, he's in a suit and looks incredibly handsome. Way too handsome for 5 a.m. His dark waves are pushed back, and his short stubble is clean and polished. His suit today is a light gray, and he's wearing a baby blue crisp dress shirt with a blue-and-gray-striped tie. He's gorgeous.

I don't even want to think about what I look like right now.

"You can't talk to Paige like that. This is her home, and she can answer the door however she likes." Not that I don't agree with him. Paige should've checked to see who was at the door before swinging it open, but in her defense, it's early and she was pissed. Not to mention this building has crazy good security. It makes me wonder how he even got up to our floor.

"Whose shirt is that?" he asks, changing the subject. His tone is a little firmer than normal.

"You're clearly not a morning person. What are you even doing here?"

"Baby, whose shirt is that?" he asks again, taking a step toward me.

I look down at the shirt. "Well, I'm wearing it, so clearly it's mine." I place my hands on my hips, narrowing my eyes at him. What the hell is going on here?

"It's really big on you."

"So?" I'm clearly not understanding the problem with my shirt.

"It looks like a man's shirt." He takes a few more steps until he's standing right in front of me. I have to lean my head back to look up at him. His jaw is set in a firm lock, almost like he's clenching his teeth.

"No, it looks like I got it in the discount bin for five dollars." I see his body visibly relax, and his warm smile comes back. I keep my glare fixed, even though that stupid smile melts my insides.

He leans down like he's going to kiss me, and I step back, making him smile more.

"I see you're still learning that if you run, I chase. Stepping back won't help you." A playful look fills his face, and I try to keep my stern expression. He came into our home, snapping at everyone, and now he's acting like nothing happened.

I take another two steps back, and his eyebrows rise right before he lunges for me. I let out a squeal and turn to run down the hallway. I only make it a few feet before I'm lifted off the ground and thrown over his shoulder.

One arm holds me in place and the other comes up to grip my ass.

"I like it when you don't run from me, but I have to say chasing and catching you has its appeal, also." The hand on my ass slips under my shirt and roams around. The soft touch is ticklish, and I can't help but squirm and laugh.

Suddenly, my back hits my bed, and he moves over me, between my parted legs. He stares down at me, making my face heat. The teasing look is gone, and now he's back to all soft and sweet.

"Fuck, you even look sexy first thing in the morning." His face drops down, and I think he's going to kiss me. Instead, his nose brushes across my cheek, then down to my neck, where he places openmouthed kisses. It makes me shiver and writhe.

"I'm still mad at you." My words come out breathy, and I don't sound like myself.

"I'm sorry, baby. Let me make it up to you."

"Oz, you can't just..." I try to protest, but he takes my earlobe between his teeth. The hand on my hip slips between us, going under my shirt. It works its way up my body, fondling my breast as my nipples get harder.

"Can't what, baby? Show you how sorry I am? You can't blame a man for trying to make his woman happy." He rubs himself against me, his hard cock moving against my pussy, making me moan.

"Your woman?" I question, liking the sound of that. I've already told someone he was my boyfriend, but hearing him say it makes it sound official. He did try to introduce me to his mother, so that should count for something, right?

"You feel that?" He drags his cock against me a little, the firm pressure hitting my clit perfectly as the hand on my breast fingers my nipple. "That's yours. You're all he wants. Since the very moment I laid eyes on you, he's been yours. So I think it's only fair you're mine, too."

"Oh, God!" I cry out, and I don't know if it's from the pleasure of his words or what he's doing to my body. His scent surrounds me, and I'm dizzy with lust. His warm fragrance invades my lungs and marries perfectly with his weight on top of me.

"I could get off listening to the sounds you make

when I touch you." Oz moves his hips faster, and I wrap my legs around his waist, wanting him closer. I'm so close, but I want to have him skin on skin. There are entirely too many clothes between us.

"Oz, please." I go for his shirt, trying to attack the buttons, but he releases me, grabbing both my hands and pinning them over my head.

"You don't have to beg, baby. I'm going to give you what you need and make you come, but the clothes stay on. I don't trust myself not to take you."

"Yes, take me." I jerk my hips against him, trying to encourage him to do that. I'm so far gone I don't know what's coming out of my mouth. I have this ache I need him to satisfy.

I'm moving my hips as much as I can, but his body has me locked where he wants me. My whole body is buzzing. My pussy clenches, and the ache that begs to be eased by him intensifies. I've never felt anything like this before. So needy for something that I've never even had.

He moans, and his face looks almost pained now.

"You have no idea how much I want you, but I want this to be right. When I take you for the first time, I don't want to think about us having a time limit. The first time I slip inside of you, I'm going to have all the time in the world to show you how perfect we are together."

His words make my heart flutter. God, can he really be this freaking wonderful?

His mouth takes mine, and I have no choice but to surrender myself to him, letting him give me what he said he would. With my hands pinned above my head, he thrusts back and forth, mimicking sex. His hard cock dragging against my clit has me tensing and ready to explode. His tongue matches the sex strokes his body is making against me as I moan into his mouth. The sound seems to work him up even more because his movements become faster and almost desperate.

All the sensations combine, and I have no choice but to go over the edge. My whole body jerks against him as he releases my mouth and I cry out into the room. Unexplainable sensations flow through me as he pinches my nipple and grinds against my clit.

When I come down from my high, my eyes fall closed and I lie there, enjoying the tingling that has taken over my whole body. Every part of me is sensitive to even the lightest touch.

He releases my breast and slides his hand down my body, stopping over my underwear. He slips one finger under my panties, gliding it across my clit. The touch makes me jerk, and my eyes fly open. I'm still too sensitive, even for his gentle petting.

His eyes are on me as he pulls his hand out, bringing the one finger to his mouth like he had before to have a taste of me. I blush even after all we did.

"I could wake you up every morning like this."

"I might let you, even at 5 a.m."

"Sorry, baby. I was excited and couldn't sleep. We didn't say what time we'd do breakfast today."

What can I say to that? He said sorry, and he was so excited to see me he came over as soon as he could. I can't even be mad at him anymore. Especially after the orgasm.

I want him to feel the same way I do right now—relaxed and happy.

"I want to make you come." I jerk my hands, which he still has pinned above my head.

"Already did." He kisses me on the lips before springing from the bed.

"Come back here," I protest, rolling to my side and looking up at him standing next to my bed.

"I can't get back in the bed with you or I'm never getting out of it. And I'm guessing I can't get you to call in sick."

No, I really can't, though a day in bed with Oz sounds wonderful.

"What did you mean you already did?" I question, going back to him saying he already came.

He smiles, leaning down over me. I grab his tie, pulling him closer, and his smile grows bigger, showing his dimples. He clearly likes me wanting him.

"I'm going to use the hall bathroom to clean myself up," he says before closing the distance between our mouths for a lazy sweet kiss that is over too quickly. I release his tie and he pulls me up from the bed. He came in his pants? The thought has me tingling again. Can men come from a little dry humping?

"I brought you breakfast. Get ready, baby." He places a kiss on the top of my head and leaves the room. I bite my lip as a smile tries to take over my face.

Wanting to have as much time as I can with him before work, I discard my T-shirt and panties and dart to the bathroom. I washed my hair last night, so I need to wash my body. I make quick work of my shower and brushing my teeth.

When I step back into my room, Oz is lying in the center of my bed, his back against the headboard as he sips a coffee. I see another sitting on the bedside table.

"It's yours." He nods to the coffee. I reach down and pick it up, taking a sip. Of course it's how I like my coffee.

He watches me take a drink, and a little flutter invades my stomach.

"How do you take your coffee?" He diverts his eyes from me for a second, then they come back to mine.

"I used to take it black."

"And now?"

"I take it with lots of cream, lots of sugar and a dash of cinnamon."

I freeze, not sure how to respond to his statement that he now takes his coffee like mine.

"I wanted to taste what you tasted every morning and now I can't stop. Can't seem to stop a lot of things when it comes to you."

Why is this so adorable? Even more so that Oz felt a little shy about admitting it. I don't think this man is shy about anything.

I make my way over to my dresser, looking at him in the mirror as I pull open the top drawer. I find a baby-blue lace bra and matching panties. I think about how it will match his shirt, and even though it's ridiculous, I want us to match.

I don't know where I get the inner power, but I look up in the mirror at him and drop my towel. I watch him as his whole body freezes. I don't break eye contact in the mirror as I bend over, slipping on the pale blue, lacy panties. Keeping my eyes locked on him, I straighten and then put on the matching bra.

I turn and look at him, but he doesn't say anything. He almost looks mad as he sits there on the bed, gripping his coffee. Awkwardly, I bite my lip and head for the bathroom.

"Don't shut that," he says in his deep voice before I can close the bathroom door. The way the bathroom is positioned, he can see the sink area from where he's sitting. "I want to watch you."

It's then I realize he isn't mad. He wants me, and he's fighting himself. It's almost empowering that I have this kind of hold on him. That I can do this to him makes some of my shyness drop away.

"You want to watch me get ready?" I ask. The request seems odd and as intimate as what we did moments ago in bed.

"Yes."

I study him for a second but release my hold on the door, pushing it all the way open. I go over to the sink where I get ready. I apply my makeup. After that's finished, I pin my hair up how he likes. Every time I look at him in the bathroom mirror, he's got his eyes on me.

When I'm finished, I turn around, leaning against the sink.

"Was that enjoyable for you?" I tease.

"Another something I could get used to doing every morning," he says, setting his coffee down next to mine on the bedside table.

He moves to the edge of the bed, and I walk out of the bathroom toward him. I go up to him and move between his legs, and this time he has to look up at me. His big hands grip my hips before he leans forward and places a kiss on my stomach. I run my fingers through his dark wavy hair, the thick locks silky between my fingers.

"I messed up your hair."

"I don't care," he says against my skin before placing another kiss there. The hands on my hips dig in a little more before he finally drops them.

I walk over to the closet and look for something to wear. I settle on black, high-waisted pants that are tight at the ankles, a gray silk top and red heels. The pants will show off every inch of the shoes, my favorite pair, which Paige got me for my birthday. They make me look sexy.

Oz continues to watch me as I get dressed.

"All ready?" I say when I'm finished buckling the heels.

Oz stands from the bed and makes his way over to me. He cups my face with gentle hands and bends to kiss me.

"You look beautiful, Mallory. Now let me feed you."

I nod and grab my phone and both our coffees from the bedside table. Oz bends, picking my discarded T-shirt off the floor. I think he's going to toss it in the hamper next to my closet, but instead he brings it to his nose, smelling it, before tucking it under his arm.

"What are you doing?" I ask, taking a few steps toward him, handing him his coffee.

"I have to leave today instead of tomorrow." Disappointment hits me. That's an extra day he'll be gone. I've really become attached to him so quickly. That thought alone should scare the shit out of me.

"What does that have to do with my shirt?"

"I'm taking it with me."

"You're taking my shirt with you?"

"Yep," is all he offers as he turns, heading down the hallway. I follow him, shaking my head. When we get to the living room area, he grabs the bag he set down earlier by the door and walks over to the kitchen. I follow suit and watch as he pulls pastries out of the bag.

"The shirt that you seemed to have a problem with this morning, you're now taking?"

He turns, taking my coffee from my hand and placing it on the kitchen counter, before grabbing me and sitting me next to it. The man easily moves me around my kitchen like I weigh nothing. It makes me feel feminine and sexy.

"I thought it was another man's shirt." He picks up a muffin and rips a piece off, bringing it to my mouth. I'm noticing this man likes to feed me. I open, letting him put the piece in my mouth. I chew the delicious blueberry muffin and swallow before asking him my question.

"You were jealous?"

"Yes," he confirms, bringing another bite to my lips. I can't help but smile before I open my mouth and take it from him.

"You like that I was jealous?"

"No, of course not," I half lie. Who wouldn't be pleased that the man you're crushing on doesn't like the idea of you and other men?

"But you don't like the idea of me with another man?" I push, wanting to know where he stands.

"No," he says sharply.

"I don't like the idea of you with another woman either."

"Good," he responds, but I want to make sure we're on the same page.

"So. We're exclusive then?" I play with the edge of the napkin in front of me, not wanting to see his reaction.

"Mallory." The way he says my name makes my eyes snap up to his. "There was never anyone after the first time I saw you. And there damn sure won't be anyone after. This is exclusive. It's so goddamn exclusive, I can't stand the thought of anyone else looking at you."

The butterflies are taking flight again, but I'm melting at his words. They should probably scare me, but they make me fall even deeper for him. I like that he isn't playing it cool and says what he thinks. Even if what he thinks is a little overwhelming.

"Good," I say, and take another bite of blueberry muffin from him.

He smiles at me, his dimples showing. "I like your answer."

"Have you ever been exclusive with anyone else?" I find myself asking. Once the words are out of my mouth I want to take them back. I don't want to hear about his past with other women.

His hand comes under my chin making me look up at him. "No. I dated when I was young but nothing serious. I've been very driven from a young age and all my focus has always been there. You'll soon notice I'm an all or nothing kind of person and I don't waste my time on things that I don't think will matter." He leans in a little more, his breath on my face. "You matter." He says it in a way that almost seems like I'm all that matters.

Just then, Paige comes strolling into the kitchen. She looks between us, not saying a word, before going over to the fridge and pulling out a Red Bull.

"Morning," I say, more chirpily then I mean to. "You remember Oz?"

"Dessert guy," she says, looking at the pastries. I silently motion for Oz to offer her one.

"I brought breakfast if you're hungry," he finally says, making me smile.

"She's always hungry," I inform him, because she is, and also I want him to know things about Paige. For them to be friendly.

"Thanks." She grabs some chocolate-looking thing before shoving it into her mouth. "I'm going to get ready for work," she says around it.

"Oz is taking me into the office. You can ride with us."

"It's three blocks," she reminds me, clearly not wanting the ride.

"I guess that's true." I look up at Oz. It would be silly to have him drop me off when we're so close.

"Let me take you, baby. I want to say goodbye before I head to the airport."

"Give that man a freaking key if he's going to be banging on this door at five in the morning!" Paige yells from down the hallway before I hear her door shut.

"I like the sound of that." He leans in again, going for my neck. I'm beginning to think that's a weak spot for me. I melt every time.

"It's too soon to give you a key." My words hold no power as I let him devour my neck. "Right?"

"You're the only one here setting a pace, sweet Mallory." He kisses right below my ear and pulls back once again.

"So, boyfriend and girlfriend?" The question seems so juvenile, but for some reason, I want some kind of label before he leaves town. He said we're exclusive, but I want to know what to call him.

"You're mine." The way he says it seems so final, and a thrill runs through me. "And I'm yours."

"You always say the sweetest things." I look down at my lap, trying to hide my warm cheeks.

"Only to you." His hand comes under my chin, lifting it so my eyes meet his again. "You going to let me take you to work and give me a goodbye?"

I lick my lips and nod, and he kisses me yet again.

ELEVEN

Mallory

Oz AND I sit and enjoy our breakfast for a few more minutes until it's time for us to go. I'm secretly glad he came over so early because it meant we got to spend as much time together as we could before he left. Getting to know each other a little more. He told me stories about him and his mother. She seems to be the only other person he really talks about. It's sweet and I find it rather endearing.

When we get in the back of the limo, I sit on his lap like the other times before. I like that he wants me close, but it's going to make being apart from him for a few days even harder.

"When are you coming back?" I ask as he kisses my neck.

"Saturday. If all goes to plan." He releases a huff, and I can tell he doesn't want to go. Whether it's because of me or the aggravation of work, I'm unsure. Either way, I can tell he doesn't want to go as much as I don't want him to.

He looks up at me with his sapphires, and I get lost in them. The bright navy blues make me fall for him a little more every day. I stroke his trimmed beard and look into his eyes as we ride the three blocks to work.

"Next time, you should come with me," he says, running his big hands down my back.

I kiss him, letting my tongue slip past his lips. He holds me closer to him, deepening it and taking control. But all too soon the limo stops.

He presses his forehead to mine, and I sit there, taking in his scent one last time before he's gone.

"It's a few days. We'll be fine. Right?"

Oz laughs as he pulls back, but he shakes his head. "I'll be fine when I have you in my arms again. Don't make plans Saturday. I want you all to myself." He runs his finger down my cheek to my chin, where he lightly grips it. "Deal?"

"Deal," I quickly agree. I want nothing more than to have a whole day with Oz, getting to know him even more.

"Now get to work before I make you late, baby. Saying goodbye is hard enough for me."

One more quick kiss and he's opening the door and helping me out.

"Promise me you'll keep your phone on you at all times while I'm gone. I'll go crazy if I can't get in touch with you," he says, pulling me in for a hug.

"I promise." I squeeze him back, before looking up to his blues, longing to get back in that limo with him.

I finally pull back and walk toward the building. I turn and look back one last time before entering. He's still there, watching me go in, and I can't help but think we are both a little head over heels in this.

It's only for a couple of days. We'll be fine. That's what I keep telling myself over and over as I wave goodbye and go into Osbourne Corp. It's Wednesday morning. I can make it to Saturday. A little distance might do us some good.

Before I enter the elevator, my phone buzzes, and I take it out of my bag to see a text.

Oz: I'll email you today, in case you can't keep checking your phone at your desk.

I scan my pass at the elevator, sending back a bunch of kisses to Oz. I smile at how silly we are being, but life is short, so why not?

I've come to realize that things in life aren't guaranteed, and I've had to work for all that I've gotten. But what's the point if there's no one to share it with? I've got Paige, who is like a sister to me. But having someone like Oz is different. Everything could be gone tomorrow, so I want to live in the moment and enjoy what I've got. And if that means letting myself fall for a guy I hardly know, then so be it. We'll get to know each other as time goes on. And along the way, I want to have fun together.

I'm confident and sure of myself as I make my way to my desk and get ready for the day.

Not long after I arrive, Skyler comes in.

"Good morning," I offer as she passes by my desk to her own, but she makes a sound like a grunt.

Thinking maybe she's having a bad morning, I go back to my stack of paperwork and get started. After about fifteen minutes, I hear Eric at his desk. Late again, as usual. He says hello over his cubicle wall, and Skyler says, "Good morning," to him over the top of my head. What the hell? She doesn't even like Eric.

"Morning," I say, and go back to what I was doing. Maybe she needed a few minutes to wake up.

I hear a ping on my computer and look up to see a new email.

From: *YourOZ@gmail.com*
Subject: Testing…
Hey, baby
Just seeing if this works okay. I'm at the airport waiting on the tarmac to take off, but I'll have in-flight Wi-Fi all the way to London. I hope your day goes well and you have something tasty for lunch. Can you do me a favor and eat in the cafeteria again today? I know you mentioned the food isn't great, but I worry about you when I'm not there. If you don't want to go down there, I can have something delivered to your desk again. Be as safe as possible while you're out of my arm's reach. I'd go crazy thinking something might happen to you while I'm away. I'll send you another email this afternoon once we are in flight and I've taken care of some business.

PS I left a package for you with your doorman. I thought since I stole your shirt, I'd give you one of mine to sleep in while I'm away.
Love, Oz

Giddy excitement runs through me while reading his email, and then gigantic butterflies as I see how he signs it. Love. He can't mean he loves me. Right? It's only been a few days. You can't be in love with someone that fast. Maybe he means it like a term of endearment. You know, when you call someone "love." Like a pet name. That's got to be what he meant.

As I look at it for far too long, I finally decide to shake it off. Live in the moment, right? Isn't that what I was telling myself to do?

From: *MSullivan@OsbourneCorp.Net*
Subject: RE: Testing
Hello to you! I like the email address. Did you come up with that?

Glad you made it to the airport safe. Now I need you to make it safe to London, and then safely back to me.

I'll grab something in the cafeteria today if it will make you happy.

I've never been to London. Are you going to bring me back a surprise?
xoxo, Mallory

I read over my email and debate changing the end of it to "love," but then hit Send. I'm sure I'll get another one from him at some point today, so I get back to work.

After about an hour of correcting Eric's forms, I gather them up to hand off to Skyler. Walking around the wall that divides our cubicle, I hope she's in a better mood.

"Here's the next round," I say, holding them out.

"Put them on the table."

She doesn't look up from her desk as she says it. She barely even acknowledges me. I put them down, but think maybe I should try again to engage her. We've only worked together a few days, but this isn't like her.

"Cute shoes. Those must be so hard to walk in all day," I say, looking at her black platform stilettos.

"Yeah," is all she says, still not looking up at me.

"I went over Eric's forms twice so they should be fine." I try again but all she does is nod.

I decide to go all in and be direct. Maybe something else is bothering her, but I think it's directed at me.

"Is everything okay, Skyler?"

She turns around in her chair and gives me a cold look. "Everything is perfectly fine, Mallory. I'm doing my job. You know, the one I fought to get. The job that I turned down the White House for. Meanwhile, I'm shacked up with the two of you." She looks past me, and I turn a little to see Eric standing behind me with a stack of papers. "Looks like I'm the only one here that did it on merit."

With that, she turns back to her desk and ignores the both of us. I'm stunned and don't know what to say. So instead of causing an argument at work, I go over to Eric and take his paperwork from him and bring it to my desk.

Maybe she thinks I'm not pulling my weight around here. But I've been busting my ass as much as she has. I've even found ways to make things faster and more efficient. I worked hard to get to where I am today.

I keep my head down and work for the next three hours, nonstop.

When I hear a ping on my computer, I look up to see an email from Oz, and also see that it's time for lunch. I decide to read my email before I go downstairs and grab some lunch and bring it back to my desk. There's plenty to do still, and I don't want to be seen as the one bringing the team down.

From: *YourOz@gmail.com*
Subject: Missing you
I'm missing you already. How am I supposed to go almost four days without you?

Of course I'll bring you something back. What would you like? Name it and it's yours. I'd love to take you all over the world. You tell me when you want to go, and I'll make it happen.

Thank you for eating at work today. Knowing you're safe makes me rest easy. Hope you're having a good day, baby.

Oh, and you inspired the email address. Thought maybe I should have one for you.
LOVE, Oz

The goofy grin on my face grows as I read his email a couple of times. I'm wondering if he wants me to sign "love," too, based on the all-caps. I'm still bummed about the incident with Skyler, but I try to brush it off while I email him back.

From: *MSullivan@OsbourneCorp.net*
Subject: RE: Missing you
I miss you, too, Oz. I could use one of your hugs right now.

Heading to lunch, so I'll be quick. I'd love some chocolate. I hear they have some good stuff over there.
XOXO, Mallory

Heading down to the cafeteria, I walk through the doors and see that it's been rearranged. There's now a fresh salad bar in the middle, and two guys over to the side making deli sandwiches. There's a menu up offering soups to go with, and I'm instantly in a better mood. Food does that to me. Maybe I was hungry this morning and taking things too seriously.

I get a half sandwich, salad and soup to go, and head up to my desk. When I get there, Skyler and Eric are gone, but I get back to work. I use the quiet time to finish all my reports, then go over to Skyler's desk, grabbing the ones she's completed, thinking I'll get a jump start on those, too.

I'm zoned out when my email pings and I look up at my computer and see an hour has gone by. Before I can read it, I hear Skyler come back to her desk, and then walk over to mine.

"Hey, did you grab those files off my desk?" she asks, looking anywhere but at me.

"Yes. They're finished." I point to a stack right beside her and wait to see if she offers anything else.

She looks at them, and then looks at me with a bit of surprise on her face. "Thanks. I thought I might have to stay late to complete them."

"No problem. Just trying to get ahead on things so we don't have to put in any extra late nights this week. The workload should be distributed equally," I say, shrugging my shoulder.

She looks down at her shoes and then up at me. "Sorry about snapping this morning."

A weight I didn't know was there is lifted at her

words. I can't stand when someone is mad at me. "It's okay. We all have our moments."

"Yeah. Thanks again," she says before walking back to her desk.

Turning around, I click on Oz's email and open it up.

From: *YourOz@gmail.com*
Subject: Don't make me turn this plane around
Is everything okay, baby? What's wrong? I'll bring you a plane full of chocolate if it makes you happy. How was your lunch? Anything good today?
I miss your lips.
LOVE, Oz

The bold on "love" makes me giggle. At this point, he's being silly, and I like playful Oz. I respond to his email quickly. I've got work to do, and I need to get to it.

From: *MSullivan@OsbourneCorp.net*
Subject: RE: Don't make me turn this plane around
Everything is fine. No need to panic. I'm okay now. I needed to grab some food, I guess. And amazing news, the cafeteria was redone and they had an awesome menu today. Totally glad I ate here!

A plane full of chocolate can't be as sweet as you. I miss your lips, too.

I've got to get to work so I don't have to stay late. I texted Paige earlier and told her I want a movie night in, so you'll be happy to know I'll have my phone next to me all night! I'll be all yours then!
XOXO, Mallory

I make my sign-off bold to let him know I saw his. I'm excited as I send the email and get back to work. It's amazing how much I've grown to care for him in such a short amount of time to the point of seeing the *L* word and not freaking out. That in itself should probably freak me out. Oh well, I'm living in the moment!

TWELVE

Mallory

"I THINK YOUR BOSS is following us." I look over my shoulder to see Captain America about half a block behind us.

"Ignore him," Paige huffs, clearly annoyed. But she grabs her ponytail, pulling her hair down and giving it a little fluff. The action catches me off guard. When we'd met in the lobby of the building to head home, they were once again bickering. She still looked pissed at him, but he had this happy smirk on his face as if he liked her sniping at him.

"He's hard to ignore." I look over my shoulder again. Yep, still there. Maybe he's going the same way we are. "I think he likes you," I add, making her look over at me. She gives me a no-go look, which only piques my interest. Men liking Paige isn't new. She's pretty and plays it down for the most part.

I think men are drawn to her because she's a challenge on top of everything. She doesn't flock to men or get all gooey-eyed. Not even over famous hot people when I show her pictures.

"I don't think it's a good idea to date someone you work with, but he's—"

"Stop right there. Just because you're on this love

train of dating doesn't mean I want to hop on. Besides, he's…" She looks over her shoulder this time, and I follow suit. He gives her a wink, making her flip him the bird. "Too perfect," she finally finishes.

"You can't flip your boss off! You'll get fired!" I gape at her.

"He isn't going to do shit."

It's clear Paige is going to do whatever she wants, so I go back to talking about the guy and not her job. "Too perfect, Paige? I mean, really? How can a man be too perfect?" I ask, even though I'd been having the same thoughts about Oz. He always seems to say and do all the right things. It's like I'm waiting for the other shoe to drop.

"This is it." She points to a little restaurant that says Big Bob's on the sign outside. It has probably seen better days. She's told me it has some of the best burgers within walking distance. She pushes inside, and I follow her. The place is slammed, but Paige manages to find us a place at the bar.

"What can I get you ladies?" an older man with thinning hair and dark brown eyes asks from behind the counter. He's in a white apron that looks like it needs a good washing.

"Two ultimate doubles with onion rings." She looks over at me, then behind her. I follow her eyes to see Captain standing outside the restaurant, leaning up against a pole. This is freaking weird. "To go?" she asks, and I nod.

"To go," she tells the man taking our order.

"Can I get you anything to drink while you wait?"

"Two beers. Whatever is cold and on tap is fine."

"You got it," he tells her as he finishes scribbling on his pad before turning around to drop the order to the cook.

"That's weird." I nod to the security guy outside. "What is Captain doing following us? I thought at first we were going the same way or something, but now it's clear he's following us. Well, following you," I amend because the guy has no reason to be after me. I don't even know his name.

"Captain?"

"Yeah, he looks like Captain America, but with tats."

Her mouth does a half smirk like she likes the name. It's not shocking, because it's one of her favorite movies. "I don't know. Maybe he's, like, testing me or something. Making sure I'm watching my surroundings. Or maybe he's a stalker." She adds the last part like she's trying to insult him.

"He can't hear you," I remind her.

"Oh, I'm sure he can read lips."

The waiter drops down both of our drinks and Paige grabs hers, chugging half of it back.

"And how is he so perfect if he's a stalker?" I ask, thinking back to her comment.

"He is. All-American boy. Probably grew up in a loving home with a perfect dad who didn't cheat on his mom and destroy her with a broken heart. I'm sure he went off to the Marines and became a war hero, and now he's back here running security for one of America's biggest companies. He's freaking perfect. It's annoying as shit."

"You like him," I say, because it's clear as day now. Paige gave away more than she realizes with her words.

If there's one thing Paige doesn't like it's asshole men or bad boys. And they seem to be drawn to her. Paige can be a little rude to men, but she likes them sweet. Men never seem to get that with her. You have to work past that first layer of stain her father left behind to find her, and I hadn't seen a man who ever tried.

She picks up the beer again, finishing off the rest of it and turning so her back is to Captain.

"God, I hope it's not that obvious to him," she grumbles.

"Paige has a crush," I say, and I'm not sure if I'm talking to myself or to her.

"It must be contagious. You infected me with your love bug and it's disgusting. We should really detox or something."

Her tone is so somber, I burst out laughing.

"Mal, I'm serious here. I can't do this."

I wrap my arm around her shoulder and pull her closer. "You don't have to do shit if you don't want to," I tell her. "He's your boss and he's following us."

She picks up my beer and takes a few sips. "You should be careful," she says, making me drop my arm from her shoulder and turn in the bar stool so I'm facing her. She continues to face forward. "Men like Oz aren't always what they seem." She actually sounds like she's sorry she's delivering this news. Almost like she knows it's true. That Oz isn't who he says he is.

"Not everyone is your father, Paige. You have got to let that go."

She cocks her head to the side, looking at me.

"I'm not saying you have to do it today, but you can't let it hold you back forever." I pick up my beer and take a few swallows myself, then hand it to her. I'm not going to tell her that she might be pushing men away, too, that the walls she built because of her father are keeping out all men. I believe that a man who really wants to be with her will break through those walls, and that will be a part of how she heals from all that. Paige is worth fighting for, and I think if she falls in love, it's going to be hard, because when Paige lets herself feel, her emotions go deep. I glance back at Captain again, and his eyes are on her before they come to me. He does a half smile, and I return it before turning in my stool again, giving him my back.

"We should have gotten an appetizer or, like, some fries for the walk back."

"I got snacks in my purse," I joke, but is it really a joke if I do have snacks in my purse?

"This is why we've worked well together all these years," she teases.

The waiter comes over, dropping off a bag of our food and a check.

"I got this one. You got pizza." I pull out my wallet and drop a few bills on the counter before polishing off my beer. Paige grabs the bag, and I put my wallet back in my purse and pull my phone out to check my messages.

I wonder how the time change is going to affect Oz texting me. He's probably about to go to bed.

I don't see any missed text messages, and it makes me a little sad.

"I'm going to call Oz real quick before he goes to bed," I tell her as we push out of the restaurant.

"All right. I'm going to use the bathroom."

He's always the one calling me and texting me. I want him to know I miss him, too.

Pulling up his number, I hit Call as I exit the restaurant. I look at Captain, who nods at me. Maybe he's waiting to talk to Paige, or maybe this is something they really do to security people. I know Paige had talked about wanting to be a personal bodyguard. Maybe he'll test her on what all she saw when she was out. Maybe he's taking notes on things he can ask her tomorrow. He's in for a rude awakening; Paige remembers everything.

"Baby." Oz's voice comes over the phone. I hear loud noises in the background like he's in a bar or something.

"Oh. I'm sorry. I thought you might be in bed, and I wanted to tell you good night."

"I wish I was in bed talking to you." It's hard to make out what he's saying with all the noise coming through the line. I hear a woman's laugh in the background and irrational jealousy shoots through me. I'm not used to liking a man enough to ever be jealous.

"Miles, come on, man. I want you to meet someone," I hear someone yell.

"You seem busy. I'll let you go. Sorry to bother you." I pull the phone away from my ear to hang up. The noise is too loud to make anything out.

"Mallory, is that you?" I look up to see my statistics professor from Yale standing in front of me.

"Oh my God. Professor Field." I end my call, slipping my phone back in my purse.

He smiles at me and shakes his head. "It's Joel. I'm no longer your professor. Or a professor at all anymore, for that matter."

"Oh. I'm sorry?" I offer, not sure if that was his own doing or not. Professor Field was one of my favorite teachers at Yale. He had a way of explaining things exactly how I understood them best. Not every teacher had that skill.

He's probably in his late thirties with shaggy brown hair and kind brown eyes. He was the typical professor, always wearing square glasses and tweed jackets. He's around six foot tall, and he always wore some kind of shirt with something funny or funky on it. He seemed like a really sweet guy while I was in school, and I know some of my friends drooled over him in class.

"I'm doing consulting work now. I'm enjoying it more than teaching, actually. Pays better, and I get to make my own schedule."

"That's always nice." I smile, genuinely happy for him.

"How's Osbourne Corp? You got an internship there, didn't you?"

"I did. I'm really enjoying it. I think the hardest part so far is getting used to New York."

"I hear you. I'm a little lost myself and don't really know many people here."

"I know the feeling, but I've met some new people at work. We're going out Friday. You should come," I offer, as Paige comes to stand next to me.

"You talk to Oz?" she abruptly asks, breaking into our conversation.

"Oh, yeah, for a second," I answer her. "Paige, this is one of my professors from Yale, Joel. Joel, this is my roommate, Paige. She went to Yale, too."

She nods at him. "You ready? Our food is getting

cold." She seems impatient and a little annoyed. I look over to see if Captain is still there, thinking that might be the problem or something. I see him still there, but now he's on the phone.

"Yeah, sorry, Joel, but we have to go. I know Friday some of us are going to Marie's Yacht Club over on 11th in Chelsea to have a few drinks after work. You can stop by and say hi if you like. Maybe meet some people. It would be nice to catch up."

"Sounds good. If I'm not working, I might do that." His shaggy hair falls in his face a bit, but his smile is bright. He looks hopeful for a chance to hang out.

Maybe he's really been lonely in the city. I can't imagine being here without Paige.

"Perfect. We'll be there around six. I hope I'll see you then," I say as Paige pulls me away, making our way toward home.

"Geez, I know you're hungry, but no need to be rude."

"Not sure your Oz would like you inviting a man out for drinks," she says, taking me by surprise. That was the last thing I thought she'd say. I thought she was hangry.

"What? He's an old professor and new to town like I am."

"He isn't old," she hits back.

Joel isn't old, but that wasn't what I meant by old. The girls at school crushed on him, but I didn't get all the hype. He kind of looks like a hip nerd or something. I guess if you scaled him compared to all the other professors that would make him hot. I always thought he was nice.

"I didn't mean *old* as in age, *old* like he used to be my teacher. Besides, I talked to Oz on the phone and he's out at a bar from the sounds of it, and I know I heard a woman in the background, so…" I shrug as if I don't care and fight the urge to check my phone. *I will not be needy*, I tell myself.

"If you say so. Just saying he doesn't look like the type that would be okay with you inviting men out for a drink."

"It's a group thing, and you're coming, too."

"Oh, I'm coming. I can't wait to see this."

"What does that mean?" I ask.

"Just saying, I can't wait to see what Oz does, is all."

"Well, I hate to burst your bubble, but Oz is out of town until Saturday, so he won't even be there."

She smirks.

"Maybe I'll invite Captain if you keep that up."

We both look over our shoulders, and Captain is indeed there, following us, still on the phone.

"Or maybe I won't have to invite him if he keeps this up."

THIRTEEN

Mallory

AFTER GRABBING THE PACKAGE Oz left me from my building's doorman, we head up to our place, where I scarf down my burger while reading over Eric's reports and making corrections. I decide when I'm done to take a long soak in the bath. We're lucky that we have our own bathrooms with nice big tubs.

I grab my phone from my purse and pick up the shirt Oz left for me. It looks as worn as my Yale shirt, but his is a faded Jets football shirt. As I take my phone and the shirt with me to the bedroom, I pass by Paige, who's on the couch, typing away on her computer.

"I'm going for a soak and then bed. I'll be up at the normal time if you want to go into work together tomorrow."

She looks up from her computer and gives me a nod. "Sounds good. You talk to Oz yet?" She eyes my phone in my hand, and then looks back at me.

"I'm about to," I say, turning to head toward my room. "'Night."

"'Night."

It's weird, but that's the third time she's asked me about Oz. It's probably because I'm usually glued to my phone or checking it obsessively when it comes to him.

Running the water, I add some bubbles and take out the pins in my hair. I pile it up loosely on top of my head and put a towel on the edge of the tub for drying off my hands.

When I slide in, I reach over, grabbing my phone to see if Oz has texted me. Surprisingly, I've got a dozen text messages from him and a few phone calls, too. Checking the messages first, I scroll through them.

Oz: Baby, answer your phone. I've been trying to call you back.

Oz: It's not what you heard. There are people here in this club, and it was loud.

Oz: Mallory, please answer me. I'm worried.

Oz: I'm sorry, baby. Don't ignore me. I left the club. I can talk.

Oz: Since you're not answering your phone, I'll leave this in a text.

Oz: There was a client that wanted to meet, and I agreed to go out for a drink to talk business.

Oz: I only agreed for business, but I wasn't familiar with the place he suggested and it was a dance club.

Oz: I was there for five minutes, and it just happened to be when you called.

Oz: Please don't get the wrong idea, baby. I care about you so much. Much more than I want to say in a text.

Oz: I would never do anything to disrespect you. Please. Just call me.

Oz: I'm back in my hotel room. I'll be up all night if I don't hear from you.

Oz: I miss you.

His messages make my heart ache and make me smile at the same time. I guess it was a misunderstanding, but I got annoyed instead of hearing him out. Hitting his number, I call him, wanting to let him know everything is okay. I'm sure he's still up and worried.

I don't think my phone makes it through the first ring before Oz is answering.

"Baby." The one word has so much need in it. Maybe even a touch of panic.

"Hey. Sorry, I stuck my phone in my purse and I just saw your messages." I bite my lip, thinking it's technically the truth. I could have picked it up sooner, but I was being a brat.

"No, I'm sorry. I tried to explain on the phone. You know I wouldn't be in a club with someone else, right?" His voice is so sweet and pleading.

"I know. I think I was hangry." He laughs at my joke, but I want him to know the whole truth. "And maybe I was a little jealous I wasn't there with you while it sounded like you were having fun."

"My sweet Mallory. I'm not having any fun without you by my side."

It makes me smile like an idiot when he says adorable things like that. I shouldn't want him to not have fun without me, but it makes me happy to know he likes it when we are together.

"I missed you today. Probably more than I should," I say, scooting down in the tub more.

"Is that water? Are you talking to me while you're in the tub?" His voice gets a bit deeper, and I tingle all over. "I missed you, too, baby. I missed you so damn much."

He yawns, and then it sounds like he's lying down.

"What are you doing?"

"I'm in bed. It's late here, and I have to be up in three hours. I waited to hear from you."

I'm overcome by guilt again for ignoring my phone because I was pissed. I apologize, but he interrupts me.

"I'm so happy you called me, baby. Listen, you enjoy your nice long soak. And if you want, maybe send me some pictures of you while you're enjoying it."

"Oz." I say it like I can't believe he asked me that. Although I've never sent nudes to anyone, suddenly the naughty idea sounds so dirty and sexy.

"I'll need something to wake up to since we can't have our breakfast together tomorrow. I'm already sad about it. Maybe if I have something sweet from you, I can make it through the day."

"I'll think about it," I say, running my hand up my leg. I consider all the dirty things I could send him, and the blush spreads across my cheeks.

"Good night, my sweet Mallory. Wear the shirt I left you. I hope I see you in my dreams."

"I will. For you. 'Night, Oz. I miss you."

With that, we hang up, and I set my phone on the towel. I soak in the bubbles for a few moments, letting my cheeks burn. He says the most romantic things to me. They make me so embarrassed, yet cherished. It's equal parts exciting and overwhelming. I want to do this for him. To show him I'm in this, too.

After my face has cooled down, I grab my phone and take a few snaps before I lose my nerve and stop myself. He's seen all of me already, right? Why should I be so nervous about sending him a few flirty pictures?

I take ten and erase all but one. Then take ten more and only keep one of those. I want to send him five different poses, so I get creative and keep at it.

Finally, after forever, I've got five that I think are suitable. One is pretty tame with me under the bubbles. The second is of my breasts above the water. The third is a pic of my legs spread with a hint of my pussy. And I blush as I debate the last two. Finally, I put my hand over my face and hit Send before I can change my mind. One of the last ones was of my hand holding my pussy lips spread so he could see my clit, and the last one was me bent over with my legs spread. I ought to get some kind of trophy for being able to get in that position and snap a picture. Thank God for timers.

After I send them all, I put my phone down and finish my bath. I think about Oz and wonder what we'll do on Saturday when he gets back. I think about going to his place and maybe telling him I'm ready to stay the night. It hasn't been that long, but I've always thought that when I finally found the right guy, I would know. And it's that way with Oz. It's like this is the guy I've been waiting on. He's the reason I passed on all the guys before. I was waiting on a man like him to come into my life and sweep me off my feet. He's done all that and so much more. I'm ready to take the next step, and that means giving myself completely to him.

Once I've finished in the bathroom, I pull on a pair of panties and then the shirt Oz left me. It makes me smile. I wonder if he's wearing my Yale shirt right now. The thing is so big it would fit him nicely. He'd fill it out better than I do.

Snuggling down in bed, I check my phone, but Oz hasn't texted back. Hopefully he's getting what little sleep he can before he has to go to work. I send him a quick text telling him good-night and sending little kisses, before turning over and falling asleep myself.

I DREAM OF OZ. We're in a tub surrounded by so many bubbles I can't find him. I'm calling his name, but I can't see where he is. I imagine his hands coming through the warm water, though, and his fingers on my pussy. He's rubbing my clit and making me feel so good that I stop worrying about where he is and enjoy it.

I wake up with my hand down my panties, my fingers on my clit and an orgasm pulsing through my body. I came so hard I woke myself up, and I lie there panting.

"Mal, you okay in there? It's almost seven-thirty. We've got to leave in fifteen minutes." Paige's words make me shoot out of bed. I stand in the middle of my room in a panic for five full seconds.

I'm in motion after that, running to the bathroom

and brushing my teeth while putting on some makeup. Thankfully, I'm pinning my hair up today, so I do that as fast as I can, too. I run around the room, yanking out some mismatched lingerie and grabbing some black slacks and a purple sweater out of my closet. It's nothing fancy, but I've barely got five minutes to throw it on with some black heels before hopping out of my room on one foot.

"Phone!" Paige yells from the kitchen, and I bolt back into my room, grabbing it off the bedside table. She stands at the front door, holding out my thermos of coffee for me, and opens the front door. "Let's go. I've already got the elevator waiting."

The two of us book it the three blocks to work, and I'm swiping my security pass on the elevator right at eight. Not too bad for having gotten up so late. I must have forgotten to set my alarm after I texted Oz last night.

The thought of him has me pulling my phone out of my bag, but then I remember what I sent him last night and bite my lip to keep from smiling. Do I really want to see what he has to say after seeing the pictures?

I decide to wait until I get to my desk so I have some privacy. I slip my phone back in my bag. I say good morning to people getting on the elevator and ride it up to my floor. Once I'm there, I greet Linda and see that I've beaten Eric to work again. That makes three days in a row now. Skyler is hanging up her bag as I say hello to her, so she must have just gotten here, as well.

"Morning," I say, testing the waters with her.

"Hey. Did you bring your lunch today? I forgot mine," she says, and I take the opening.

"No, I was running late. I forgot mine, too. Want to eat in the cafeteria?" I offer, hoping she'll say yes.

"Sure. That new salad bar was dope yesterday. I'm in."

I smile as I sit down at my desk, happy that my work friendship is back on course. I don't know what rocked the boat yesterday, but it seems Skyler respects hard work, and I can understand that. Especially when working with someone like Eric, who seems to be skating by.

Taking a deep breath, I pull my phone out and tap on my text messages. I see only one from Oz, and disappointment hits. I click on it, and then I smile.

Oz: If you're reading this, then I've surely died and gone to heaven. You, my gorgeous Mallory, are more stunning than my pathetic words via text are able to say. Grrrrr.

I imagine the sound of his growl. It makes the ache between my legs return, and I think about the orgasm I apparently gave myself in my sleep last night. Jesus. I send him a quick text, thinking he's probably in a meeting. The time difference is so vast, I don't know what he's up to.

Me: Good morning! I'm happy to see you liked the pictures. Maybe I can get some in return today? I've yet to see what's under your sexy suits. I miss you... XXXXX

I slip my phone in my bag and get to work. It's a busy day, and Linda has given us some new information to add to the statistical data we're going through. It's more busywork. But I'm happy to be here and happy to be a part of the team.

RIGHT BEFORE NOON, Linda comes over and gives each of us a breakdown of a new program they're integrating and asks if any of us are familiar with it. I did some side projects for data research in college and it was one of the ones I used. Linda actually beams at me when I tell her, and I think it's mostly because she won't have to train me on it. She puts me in charge of our intern team. I'm to explain to the others how to use it in order to maximize the program. We all agree to break for lunch and then come back afterward to start. Just before I grab my bag to go downstairs, there's a ping on my computer alerting me to a new email.

From: *YourOz@gmail.com*
Subject: Long day…
Hey, baby. I got your text. Sadly, work has been brutal today, and I'm only now getting a break. I see it's lunchtime for you. Are you still planning on staying in like I asked? Please tell me you are. You know I worry. I want some alone time with you tonight…your time around 8? Give me the all clear, my sweet Mallory. I ache for you.
Love, Oz.

I know Skyler is waiting on me, so I type out a response quickly.

From: *MSullivan@OsbourneCorp.Net*
Subject: RE: Long day…

Heading to the cafeteria now... I'm sure I can clear my
schedule for you tonight ;)
Miss you more!
XoXoXoXoXo Mallory

After I hit Send, I lock my computer and grab my
bag. It's a quick lunch because Skyler wants to get a
jump on the program and doesn't want to slow down
when I have to explain it to Eric, as well. When we get
back, we hit the ground running and don't stop until
Linda walks over to us.

"Hey. It's after five. You two need to get out of here."

"Really?" I look down at my watch and see that she's
right. Eric had said he was going to the restroom a while
ago, but it looks like he never came back. Skyler and
I have been plugging away all day, and I guess we got
lost in our work.

"Good job today, ladies. I'm really impressed with
your work." She smiles at us before turning and going
back to her office.

"Thanks for the help today," Skyler says as I gather
my things.

"No problem. I'm down for sharing information if it
makes it easier for everyone."

We take the elevator down together, and I see Paige
in the lobby before me.

"Hey, Skyler, meet my roommate, Paige. Paige, this
is another of the interns, Skyler."

They shake hands and say hello, and I'm reminded
of how Paige acted yesterday with Joel. But then I remind myself that she doesn't like men.

"Yeah, I think I've been invited out with you guys tomorrow night, right?" Paige says, looking at me.

"Oh, good. Guess I'll see you then. You two have a good night," Skyler says, and takes off.

"Can we order food tonight? I'm beat," I say as we make our way outside and head home.

Checking my phone as I walk, I see I have a couple of texts from Oz telling me to be safe going home and that he looks forward to our chat tonight. I notice Captain America is following us again, but Paige doesn't comment, so I let it go. I'm ready for some pajamas and lounging, and I'm too tired to get into men with her tonight.

FOURTEEN

Mallory

IT's BEFORE EIGHT when I close my laptop and grab my phone and head to my bedroom. I spent the last hour looking up new updates on the forums for the new program at work. Learned some stuff that I really think will help. I want to talk to Oz in private, and I'm not sure how long this will take. Paige said she had some work to do and went to her room right after dinner, so I cleaned up the last of the dishes and got things ready for the morning.

As soon as I lie back on the bed, the phone vibrates in my hand. My goofy grin appears as I see Oz's name on my screen.

"Hello there," I say, sinking against my pillow.

"Mallory." My name on his lips sends tingles down my spine, and I wish for the millionth time today he was here by my side.

"Miss me?" There's a playfulness in my voice, and yet there's heat there, too.

"More than you can possibly know."

"Tell me about your day. Maybe it will make me miss you less. I'll feel like I was with you."

"I love hearing you say you miss me." His voice is deep and sounds so close. It's like he's lying next to me in bed, and not on the other side of the world. I smile, thinking no one has ever made me smile so easily with only a few words.

"I bought a company here last year and I was wrapping up some stuff to finish selling it."

"You sell them that quickly?"

"We did some fast big changes to it and a few buyers were jumping to get it. Turned into a little bit of a bidding war. We settled a price so he got the final bid. Spent the day finalizing things."

There's a pause, and I hear a rustling, and then hear him let out a breath like he's lain down. "Now let's discuss the pictures you sent me last night."

My face probably looks like Rudolph's nose, but I decide to own it. He asked for them, and I followed through. Might as well put my nudes where my mouth is. Trying to be a little more confident than I actually am, I go for it.

"Which one was your favorite?" I'm new to flirting, but as long as he's the one doing the talking, I'm sure I'll manage.

"The first one. You're smiling so beautifully, it makes my heart ache. I've stared at it all day."

I'm surprised by his answer, thinking he'd like the dirtier ones better.

"Really?"

"Yes. Really. I wish I could see it now. Your soft lips and sweet pink cheeks. I can picture you now, lying on your bed, talking to me. Your hair's probably up in a messy ponytail like in the pictures. Your perfect neck exposed, waiting for my kisses. What are you doing right now, Mallory? How close am I?"

His words send heat running through me, and suddenly it's one hundred degrees in my room.

"You're very close. I miss my T-shirt," I say, teasing him. "Are you keeping it company?"

"I'm wearing it as we speak, my sweet girl."

"You're joking." There's no way he has it on.

"Oh, but I'm not. I've got it on right now, and not much else. I wanted to smell you while I talked to you. I've slept with it every night since I left your side."

Something about this should be silly, but instead it's turning me on more.

"What else are you wearing?" I ask, pushing for him to tell me more.

"Your shirt, Mallory. And nothing else. Your pictures have had me in a state of pain all day, and I've been needing release. Not to mention, your shirt wasn't the only thing I took. I took the panties, too."

I hear a deep breath and picture him smelling my panties as he strokes himself. My pussy clenches in response. I want to help him. I want to make him feel as good as he makes me feel.

"What can I do?" My words are breathy, and my breasts tighten as my nipples ache.

"I want you to slide your hand down the front of your panties and gently touch your pussy, baby. Tell me if you're wet."

His dirty words make me clench again, and I can guarantee I'm soaked. I've never been talked to like this, and it's turning me on more than I ever imagined.

I do as he says, sliding my hand down into my panties and touching my wet pussy lips. I gasp at the sensation. They're so sensitive to the touch.

"You're wet, aren't you, baby? Your sweet pussy is missing my attention."

I moan into the phone as I spread my lips and rub my clit.

"My cock has been so fucking hard all day thinking about how good your pussy tastes. I missed it so much this morning. Getting to hold you and getting you off. I've leaked come into my underwear all day thinking about what I want to do to you."

"Oz," I whisper, and pulse around my fingers.

"That's it, Mallory. I'm rubbing my cock as I listen to you masturbate. I'm going to come when you do, baby, and not a second before. I wish I was there to put my mouth between your legs and lick up all your honey."

"Oh, God." The image of him between my legs is nearly enough to send me over.

"That's what I dream about, baby. Eating your tight little pussy until you can't walk in a straight line." I hear the sounds of him jerking off his cock, and I don't know how much more I can take. I'm so beyond turned on that I can't think straight. "Is it virgin, baby? Is your wet pussy untouched?"

"Yes," I moan, his filthy words sending little tremors through my body. I would confess anything to him at this point. I'll promise him anything, as long as he keeps talking to me.

"Good girl, Mallory. That's what I want to hear. That I'm the only one who's ever going to touch you. That you've been saving it for me."

"Yes." My moan is louder this time, my body tensing, so close to release.

"Come, my love."

His words send me over the edge, and I contract around my fingers as my back bows off the bed and my legs tense up. It's powerful, and hearing his grunts of release on the other end of the phone only drags out my orgasm more.

I'm lying on the bed, a complete mess. I'm sweaty without a bone left in my body, and I'm trying to catch my breath.

"Baby? Are you alive?"

I laugh into the phone and my cheeks heat. How can I possibly be shy after that?

"Barely. You?"

"I believe I've found heaven for the second time today." I can hear the smile in his voice, and it makes my heart ache for him.

"I miss you. Is it too soon to ache like this?"

"My sweet Mallory. You have no idea how happy it makes me when you say that. You'll be back in my arms before you know it."

"Good. I didn't like my morning routine today."

"Then I'll make sure to spoil you every day when I get back."

"Deal."

"I'm going to get some sleep. I've got to be up in a couple of hours."

Looking over at the clock, I see it's after nine. He must have gotten up to call me. It's early for bed, but I'm so exhausted all of a sudden.

"I think I'm going to turn in early, too. I've got a late night tomorrow, so I should catch up on sleep."

"Late night?" Suddenly, he sounds wide-awake.

"Yes, remember? I'm going out with some people tomorrow after work. It's to the bar next door." My tone sounds like I'm asking for permission. "Paige is coming with me," I say, trying to let him know I'll have a friend.

He's quiet for so long, I pull the phone away from my ear to check to see if I've lost him.

"Oz?"

"I'm here," he says, but I can't read his voice. "I must have forgotten you mentioned that."

"It's no big deal. Just a drink after work, and then I'm home. Maybe we can have another phone chat?" I offer, thinking maybe this will bring back his good mood.

"Sure. We'll see." There's a pause, and it sounds like he's pacing. "It's fine. Get some sleep, baby. We'll talk in the morning."

"Are you sure?" It's weird to check in with him, but I remember how I felt the other night when he was at that nightclub and I tried to talk to him. I don't want to do the same thing to him, so I try to smooth things over. "I'm sure I can reschedule—"

"No. Really. It's okay, baby. We'll talk in the morning. You worry about getting a good night's sleep. Set your alarm this time."

I laugh, thinking about my running around this morning. "I'll do my best."

"I miss you, Mallory."

"I miss you, too, Oz."

When we hang up, I set my alarm and pull the covers over me, thinking that saying "I miss you" sounds an awful lot like something else. And before I fall asleep, a thought crosses my mind.

I don't remember telling him that I forgot to set my alarm.

FIFTEEN
Mallory

I REFRESH MY EMAIL again before picking up my phone to check for a new text message.

Still nothing.

I haven't heard a peep from him all morning, and it's a little after noon now. I've really become too dependent on these messages. But still, this isn't Oz. It's not like him, based on what I've learned about him over the last week. He's always sending me something, even if it's a small note or a cute picture. It's also weird to think how I've only known him for a week, yet he's so vital to my everyday life now. I guess he is, though, when it comes to my new life here in New York. He's been a part of it since the very first day. Even now, he isn't ever far from my mind. He slipped in so easily, and I grabbed on to him, experiencing things I never had before.

He makes me feel so important to him. I'm special to him with all the little silly things he does. Like having to see me, wanting to bring me breakfast or needing to hear my voice. What has me melting most of all is the way he's always checking on me. That isn't something I've ever had. I know I'm well past the age of needing someone to look out for me, but it's good to have it for once in my life. Someone making sure I eat and being worried about me going out. I should be annoyed, but all it does is show me that he loves me, cares for me.

The only person I've ever loved is Paige. She's the only one who's been in my life long enough for that to even happen. Everyone else seemed to float in and out too quickly. A few teachers stood out from time to time, but living in the system, sometimes people bounced too fast. I could never latch on to anyone. I'd taught myself not to, because it only led to heartbreak. But with Oz, it's something deeper, something that's growing. It will be different to how I love Paige. This is life-changing. Just having these thoughts scares me, too. It's so early to be having them. I try to push all that from my mind. It's about living in the now. I can't think about getting hurt or I'll never have a relationship. I'm grabbing on to this and seeing where it will take me.

Maybe he's really busy today. He's working, like I should be doing and not checking my phone every five minutes and evaluating this relationship like it's a math problem I can solve.

"Sale at Nordstrom," Skyler says, popping her head up over the cubicle wall and taking me by surprise. "Like, big." She spreads her arms wide, indicating how big the sale is. "Only two blocks that way." She points over her shoulder.

"We're skipping lunch, I take it?"

"It's worth it. Plus, the place we're going after work has small plates, so we can load up to make up for skipping lunch."

"Now that's some math I can get with," I say, making her laugh as I lock my computer screen. But not before refreshing my in-box one more time. I clearly have no self-control when it comes to Oz. "I do need some new clothes to keep up around here," I add, grabbing my purse from the bottom drawer of my desk and slipping my phone in it.

"I know. The women around here have the nicest stuff. And my freaking girlfriend and I are different sizes, so we can't even share clothes."

We make our way down the hall toward the elevator.

"I understand. My roommate is tiny. I'm not squeezing into anything of hers. I'm happy we wear the same shoe size."

"At least you have that," Skyler says, hitting the button for the elevator. "You wearing that tonight?" She nods at my outfit. I'm wearing simple black pants and a white silk blouse that has a big bow at the neck.

"Actually, I've got this cute purple-and-silver dress I'm going to wear tonight. I'll change into it before we head out, but I'll wear these shoes."

I lift one of my heels. They're a deep purple, but the heels are covered in diamonds. Paige got them over a year ago, but they're basically mine now. I'm obsessed with them and always try to find clothes that match them. Now that I'm thinking about it, I bet a purple bra with matching underwear with them would be crazy hot. I'll be looking for that for sure at Nordstrom. Maybe I could take a picture in the dressing room and send it to Oz. Maybe that would get me a text back.

"Those are hot," she agrees, looking at them.

The elevator dings on the lobby floor, and we both exit.

"How about you? What are you wearing?"

"Mallory?" I hear Paige yell across the lobby, cutting

Skyler off before she can answer me. We both turn to look at her as she hurriedly walks over to us.

"Where are you going?" she asks when she's finally standing in front of me.

"Nordstrom. They're having a sale. I would've invited you, but you said you had lunch, like, an hour ago."

She shifts a little on her feet before looking over her shoulder. I follow her line of sight to see Captain staring at all of us.

"Does he follow you everywhere?" I would think this Captain guy is creepy if I didn't know he was the head of security here. And the fact that Paige is kind of crushing on him.

"We're sort of teamed up," she says dismissively, clearly not wanting to talk about him. "But you can't go. I need to talk to you." She almost seems a little out of breath and rushed.

"It's cool. Do what you need to do. I can head out on my own," Skyler says.

"Sorry. Next time," I offer, disappointed that I'm ditching her, but it's clear Paige needs to talk.

"Don't hate me when I come back with a bag full of goodies that only cost me half the price," she teases before doing a mock salute and heading out the door.

"Over there?" I point to a bench in one of the corners in the giant lobby.

She nods, and I follow her over and sit down with her.

"What's up? You're kind of freaking me out."

"I think we should get a pet."

"You think we should get a pet," I repeat, making sure I heard her right.

"Maybe a dog."

"Maybe a dog," I repeat again, unable to stop myself, because this isn't adding up.

"Stop that."

"What? I'm making sure I'm hearing you right. You know, the person who said they'd never get an animal because they're a pain in the ass."

"Maybe you're right. Never mind." She stands up. "Glad we got that worked out."

She walks off, leaving me sitting on the bench. What the hell was that? "You coming?" she says when she reaches the elevators.

I stand up, pulling my badge out and flashing it to the front desk. They probably know who I am by now, but I'm still pretty new.

"You're acting weird," I tell her as we wait for the elevator to arrive.

"We meeting in the lobby to go out for drinks?" she asks, ignoring my comment.

"No. Come to my floor. We have a nice bathroom, and I want to change and touch up my makeup."

"Sounds good."

The elevator dings, and we both get on. I hit the floor for the cafeteria since I have some time to eat now. I might as well get a little something.

"I'll be at your desk a little after five," Paige says as she gets off on her floor. I shake my head at her. She's acting like a weirdo. Maybe this crush is messing with her head or something. I can relate.

When I get to the cafeteria, I get a salad and take a seat at one of the tables.

"Did you hear there's some big meeting on Monday?

I wonder what's going on. We hardly ever have those. Wonder if the big boss will be there," I hear a girl from a table behind me say with a dreamy sigh in her voice. Wondering what she's talking about, I pull out my phone and check my work emails.

In my in-box is indeed an email about a meeting that everyone is required to attend. It's going to be on the first floor early Monday morning.

"He never comes to any of the meetings. I've maybe seen him around four times in the year I've worked here. He stays holed up in his office. I hear he's a giant asshole, which I'm guessing is true because the times I did see him, he was pissed off, so…"

I shrug off her words. I've been here a week, so I should be in the clear if there's any backlash about anything in the last-minute meeting.

"Even when he's all pissed off, he's still crazy hot. I hear he's single." The women continue chatting. "Maybe if he got laid he wouldn't be such an asshole."

"I think he is single, because he's always on his own at big events. I check online for him sometimes, but all the red carpet shots are solo. Either that, or he has that secretary of his with him who guards his door like a pit bull. Maybe he's sticking it to her." They both laugh, and I roll my eyes at the cliché gossip.

"I think she's married though."

"Like that ever stops them." They both laugh again.

I take a few more bites of my lunch before picking up my tray and dumping it. I head to my desk, but when I get back, I see neither Skyler nor Eric have returned.

I decide to jump right back into my reports, still a

little sad about not hearing from Oz today. It's like it's put a damper on my day.

Twenty minutes later, Skyler comes strolling in with three bags in her hands.

"Everything cool with your friend?" she asks.

"Yeah. She was having a weird moment." I eye her bags.

"Three shirts, two pairs of pants and a pair of shoes."

"Damn, you made out."

"Yeah, but the shoes are for my girl."

"She still coming tonight?" I ask, wanting to meet her. Skyler brings her up all the time, and every time she talks about her, her face lights up. I wonder if I look like that when I talk to Paige about Oz.

"Yep. She's meeting me in the lobby."

"Nice. Paige is going to meet me up here so I can change first."

"Your man coming tonight?" She smiles, but her tone seems a little wary.

"Nope, he's out of town. But I did invite an old college professor who's new to the city, too, but I'm not sure if he's going to make it."

"This professor a man?" She raises her eyebrows as she asks, making me think back to Paige's reaction about it, too.

"Yes, why is that weird? Paige acted like it was weird, too."

"Just curious," she says, putting her bags next to her desk. Now I'm second-guessing myself. It's not like I have a crush on Joel. In fact, he wrote me a crazy good letter of recommendation when I applied for internships. If anything I'm thankful.

"I got you a cookie." I pick it up from my desk and hand it over the partition. "Thought you might be hungry after all that shopping. It's an I'm-sorry-for-the-last-minute-ditch cookie, but maybe not after seeing your bags. I'm not sure I should give it to you."

She snatches it out of my hand.

"I forgive you." She unwraps it from the napkin and takes a giant bite out of it. "Let's bust these reports out so we can get out of here."

SIXTEEN

Mallory

LEANING OVER THE SINK, I put on a heavy shadow and an extra layer of mascara.

"Will you stop that?" I say, looking at Paige in the mirror. She's pacing the bathroom and it's making me nervous. "What's wrong?"

She stops and looks over at me, shaking her head. "Nothing. Just ready to go."

"I'll be done in a second. Pump your brakes." I wink at her in the mirror. She hates when I say that. "Is this about Captain America?"

"No. Maybe. Sort of." She goes back to pacing, and I smile.

Pulling out the pins in my hair, I let my brown locks fall to my shoulders. They're a bit wavy from being up all day, but I think it gives me a sexy look. That makes me think of Oz and of how I didn't hear from him today. He's probably super busy with work, and I'm sure I'll hear from him tonight.

I watch as Paige comes over and stands beside me while I pack my makeup bag.

"Hey. I love you. You know that, right?"

Looking up, I see there's a worry in her eyes.

"Yeah. I love you, too, Paige. Is everything okay? You were weird today in the lobby, and now you're off."

She smiles as she lets out a deep breath. "I'm good. You're the best friend I've ever had, and I want to make sure you know it. Life is short, right?"

I let out a little laugh, thinking I've been telling myself the same thing all week. "Yep. I completely agree." I reach out and wrap her up in a hug. We're like sisters, and sometimes you need a hug from your sister.

"Now," I say, pulling back from her, "let's go have a drink and shake some tail feathers."

"Okay," she says, and it sounds like there's still a bit of sadness to her tone.

Personally I think she's all twisted up about her man and needs to let it go. Live in the moment and enjoy herself. That's what I plan on doing. And tomorrow, when Oz gets back to town, I'm going to spend the day showing him how much I missed him.

We head out of the building and around the corner to Marie's Yacht Club. A lot of people from work come here to catch a drink before they head home. When we walk in, I spot Skyler at a table in the back with a group of people around her. Paige and I make our way over, and I introduce her to the people I know, along with being introduced to the ones I don't. There are about fifteen to twenty people total, milling around in the back, so Paige and I head to the bar to grab a drink.

"A lot of people came," Paige says as she looks around the place.

"Yeah, it should be fun this way," I say, grabbing our beers and passing her one. "Let's order some food. I'm starving."

"You're in charge," she says, and follows my lead.

WE SPEND A couple of hours at the bar, ordering food and hanging out. I have a few beers and then switch to Jameson, wanting something a bit stronger.

"You sure you should be drinking so much?" Paige asks me after I finish my whiskey.

"I wanted to get a good buzz before we go dancing." I shrug like it's no big deal. It usually takes me a few drinks before I can get on the dance floor. Paige sips her beer and leans back in her chair.

"I think it's time to bust some moves," Skyler's partner, Jamie, says. She stands up, shaking her hips, and we all laugh.

I get up to follow her and Skyler, but Paige grabs my arm on the way out.

"I'm not feeling so well, Mal. Can we go home?" There's concern in her eyes, and I take a step toward her.

As I do, I see Captain America out of the corner of my eye. He's standing outside the bar, like he's been waiting for us to leave.

"You're in luck. Your man is outside, and I'm sure he'd love nothing more than to take you home."

"Hey, Mallory, I thought I'd miss you." Just then, I turn around to see Joel approach us.

"Hey!" I say, overly excited. I know I've had a few too many drinks by how happy I'm sounding. Whenever I drink too much, I get goofy.

Walking over to him, I reach out and give him a high five. I laugh because it's a silly thing to do, but I'm genuinely happy he came out.

"You guys ready?" I hear Skyler say, standing with Jamie.

I laugh, looking around and thinking this needs to get sorted out.

"Captain America. Paige isn't feeling so good. Can you walk her home?" I yell to him as he enters the bar, getting his attention. I turn to Joel and smile at him. "We're going dancing next door. You in?"

He says yes, and both Skyler and Jamie hoot with excitement. He walks with them, and I take a step in that direction, but again, Paige grabs my arm.

"Mal. Come home with me. Let's call it a night."

I lean in, whispering, but I'm sure it's way too loud after all my drinks, so Captain America hears everything. "Let him take you home. I bet he'd let you rock that body of his."

She rolls her eyes and tries to pull me with her. Suddenly, I'm irritated that she's trying to keep me from having fun.

"Stop it, Paige. I'm going to dance for a bit, and then head home. I'll call you when I leave."

At my words she drops my arms and squares her shoulders. "Fine. I'll go with you."

When she takes a step in my direction, I hold my hand up. "No, I think I'm good on my own tonight."

I'm pissed off as I walk away, wondering why she keeps trying to make me go home. I'm a grown woman blowing off some steam after a hard day at work. Jesus, it's not like I'm kicking a puppy.

When I walk around the corner, I see Skyler, Jamie and Joel up ahead and I take long steps to catch up with them. Once we're at the entrance of the club, I shake off the aggravation from a second ago. I like being happy Mallory when I'm buzzed, and I don't want to let her weird mood spoil tonight. My first week of work rocked, and I want to let my hair down. Whenever we went out in college, we always cut the nights short, more focused on school than anything.

As soon as we're inside, Skyler pulls me onto the dance floor while Jamie and Joel shove their way to the bar to grab us drinks. The DJ has got the bass thumping, and I'm all kinds of wonderful. Skyler and I are silly as we dance, doing the robot and laughing.

I'm sweating by the time Joel and Jamie get back from the bar with our drinks. He hands me another whiskey and a bottle of water, and I thankfully chug both, the whiskey burning my throat, but warming up my body, and the cold water probably a good idea at this point.

After both of my drinks are drained, I'm back to dancing, and this time Joel dances, too. Skyler and Jamie are dancing with us, so it's more like a group dance than us coupling up. I'm laughing and having a good time, really happy to shake off the blues from today. Not only with Paige now, but my funk about Oz being quiet for so long. I'm going to head home tonight and take some dirty pictures for him. He'll love getting them in the morning.

Suddenly, the music turns from fun and bouncy to a slow, sexual beat.

I look over and see Skyler and Jamie wrapped around each other as the crowd moves in closer. Joel reaches for me, and I laugh it off, but as bodies move on the dance floor I'm pushed into him.

He grips my waist and moves against me. I take his hand off me and put a little space between us but keep dancing. He grabs my hips again pulling me into him. I'm about to tell him I've had enough dancing, when there's a break in the crowd and a fist comes flying.

The music keeps playing, and I watch in shock as Oz leans down and punches Joel in the face again. It takes me half a second to react.

"Oz!" I shout over the music, and he turns to look at me. His dark waves are all awry and he's breathing hard. He's dressed in a pair of jeans and a T-shirt, and he looks like he's sweating. Jesus, did he run all the way from London?

Out of the corner of my eye, I see Joel sit up and I reach out to help him up. Oz moves to step in between us and I give him a death stare. He freezes, and Joel stands, putting his hand to his face. I think there's blood running down his chin, and I'm so angry at Oz I could spit nails.

I look over to see Skyler and Jamie, both with their mouths open. Then Jamie smiles and leans over to yell, "Your boyfriend is so hot!"

Skyler rolls her eyes and pulls Jamie back to her, but then comes over to me. "You got this?"

"Yeah. I'm good," I shout. I turn to Oz and push past him.

"Are you okay?" I ask Joel over the music. Oz's hands grip my waist, pulling me gently back to him, and I'm getting even angrier that I don't hate his touch.

"Yeah. Sorry, I didn't know you had a bodyguard. I'll talk to you later." He glares at Oz over my shoulder before making his way out of the club.

Everything happened so fast. Most of the people on the dance floor didn't see anything happen. Not even a bouncer comes over to stop the shit, and that's what they're hired to do.

Oz wraps his arms around me tighter. He leans over me, trying to blanket my body.

"Get off me," I say, pushing at his immovable hands. "I can't believe you did that." I actually stomp my foot, thinking it will get him to let me go, but he places his warm lips on my neck and gives me a gentle kiss.

I will not lean into him. I will not give in to this. I will not like this one bit.

His big hands flatten on my stomach, and his hips push into my ass. The sexy bass runs through my buzzed blood, and I'm reminded of how much I missed his touch. One of his palms runs up my body, cupping my breast as he kisses my neck more. The other slides down my thigh, his fingers tracing the hem of my dress as his big body moves with mine.

"I'm sorry, baby. I was going to surprise you, but then I saw someone with his hands on you and lost it. I missed you so much, Mallory. Please don't be mad."

"You bust in here like you own the place, and think it's okay for you to punch my friend? You can't steamroll me, Oz."

"Mallory, nobody puts their hands on what's mine. Nobody."

I push away from his grip, hating the loss of his hands on my body, and immediately wanting it back. But I have to stand my ground. I can't have him thinking that he can get away with this kind of behavior without me putting up a fight. I whip around and the sight of him is nearly impossible to resist. Gritting my teeth, I turn to walk away. I'm a little too tipsy to try and figure out what it is I want to say. I know I'm mad.

Before I make it a single step he's pulling me into his arms. I hold both my fists up against his chest and try to push off of him. But this time he doesn't let me go.

"Stop it, Oz. You're being a...a..." I can't think of something mean to call him, because I don't want to hurt him. I want him to know I'm mad. "A panda."

He laughs and holds me tighter. "A panda?"

I think for a second, and then get mad at myself. "I was trying to think of a bear. Damn it, I messed it up."

I fall against his chest and let out a sigh. The rumble of his chest resonates as he pulls me close.

"Baby, you can call me whatever you want. As long as you don't try and run from me."

I melt into his body, not wanting to fight. I missed him so much I can hardly stand it, and I hate to admit how much I don't want to resist. His hands move up my back and the hum of excitement rolls over me again.

"Don't do it again," I mumble into his chest.

His mouth moves to my neck, and then his lips are on me there. "I'll always keep you safe, baby. That isn't up for debate. Ever. But next time I'll try not to hit someone."

His promise, although not exactly what I mean, is good enough for me. I squeeze my arms around his neck and his hands palm my ass.

He licks behind my ear while his words melt over me like hot fudge, and I'm a slave to him once again. I fall into him, giving my body over and loving him against me.

"Oz," I whisper, and I'm in a cloud of lust.

Now with him around me, I'm sexual and wanton and I stare at his face, looking into those sapphires I've missed so much. I run my fingers through his hair and stare at him. It feels like it's been months since I've seen him, rather than days. He pulls me in close and leans down, placing his lips on mine.

The kiss is like coming home, and my body responds instantly. The sexual thump of lust around us and being deprived of him for so long makes me bold. Pulling myself up on him, I wrap my legs around his waist, and he grips my ass.

He breaks the kiss, looking around, then he's in motion.

"Where are we going?" I ask, kissing his chin and down his neck.

"Home."

"Mmm," I hum as he carries me out of the club and into the back of his limo.

I know it's his immediately because it smells like his warm honey and amber. The scent surrounds me as he shuts the door. I grind on his lap, wanting him against me.

"I missed you so much," I whisper against his neck as his erection presses in the right spot.

"How much, baby?" he asks, reaching between us and pushing my dress up the rest of the way.

His fingers are at my panties, and then the cool air hits my pussy. It's dark in the back of the limo, but he's got my panties to the side as his finger pets my clit, and then dips inside me.

"A lot," I moan, throwing my head back and riding his thick finger. A tiny pinch of pain stings as he puts in a second one, but I've had enough alcohol to make me forget about it.

"That's it, Mallory. Ride my hand. Come for me, baby. Let your body show you who you belong to."

He's got two fingers in my pussy and his thumb on my clit as my hips rock back and forth on his hand. I didn't realize how horny I was until I was next to him again. It was like my body shut off until I could be with him again.

Then he pulls back making me whimper. I was so close. It was right there.

"Who does this belong to, Mallory?" The palm of his hand cups me, lying against my clit. I try and push forward wanting the friction but he only pulls back more. "Say what we both know to be true and I'll give it to you."

"It belongs to you," I moan in a begging plea. Not fighting what he's saying because it feels so right and he gives me what I need.

"Oz!" I shout as the orgasm rockets through me. It's fast, but it's so good that I nearly collapse on top of him afterward.

I whine when he takes his fingers from inside me. I want his warmth back. But when I hear him licking his digits clean, I remember how much he missed my taste, and I can't be mad.

I'm half-asleep when the limo comes to a stop, and Oz carries me out of the car.

"I want to sleep with you," I mumble against his chest.

"You are, baby. I told you I wanted a whole day. And I'm getting it. Starting now."

Smiling, I throw my arms around his neck and let him lead. It's good being in his arms again and knowing that he'll take care of me. There's nothing like trusting someone completely to make you fall in love.

SEVENTEEN

Mallory

MY DREAMS ARE SCATTERED, and I can't make anything
out clearly. I'm in a sea of people, and suddenly Oz is
there. He's the only thing I can focus on, and I run to
him. His heat is against me, but he's so far away. I want
to pull him closer, but he's out of reach. I'm aching for
him, but I can't get there.

Opening my eyes, I see the room is pitch-black and
I have a tiny moment of panic. But then his smell fills
my lungs, and his strong arms tighten around me and
I know I'm safe.

The cool sheets brush against my skin, and I discern
I have on panties and nothing else. I must have passed
out in Oz's arms when he carried me inside his home,
because I don't remember anything beyond the limo.
Looking at the bedside table, I see it's four in the morning. I can never sleep through the night when I drink,
but on the plus side, I don't have a hangover.

I'm lying on my back with Oz wrapped around me,
and it's the most wonderful feeling in the world. His
warm skin against mine is making my body come alive,
and I want him. His head is against my neck, and his
breaths on that sensitive spot are driving me wild. His
big hand is on my naked breast, and I'm reminded of

how he played with my nipples when he got me off. Suddenly, desire is pooling between my legs, and I'm yearning for him like never before.

I reach out and run my hand across his forearm and up his biceps. He moves under me as he lets out a little hum, so I keep going. I run my hand down his side, then move it lower to his hip. When I don't come into contact with any underwear, my pussy clenches. He must have left my panties on to try to keep himself from taking me. The thought makes me happy. And naughty.

As my hand moves down his hip, he thrusts against me, and it's then the steel-hard ridge of his naked cock rubs against my thigh. Behaving boldly, I move my hand between us to where he's hardest and wrap my hand around him. The long, thick shaft is heavy as I move up and down, testing his size. His cock pulses in my palm, and I try to squeeze my thighs together for relief. I ache for him, long for him to be inside me, and I don't think I can wait another second. This is what I've been wanting, and now I have him lying naked in bed next to me.

"Mallory," he moans against my neck, and thrusts his cock into my hand.

"Oz. I need you," I whisper, his lips kissing me below my ear.

"What do you need, baby?" His voice is sleepy but deep and filled with sex.

As I grip him tighter, he shudders beside me. "You. I want you, Oz. Please."

"Be careful what you ask for. Because if I have you, I won't stop."

The threat in his voice sends a thrill of excitement

though me, and makes me desire him more. It should be impossible to be this turned on, but lust is raging through me, and I'm unable to quiet it.

"Don't stop. Please."

He grunts and kisses down my neck, moving his big body over mine. In the dark, I can't see anything, but it heightens my passion. Making me aware of every little detail beyond sight. He works his way down my chest, and his cock slips from my hand. I miss holding it, but the warm slick heat of his mouth is driving me crazy.

His body moves between my legs and he knees my thighs apart. He's rough as he does it, and I like that he isn't being delicate. It's not painful; it's the complete opposite. It's as if he's taking what he wants, and the thrill of his possession is intoxicating. The weight of him on me, with his stomach against my pussy and his mouth on my breast, is overwhelming. My nipple is sucked into his mouth, and my back nearly comes off the bed to follow the sensation. I've never felt anything like this before, and my body arches to get closer to the warm heat.

He releases my nipple with a *pop*, and I cry out at the loss.

"I'm going to do so many things to your body, baby. Lie here and let me love you and give you what you need. Let me own every inch of you."

I grab his hair, gripping the wavy locks between my fingers. I tighten them in it as he returns to my nipple, sucking it into his mouth again. He licks me, then bites a little. The sensation forces me to take in a sharp breath, and I moan his name. His mouth tortures me, going back and forth between breasts, making sure each has equal attention.

"Slow down," he whispers, and I don't know if he's talking to me, to himself, or to time.

I want this to last forever, but I also want more.

Oz moves down farther, kissing my belly along the way. He pauses there to kiss my sides and across my belly button. The wet heat on one hip makes me moan as he moves to the other, tasting me there.

"So soft. So fucking perfect." His voice is gruff, making goose bumps scatter across my skin. "You're mine now, Mallory. I'm going to make you cling to me until there's never a question of who you belong to."

His hands push my thighs open farther, and I'm a little grateful it's dark in here. I can't see what he's doing, and he can't see my blush as he places a kiss over my panty-covered pussy.

"I can't keep my mouth off you," he says, repeating the action.

This time when he kisses my pussy, his mouth opens over the material and the warm wetness seeps through my panties.

"I can taste your sweetness on them. You're so wet you've soaked through. It's all for me, isn't it? Every inch of you is just for me." The possessiveness is thick in his voice.

I raise my hips, wanting his mouth again, but he doesn't give it to me. Instead, he reaches up to the front of my underwear, grabbing the waistband and giving it a firm tug. The lacy material gives way, and he tears them off me. The aggressive move heightens my arousal.

Cool air hits my pussy, but I'm quickly warmed when he covers my tender, wet flesh with his mouth.

"Oz!" I shout, as slick heat rolls across my clit, circling it and giving it pressure. The sensation is unlike anything I could've ever imagined, and I spread my legs wider giving him as much of me as he wants.

He slides his thick fingers up my thigh and penetrates me as he bites down softly on my tiny nub. The pinch of pain mixed with overwhelming pleasure makes me dizzy with lust.

Hot breath tickles my pussy as his fingers curl upward inside me, rubbing some perfect place that has me mewling with need. The intensity of the touch is indescribable, and Oz holds me down as he pulls the pleasure out of me.

"So sticky sweet," he says, and I can hear how wet I am.

My face burns from the blush, but I'm so far gone I don't care. I'm lifting my hips and begging him to put his mouth on me. Embarrassment has left the bed.

"Fuck, I can't wait to do this with my cock. I'm going to own you, Mallory. Every inch of me is going mark every inch of you."

He thrusts his fingers in and out of my wet channel, and my thighs shake. This is pleasure unlike any I've ever known, and I never want him to stop.

"I've waited so long to taste you, to have you. Now you're all mine." He sounds aggressive as he says it. Almost impatient, like he's waited forever.

He latches his mouth back on to me, and the flat of his tongue keeps licking over and over. He's like a tiger giving me a bath as he laps up my dripping pussy. It's the perfect tempo, and I writhe on the bed. The even, firm strokes repeat until my pleasure can't build any higher.

Gripping his hair tightly, I throw my head back and shout his name as I come on his fingers and against his face. I ride his hand and mouth, stretching out the orgasm as long as I can. It's earth-shattering, and I've gone weak when I come down and catch my breath. The orgasm was fast but no less fierce as it echoes through my veins.

Oz pulls away only slightly to kiss the top of my pussy, above my clit. Then he slips his fingers out of me and I clench at the loss. I can hear him lick them clean as he moves up a little more.

He kisses my hips again, and then my stomach, making me moan. He nuzzles me there, and the prickles of his day-old shave abrade my oversensitive skin and create shivers in their wake. I'm sure I'll have a burn on my pussy from it, too, though it's the last thing I'm worried about now.

"I need inside you, Mallory," he says against my soft belly. "Are you on the pill?" He places a gentle kiss on my belly button, but I want to cry at his question.

"No. Do you have anything?" Jesus, I can't even bring myself to say the word *condom*. Why didn't I think of this before? I'm cursing myself as he shakes his head.

"I don't want to use one with you." He licks over to my hip, and my desire is building by the minute. "I'll pull out, baby. I want you bare."

I'm not an idiot. I've attended Sex Ed, and the foster system taught me what unplanned pregnancy can do.

But I'm a puddle of horny lust, and I can't tell him no. This is when I should be clearest, but I'm so beyond reason when it comes to him that I'll give him anything he wants. Including unprotected sex.

"Okay," I whisper, quietly giving power over to him.

He growls and moves up my body, kissing every inch of me along the way. His hands are all over me, and his mouth won't leave my skin. It's as if he is trying to devour me, and I do nothing but lie there and let him.

When he gets to my breasts, he torments my nipples, loving each one with his tongue and teeth. They are going to be sore later, but I can't think about that. I can only think about now.

The hard head of his cock comes up against my opening, and I moan at the heat between us. He teases me, rubbing the tip on my clit as his mouth moves to my neck. He's everywhere, and my nerve endings are ablaze. He's got them all charged, and each touch is like sweet fire.

"Mallory." He says my name as if it's an ache deep in his chest. He's demanding, and I have no power to tell him no.

"Please, Oz. Make love to me."

He thrusts inside at my surrender, and his sudden girth is painful. But his fingers pinching my nipple and his mouth on my neck keep me distracted enough to breathe through it. He holds himself fully inside me, letting me adjust, and the distractions are working.

"My sweet girl. You don't know how long I've waited for this." His words are through pained breaths, and he sounds so close to the edge. I wrap my arms and legs around him, holding him tightly to me. I want to offer my body to him as a reward, and give him what he gives me. A sense of belonging and of coming home.

It's as if we've both waited our whole lives to get to this moment, and something special passes between us. His familiar scent washes over me, and his mouth continues to kiss every inch of my exposed skin.

He moves slightly, and the sweet drag of his cock sets my body alive. The thin layer of sweat on my skin makes Oz slide against me as he thrusts, and it's beyond erotic. It's as if the passion that has formed between us helps our bodies connect in the most primal way possible. The need between us so elemental that nothing could stop us.

His bare cock inside me feels taboo, as if we're breaking some kind of rule. Not using protection adds to the element of secrecy, and it's turning me on even more. The irresponsible part of me relishes it. I've never done it before, and it feels so fucking dirty sweet. I raise my hips, wanting all of him as deep as possible, and he grunts on top of me. Both of us know what we're doing and what it could lead to, yet his bare cock keeps thrusting away.

The thought has my pussy tightening around him, ready to come again. "Oz," I moan, and even I can hear the need in my voice.

He takes his mouth away from my neck, moving to my ear.

"Let me come inside you, baby. Don't make me pull out." His deep voice is telling me all the things I shouldn't want, so why am I so turned on by it?

His words make me bear down on him harder as

he grinds himself into me. It's as if I'm begging him to do it.

"I'll take care of you, baby. I take care of everything." His hands come up to brush the damn hair out of my face as he licks my neck. "You're mine, Mallory. I'll never let you go."

"Oh God, Oz." I clench again, and I know I'm going to come. It's building so high, and his thick cock is filling me so perfectly.

He growls as he grinds against my clit. He's not even pulling out to thrust now. He wants to be inside me as much as possible.

"Please, baby," he says, licking the shell of my ear.

I'm overwhelmed with want, and playing on the edge has heightened my need. This is so wrong. But being with him in this way is so right. It's like I've finally found my other half, and sharing my body with him is natural. Doing this together, both of us bare, is perfect.

"Yes," I whisper.

The capitulation has me falling over the edge, giving him what he wants most. Me.

His strong, smooth back tenses under my palms as he holds himself in me, as deep as possible, and I come on his cock.

"Oz!"

I shout as my pussy pulses around his throbbing length, and he comes inside me. I continue to orgasm, knowing it's so wrong that we did it, but not being able to stop my body's reaction. The raw sex was so good and so dirty, but still sweet at the core. It was possessive and primal, and I had the strongest orgasm I've ever experienced.

We finally shared ourselves in the most intimate way possible, and I don't think about what it all actually means. In this moment, I'm falling for him, and I let myself be in the moment. It's the closest I've ever been to someone, and I refuse to think about anything other than the bliss between us.

I'm suddenly exhausted. Wiped out from the orgasms, my body is depleted of energy. I try to cling to Oz, but my fingers slip from his back, and my legs have no strength left to hold him to me.

I don't know if I fall asleep before he pulls out or if he stays in me all night. What I do know is that when I find Oz in my dreams, he holds me and tells me he loves me. Or maybe that wasn't a dream at all.

EIGHTEEN

Mallory

I LIE ON my back, the morning sun creeping through the tall windows that span the far wall. Oz is on his stomach with one arm wrapped around me as the night before plays through my mind. I think about my little spat with Paige and how I was a brat to her. I'm really going to have to apologize for that. I snapped at her when I shouldn't have. All through college she was always pulling us out of places, wanting us to go home, saying we would live it up after we graduated, and I think some of that came to a head last night. It was something I both loved and disliked about Paige. She cares so much and sometimes she mother-hens me. It's not something I'm used to. At the same time, though, I want to be able to let loose every now and then.

Maybe on my way home I can stop and get a supreme pizza and a case of Red Bull as a peace offering. Talk things out a little.

Then there's Oz. I run my finger along the tattoo that runs up his arm; the one I didn't even know he had. He's always buttoned up in his suits. It reminds me how little I really know about him and how far I'd let things go last night. I wanted the sex, but I'd let him come inside me. I can still feel the wetness between my thighs, but

I can't bring myself to regret it. I've never in my life felt so connected to someone.

I think about Oz punching Joel, and I think about something I saw in his eyes. Something deep and dark, lurking underneath. Was it a moment of jealousy, or was it more? It had to be something that happened in the heat of the moment, because everything about Oz is sweet and loving. Every touch and every word he gives me. That anger is the first flaw I've seen in him. But the way he was with me last night was completely different. He worshipped my body, like he was starved for me. His mouth never really left my body as he made love to me.

I'd still have to talk to him about it. In the fog of my drunkenness, I'd brushed it off too easily and got caught up in Oz being back after not seeing him in days. That and not hearing from him all day Friday, which wasn't normal for us. He can't go around punching people in a jealous rage.

Pulling myself slowly from his bed so I don't wake him, I slip off and quietly walk to the bathroom. I close the door behind me, flip on the light and look around. I must have been half-asleep when Oz brought me home with him last night, because I don't remember any of his home. In fact, I don't even know what part of the city I'm in.

The bathroom is giant. A glass shower that looks like it could fit ten people takes up one wall. On the other wall is a bathtub that someone could possibly do laps in. This bathroom is bigger than our freaking living room. I debate taking a bath in it now because I can feel every achy muscle in my body as I move. It's a sweet pain that makes me smile. I even like the tenderness I feel between my legs. Like Oz marked me as his. Feeling the blush hit my cheeks, I try to shake off the shyness about what we did last night. No use in being embarrassed now.

I glance in the mirror. My eye makeup is smudged, and my lips still swollen from the kisses he'd given me. Taking a step closer to the mirror, I see little red marks around my breasts. Flashes of Oz kissing and sucking on them flip through my mind, and I recall the feel of his whiskers there, too. I look well loved, and I want to spend the weekend doing it over and over again, not caring that my body is still sore.

A beeping noise draws my attention to the bathroom counter. Oz's phone is plugged into the charger and the screen lights up, showing he has a voice mail message. The name *Paige* shows across the screen.

My Paige?

Shit, I didn't even tell her I wasn't coming home. Damn it, she's probably crazy worried. Guilt hits me again about last night and how things went with us. I can't even imagine what kind of message she would leave on Oz's phone or how that crazy woman tracked down his freaking number.

Picking up the phone, I slide my finger across the screen and smile when I see the picture I took of myself in the cafeteria at work as his home screen. Clicking the voice mail button, I get ready for a serious scream-fest from Paige.

"Miles. What the actual fuck? I had that shit under control. I was going to get her out of there. You storming in the club and punching someone in the face in a jealous rage is going to get your ass on the fucking

cover of some gossip column, you dumb shit. Not only that, but blow the plans you've had in place for over four fucking years. Oh, and let's not forget that all the enemies you've made owning Osbourne Corp are likely going to know you have a thing for Mallory. Now that's going to put her right in the fucking spotlight. You better hope no one got any pictures!" She yells the last part before ending the message.

All the blood rushes to my ears as I try to piece together what Paige said. Why was Paige's number saved into Oz's phone? How did I not even catch that? Oz owns Osbourne Corp? Paige knows Oz? Wait. Oz has had a plan for me for four years?

My hands shake, and I drop the phone. It hits the white tile floor with a crack, but I don't care in the least. I have to get out of here. Now.

I want to run, but I have to be quiet. My heart is pounding in my ears. I need to sneak out. I head back to the bedroom and quickly find my dress and slide it on. I see my purse and shoes over by the dresser and I grab them. I look over at Oz, who's now on his back, the sheet covering the lower half of his beautiful body. I want to scream at him and ask what the fuck is going on. I step forward, about to do it, my emotions getting the best of me. I feel the angry rage bubbling inside me, and as I get to the side of the bed, I look down at his bare chest.

My eyes roam over his left pec, right where his heart is. The name Mallory is tattooed there in cursive script.

I feel like someone punched me right in the stomach. My hand goes to my mouth to stop myself from making a sound. The tattoo doesn't look new. I slowly and quietly back away from the bed until I reach the door. When I'm there, I silently open it and run down the hallway. When I reach the end, I spot the elevator. I hit the button in a panic and pray I make it out of here before he wakes. I don't want answers from him. I want them from Paige.

When it dings, I get on, hitting the button to the lobby over and over until the doors close. It's then I realize this elevator looks familiar, and it's not because I'm remembering it from the night before.

"No," I whisper to myself, clutching my purse and shoes to my chest. When the elevator hits the bottom floor, the doors open, and I see Chuck, the security guard who always smells like he drowns himself in Old Spice. I close my eyes and open them again. I pray I'm dreaming, but Chuck is still there with a giant smile on his face.

"Morning, Miss Mallory," he says, giving me a little wave.

"Morning, Chuck." I hit the button for the third floor and he gives me a strange look. Probably because I'm not getting off and I'm sure I look like I'm doing the walk of shame.

I dig in my purse for my keys as the doors close. When the elevator stops, I get off, going straight for my door and unlocking it.

Paige's head pops up from the sofa, and I turn, locking the door behind me. I give her my back and take a few deep breaths. I don't know what to say or where to start. I'm not even sure I want to hear her explanation. I'm terrified of the reality I'm about to face and what this will mean to the world I've built.

When I turn back around, Paige is standing up from the sofa.

"Jesus, Mal, you could have at least—"

She stops talking when she sees my face.

Then her eyes close likes she's in pain, which only pisses me off more.

"He told you," she whispers, opening her eyes.

I feel wetness hit my cheeks and a burning in my nose. I'm so angry I'm crying.

Paige comes around the sofa, but I can't let her get close.

"Don't come near me." I drop my purse and shoes, holding my hands out in front of me. The words are ripped from my throat and make her stop in her tracks. I watch as her eyes water, and Paige does something she hardly ever does. Tears flow down her cheeks, matching my own, but I'm indifferent to them. This isn't about her.

"How do you know Oz?" I shake my head. "Miles," I correct myself.

God, I'm so fucking stupid. *Call me Oz*, he'd said. *Osbourne Corp.* How could I be so dumb?

She looks around the room like there might be an answer for her here. "Paige," I snap, jolting her, and the words pour from her mouth.

"I've worked for Osbourne Corp since the moment I met you. I was assigned to guard you during your freshman year in college. I was hired to report back on what you were doing, keep you out of harm's way and to make sure you had anything and everything you might need."

"I don't understand." Why? I don't get any of this.

I swipe at the tears on my cheeks. Oz has had a guard on me for over four years? That doesn't even make any sense. I only met him— Then it hits me. My scholarship to Yale was from Osbourne Corp, too. The man behind the curtain was a bit too real.

"Mal, please. I love you like a sister."

"Don't you say that. I was a job to you." That much is clear in what she said. Everything we shared is a lie. All of it. Here I thought I was getting everything I ever wanted, but it was all fake.

"At first, yes, but listen to me. Over time it wasn't like that. I love you, and that's why I'm going to tell you the truth. Fuck Miles. It's more complicated than you know."

I shake my head. I can't believe anything that comes out of her mouth. I don't even know what's real anymore. The one person who's ever meant anything to me isn't even real. I'm clearly shitty at reading people. I can't see what's right in front of my face. I feel like I can't breathe.

"Miles is obsessed with you." She lets out a humorless laugh. "*Obsessed* is putting it mildly."

A loud pounding comes from the door, making us both jump.

"It's him," she says, before Oz calls my name from the other side of the door.

"Mallory, baby, are you okay? Open the door." The door handle rattles, and we both stand there looking at each other. I thought she'd go over and open the door, but she doesn't. She keeps staring at me, those stupid tears running down her face. She doesn't get to be hurt. I was the one who was fooled here. I can't look at her because even though I'm hurt, it hurts even more see-ing her cry.

"I'm leaving." I turn, heading down the hallway, but Paige grabs my arm.

"Don't touch me!" I scream louder than I mean to, and a sob follows it. I feel like all my emotions are try-ing to escape my body at one time and it's taking ev-erything in me to keep myself together.

"Mallory!" Oz yells from the other side of the door. "Baby, are you okay?" His voice is panicked now and getting louder.

"Miles, it's fine. Go home," Paige yells back, letting go of my arm.

He's quiet for half a second, then the handle begins to rattle again.

"Open the door, Paige." This time his voice changes. It's hard, and the order is clear. He isn't asking.

I cock an eyebrow at her, wondering what she's going to do.

"I choose you," she says, answering the silent ques-tion. I feel a touch of relief at her words, but they really don't matter. Our friendship is over. Well, the friend-ship I thought we had.

"I'll kick in this door," Oz says when no one responds to his command. This is a side of him I don't know. He showed that side last night when he punched Joel.

"He owns the whole building. Even the lease," she admits. "I can't stop him from coming in."

"Doesn't matter. I'm leaving."

"Goddamn it, Paige." Oz hits the door so hard the whole thing shudders, and I'm surprised it doesn't buckle.

"She knows, Miles." Paige's words are quiet, but he must hear them because he stops banging on the door. The silence thickens.

"You said you'd let me explain." The hardness has gone from his voice, and now he's speaking with the softness with which he always talks to me. "That if anything ever happened, you'd let me explain. You promised."

He says my words as if they're his loophole.

"Guess that makes us both liars then," I throw back at him.

"I never lied to you, baby. Never." His voice sounds pained, and it pulls at my heart. Even if this whole thing was a lie; him, school, my job, all of it. Even if this wasn't real, I'd still want to fall head over heels in love with him. Hell, maybe I am in love with him, because it feels like my heart is being ripped from my chest. Part of me wishes I'd never found out.

"You broke my heart. I broke my promise," I say, before turning and heading down the hallway to my room to pack a bag.

When I turn, I expect to see Paige behind me, but she isn't.

I hear yelling down the hall but can't make out any of the words. Ignoring them, I rush around the room. I need to get out of here. I'm barely holding it together, and I don't want to crack here in front of them. The people who did this to me.

"I got him to leave," Paige says, standing in my doorway. "Okay, maybe not leave, but he isn't coming in."

"I don't care. I don't want to be here with you either."

She makes a sound as if I actually hit her with more

than a verbal blow. It makes me want to reach out and grab her and pull her toward me in a tight hug. I have to clench my hands to stop myself. But she lied to me, and she isn't really my friend. I won't let them make a fool of me again.

"You're pissed. I get that."

"You get that?" I say mockingly, turning to look at her, and she lifts her hands, making it clear she doesn't want to argue with me.

"Be smart here, Mal—"

I cut her off. "Be smart here?" I throw the clothes I have in my hands onto the bed. "It's clear I'm fucking dumb as shit."

"What I'm saying is I don't know if anyone got wind of what happened last night. If they did, your face is about to be everywhere. And Miles has enemies. You don't get to be where he is and not have them. Hell, even his own dad is one."

"Not my problem." I turn, going back to pulling clothes from my closet. I have no idea where I'm going. I don't have a ton of money, and I don't even want to think about how fast hotel bills are going to add up. Oh God, my job. I work for him. I curse myself for spending all that money on stupid clothes for the job I'm going to have to quit.

"It will very much become your problem. Not only that, but where are you going to go? I know you. You're probably planning to quit your job now, too. Be smart," she says, making me turn to look at her. "He won't let you go, Mallory. Like I said, he's obsessed with you. I have a very strong feeling he'll pull every string he has to, to make sure you don't get hired anywhere, and it won't help that you quit an internship a week after starting. That never looks good."

I drop down on my bed, defeated because everything she said is true. I'll burn through my savings faster than I can find a job. I also wonder if this was part of his plan. To give me no options.

"You're mad. Use it. I'll leave. I know you want me to go, and I'll give you that because I do love you. Keep your ass here, go to work and save some money. Then leave if you want to, but make a plan, Mal. Don't put yourself on the streets."

I hate how much truth is in her words. I can't be stupid, but I have no idea what I'm going to do.

"Get out," I tell her. She stands there for a second, then turns to leave. Before she can walk out, there's something I need to know. I hate myself for the question, but I have to ask it.

"Why is he obsessed with me?"

She turns to look at me, a sympathetic expression on her face. "I don't know. But I don't think he'll ever let you go."

With that, she leaves. After a few moments, I hear the front door close, and the dam breaks. Everything comes flooding out, and I can't hold it back. The pain of being alone again takes over, and it's as if I'm a foster kid all over again. It's a feeling I thought I'd never have to experience again. Maybe I'm meant to be alone forever.

NINETEEN

Miles

PAIGE OPENS THE DOOR, and I push away from the wall,
walking over.

"I told you this was going to happen," she says as she
locks the door behind her and pockets the key. I should
have changed out that goddamn lock she put on there
the first time I saw it, but I thought I had time.

This was all supposed to come out later. Long after
I had Mallory to myself and had made her mine. I was
supposed to have her tied to me in every way possible
before her world came crashing down. Make her love
me, need me, make her feel a little bit of what I felt
for her.

"How did you fuck this up?" I snap at her. I want
to blame anyone but myself for this. My fucking plan
was perfect. *Was* being the key word until I fucked it
up a little myself a week ago, that first night at the bar.
I wouldn't have had to do that if Paige would have kept
me better filled in. Paige shouldn't have taken her to
that bar in the first place.

"I don't know." She looks away, and I see the tears
roll down her cheeks. I forgot how long she's been with
her and how close she'd gotten to Mallory. That she

wasn't there to protect her. Not anymore. My sweet Mallory got to her, too.

"Where are you going?" I look at the bag over her shoulder, wondering what the fuck is going on. "Get back in there and talk to her."

"She needs time, Miles. She's heartbroken. Can't you understand that? Try and put yourself in her position. I think she fucking loved you. She was like a sister to me. And now all of this is broken. She's going to need time," she says, emphasizing her point. I can be bull-headed especially when it comes to Mallory.

She walks past me, and I reach out, grabbing her arm to stop her. She looks at me with watery eyes, and it's the only time I've ever seen her cry.

"Apologize, Miles. Apologize a lot. But give her time." With that, I drop my arm and she passes by me. Before she gets on the elevator, she turns back to me. "I think she's going to go back to work. I'll still be watching her." She gets on the elevator, the doors shut and she disappears.

I look back to Mallory's apartment door and I walk over to it, unable to leave. Pressing my palms to the door, I try to feel her inside. She's the other half of my soul; I should be there to help her with the pain. Pressing my ear to the door, I close my eyes when I hear the sounds of her sobbing. The sound hits me right in the gut. A sound I'd heard before, from another woman, a sound I told myself I'd never hear from Mallory. But here I was, all my plans falling apart, causing the very thing I'd promised I'd never do. Be like him.

"Mallory. Please. Let me in, baby. Let me explain." I try not to shout but still make my voice loud enough so that she can hear. I wait a few moments, and nothing changes. I hear the sound of her cries, and I can do nothing to fix it.

I've broken the single most precious thing in my life, and nothing can mend it.

I fall to my knees and press my side against her door. I deserve to hear her heart being ripped to pieces. I've caused this pain, and I should have to hear every sob. Putting my head in my hands, I cry with her. Because all I ever wanted to do was to love her and have her love me. Everything I've done has been so that she could have only the best. But in turn, I've stolen away all that was good and left her in ruins.

It's hours later when her cries quiet and I can no longer hear her. I hope that she's found sleep or that maybe she's gotten some peace and has been able to pull herself together.

My legs cramp and my back aches, but I don't move away from her door. I won't give up the chance to talk to her, even if it's her yelling at me.

I SIT IN FRONT of her door all night.

And all day Sunday.

And all night Sunday.

I don't eat. I don't sleep. I barely move.

She cries off and on, and each time it rips me apart all over again. But I sit and I wait, never leaving my post. I would do this for a thousand years for one more chance with her. She probably doesn't even know I'm here, but I've always been with her, even when she didn't know.

Monday morning, I'm still in the same place, stand-

ing sentry. I know it's morning when I see light creeping in at the end of the hall. I watch the sun rise and
wish I could see her face.

Then the front door finally opens.

I nearly fall over into her apartment, but catch myself in time. I look up into Mallory's eyes, and I see so
much hate there, it burns through me. I'll take it. It's
better than indifference.

"Baby."

For a split second, I think she's going to say something, but instead she steps over me and walks to the
elevator, hitting the button. It takes everything in me
not to grab her. A control I never knew I had. Pick her
up and carry her back to my home until I make her see
reason. Make her understand there is no leaving me.
This will end with her being mine. There is no other
option. I won't allow there to be. Period. But I know
she needs soft right now. She's already gotten too big a
dose of how deep my obsession runs.

I jump up, running after her, but she doesn't so much
as glance at me. I drop to my knees in front of her, not
caring how pathetic it makes me look. I want her to see
that I'm willing to grovel. That I'm willing to put my
pride aside and literally beg her to listen to me. She is
my life, and I refuse to let her go. Losing her isn't an
option, and I will demand she listen, even if it's from
my knees.

"Mallory. You're going to have to hear me out sooner
or later."

She hits the elevator button again, like it can't get
here fast enough.

"Mallory." I say her name in a warning.

The elevator door opens, and I reach out to her, so close to touching her, but she steps onto it and turns to face me. She looks painfully beautiful. She's wearing a black fitted dress with deep purple heels. I notice her hair is down, and it annoys me. Like she's done it out of spite.

Soft, I remind myself. "Baby. I need you. Don't go. Let me explain." It takes everything in me not to tell her I'll never let her go. That one way or another, she'll be mine again.

She looks down at me, and then looks away, like the sight of me hurts her.

"Might want to get that tattoo covered."

With her words, the doors close, and I'm left alone. Looking down, I see I'm shirtless, only wearing a long pair of sweatpants. I hadn't given a single thought to myself or what I looked like when I ran out of my place. Only that I needed to get to her.

I get to my feet and hit the arrow to take me up to my floor. I need to get ready for work. I need to get my head on straight and figure out how the fuck I'm supposed to win her back without getting kidnapping charges. I've got a shareholders meeting today that I'm nowhere close to ready for, but I couldn't give a fuck about it. The only thing I care about is getting my woman back. In order to do that, I need a plan.

I get on the elevator and rub the place over my heart. I got the tattoo after the first time I saw her, and I never once regretted it. It will stay there until the day I take my last breath, like my love for her will.

I'll win her back, or I'll die trying. There is absolutely no room for failure.

TWENTY

Mallory

I STARE AT the computer screen, the numbers seeming to mush together. I was thinking I could come into work early and maybe lose myself here. I thought I could get my mind to stop racing, but all I can see is Miles on his knees in front of me as the elevator doors slid closed. It took everything in me to not reach out and touch him.

I made sure I looked as perfect as I could before I opened that door this morning, even if it took an extra layer of foundation to hide the bags under my eyes. I didn't want him to know I'd been on the other side, miserable and crying the whole time.

He sat there all weekend. I couldn't stop myself from checking every few hours, thinking he'd leave at some point. I was certain he'd give up, but he never did. The worst thing was so many times I wanted to open the door. I wanted to get in his face and yell at him. I wanted to direct all this anger I had at someone or something. I wanted to figure out what was going on, because my mind was running wild and nothing was adding up.

Osbourne Corp has been a part of my life for a long time. Since I was a senior in high school. First the scholarships, then the internship. These are things I thought I'd earned on my own, and now I'm finding out I hadn't.

My mind can't seem to shut off as I try to remember as much as I can. Like the fact that I was the recipient of the first scholarship the company ever gave out. That I got the coveted internship so easily, yet didn't get any other offers.

The truth of Paige's words hits me. If I did leave, he'd make sure no one else would hire me. He had done so once already. What's to stop him from doing it again?

All these things floated through my mind this weekend. The little things he'd said about how long he'd waited for me. The way Paige never stonewalled him like she'd done to other men who tried to date me. I didn't know what to do with all these odds and ends. They didn't make any sense.

The one thing that keeps taunting me is why did he do this?

I can't wrap my mind around the idea that he was obsessed with me. I'd never seen him before I came to New York. I would have remembered him, I'm sure of it. But he knew me somehow. Probably knew everything there was to know about me.

Worse, after I really knew who he was, I couldn't stop myself from digging into him. Looking at every article I could find on the *Elusive Billionaire Miles Henry Osbourne*, they called him. There wasn't much in the gossip magazines. Every picture I found of him he was either alone or with his mother. Except for one that looked to be when he was in college with a woman named Ivy Lennox. The picture didn't make them look like a couple. I recognized the background of the picture and knew they were at Yale when it was taken. The tagline read *The Next Big Power Couple?* I had to admit they did look good together. She was completely different from me in looks. Tall, long blond hair, a waist that could rival Paige's and a wardrobe to match her perfection.

"Still mad at the boyfriend?" Skyler asks, startling me as she looks over the top of the cubicle wall at me. Her perfect eyebrow is raised in question. I must have been lost in thought because I didn't even hear her walk past my desk.

"That's putting it mildly." I know she's only talking about the fight Miles got into with Joel. I'm actually a little worried about who else might have seen it and if anyone but her knows that I've been dating the boss. I don't even want to think what those rumors will turn into.

"It was a dick move, but I have to say sometimes that whole caveman thing works for people. I know Jamie likes it when I get all territorial over her." She smiles like she does it on purpose to get her girlfriend all worked up.

"At least you won't have to see him much. Not like he's ever around here. I've only seen him once in real life and it was when he was picking you up." She shrugs like it's not a big deal, but it is.

To me it is, anyway. I can't see him or I might crack. Hell, who am I kidding? I'll fucking shatter. I drop my head into my hands in despair. I groan and look back up at Skyler. "God, I'm so stupid. You knew who he was, didn't you?"

"Well, yeah." She looks at me like I'm crazy.

"I didn't know who he was until yesterday," I admit.

"Are you fucking kidding me?" Her eyes look like they're about to bulge out of her head.

Then it finally clicks into place. The day she was short with me. She must have been thinking what everyone else would be thinking if they found out about Oz and me. That I was banging the boss for my job. The sad part is I'm not so sure it's not true. If Oz didn't have his sights on me, I probably wouldn't be here to begin with. I don't know if that should make me mad or not. It's not like I'd gotten a scholarship they'd been handing out for years. This was something new and apparently created for me. I'd gotten a few small grants from community colleges, but nothing like the full ride to Yale they gave me. It had all the odds and ends, of boarding, books, a meal pass, plus some.

"I know." I suck my bottom lip between my teeth, biting it as I look back at my computer screen.

Skyler comes around, leaning against the edge of my desk. I look over at her. What sucks is I don't even know if I can trust her. I'm clearly terrible at telling who my true friends are and who's being paid to watch me.

"Did you end it with him?"

I nod. For some reason I can't bring myself to say yes. The simple nod is all I have in me.

She's silent for a second, and then lets out a little sigh. "Is it really so bad he didn't tell you he was a big-time billionaire? I can think of worse things you could find out about your boyfriend," she teases.

Oh, I have a list I want to tell her, but instead I give her a half smile. I don't want to be the girl that cries in the office, and if I start talking, that will likely happen. Worse, I'd be crying over the boss. I couldn't get more cliché.

"God, I bet this meeting is going to be so fucking boring." I turn my head to see Eric standing by my cubicle. He looks like he just rolled out of bed, or maybe that's the messy hair thing I've seen some guys doing. I don't get it. It looks sloppy for work.

"I think it's a general meeting, going over random company stuff. I hear they do them periodically," Skyler adds.

Eric shrugs and goes over to his desk.

"Think he'll be there?" I say quietly so no one else can hear us.

"Is he mad you wanted to end it?"

I nod.

"Yep. He'll be there." She reaches out, squeezing my shoulder. "Act like you don't care."

If only it was that easy. My cold act this morning, walking five feet from him, was hard enough. I wanted to be indifferent and pretend I didn't care at all. I thought that would hurt him more than giving him anger or tears. Indifference made it seem like he wasn't worth any emotion. I wanted to hurt him, and I wanted him to be as miserable as I was.

Because if there's one thing I can be sure of, it's that while I might not get what Miles is doing, he wants me. *Wants* might not even be the right word. *Obsession* seems to fit better. It's clearly unhealthy, but the worst part is a little flutter hits me when I think about him being obsessed with me. Even though I know it isn't right. Even though I know it's crazy. I'd be lying if I denied that a deep part of me is intrigued by it.

I go back to looking at my screen. I should really try to get something done before this meeting. It's the whole reason I came in early, to not think about Oz.

I hear a ping on my computer and look up to see a new email.

From: YourOZ@gmail.com
Subject: I'm sorry

I hold my mouse over the email, wanting to click it so bad. I move my cursor over to the trash button and click, then go in and block his email. I'll crack too easily right now. It's best if I avoid him, because I know I can stay away. It's moments like now, when my anger isn't at its height, that I feel weak. I want to talk to him and ask him so many things to try to stop all the questions bouncing around inside my head. Maybe then I can think. Or maybe I'd only make it worse.

I want to go back to Saturday morning and not get up from the bed. I wish I could have enjoyed that moment a little longer before the lies came crashing in and took not only Miles from me, but Paige, too. The only family I'd ever had. I lost them both in a matter of minutes. Or maybe it was me being stupid again to think I even had them to begin with.

"You ready?" Skyler asks, popping her head over my cubicle again. I glance at the clock on my computer screen, realizing I've been staring off for twenty minutes. Hey, maybe I don't need to quit. At this rate, I'll probably be fired by the end of the week.

"Yeah."

Reaching under my desk, I grab my purse. Eric

comes around to join us as we make our way down the elevator to the bottom floor of the building. We file into what looks like an auditorium. The room fills up quickly with more than two hundred people.

I take a seat between Skyler and Eric, pulling a notepad and pen out in case I need to write something down. I look over and next to the stage against the wall, I see Paige wearing all black. Today her reddish-brown hair is tied into a loose ponytail, but something about her is off. She scans the crowd, and after only a second, she's looking right at me. Our eyes lock and a lump immediately forms in my throat. I don't think Paige and I have spent more than twenty-four hours apart in the last four years.

I should be mad at her. I should be fucking pissed, but it's hard when she's giving me that look. She's hurting. I can see it all over her face, and it's not a look I'm used to on her. Not Paige. She's strong and doesn't need anyone or anything, but she doesn't look that way right now. Right now, she looks like she needs me.

Captain reaches to tuck a strand of her hair behind her ear, drawing her attention to him. She smacks his hand away, making him smirk. I look down at my notepad, wanting to look away from the two of them because what I really want to do is send her a text teasing her about her crush, about what's going on with the way he touches her, but I can't. I shouldn't want to either. I should hate her for lying to me.

I reach into my purse, pulling my phone out and seeing I don't have any missed calls or texts at all. That bothers me, too. Jesus, I'm a mess. Now I'm mad he hasn't texted me after I deleted his email without even reading it. I have serious issues right now.

Skyler nudges me, and I look over at her and see she's looking at the stage. I follow her line of sight and there he is, staring right at me. His dark beard is a little longer than normal, probably because he didn't shave all weekend and he still hasn't taken the time. He's in dark blue slacks and a light blue button-up shirt that's rolled up at the sleeves.

He looks tired. The lack of sleep shows under his eyes as he stares at me. Everyone else is taking their seats at the long table on the stage. He sits off to the side like he's only there to observe.

"Hey, is that Miles Osbourne?" Eric asks, leaning over toward me. I look at him and shrug, like I have no idea. When I glance back at Oz, his eyes are still on me. Intense. It's clear that he doesn't care if anyone notices he's staring at me. He glances over at Eric, then back at me, and even from this distance I can actually see his jaw tick as he clenches it.

I watch as Oz reaches into his pocket, pulls out his phone and types away. I feel mine vibrate in my lap, but I don't look down or reach for it. I look away from him and over at Skyler.

"Wow. He looks pissed." Skyler says it without moving her lips. She tilts her head a little—I'm guessing so Oz won't know what she's saying.

I glance back at him and his eyes move from me to Captain and Paige up against the wall. He and Captain seem to have some silent conversation before he looks back at me. I look between them and I know he's going to do something. Grabbing my phone, I open my text messages.

Oz: Don't make me have him removed from this building.

I see Captain moving around the side of the auditorium and I panic. He's going to make a fucking scene! This is how he's sorry, by embarrassing me? This is freaking ridiculous. He really can't be this jealous.

Me: Knock it off right now, or I'll walk out of here and never come back.

I hit Send and look up. He looks down at his phone and I glance over to see Captain has already stopped. Paige has him by the arm and is talking to him as he looks down at her. She glances at me, and I know she's stopping him from coming over here. I sigh in relief as she gets him to move back toward where they were standing before.

"Good morning, everyone. Some of you may know me already, but I'm Samuel Black, CEO of Osbourne Corporation."

I lean back in my chair, relieved that Oz isn't making a scene, but I don't look at him. I keep my eyes on Mr. Black as he goes on about future plans for the company and the direction they want to take.

After what seems like years, I finally crack and glance over at Oz. It was all I could do to hold off from looking at him for five minutes, and I hate how pathetic that makes me feel.

When I look to him, I see he's still staring at me.
It makes me squirm in my seat, and I want to shout
at my body for its reaction to him. To those deep sapphires staring at me so intimately. Grabbing my phone,
I text him.

Me: Stop staring. People will notice.

Oz: I don't care if people notice.

Me: I do.

Oz: Have dinner with me and I'll stop staring.

I glare at him before putting my phone back down.
This is a little different Oz than I'm used to. Some of
his softness has bled away, a hard dominance coming
through. I'd seen it before but never coming for me
like this. Before I felt like when he did something there
was a question if I was okay with it. That seems to be
gone. He's always been intense but now it seems like
he's cracked a little or maybe the real him is coming
out and this part of him is on a mission to steamroll me.
Is this some kind of weird blackmail or something?
He's holding me hostage by making me feel like I don't
have control over anything. I'm not used to this, even
if my freedom before was only an illusion. I'd never
known anyone to take the time to get to know me like
this. But it's been happening all along without my
knowledge. I assumed it's been me watching out for
me as long as I could remember.
Until Paige came into my life, and then I thought we

were watching out for each other. While I know she has a father, he was never around, nor did she seem to want him around. So when we became close, I thought it was because of our shared past. Not because she was paid to be there.

I breathe a sigh of relief when the meeting finally ends. Basically, this was a company announcement to talk about our quarterly goals for the end of the year and keep our shareholders informed of future plans. I didn't absorb much of what was being said, what with feeling his eyes on me the whole time.

I glance over and Oz stands up, looking like he's going to come toward me, and I'm out of my chair, working my way through the crowd of people.

Before I get more than a few steps, Skyler grabs my arm.

"Lunch?"

"Not here," I say, and even I can hear the desperation to get out of here in my voice.

She nods and I follow her out past the crowd and through the glass lobby. Once we get outside and fresh air greets my lungs, I can breathe. We walk down the street to a little bakery. I get a banana nut muffin and coffee. We sit down, and I pick at the muffin, not wanting it even though I should be hungry. I didn't eat much this weekend, but my body doesn't care. An anxious ball still sits in my stomach, squeezing sporadically.

My plans are not working out like I wanted them to. Go to work, do your job and quit after a little while seems easier said than done now.

Skyler plays on her phone while she eats her sandwich, smiling away at whoever she's talking to. I look down at mine and see another text from Oz, but I power it off, tossing it into my purse. When we're done, I throw my coffee cup and the rest of my muffin in the trash. I look up afterward and see Captain leaning against the far wall of the coffee shop, looking my way. He's wearing a perfectly tailored black suit, and all I can think about is how he almost looks like an FBI agent or something. He's way too big not to stand out, and if he's trying to blend in, it's not working.

I study him for a second before turning and following Skyler out of the coffee shop and back to our office. I wonder if he's following me or getting coffee. A lot of people that work in the building come here because it's the closest. So I try to pretend his being there isn't about me.

When I get back to my desk, I drop my purse in a drawer before heading to the ladies' room. I don't make it two feet into the bathroom and Oz is on me, shutting the door behind him.

"Don't." I try to move around him, but he blocks me from leaving. Caging me in.

The next thing I know, his mouth is on mine.

Like every other time he's kissed me, my body melts into his and I open for him easily. It's as if I have no control over my body. I forget that I'm mad at him. His lips are warm and needy, filled with so much possession and claiming, like he is trying to consume me with his kiss, and I want to give him what he's asking for. I want to comfort him and make it all better, but then I remember why I hate him.

I push on his solid wall of a chest, but he kisses me deeper like it's impossible to separate us. Soon I'm wrapping my fingers into his shirt and kissing him back hard. It's nearly punishing, and all he does is take. It's everything I want, but shouldn't.

He moans into my mouth then pulls away and kisses down my neck. He moves his lips lower, going to the V of my blouse, down to the valley between my breasts. "I've missed you so much," he whispers, giving me soft flicks of his tongue. "You can't leave me."

His words are like an ice bath and bring me back to reality. I push him hard this time and release my fingers from his shirt. He goes back half a step, and I look up at him, reminding myself I don't know this man at all.

"Don't push me away, Mallory." His tone is firm. A warning just like this morning in the elevator.

"Just leave me alone. I can't do this right now. And I definitely can't do it here," I bite out at him, having forgotten for a moment where we are. Then I wonder if anyone saw him slip into the bathroom with me. It's not like the man isn't noticeable, and I'm sure people pay attention when he walks through the department.

"I can't leave you alone." The way he says it makes a chill run up my spine. There's so much need in his voice. Possession. It's like he can't live without me, and I don't know what to do with that. "You'll hear me out." He moves back in, crowding into my space again. One hand comes up to my cheek, cupping it, and it takes everything in me not to lean into his touch. "I never meant to hurt you. All I've ever wanted from the moment I laid eyes on you was to give you everything."

I close my eyes tightly so his deep blue eyes don't pull me back in. When I open them back up, I'm determined.

"Give me time," I say, the words paining me as they come out of my mouth.

His hand drops away and he nods, taking a step back. He grits his teeth, and it looks like he's a breath away from snapping.

"I've given you a lot of time, Mallory. More than you know. I'll try, but you do things to me. Things…" He waves one hand in the air like he can't find the word he's looking for. "Things I can't explain." So much emotion plays across his face, I have to look away and remind myself he's not who I think he is.

I can't see him as the man who lit up my life for the past week. He isn't the man who had me falling hard and fast for him. He isn't the man who made the sweetest love to me, like he'd been waiting his whole life to do so.

I'd never felt more cherished than when I was with him. It was something I'd never experienced before, and maybe never will again.

As if he can't help himself, he leans in, running his nose up my jaw. My breath hitches, and I want to curse at not being able to restrain myself. His warm scent surrounds me, and I'm conditioned to crave him now. The dampening between my legs is beyond my control, and I try to hold my breath to make it stop.

He places a soft kiss right next to my ear. "I'll try, baby. For you, I'll try anything. But don't let anyone else touch you. I won't be able to stop myself if that happens." He places another soft kiss. "I will try but one way or another you'll be mine. Don't fight what will be. I've been holding back for you but I can only hold it for so long." Then he's gone.

I don't know how long I stand there before I'm fi-

nally able to breathe again. I use the bathroom and try
to put myself back together as much as possible. Inside
I'm a mess, but outside I seem to be holding up okay. I
go back to my desk, losing myself in my work and trying not to think about Oz's dark promise.

I'm actually glad when Linda piles more work on my
desk, making us work long past normal hours. I don't
think about anything other than what's in front of me,
and the distraction is pure bliss.

Skyler and Eric took off an hour or so ago, and finally at nine I decide to call it a night. I shut down my
computer, grab my purse and head out.

When I get to the lobby of the building, I don't make
it five feet before the big guy, still dressed in his suit,
steps out to let me see him. Captain is clearly following me.

My anger spikes because Oz said he's giving me
time. I pick up speed as I make my way the three blocks
toward my building. Walking in, I give Chuck my normal wave and look behind me to see Captain loiter at
the entrance. He's watching me get on the elevator. I
want to hate him, too, but I don't know if I have room
with everything I have going on in my heart.

I know Miles owns the whole top floor, and to get
to it you have to have a key. I pull out my set of keys
for our apartment and notice the ring holds three keys.
One is for our mailbox, one is for our apartment and
the third Paige said was for storage. But the more I look
at it, the stranger it looks. It appears to be too small.
In fact, it looks more like one you'd need for the elevator. Curiosity gets the better of me, and I slowly slide
the key in. It turns smoothly. Before I can stop to think

what I'm doing, I hit the button for the penthouse and it lights up. The elevator moves toward the top floor.

"Holy shit," I whisper to myself.

I panic, but then I think, why should I be upset? I did nothing wrong. I'm the victim here, and I should be allowed to do what I want. Fuck it. I'm going to give Oz a piece of my mind about this not-really-giving-me-any-space shit. I asked for some time and he sends his security to tag around and watch what I do.

By the time the elevator begins to slow, I've worked myself up into a ball of anger. How dare he take over my life without my permission! Who the hell does he think he is?

When the door slides open, I take three steps in and come to an abrupt stop when I see Paige standing in the living room in her workout clothes. She's got on a sports bra and tight yoga pants and is covered in a light sheen of sweat.

She turns to look at me, and I stare back, shocked.

What is she doing here? Why is she in Miles's home?

The way she looks, it's as if she's comfortable here. Like she's been here lots of times, and my stomach drops. I think I'm going to be sick. Before I can say anything, I turn and get back onto the elevator. I see her bolt toward me, and I hit the close button over and over. But she makes it as the doors close, squeezing in beside me.

I hit the button for our floor and don't look at her. Sparks of jealousy are flying, and I'm feeling the betrayal all over again.

"Why were you at his place?" I bite out, unable to stop myself.

"I'm staying there."

"Why the fuck are you staying there?" I snap, finally turning to look at her.

Her hair's a mess on top of her head, and her eyes are red-rimmed like she's been crying. She's not looking at me, but I can still see it. My heart aches for her, but at the same time I'm so mad I can't give her the comfort she needs.

"How close are you two?" My implication is clear, and I cross my arms over my chest, waiting on her defense.

Paige takes a deep breath, and her eyes finally meet mine. "He's my brother."

That little bomb drops, and so does my jaw. And that's when I notice it. The same sapphire-blue eyes. How had I never put that together before?

"Half brother. Same dad, different mom and all that jazz." Her jaw ticks a little, something that always happens when she talks about her father.

The elevator dings, and I step off. I look at Paige, and without a word, she follows me to the apartment. I unlock the door and hold it open for her, closing and locking it behind us. I drop my bag by the table and make my way over to the couch. She follows right behind and sits down next to me.

I put my hands in my lap and wait for her to talk first. I don't know what I was expecting her to say, but I'm in shock.

"This is so fucking hard, Mal." Her voice cracks, and my fingers twitch. I want to hold her hand and comfort her, but I need to hear this. I love her, but I deserve the truth.

"I thought Miles was all I had, and I latched on to that," she finally says after about a minute. "You know I hate my father. Fuck, *hate* isn't a strong enough word. Then Miles found me when I was seventeen and offered me something I'd always wanted. A family. Revenge."

"You want revenge on your father? Why?" She's never told me anything about him, and sitting here now, maybe I'll finally understand.

"Well, Miles wants revenge." She takes a breath and her eyes meet mine. "I want—" She stops herself abruptly.

"You want more," I finish for her. I've seen the hate in her eyes when she talks about him. She's out for blood. Paige has always had this slight distaste for men, something I'm guessing her father must have given her, because it's all over her face right now.

She nods in agreement. "When Miles found me, he showed me that I could have more than this consuming hate in my life. He offered me a little bit of a family. And he told me if I helped him, he'd work on getting our revenge."

"You're his sister. He should have helped you, not used you." I feel a pang of anger toward Oz on Paige's behalf.

She lets out a small laugh. "It's not like I fought him. I was seventeen at the time, and he gave me a job that sounded pretty kick-ass. He paid for my college, and then paid me a salary on top of it. He promised that when I was finished I'd get a job with his security team. Miles took over, and I could cut all of the bad shit out of my life. He saved me."

We sit in silence for a moment, and I finally let out a

breath. "I hate fighting with you, but I feel like you've been lying to me, and I don't know what to do with that. It's hard to be mad at you, but I am." I reach out, taking her hand, and she grips mine tightly. I remember reading once that forgiveness isn't about the other person, it's about self-healing. She had her reasons for doing what she did, and I can't blame her for it. It hurts to know she deceived me, but I also know in my heart that she did it with the best intentions.

"You're all *I* have, Paige."

"I know. I feel like such an asshole. You have to know it started off as a job, but it became real. Our friendship was real. *Is* real," she corrects. "You mean more to me than anyone else in the whole world. I know I was happy when I found Miles, but we aren't even that close. Not like you and me. I can't lose you, too. Please don't let me lose another person I love because of my father."

A tear slides down her face, and I pull her into a hug. "Jesus, Paige, what did he do to you?"

Her arms come around me and we sit there for a moment, holding one another.

She shakes her head. "I've never told a soul," she whispers, breaking my heart a little, because this isn't a side I've ever seen of her.

Pulling back, I look into her tear-filled eyes. The blue looking so much brighter. "You can tell me anything, Paige."

"I—" Her voice breaks. "I used to think I never told anyone because I was scared of him. Maybe I was, but I think it's more because I was ashamed. Ashamed I didn't save her."

My eyebrows draw together as I wonder what she means. *"Please don't let me lose another person I love because of my father."*

"My mom isn't missing. She's dead." A tear escapes down her face. "I watched him kill her and I stood there."

"Oh, Paige. You had to have been young."

"Fifteen."

Tears run down my face, thinking about Paige having to see something like that. I couldn't imagine. So much of who Paige is really makes sense now.

"What happened?" I ask, wanting Paige to open up to me more.

Her bottom lip starts to tremble and I can tell she doesn't want to talk about it. Not yet anyway but this is a start.

"You could report it now," I try. Worried about what she might have planned. When Paige gets on something, she goes at it like a dog with a bone. Another thing that reminds me of Oz. They are a lot alike it seems.

"No!" she snaps. "You never tell anyone this." She grabs my hand, her face pleading.

"Of course I'd never tell anyone, Paige," I reassure her. "I just—" I'm not sure what to say. I want her to find some kind of closure on this but it's clear it's something she wants to handle on her own. That scares me, but I want her to know I'm here for her. I'll always be here no matter what. Even when I was upset with her, deep down I knew we would come back together.

I look at her and let go of any anger I have. I know what's in her heart, and I know what's in mine. I don't want to hold on to something that makes me so sad.

"I forgive you, Paige." I shrug and give her a half smile. "I'm shocked I lasted this long, to be honest."

She smiles at me, and it's the first time in days some of the weight on my shoulders lightens.

"Just don't tell Oz any more shit about me."

She shakes her head, and I know she means it. "I won't. I told him I was done with everything. Please don't tell him what I told you."

"He doesn't know your dad killed your mother?" I ask, wanting to make sure I understand her clearly.

"This is my secret to keep."

I know she doesn't like talking about it but to have never told a soul. To have had no one to give her some kind of comfort breaks my heart even more for her. No wonder she can't talk about it. She doesn't know how. We'll get there, I remind myself so I don't push her.

"I went up there because I think he's having me followed, and I was going to scream at him."

"He's having you followed," Paige confirms. "I'm not on his side, but I know our father has gone after people close to Miles before, done things to hurt them in hopes of hurting Miles. Not to mention he's probably trying to keep the press off you. If some people find out what you mean to him…" She pauses and looks away. "Well, I get why he's doing it."

"How long has this been going on?"

"I only know from when he asked me to keep an eye on you. He doesn't really talk to me about you. He doesn't say why he's doing it, so I can only guess. He always asks how you're doing, if you need anything, and of course, to keep men away from you." She pulls the tie from her hair, letting it fall in soft waves.

"At first I thought maybe you were connected to someone important and he was keeping an eye out or something. But every now and then, I'd pick up flares of jealousy, and I started to think it was something different altogether. Not to mention I've never seen him show interest in a woman before. Not even a drop. Then I saw you together and he was a totally different person."

I bite my lip, looking down at my lap to keep from asking.

"I'll tell you, Mal." I look back up at her, and now every time I see her eyes, I think of him. Who am I kidding? He's all I seem to think about anyway, even without the reminder.

"Miles is kind of cold except when he's with you, and the few times I've seen him with his mom. He didn't seem to do anything but work, but now here he is, running all over the goddamn place, giving Captain an aneurysm." She adds that last part and smiles as if she likes the idea of him driving Captain nuts.

"So do I think he wants you? Yes. In fact, I think he might be a little crazy about it. It's creepy how he can go from yelling at us to being all sweet and gushy with you at the drop of a hat. So with you, I'm thinking he's a little crazy, but in other aspects of his life, he seems pretty normal."

"That's reassuring," I say drily.

"I don't know what to tell you to do with that. I have trust issues and even worse issues when it comes to men. The rich ones are the worst, and it's been slowly eating away at me that I can't get a solid read on Miles and what he's doing with you. I saw him as a rich man using his money to get what he wanted, but I let it go because we were so far away. He wasn't around, and to be honest, I didn't think about it much. You and I went to school and we did us. That was, until we landed here. You got the internship. Then he and I started to have this back-and-forth struggle. I wasn't giving him the information he wanted anymore, and I think I made him miss a step. Like an addict who wasn't getting his fix anymore, so he showed up that night at the club and tipped his hand a little too soon."

"I was falling for him," I admit. "I had sex with him. Unprotected sex." I drop my head into my hands, still not believing I'd done it. In the moment, I felt so connected to him. I didn't want anything between us. The way he was worshipping me, I felt like he was going to be my forever. That I'd finally found a little piece of a fairy tale. That I'd been saving myself for him.

Paige grabs my wrists, pulling my hands down so I have to look back up at her. "Do you regret it?"

"No." I shake my head. "It was wonderful, actually. He was so sweet and it was perfect. Until it wasn't. He makes me feel so important and special. Like he'd do anything for me. That he can't breathe without me. It's intoxicating to think someone feels that way about me, but it's overwhelming, too. I don't know what to do. I mean the man has been controlling my freaking life!" I half yell the last part, emotions taking over.

"You don't have to do anything right now. Not a damn thing. You want to talk to him? Talk to him. If you don't, then don't. We'll go to work and do us."

"Can 'doing us' be eating ice cream?" I ask, hungry for the first time in days.

"You read my mind." Paige stands, pulling me with her.

"You moving back in?" I ask, following her into the kitchen.

"I didn't really take much with me, so I'm still kind of here."

"Good, because I need your shoes."

TWENTY-ONE

Miles

I STARE AT the closed elevator, and an inner battle rages inside me, like it's been doing all day. I thought the years waiting for her were bad. That was nothing compared to now. Knowing what she feels like under my hands, the way her skin tastes, how her lips part when I'm turning her on.

I thought I'd learned almost everything about her, but really I only knew the outside. Now I'm drowning in the details, trying to soak them all in, and I want more. My obsession has only worsened.

TURNING, I STRIDE back into my home office, pulling my phone out of my pocket. I glance at the monitors that line the wall next to my desk. Normally they're filled with reports and stock charts and even the news. Now they're filled with the building's security footage.

"Mallory and Paige are on their way down," I bark into the phone, louder than I mean to.

"On it, sir." I can hear Ryan, the man I've had shadowing my Mallory, start to run. He was probably en route back home thinking Mallory was in for the night, but now I know what she's going to do. I watch the elevator footage, wishing I'd had audio installed. I want to hear her, want to hear what she's saying.

I know Paige is going to tell her who she is to me. Relief fills me at that. I don't want Mallory to think I allow women into my home. The thought of her letting some man into her place makes me clench the phone I still have pressed to my ear.

Reaching out, I touch the monitor, wanting to wipe away the furrow between her brows. She turns to say something to Paige, and I see tension leave her body at whatever Paige says to her. I'm guessing the truth.

"Sir, the elevator looks to have stopped on her floor," Ryan says as I watch them exit the elevator and Mallory opens the door, holding it for Paige. Another sliver of relief rushes through me.

I don't like the idea of sharing my Mallory with anyone, but it's clear how much they love each other and how close they've become. If Mallory isn't going to be sleeping next to me at night, the next-best thing is for her and Paige to be sharing an apartment.

"Yes. Mallory went into her apartment," I confirm for him.

"Paige?" he asks. I hear the ding of the elevator and glance at the monitors to see him getting on.

"With her," I confirm, ending the call, knowing he's on his way up here. Tossing the phone on my desk, I come around to sit in my chair and flip on the camera that faces her door. The doorman is under strict instructions to let me know if she leaves. I know it makes me seem fucking crazy, but I don't care. I stopped caring a long time ago. Fighting it is pointless, and it only makes me more edgy when I do. I've learned to embrace it.

Sighing, I lean back in my chair, running my hands through my hair. The tension in my body is going to kill me. I should go for a run to work it off, but my lack of sleep is weighing on me. Like everything else about this fucked-up situation. Which it is. I fucked up. Something I never do.

I make plans and follow them through. Always three steps ahead of everyone else. It's why I'm where I am today. It's the only way to be if you want to get ahead, but I should've predicted things. I should've known I wouldn't be able to go slow with her so close. I fucked up and went in too early.

"You look like shit," Ryan says, pulling me from my thoughts. He strolls into the room, dropping down in the chair on the other side of my desk.

"Paige isn't going to work with us," I tell him, leaning forward and ignoring his statement.

"She's never really worked with me to begin with."

"I'm not firing her, so don't even fucking say it." I shoot him a hard look, one that works with most, but he's completely unfazed by it. I'm not sure anything intimidates Ryan, but that's part of why I hired him to be head of my security. One of the many reasons.

"Didn't want you to," he responds easily, like he doesn't care that he has someone on his team he can't seem to control. It isn't normal for him. One fuckup with Ryan and you're gone. Part of our agreement when I hired him was that he picked who worked security. He hired and fired. I thought making him agree to hire Paige would be a fight, one I'd win, but still a fight.

"Besides, I can't go firing your sister, now, can I?"

I don't give him a response as I tilt back in my chair.

Paige being my sister isn't common knowledge. In fact, I had no idea about her until Ryan brought me the information.

At first I was pissed when I found out about her. Then I got a better look. She hated him as much as I did. The enemy of my enemy is my friend. And in this case, it was family.

"It's better to keep her here." He looks away from me, and for a moment I see a look pass through his eyes.

"I suppose so." I get up from my chair, walk over to the bar and pour myself a drink. I raise it to Ryan in invitation, but he shakes his head.

"You know, you look at the monitor about every ten seconds. If you're wondering if you have a tell. But I guess it doesn't matter with how you were staring at her through the whole meeting this morning."

I shoot my drink and slam the glass down on the bar harder than I mean to. "You're supposed to be watching her, not me," I bite out.

Ryan smirks. "Watching her means watching everyone who's watching her."

Part of me wants everyone to know she's mine, but another part doesn't. Right now, people aren't paying attention, but when the whispers start, they'll be looking. Looking at my Mallory. It's coming either way, so I might as well rip the Band-Aid off. Well, as soon as she'll let me. I promised her time, space. It's going to take everything in me to give her that, but I'll do it for her.

I'd do anything for her…but give her up. Which brings me back to where we are now.

"Paige isn't going to help us anymore," I reaffirm.

"We'll need to be prepared for this. I know she'll keep an eye on her, but she won't give me anything. Hell, she barely has since they arrived in New York."

"I'm alrcady on it. I'll make sure we have eyes on her if she isn't in her apartment or office. But, sir, I'd like to let Jordan do that. I should be on you. You're at higher risk and—"

"No," I cut him off. I might be at a higher risk, but Mallory is more important. Ryan is the best, and that's why he wants to be on me. I want the best on Mallory. Without her, I wouldn't last. If something happened to her, I'd be done for. I don't tell Ryan this because it's fucking crazy and I know it. He already thinks I'm losing it as it is. I need him to do as he's told.

"Are you saying your team isn't good enough?" I look over at him and watch his jaw tighten. No one is more anal about their work than Ryan.

"I'll make sure I'm on her detail." He rises from his chair. I give him a nod as he exits the room, and then look back at the monitor. Paige still hasn't come out and I'm not thinking she will.

I go over to the couch, kicking off my shoes and unbuttoning my shirt, getting ready to lie down. I don't want to go back to my bedroom. The bed is unmade from when we made love. I'm not sure how I'd react if I still smelled her on the sheets, or worse, if the smell was gone.

I think back to the bathroom today. I'd waited for the perfect moment to corner her. Ryan had told me she was on her way back up to her desk. I needed to talk to her. Just a little taste to take the edge off. Even more so after I'd seen how the little prick next to her in

the meeting was looking at her. I need to remember to
have Ryan pull his file for me.

"Time," she'd said after she kissed me. And she *had*
kissed me. I may have taken her mouth first, but she
came back at me just as hungry. It was there. I know she
felt it. There was no way I was alone in this.

I'd give her what she asked for, but I'd do what I'd
planned to do from the beginning: try to get her attention, date her. Slowly make her fall in love with me. It
was going to be damn hard after I'd rushed so much
already. Now I know what it's like to have her in my
bed and under me, where she belongs. Her legs spread
for me as I come inside her, never taking my mouth
from her body.

My cock jerks at the reminder. Reaching down, I pull
myself from my slacks and think about the next time
I'll get her to myself. Maybe this time I'll tie her to the
bed so she can't slip away in the middle of the night.
Crawl between her legs and bury my face there. Make
her beg me to eat her until she begs me to stop. Until she
can't move because I've exhausted her with pleasure.

"Mallory."

I moan her name as the erotic thoughts flash through
my mind and come lands on my stomach.

"Fuck," I growl, sitting up.

I'm never going to make it.

TWENTY-TWO

Mallory

Tuesday

"DELIVERY FOR A Ms. Mallory Sullivan."

I turn to see a man standing in our office and holding a bouquet of pale pink peonies. Skyler stands up, leans over to my cubicle and lets out a whistle.

"Right here," she says, pointing at me, and I stand too, a little shocked.

I take them from him and he makes me sign a form before giving me a small salute and walking out.

The blush hits my cheeks as I turn and place them on my desk. There's a small envelope attached, and I unpin it from a leaf, looking up to see Skyler waiting expectantly. I raise an eyebrow at her, and she rolls her eyes and laughs as she gives me some privacy.

Last night Paige and I talked some more before I went to bed and had a better night's sleep than I'd had in days. It wasn't anywhere close to as good as the one I'd had with Oz, but I'll take it over being a zombie any day of the week. I left my phone off, not really ready to talk to him yet. I still need to think things over and get my head on straight. But I guess Oz found a way around my silence. At least he's giving me space, in his own way.

When I saw the flowers, I knew right away he'd sent them. No card was needed, but I pull it out anyway, wanting to see what he has to say for himself. Seeing his beautiful, neat handwriting does something to my insides, but I try to ignore it.

Mallory,
Nothing is as lovely as you.
Missing your beauty.
Love, Oz

The blush on my cheeks deepens, and I sit in my chair, trying to think of what to do next. Do I thank him for the flowers? I've never gotten flowers from anyone before. God, why does he have to be so…so…charming? He makes it hard to be mad and I want to hang on to that anger. I can't let him steamroll over me.

Placing the note in my bag, I go back to work, wanting to think about my response before I give him an answer. If I even will.

It turns out I don't have time to think of a response before the next bouquet is delivered. This time it's a larger arrangement of lavender dahlias. Eric perks up at this and asks if it's my birthday. Skyler rolls her eyes at him. I wait until I have a moment alone before I read the note.

Mallory,
Nothing is more precious than your touch.
Missing the feel of your softness.
Love, Oz

I grab my phone from my bag and squeeze it. I want to turn it on and text him, but I know I have to stay strong, too. This man lied to me, and I need some space to think over what I want. But instead he insists on doing things that are going to make me break; I know it, and a small part of me wants to know what he'll do next.

The next delivery of flowers arrives an hour later, and so goes the rest of my day at work. I spread them all over the department, so I won't have all of my work space taken up. People ask questions, but Skyler helps me out with that. She says it's a joke, and people shrug it off.

All day the notes come, and I keep every one of them, each one melting me more and more, breaking down my anger. He sends red tulips, peach plumeria, violets, hydrangeas, and even a bouquet with bells of Ireland. Every arrangement is beautiful and special. They aren't your typical flowers—each of these looks to have been specially picked—and I know in my heart he did that.

Finally, before quitting time and hopefully after the last delivery, I turn on my phone to send him a quick text. I don't know if I'm strong enough for more.

Me: Thank you. For all of them. They were overwhelmingly beautiful.

His response is instant. Like he's been waiting all day, and maybe he has.

Oz: You deserve a thousand more.

Me: I wouldn't know where to put them.

I smile and it feels nice. God, I want to forgive him and run into his arms. But I asked for space and I need to take it.

Oz: I would build you a castle, if only you would ask.

Me: Maybe one day.

I bite my lip, thinking maybe I shouldn't have said that. Damn it. I have to be stronger, I tell myself, but it's hard when someone makes you feel like you're so important to them. But then I let out a sigh and put my phone back in my bag. I decide to leave the flowers at work so I can enjoy them longer. I head out and meet Paige in the lobby. I don't need her for the walk home, but it's nice walking with her again.

When we get to the apartment, she pulls out her key, unlocking the door and stepping inside.

"Holy shit," she says, and I try to look around her.

The scent hits me before I can see what's beyond her, and when she steps to the side, I see it.

"He said I deserved a thousand more," I whisper as I look around the room.

Flowers are on every inch of every surface, and they're all exquisite. I stand there stunned and tears sting my eyes. My man behind the curtain will not give up so easily.

Wednesday

"Delivery for—"

"Right here," Skyler says, standing up and looking over our cubicle wall.

I put my bag away and turn around. I haven't been here ten minutes and it's started again already? When I see the man standing there without flowers, confusion hits me.

"Mallory Sullivan?" he queries.

I nod and wait.

"Sign here, please."

He hands me a small clipboard and I sign for whatever it is I'm supposed to get. He takes the paper and hands me a long, slender, black box tied with an ivory ribbon. It's an odd size, but I take it to my desk and sit down with it. Looking up, I see Skyler sigh and duck away again. I hear Eric coming in late, and I wait until he's seated, too.

I untie the ribbon and open the box and see a piece of paper and a pen inside. I read the note and look up to see the deliveryman still there. And then I laugh. It's the first time I've laughed in days, and it feels foreign but so nice.

I read the note again, debating if I should play with him but I can't deny the smile and flutter that strikes me. It's nice to not be so sad and I want to soak this moment up even if I'm still mad at him. I tell myself this is for me and not for him. I pull out the pen, doing as the note instructs, and put the paper back inside the box, tie the ribbon and hand it back to the delivery guy. He takes it and turns on his heels.

On the note was a hangman's pole and blank spaces at the bottom. Oz said he wanted to play a game with me, and though it sounds ridiculous, it was so adorable I couldn't help but melt a little more. He's slowly chipping away at the anger I'm trying to hold on to.

I go back to work, pushing Oz out of my mind, keeping busy. About an hour later the delivery guy is back with the same little box. I sign again and he waits while I unwrap the ribbon and read the note.

I'd guessed the letter *L* and it was no good. So I try the letter *S* this time and send it back with the delivery guy.

All day Oz and I play back and forth. Each time I got one wrong, he drew a piece of the man on the hangman's pole. When I got one right, he would fill in the places where the letters went.

Right before five o'clock, I get the last delivery of the box and solve the puzzle.

A DREAM IS A WISH YOUR HEART MAKES

I'd solved it long before lunch, but who would stop a game like this? I'd smiled all day, feeling lighter than I have in ages.

When I get home, there's been a delivery of dinner from this amazing Italian place, and Paige and I eat until we can hardly walk. She doesn't ask who it was from. We both know.

Thursday

I'M STARTING TO CRACK. But I've made it this long. I didn't text or email him all day yesterday even though I'd wanted to. I would start to, then stop each time. I feel like I'm fighting more with myself at this point than Oz. I can wait a little longer. Every time I try and remember why I'm mad at him, I end up defending him. Maybe because of what Paige had told me. All Oz wanted to do was protect me. Something no one has ever cared to do for me in my life. I'm excited to see what he has in store for today.

I'm at my desk sipping my coffee when a woman dressed in a black suit comes over to me.

"Ms. Sullivan?"

I nod a little nervously. I wonder if I'm in trouble. She pulls out an envelope and hands it to me, walking away right after.

"Another game?" Skyler asks as she walks by my desk.

I smile and turn away from her, opening the envelope. Inside I find two pieces of parchment paper and a pressed four-leaf clover in between them.

The clover looks old but perfectly preserved between the pieces of parchment. I look back down inside the envelope and see a note I'd missed the first time.

Pulling it out, I see Oz's beautiful script and begin to read.

My Mallory,
The first time I saw you was a long time ago. I'd love to tell you about that day and every day until the moment we met. When you're ready, I will, but until then I want you to have this.

I found this clover the day I saw you, and I kept it in my wallet ever since. I felt like it was a sign of things to come. That if I did everything right, maybe one day I could have you.

If you exit out of the south side of the building, there's a small garden nearby. Go there when you get a moment today. I've got something for you.
Love, Oz

I place the clover carefully inside the papers and take out my wallet. I have an empty pocket behind my driver's license and I slip it inside. It's as if the space was waiting for the clover, and something about it makes me ridiculously happy to have it.

I can't stop smiling but there's also a lump in my throat. This man means so much to me and it's eating at me that I'm mad at him. Worse, I'm now worrying about how it's eating at him, too. I'm making us both miserable.

A few hours later, Skyler asks me to lunch, but I've got plans. I need to find this garden and see what's there.

Making my way past the security desk and to the back of the building, I look around for an exit. There's a guard by the door with an earpiece in his ear, and when he sees me, he opens a hidden door I never knew was there. Has he been waiting on me all day? I idly wonder if he would have stood here waiting on me until nightfall.

When I walk through the door, there's a winding stone path that's covered by a wooden pergola. A lush wisteria vine weaves through the wood, creating shade and pops of lavender. The garden is cool, despite the New York heat, and there's even a slight breeze.

The path continues to curve, and I walk what seems like a long way before I finally come around the last bend.

At the end of it, I look around and put a hand to my mouth in shock. It's absolutely beautiful. The path ends, revealing a large, round grassy area. There is a wooden bench and a linen-covered table that sit across from me, with lunch set for one. There are trees surrounding a low stone wall and a small waterfall off to the side. It's peaceful and completely private and so incredibly beautiful. I can't even hear the noise of the city and I'm outside. Looking down at the thick green grass, I decide to take my shoes off. I take a step and it's then I notice clovers cover nearly everything, all of them dancing in the soft breeze. I smile and walk to the table.

Before I sit down on the bench, I notice the sun catches a gold plaque on the wood, and I read it.

To Mallory,
Everything for Her

I run my thumb over the words and take a deep breath, trying to hold back the emotions. I look around the secret garden and try to take it all in. He's done so much for me that I'd never known about, and I wonder if I should be upset about it at all. The thing that strikes me the most is that this place isn't new. This has been here for some time. How long, I have no idea. I know that this didn't happen overnight.

I spend my lunch in the garden, enjoying the food and listening to the waterfall. I think about him, and then I wonder how many times Oz sat in this very same spot and thought of me.

Friday

I'VE BEEN AT WORK for about two hours, and I have to admit I'm a bit disappointed that there haven't been any deliveries. I haven't responded to any of his texts in the past forty-eight hours. For a moment I fear he might have given up but I quickly push that aside. I know he won't and something about that is so reassuring and makes me feel safe. I sink myself into reports, and only when I hear a small hum do I look up.

A man in an old barber's costume blows into a tuning device, and I look around to see three other men with him.

"Oh my God," I say as the barbershop quartet starts to sing.

Everyone in the department comes over, and my face is as red as a fire hydrant. And to make matters worse, they're singing "Call Me Maybe" by Carly Rae Jepsen. If there was a hole close to me, I'd crawl inside of it and die of embarrassment.

But as they sing, I find myself laughing again, and all I can think about is Oz and how much he's made me smile through this whole week, even through my anger.

After the guys leave to resounding applause from the entire accounting department, we all go back to work. I have my phone in my hand again as I try to decide what to say, when I hear another hum.

"Oh, God," I say, and put my hands on my head as another singing telegram begins a song.

All day Friday, I have people singing to me, one even dressed as a gorilla doing Britney Spears. It's insanity, and I'm mortified. But at the same time, I have to give it to him. The man knows what he's doing.

A phone call isn't going to cut it this time, and he knows it. I need to see him.

TWENTY-THREE

Mallory

I TAKE A deep breath and try to keep my knees from knocking together. Pressing my hand to my stomach, I try to keep the butterflies at bay.

Pressing the button for the top floor, I steel myself. This won't be easy, but I've got to keep it together.

When the doors open to the executive floor, I step out and see a young woman sitting behind a large wooden desk polished to perfection.

As I step forward, I see her with her head down, writing furiously in a notebook, not even noticing that the elevator opened or that someone is now waiting in front of her. I clear my throat, and the young woman nearly jumps out of her seat, clutching her notebook to her chest, and then immediately hiding it away.

"Yes, sorry. Hi," she says, clearly flustered as she pushes her glasses back on her nose. "Welcome. May I help you?" She finds her footing and sits up straighter.

"I'm here to see Miles," I say, and find the situation has put me a little at ease. I don't know what I was prepared for, but certainly not this. I think I expected an old rigid assistant or a young bimbo, but this woman seems kind of dorky in an adorable kind of way.

"Do you have an appointment?" she asks, turning to her computer and scanning the screen.

"No. Can you tell him it's Mallory?" I try. Maybe if he knows I'm here, he can make time to see me.

"Ms. Mallory Sullivan?" the assistant asks.

When I nod, she stands up out of her chair, nearly knocking it over in the process. "Please. This way." She sounds hurried as she leads me over to large double doors with ornate carvings. She knocks half a second before opening the door and announcing our entrance. "Mr. Osbourne, Ms. Sullivan is here."

I take a step around his assistant and see Miles on the other side of the room. He stands slowly, almost in shock that I'm here.

"Thank you, Jay. Please see that I'm undisturbed," he says, not taking his eyes off me.

"Yes, sir," she says, closing the large door behind us.

I hear the locks engage, and I narrow my eyes at Oz. He holds up a remote in his hand and shrugs one shoulder. It's as if he knows he's crazy, but he either can't help himself or can't be bothered to care about his behavior. He takes a step toward me, but then seems to think better of it and stands still.

The silence hangs between us, heavy with unspoken words.

After what feels like an eternity, but is really only a heartbeat, I decide I have to be the one to speak.

"Thank you."

"You're welcome."

"You don't even know what I'm thanking you for," I say, letting out a little laugh.

"If something I did made you happy, then I hope to do it again. Often."

As if emboldened by my words, he comes out from bchind his desk, coming to stand in front of me. He's not within touching distance, but that has never mattered before. We could be on separate tectonic plates and I think I would still sense his presence.

"Singing telegrams are over-the-top," I say, almost accusingly, but can't help my smile as I think of all those people dressed up and singing to me today.

"Yes," he agrees, not denying it was inappropriate. His eyes crinkle at the edges, and his smile shows the dimples I've been missing.

"I thought the man behind the curtain was supposed to be mysterious."

I finally look away from his penetrating sapphires because I fear that if I look at him a second longer, I'll end up in his arms. I have to stay strong. We have to talk about all of this.

"I think we're past the mystery, Mallory. I think we've reached the point where there should be no secrets left between us."

Looking around his office, I see that he has a beautiful view of the city behind him, but nothing much else in the room. There's a bookshelf to my left, and a giant television to my right. The screen is split into sections, each scrolling stocks and investment channels.

"The garden was beautiful," I whisper, looking anywhere but at him.

He steps forward, and his scent assaults me. The warm amber and honey surrounds me in a comforting embrace that I didn't know I needed.

"I want to tell you about it. About everything. Let me explain, Mallory. Please."

He still doesn't touch me and I'm thankful for it. Because I'm not sure I'm strong enough to push him away again. I can tell he's fighting himself, see the tension in his shoulders, his fist clenched tight as he stands there trying to play it calm and cool, but I can read him better now. See how he holds himself back with me, for me. I've missed him so much. Not talking to him the past few days has hollowed me out. A piece of me missing.

"Oz." I say his name, but I have no idea what I want to say after. Take me? Leave me alone? Push past all this bullshit and make me understand?

"Have dinner with me. I'll explain everything to you."

I look up and see the pain in his eyes. Hating seeing it there because no matter what I might have told myself, I care about this man and it hurts to see him hurt. How can a man who hardly knows me love me like this? He's fighting himself for me. This is insane, and I want to shout that it's also completely impossible and he should snap out of it. But then my heart chimes in, and I can't. I know what he's feeling isn't one-sided, and I don't know what to do with all of these emotions.

"Just dinner, Mallory. Please."

Releasing a breath, I nod. If I want answers, I need to hear him out. I've never wanted anything as much as I want him, and that feeling isn't going away. He gave me the space I asked for, in his own way, and nothing has changed. I want the truth, and in order to get that we need to talk.

"All right, dinner. Saturday night. You can pick me up at my apartment at six."

He looks like he wants to say more. I know he probably wants to push for tonight, but I need to have the upper hand while I can. If I give in to him, I'll never have a say over anything again, so I need to make damn sure that when I do it, I'm ready for that again.

His fists clench even tighter at his sides and his jaw twitches, but he nods. "Okay. Tomorrow night at six."

"Thank you," I say, tension leaving my body. It's as if now that the plan has been set and he didn't fight me on it, I can relax.

His hands unclench, and he acts as if he's going to reach for me, but then lets them drop. The air is charged between us, and anything could set us off. It's like a gas leak waiting on a match to strike before the whole thing explodes.

So instead of giving in to the flame, I take a step back and then another, until my ass hits the large door behind me. I turn to pull it open forgetting about it being locked and feel Oz's body press against mine, his smell filling my lungs, wrapping around me like I've been thinking about for days. I didn't even know you could miss a smell.

He places a kiss on my neck softly and I tilt my head, giving in to what we both want. Before I can even take another breath he's turning me, my back hitting the door once again.

"I'll give you until Saturday but you'll give me something to hold me over." His mouth takes mine before I can even ask what he wants. Taking what he wants. Demanding my lips to open to his and they do. I'm starting to think he owns my body more than I actually do.

I moan into his mouth and he eats my passion like he can't get enough of it. Before finally pulling away, leaving us both breathless. I'm almost in a daze from everything I felt from one kiss.

"Go now, or I'll never let you leave this room."

Oz reaches into his pocket, and I hear the clicks of the locks disengaging. He's letting me leave, and for some reason, it makes my heart ache.

"Tomorrow," he says, and for a second it sounds like a threat. But even as I think it, my excitement grows.

TWENTY-FOUR

Mallory

WHEN I GET back to my desk, I see a medium-sized plain white envelope sitting on it, and I immediately think it's from Oz.

"Paige gave that to me to give to you," Skyler says, looking down at the package with clear interest. "Okay, so maybe she jumped me in the bathroom and forced it on me."

I laugh, picturing Paige waiting in the bathroom for the perfect moment. I pick up the package and rip it open. A cheap-looking phone slides out. One text message is visible on the screen.

Red Bull Whore: Operation Ruby Slippers is a go, Dorothy.

I can't help but laugh.

"She got you a phone?" Skyler eyes me because it's clear it's one of those cheap phones you get inside a gas station or something.

Leaning forward, I whisper, "We're going out tonight."

She probably thinks I'm being crazy. "Simon's Wine Bar. Up East Street, four blocks." I nod, probably in the wrong direction. I still get a little turned around being so new to New York.

"Everyone else is going to Marie's Yacht Club like always," she says.

I shake my head.

"I don't want to go where everyone is going," I admit, knowing Oz would find us in point two seconds. We'll at least give him a good chase by not following the crowd.

"Ah. Dodging the boss, I see." She leans in a little farther and whispers, "I'm in."

I smile back at her. I don't know why this is so fun. Maybe because I feel like I'm sneaking out, which I never did because I never had anyone who would have cared if I did. The thought that I do now makes my stomach flutter, but I ignore it.

I text Paige back.

Dorothy: I really think your name should be Peggy Carter. Just sayin'.

I laugh when I see she actually programmed my name as Dorothy and I even have a little picture. If I'm going to be Dorothy, she should have to be Peggy. This math adds up to me. After all, we are trying to skip out on Captain.

Red Bull Whore: Not happening.

Dorothy: Too late. I already changed your name in the phone.

I send a pic I find on Google real quick of Captain America kissing Peggy Carter.

Peggy Carter: Grrr... Whatever. Peggy doesn't even end up with Captain America! She, like, all dies and shit. Don't put that dead voodoo on me!

Dorothy: Well, there is a chance we'll die and shit if we get caught tonight.

Peggy Carter: I think you mean WHEN. They might not find us until we come back home, but they will know we went MIA for a while.

Dorothy: Does it make me terrible that I kind of can't wait for Oz to flip his shit?

Part of me is doing this because I want to show him I can do whatever I want, whether he likes it or not. He can't always have eyes on me. Call it an act of rebellion, but I want to assert myself.

Peggy Carter: No. Leave your normal cell in your desk.

I pull my cell phone out and put it in my desk before taking my seat.

"I'll meet you there if my girl feels up to going out," Skyler says before going back to her chair. I lose myself in work for a few hours until my secret phone dings again.

I pick it up and see a pic of Captain, studying a computer screen. He doesn't look like he normally does in a suit. This time it looks like he just got done working out. Jesus, no wonder Paige has a crush on him. He has this whole I'll-snap-a-man-in-half look mixed with I-always-call-women-ma'am-and-open-doors-for-them. It's oddly appealing.

Peggy Carter: Look at him. He doesn't even know in a few short hours he's going to want to murder me. *evil laughs*

I giggle, and then the laughter takes over.

Dorothy: WHY IS THIS SO FUNNY?!

I can't stop laughing. I have no idea why this secret operation thing keeps making me laugh. We've been planning on doing something Friday night for the past few days and it's slowly morphed into this whole big thing.

Peggy Carter: Because they're always two steps ahead of us and it makes me want to throat punch them.

Dorothy: Time check, PC.

Peggy Carter: 5:05 sharp. I have a mission planned for Captain. Operation GOOSE CHASE.

Dorothy: I don't even want to know what Operation GOOSE CHASE is.

Peggy Carter: …

Dorothy: Okay, I totally want to know.

Peggy Carter: I may have asked the door guy in our building to feed our cat at 4:55 sharp.

Dorothy: We don't have a cat.

Peggy Carter: I may have also given him the wrong security code.

"Oh, God," I whisper, and then laugh to myself. Putting the phone back down, I think about the alarm going off and Captain—and possibly Oz—panicking, thinking someone broke in while we are at work. At least they'll know we aren't there, that someone should check it out.

I work for the last few hours until it's time to head out. Skyler asks if I want to walk out with her, but I shake my head and tell her I'll hopefully see her at the wine bar after she's finished having dinner with her girlfriend.

Grabbing my stuff, I make sure I leave my cell phone and grab the one Paige got for me. I'm a little disappointed that I didn't hear from Oz after meeting in his office and agreeing to a date. But I could tell he was holding himself back. I could see it with every strain in his body that he hadn't wanted to let me out of his office. That he wanted to finish what we started, and I know I would have let him. I can still feel the slight soreness on my lips from his demanding kiss.

I loved that he was trying to keep it together, but another part of me, a dark part, wanted him to snap. How can I get so mad at him for what he's doing, then get so turned on by it? It's like my brain, heart and vagina can't agree on one thing.

I hit the elevator button right at five o'clock. It only takes a minute to hit my floor, but stops several times on the way down to the lobby. I finally get to the lobby floor at five-oh-five, and I slip out, heading for the front door and moving with the crowd. I only make it a few short feet outside the building and I'm being pulled by the arm into a small nook.

"I think we did it," Paige says, her whole face lighting up.

"Are you sure?" I whisper, leaning out to look to see if anyone is following us.

"I think so. Captain took off before you got off the elevator. He told me to keep my ass planted and he was calling Miles as he was leaving," she whispers back. I look her up and down and laugh. She has on big sunglasses and a trench coat.

"What are you wearing? Why am I whispering? Why didn't I get something like this to wear?" I keep whispering. I can't seem to stop myself.

"I don't know," she mouths back and we both burst out laughing. Tears leak out the corner of my eyes. I can't remember the last time I laughed like this. It feels good. Normal. Us.

"Let's go." I grab her hand, heading to Simon's, but she pulls at my hand and walks the other way. I'd make a terrible spy. My sense of direction is the worst.

"Where did you even get that thing?" I ask her, looking over at her trench coat. It's super cute and I would have noticed it before now. It looks a little big on her. In fact, it would fit me nicely.

"Lunch. I hate it. You can have it. I wanted to hide this." She turns, walking backward, and flips open the coat. People jump out of her way so she doesn't knock into them. Under the coat she's wearing tight black pants, knee-high black boots and a tight black tank. She looks hot. Hotter than she normally dresses.

"What's happening here?" I ask her, and she smiles before turning and walking forward with me.

She shrugs. "Maybe I wanted to look nice. Or maybe I always wanted to do that flip-your-coat-open thing, like in the movies." She reaches up, pulling the tie from her hair, letting the glossy waves fall to her shoulders and down her back. I do the same, unclipping my hair, running my fingers through it.

"You thinking about dating or something? When we were at school, you always said you'd worry about that later. It's kind of later." Maybe that's what's up with this slight style change. Paige never plays up her sexy. She doesn't have to. Men always take notice of her.

She shrugs again. "I don't know." She shakes her head as if telling herself no. "I should be focused on other things, but it would be a lie if I didn't find it intriguing the way Miles looks at you sometimes."

We step into the wine bar together, bypassing the hostess and grabbing two chairs at the bar.

"It's a little intoxicating. To have someone obsessed with you. Like you're their everything. I've never had that. Not in foster care. I'd be lying, too, if I said something about it isn't sucking me into him."

"Drinks?" the older bartender asks, cutting into our conversation.

"I'll have a glass of rosé, please." I give him my card to get a tab going.

"Same," Paige adds, and orders five small plates for us to eat while we sit and talk. I don't know how long we're here, but the bar slowly fills and someone in the back plays a piano. Some people sing along and request songs.

"Think they're freaking out yet?" I ask Paige.

She looks down at her watch. "Oh, I'm sure. They'll live. I'm with you, so they can cool it. Well, they might be pissed if they knew this is my fourth glass." She finishes off her glass and orders another one.

I've only had two, enjoying the warmth of the wine. Wine always goes straight to my head, so I try to keep it light. The fact that I could be pregnant sits quietly in the back of my mind.

Paige doesn't normally drink much, and it makes me smile that she's letting loose a little tonight.

More people trickle in and it's not long before I can barely move without bumping into someone. Unlike our other nights out, Paige doesn't shut down men who talk to us. She talks back and even jokes a little. It's probably the wine.

"I didn't know you came here," someone whispers in my ear, and I turn slightly in my bar stool to see Eric. "I was hoping to see you at Marie's Yacht Club, but you weren't there tonight."

"Wanted to try something different," I say, turning a little more so I can look at him. It's hard to hear in the once-quiet bar with all the people and the piano playing.

His hand comes to my hip, and I'm taken aback by the intimate gesture. I'm not sure if it's because people are pushed in so close and he's making room, or if he does it on purpose to touch me. I glance over at Paige, who's talking to a well-dressed man in a suit. She looks over at me as if sensing my eyes on her.

"Want to dance?" Eric asks, but his other hand grabs my other hip, pulling me off the chair before I can respond.

"I'm not sure we should." I don't want to cause a scene with the crowd around us, but his grip on my hand is tight. I want to shout the word *no* but I'm on the dance floor before I have a chance.

He pulls me closer, but my body freezes up when, out of the corner of my eye, I spot two sapphires locked on me.

TWENTY-FIVE

Mallory

OZ STALKS OVER to us, and I'm frozen in place. I don't even register Eric leaning down and putting his lips on my neck until it's already happened. I pull back from Eric's grip instantly, sick from his unwelcome advances.

He gives me a greasy smile and holds me tighter. His Abercrombie good looks contrast with the creepy feeling he's giving me. I'm about to tell him exactly how to fuck off when a fist comes flying across his face.

For a half a second I think, *here we go again*, until I see Paige standing over him and shaking out her hand.

"You keep your hands off of her, you spoiled piece of shit."

Eric lies on the floor, unmoving. She knocked him out cold.

I'm in shock, unable to move. After a heartbeat Paige turns to me and looks me up and down.

"Are you okay, Mal?"

Unable to find my tongue, I nod. A crowd has formed around us, and some guys have come over to check on Eric. As I'm about to speak, Oz breaks through the crowd and comes to me.

I'm in his arms for a second before he's looking over at Paige. "You okay?"

She shrugs and gives me a half smile.

I hear a commotion behind her and look around Oz to see Eric getting hauled off the floor as Captain yells at Eric's friends to get him the fuck out of here.

When did he show up?

Oz throws some bills on the bar behind me and turns to give Paige a stare. He doesn't say anything before taking my hand and pulling me from the place.

Everything happens so fast. One second I was laughing with Paige and the next I'm being dragged away from all the fun, the night ruined by some sleazy guy trying to put his hands on me. Even if Oz hadn't shown up, Paige knocking Eric out cold might have spoiled our good vibe.

The summer heat hits me as we exit the building, but it's quickly replaced by the cool air in the back of Oz's limo. He shuts the door and walks around, climbing in on the other side, and never once have I given him permission to do this.

His scent assaults me, and suddenly the two small glasses of wine I had are making me dizzy with lust. Or at least that's what I'm telling myself. He gets in, and the sight of him so close to me makes me weak. God, I hate that I'm not strong enough to tell him no, because if he touches me, I'll dissolve. Everything I've said about waiting and talking and wanting to know the truth will go right out the window. And he knows it.

"Oz." I stop. I don't know what I'm going to say. Apologize for sneaking away from him? Beg him to hold me? Beg him not to?

He shakes his head and I stop the words. I know

ALEXA RILEY 257

they're useless when it comes to him. He crooks his finger at me to come to his lap, and like the slave I am, I go.

I crawl onto him, sitting with my legs together and my ass pressed against his erection.

"Did you drink tonight?" he asks, looking down at my mouth.

I nod, knowing his meaning. We've had sex. Unprotected sex. And this could very well mean I'm carrying a baby. I know where his train of thought is going, so I try to put him at ease.

"Two small glasses."

He nods, and then runs his hand down my cheek. "No more. Not until we know for sure."

His words are whispered in the dark, and if I close my eyes, I can almost pretend I don't hear them. But I do, and I know that I'll give him what he wants. Like I always do. I've been fighting a losing battle. As much as I pretend to hate how overbearing he can be, a part of me loves it, too. My rational brain tells me all these things aren't okay, but deep down I know I'm only lying to myself. When I think of all the things he's done for me, and how he'd do anything and everything to have me, I love it.

His big hands, which could nearly span my waist, rub up and down my back. The air in the limo grows thick with desire. I need to talk to him, but when his hands are on me, I can't form a coherent sentence, let alone stop the tidal wave of need that is about to crash on me. If he kisses me, I'll beg him to take me right here on the floor. That's how much I need him right now. I've gone too long, and I'm a drug addict coming off the wagon and looking for a fix.

"Oz." His name is nearly a moan as he pulls me closer. My voice is pleading, and he knows he's got me right where he wants me.

"Shhh."

His sapphires look my body up and down, devouring me every inch of the way. He stares at my neck, and he reaches over and grabs something. He pulls out the orange linen pocket square from his dark gray suit and dips it into a glass of water he has sitting on the side bar. Then he proceeds to wipe my neck, where Eric put his mouth.

He doesn't say a word as he cleans me, and then throws the linen to the floor in near disgust.

The next thing I know his mouth is on me in the same spot, his teeth grazing the sensitive skin and his full lips sucking me into his mouth. He's angry that someone else touched me, so he has to cover it up with his own touch. In a weird, twisted way, I understand it. And I welcome it.

I cling to him as he assaults my neck. Moaning into the quiet of the limo is all I can do as I take what he gives me. His hand runs between my legs, and the heel of his palm grinds against my panty-covered pussy. I shudder against the feeling, needing him. He puts more pressure in the most perfect place and I grind my hips against him while his mouth devours my neck.

"Oh, God," I gasp, nearing a climax I'm not prepared for. It's been too long since he's really touched me. A wave of emotions floods me. The building pleasure is close, and I dig my nails into his suit jacket to try to keep it from happening, or to try to pull it closer. I have no idea which. But as he kneads his palm against me, he bites my neck and I come apart in his arms.

I cry out as the pleasure of my orgasm liquefies my bones, and I'm left a wrung-out heap of warmth in his arms. What he does to me is too good, and I won't ever be able to get enough. Even now, as my climax gives its last pulse and soaks my underwear through, I'm already thinking about how many more he can give me before I pass out.

Before I realize what's happening, Oz is carrying me out of the limo and into my building. Well, *our* building. I try not to blush as the night doorman waves at us and Oz nods to him.

When we get to the elevator, I expect him to put me down, but he doesn't. He walks in and stands there, cradling me in his arms.

"I don't suppose you're taking me to the third floor?" I ask, looking up at him through my lashes.

"No."

There's finality in his words, and I know now is not the time to fight him. So instead I put my key in for his floor and hit the button.

The elevator shoots straight up without pausing, and my stomach flips as we come to a stop. He's taking me back into the land of Oz, only this time I fear I won't be able to slip away so easily.

TWENTY-SIX

Miles

I CARRY MALLORY to the bedroom and sit her down on the edge, kneeling in front of her. Reaching down, I unbuckle her deep blue suede heels and slip them off. I rub her feet for a moment, helping to ease any of the ache she may have felt from walking on them today.

The small moan she lets out as I squeeze her foot has my already-hard cock throbbing against my thigh. I try to ignore it, although I can feel my heartbeat inside it.

Moving to her other foot, I remove that shoe and give her foot the same attention.

"Oz."

Her voice is hesitant, but I wait, letting her say what she needs to. I've been crazy with worry for most of the night, and I'm afraid if I start talking I'll get angrier.

I knew something was wrong the second I arrived in the lobby of our building. Chuck, working at the desk, showed me the request, and I cursed my own stupidity. I should have seen this coming. But when I checked her tracker, it said she was still at work.

I went to her desk only to find her phone sitting there, and I cursed again. Ryan couldn't get hold of Paige, and I had a feeling they'd done this on purpose. It didn't stop the absolute panic flaring through me as we searched everywhere for her. I called around to every bar within a ten-block radius as we rode around the city hoping to catch sight of them.

We finally got lucky when Ryan got a call from one of his friends who works security at a wine bar. He said there were two women there who fit the description, and he sent us a picture of them. I nearly ground my teeth to dust looking at her sitting there. She was so beautiful, and it killed me that she was out of my grasp. We made it there in record time, but not before some asshole put his hands on what's mine. The same little fucker I knew sat next to her Monday in the meeting. Thankfully, Paige was there. I don't know what I would have done if I'd gotten my hands on him.

I know who that little worm is, and I'll be taking care of him later.

As Mallory's hands run through my hair, I close my eyes and let some of the tension leave me. At her simple touch, all that I've been worried over falls away. She's the cure for all my aches, and I lean into her touch, wanting to be soothed. I take her wrist in my hand and turn her palm to my mouth.

"Stay with me," I whisper against her skin. Opening my eyes and looking into her gray-blue pools of love, I confess what's in my heart. In every part of me. All I seem to know anymore. All I can think about now. "Please, Mallory. I need you."

"We need to talk. You said dinner Saturday." She bites her lip, and I want to be the one doing that to her lip.

I nod over to the clock beside the bed. "It's after midnight, baby. You're all mine." She glances over and her cheeks flush. "I said I'd wait until today. We'll talk, and I promise to tell you anything you want to know. I'll answer all your questions about everything, but not tonight."

I place my hands on her thighs and let them travel upward, until I reach the hem of her dress. It's a light tan linen material with buttons all the way down the front. It flows loosely around her thighs, and I bet if she twirled I could see her panties.

"Don't deny me, Mallory."

Looking up, I see the small nod she gives me as her legs open a little wider.

I move down and rub the stubble of my beard on the insides of her thighs, and again her legs widen for me. As if listening to my desires, they give me what I want. And right now what I want most is between her gorgeous legs.

Pushing up her dress the rest of the way, I see the wet fabric clinging to her pussy and showing me the outline of her needy sex. I peel off my suit jacket and throw it on the ground as I loosen my tie and unbutton the top two buttons of my shirt. That jacket probably cost thousands, but I'd burn it if it got me to Mallory faster.

Without teasing, I reach up and grip the thin cream straps of her panties, ripping them at her hips. Pulling away the ragged lace, I stuff them into my pocket and think about the small collection of her panties I'm starting to assemble.

Mallory gasps, and then leans back on her hands as I pull her ass to the edge of the bed. "You keep ripping them off me and I'll make you replace them."

I hover right over her pussy, breathing in her heady

scent. I lick my lips so the drool doesn't run down my chin. I look into her eyes. "You could stop wearing them, stop keeping me from my sweet pussy."

My mouth descends on her warm, wet heat, and she cries out, nearly lifting off the bed. Reaching down, I slide my hands into my pants and squeeze my cock hard, trying to keep myself from coming too soon.

Her sticky nectar coats my tongue and lips as I move my tongue to her opening and fuck her with it. Her hands move to my hair and she grips it tightly. When I replace my tongue with my fingers and move my mouth to her hard pearl, she says my name. Hearing it echo through the bedroom fills me with insane need, but I have to get her off like this. I need to give her this, and I need to have it. Something primal inside me is demanding it, and I have to give in to my inner beast.

My fingers move in and out of her incredibly tight channel, and I moan right along with her. The feel of her velvety soft pussy on my tongue is driving me to the edge.

"Oz." She's out of breath and pulling me closer. "I'm… I'm *coming*."

She shouts the last word as she tenses against me, her legs tightening like vises around my head. I couldn't care less if she stabbed me in the heart right now, as long as I'm able to make her feel anything close to what I feel for her.

Giving her gentle slow licks, I help wring her orgasm out of her. Giving her every little pulse of pleasure I can before kissing the insides of her thighs. She's so soft and delicate here, and knowing no other man has ever laid a hand on this part of her goes a long way toward calming both my need for her and all the jealousy I seem to have when it comes to her.

Standing up, I look down at her and take off my shirt and slacks, kicking off my shoes as I go. When I'm standing in front of her in boxer briefs, she sits up and her eyes lock on my chest. It's late, but there's a lamp on beside the bed, and she can see the tattoo of her name over my heart.

Tentatively, she reaches out and delicately touches the space there. I've got defined muscles, but I also have chest hair and some of it slightly covers her name. When her fingertips touch me, it's as if she's brushed a rose petal over the letters. She's so soft and delicate, and having her hands on me is my own personal heaven.

Reaching out, I place my hand on top of hers, flattening her palm to my chest. I lock eyes with her beautiful bluish-grays, and feel my heartbeat against her hand. If only she knew that it was beating in time to tell her I love her. I wonder if she would still want to feel it?

"Why." Her whisper is soft but I can hear the awe in her voice.

"I knew I couldn't have you the first time I'd seen you so I wanted something of you on me. To always have until I could have you."

Her hand stays on my chest as she takes in my words, and I move mine away, running my fingers down her arms and to her chest. I unbutton her dress all the way down, never taking my eyes off hers. There's so much in her eyes, and I can't look away. Not even when I remove her dress and unclasp her bra. Not even when she's completely naked in front of me.

Wrapping an arm around her hips, I lift her up and

place her in the middle of the bed. She slips her fingers in the waistband of my underwear and pushes them off my hips. I help her the rest of the way, and then we're both naked. Warm, soft skin against my hard-angled body. She molds to me in every way possible as I settle down between her hips and press my hard cock against her wet clit. I run the length of it slowly up and down as I look into her eyes and brush the stray hair away from her cheeks.

"My God, you get more beautiful every time I see you." Her delicate fingers come up to trace the dips and flex of my back.

I want her, and I want nothing between us. I know what happened last time, and I know that she could be pregnant right now. This would be irresponsible to some people, but Mallory is my whole life. She has been from the moment I saw her. And if a baby were to be created while we made love, then it's meant to be. I want a life, and yes, a family with her. Whenever that day comes, it will be another piece of her to love. A piece of us to cherish and nurture. How can that be bad?

"Oz." Her eyes look into mine and I see the uncertainty, but there's also need there. And I'm hoping the need wins out.

"Let me inside, baby."

Her eyes roll to the back of her head as she closes her eyes and moans. I run the thick vein of my cock up, and then slowly run it back down, making sure to rub her clit with every pass.

"We have to be careful. We can't keep doing this," she says, lifting her hips up to meet my strokes.

"Mallory, if you can't tell by now, I'm crazy about

you. And there isn't anything I wouldn't do to protect and care for you. Especially if you were to become pregnant with my baby. I'll take care of everything. Always."

She hesitates for a second, and then nods up at me. It's then I take her mouth, letting the small taste of her pussy pass between us. Her warm lips part for me and I dip my tongue inside. The kiss is deep and passionate, and it's fucking perfect. Like every inch of my Mallory.

Moving my hips, I press the tip of my cock into her wet opening and push past her tight folds. She's wet, but she's incredibly tight, and my thick cock barely fits inside her. There's still an inch that I can't push in yet, but I don't care. Having her, even a little, is more than I dreamed about.

I move my lips down her neck and slowly rock in and out of her, helping her get adjusted to having my cock in her again. Her tight pulses are vibrating down to my balls and I ache to empty inside her.

I can't seem to keep my mouth off her as I lick my way to her breasts and suck on her nipples. I lave one, and then turn to do the same to the other. Sucking each into my mouth and giving them both a small bite. I lick the space between her breasts, and then suck on the delicate flesh there. I know I should be more gentle, but the way her nails dig into my back tells me to keep going.

My thickness slides in and out of her easily now, her muscles relaxing and taking all of me. Her feet come around my waist and her hips rise to meet every thrust.

"Mallory," I grunt against her neck. "I can't hold off much longer."

I should do the right thing and pull out. I could come

on her soft belly and mark her creamy skin as my own. I should do that for her.

"Oz," she whispers, and pulls her legs tighter around me.

I know her orgasm is nearing and I don't have much time.

"Baby, I need to pull out," I choke, trying to breathe through it.

"Inside me," she moans as her pussy clamps down on me and her orgasm bursts through her.

I have no choice but to stay in her warmth and spill my come into her waiting womb. It's long and loud as I roar my orgasm into her, giving her every drop of me. It wasn't my intention, but fuck does it feel so good coming inside her. Where I belong.

When I've given her all of me, and she's panting with her own release, I roll us over so she's lying on my chest. We're both breathless, and I wrap my arms around her, kissing her forehead.

"Promise me you won't sneak out," I say, squeezing her a little tighter. "I'll tell you everything. Please don't go."

She brings her hand up to my chest and pets the place where her name resides.

"I promise."

With her words, I drift off to sleep, and for a second I think I tell her what I've been longing to say.

I love you.

TWENTY-SEVEN

Mallory

"I CAN'T SEEM to stop," Oz says into my ear in a half moan half grunt. He has one hand gripped on my thigh, keeping it in place over his leg, his other arm under me with his hand gripping my breast as he thrusts in and out of me from behind. His big strong body molded to mine. This is how we've been most of the night, and this is the second time he's woken me. The first was with his mouth between my legs, and now this. I'm not sure which I prefer. Both are equally wonderful.

He slowly thrusts in and out of me, making me moan with him. I swear him moaning my name could get me off. I had no idea something could be such a turn-on. But hearing my name come from his mouth like that does things to me everywhere.

"Then don't," I encourage him, moving my hips with his and taking him deeper into my body. Wanting him there. Every time he's locked inside me like this, it's like I'm home. A place that's only mine. A place I'd been missing all week. How I managed to keep away from this I have no idea.

"Every time I wake up, I have to make sure you're real," he says before he's licking and kissing my neck again, making me arch my back, pushing my breasts farther into his hand. "Make sure I didn't dream you were here with me." He thrusts again, and his teeth graze my neck. "You're going to come for me, aren't you?"

It isn't a question, so I don't answer him. I should get annoyed with how he's always bossing me around and making me do what he wants, but my body isn't getting that message. My pussy clenches around his cock harder and begs him to make me come.

I reach behind me, sliding my fingers into his hair, needing to touch him. I need something to grab on to, because I sense it getting closer. The orgasm is almost here, and I know I'm going to explode.

"You like when I talk dirty to you, don't you?" I moan his name in response, still feeling a little shy saying what I want. I'm getting the hang of the sex thing, but my dirty talk isn't there. But I want him to keep going, because he's right. I like it. Hell, I think I might love it.

"That's really good, baby, because I've been thinking about the things I've wanted to do to you for years. I can't wait to tell you what I'll be doing to this body for the rest of our lives."

"Please," I beg.

"Fucking love when you beg me. It makes me feel like you want me as bad as I want you. Beg me. Beg me, and I'll give you anything."

"Please, Oz, make me come. Please," I plead. I'm so close, a little more. He's slowed down his thrusts, and I'm going insane. A little harder is all I need.

"Ask me to come inside you," he moans against my ear. His words make my stomach do a little flip. He releases my leg, but I keep it in place while his hand travels down to my clit and his finger brushes over it, not giving me the pressure I need.

"Come inside me, Oz. Fill me up with you," I cry out, and he does. Thrusting deep, his fingers finally give me what I need and he sends me over. He jerks behind me as I clamp down around him, my orgasm taking me. His warm release fills me and my desire deepens from the sensation.

I don't know how long I lie there, enjoying the aftermath of our pleasure while he places soft kisses along my neck. Since I hit this bed last night, I think at least one part of him has been touching me nonstop. Almost like he can't help himself.

"You didn't leave," he finally says, making me giggle. I don't think I could've gotten out of this bed even if I wanted to.

"I could barely move with how you were wrapped around me last night." I was lucky I could breathe at a few points.

"Sorry," he mumbles against my neck, and I don't believe for a second he's sorry at all. I wiggle against him and he tightens his grip, proving my point.

"I really do need to use the bathroom."

He sighs, reluctantly letting me go, and I shyly stand. The curtains in the room are pulled back and the morning sun fills the room, exposing every inch of me. Once on my feet, the moisture of our night together runs down my thighs.

"Fuck, I like seeing that." Oz's eyes are trained between my legs, and after a second he lunges for me. He pulls me back toward the bed, saying he wants a better look. My cheeks warm, which is silly because Oz has seen me there more than a few times now. He runs a finger up my thigh into the wetness, and damn him.

"Bathroom," I whisper, making him look up at me.

He nods. "Don't shower. I'll cook for us, then we'll shower," he says, pulling himself from the bed and giving me a quick kiss. I try to deepen it, but he pulls back. "You'll end up back in the bed, sweetheart," he warns, making me smile. I like how I seem to test his control.

He walks over to a closet, pulling out a shirt and handing it to me. "You can wear this." He slides it on over my head, not really giving me an option. But it's not like I'm about to put on the dress from last night. It's in a pile on the floor, and I'm not sure I'm ready to walk around naked, so I let him dress me.

"Scrambled eggs and bacon?" he asks, before giving me another quick kiss.

"Yes." He kisses me on the cheek this time before turning to grab his boxer briefs off the floor and sliding them on. He walks out of the bedroom door, and I can't help but watch him go. He's got a great ass.

Pulling myself together, I make quick work of taking care of business in the bathroom, but stop to look at myself in the mirror. Leaning in closer to the mirror, I see something on my neck that makes me gasp.

I turn, storming out of the bathroom and toward the kitchen. He left a hickey on me! It might be light and I'll probably be able to cover it with makeup, but still. A freaking hickey like I'm in high school or something.

"Miles!" I snap, making him turn from the stove, spatula in hand and a stupid, perfect smile on his face. No one should look that good in the morning, or while cooking. Who cooks in their underwear anyway? He's trying to kill me.

"Yeah, baby?" he says easily, like he's not worried about my temper.

"I'm about to yell at you, so stop smiling," I snap again, which only makes him smile more. He turns, flipping off the stove and putting the spatula down before turning to look back at me. Still smiling.

"Hard not to smile when you're standing in our kitchen, in my shirt, looking like I made love to you all night. As long as you're not trying to slip out on me, I don't think there's anything you could be doing in here that won't make me smile."

I ignore his sweet words because, well, because they're too freaking sweet. Like everything that comes out of his mouth. It's utterly mind-blowing how he does that, so I choose to ignore his words and to keep my anger. I don't savor any of his words. Especially not the one about *our* kitchen.

"You gave me a hickey." I point to the spot on my neck. The same spot he attacked last night in the limo.

He lets out a breath, like he's trying to stifle a laugh.

"This jealousy thing you've got going on isn't going to work," I tell him, putting my hands on my hips and standing my ground. We haven't even been together that long and he's lost it multiple times when guys have gotten too close to me.

He moves toward me, and I don't budge until he's right in front of me. He picks me up, and I can't help but squeal. My butt lands on the kitchen counter, and his hands bracket my thighs. He drops his head and I watch his movements as he breathes. I can't stop myself from running one hand into his hair, finally making him look up at me.

"It's hard," he finally says. "I've wanted you so fucking long. You have no idea. So fucking long," he says. "Then when I see someone trying to move in on that, well, I slip. I get pissed, and something takes over. I know it's crazy, but I can't seem to stop it, no matter how hard I try. I can't." He says the last part like he's pleading with me to see it, too.

"How long have you been waiting?" I ask the question that's been sitting with me for days. I know for sure he's been waiting since I started college. I have a good feeling it was before that with how Osbourne Corp had been a part of my life before then.

"I first saw you when you were in high school competing in the state math competition. I was in college at the time and was asked to be one of the judges."

I try to think back to that day. So many names and faces, but I can't believe I would have missed him. I try to count the years. How long ago was that?

"Five years," I mumble to myself, trying to wrap my mind around this piece of information. "You've been watching me for five years." I shake my head at the words, still not believing it, even though I know it's true. It all adds up.

"Sometimes it feels like longer. I can't seem to remember a time before you, really." His words are soft and sweet and filled with something I don't understand.

"Why?" It's the one thing I really don't understand. I'm not a terrible catch, and I know I'm pretty. I've never had problems with men asking me out, but Oz is in a completely different league. I saw so many girls throw themselves at the guys with money around campus, and I have no doubt Oz's bank account would get him the same attention. Even more so because not only is he rich but he's also not bad on the eyes. At all.

He stands up a little taller, my hand dropping from his hair so he's now looking down at me.

"I'd gone to the competition because sometimes you have to rub shoulders with the right people to get places. Back then I had to do it a lot more because I was still making a name for myself. Trying to make my empire bigger and better." He shrugs like he doesn't really worry about that anymore. He's done that already, in the past five years. Everyone knows what Osbourne Corporation is.

"Mainly I was trying to be around some of the people I knew my father was close to. He went to Yale and so did a lot of the people he chose to work with."

"You hate him, too." Just like Paige, but he doesn't seem as angry as she does.

"Since I was eighteen and my mother told me all the horrible things he'd done to her." His jaw clenches and I wonder what his father did to his mother. He'd killed Paige's. "I wanted to be like him. He was so smart and seemed like he knew what he was doing in the business world. I was intrigued and I always tried to make him proud. I wasn't seeing what was right in front of my face. How could I have not noticed how he'd treated my mother? She sobbed when she told me what he'd done to her. And there was nothing I could do that day to make the tears stop. I never knew about how he abused her. I hadn't seen it before then, or maybe I could have done something sooner. But I sat there and listened to her tell me about their years together and that she was leaving him. And then I found out what he was truly capable of." He shakes his head like he still can't believe it. "There's so much about him you don't know. And I don't know if I can tell you. I don't want his dirt to get on you, Mallory. I promised myself I'd never be that man, and even talking about it makes me fear I'm pulling you into that world." His eyes close, and I think about him listening to me cry. How close to home that must have felt for him. How he listened to his mother cry, feeling helpless.

"Oz." I reach up, placing my hands on his chest. "It's not the same. You know that, right?" I can tell by the look in his eyes he doesn't believe that.

"I told myself I'd never be like him. I'd never hurt the people I love. I'd be better. I'd give my mom a better life than he ever did, then I'd make him regret ever making her cry even one of those tears, and that's what I did. I took my trust fund and poured my life into making sure he never hurt anyone again." His mouth turns up at one corner, like he's remembering. "Then you walked into my world."

He reaches out, tucking a piece of stray hair behind my ear.

"Revenge wasn't the only thing I wanted anymore. For the first time I felt like I'd come alive watching you. But you were so young, so I told myself I'd stay away. I found out who you were, and then I wanted to make sure you'd get into a good school. Then I wanted to learn more and more about you. The more I found out, the deeper I kept falling into you. It was one thing after another. I kept sliding down this hill. I couldn't stop thinking about you. Every time I'd go to a dark place, I'd think of you and it always pulled me back. That's when I knew I couldn't let you go, because you were the only thing that really shone light in my life. You were a part of me that wasn't fueled by revenge, so I told myself it was okay. That I'd be good for you. That I wouldn't be like my father. I'd give you everything and build a perfect life for you. That I would be the one for you when the time was right. That I'd never make you cry."

His words rain down on me, and I try to take it all in.

"You paid someone to be my friend," I remind him.

"I'm not saying what I did wasn't a little much, but I was going insane worrying about you. Without knowing someone was watching you, I don't think I could have stayed away from you for as long as I did. I would have cracked, I know it. Paige kept me sane. At least then I knew you were okay. She was making sure nothing could hurt you at a time when I wasn't there to do it myself."

"No one is trying to hurt me," I try to tell him, but he doesn't really hear me.

"Mallory." He says my name with so much emotion it makes my heart clench. I don't think anyone has ever said it with so much tender need. "I know I'm a little crazy when it comes to you. Trust me. I know I'm not great with reason, but I can't control it. I've tried. I've fucking tried, but it is what it is."

"What if I don't like it?" I ask, shifting under him. His eyes roam over me as he moves in a little more.

"I think you don't want to like it, but a part deep inside of you does, or you wouldn't be here right now."

I let his words sink in because I can't think of an argument against it. I do like his overbearing, controlling ways, although my head thinks I shouldn't. It makes me feel important to someone. Maybe I'm a little bit crazy, too, wanting and liking that kind of attention. Attention I've never had from anyone. The only person other than Oz to give a shit about me is Paige.

"I like parts of it, but, Oz, you can't control everything. I have to have a little of my own life. Like my job. You'll stay out of that, right?"

A smile spreads across his face, but I point my finger at him.

"I know I've gotten where I am today because of you."

"That's not true," he interrupts. "You're incredibly smart and would have gotten into any school in the country. I wanted to make sure your path led to me."

Part of what he's saying might be true, but I wouldn't have gotten a full ride to Yale or gotten a job at Osbourne Corp without him. Osbourne Corp didn't even have internships before last year. I have a suspicion that program was created for me.

"That said, you're still going to let me do my job and stay out of it," I tell him, holding firm on this.

"I have to have a guard on you, sweetheart. When word gets out we're together, that puts a target on your back, and not just for my father, who knows I'm after him. I'm worth a lot of money, and if people know I have a weak spot, they'll go after it."

"I'm your weak spot?" I'm not sure how I feel about that. Should I be offended?

"You're my everything," he says simply, making me smile.

"It's hard to be mad at you when you say the sweetest stuff to me."

"It's better to give in, baby. I won't stop coming for you until you do."

"Promise you won't interfere with my job," I ask him, wanting his word.

"I promise to try my best."

"Miles!" I snap.

He shrugs. "I'll stay out of your way, but if someone fucks with you." He shrugs again, like anyone who does fuck with me is fair game.

I roll my eyes because in this moment I see a flash of Paige in him. That's something she'd say or do. Even she wouldn't be able to help herself if someone were to *fuck* with me. But it's a freaking office internship. I don't think anyone will be fucking with me in the way Oz is referring to, so I let him have that one.

"I'm still mad at you," I tell him, folding my arms over my chest.

"Good," he says, picking me up off the counter and carrying me over to a sofa. "I can work on you not being mad at me for the rest of the weekend." He drops me onto the sofa and falls to his knees in front of me, then spreads my legs with a hungry look in his eyes. "I'll start by eating your pussy until you come in my mouth, and then I'll finish making you breakfast."

I want to protest, telling him that it won't work, but the only thing that comes out of my mouth is his name.

"WHAT'S WITH YOU?" I look over at Paige, who looks like she's got lipstick on as we walk into work. Oz is behind us, giving us a little space. I slipped downstairs early this morning to get ready for work, reminding him that I was walking to work with Paige today, something we'd agreed on after I stayed the night on Sunday—the third night in a row.

Now we're in the Osbourne building, and I'm trying to get answers from her.

"What?" She shrugs one of her shoulders like she has no idea what I'm talking about. I glance back to see Oz stopping at the front security desk and talking to one of the guards. He gives me a wink as I get on the elevator with Paige.

"You have lip gloss on."

"My lips were chapped and it's all I had," she says defensively. I give her my *yeah right* face, then I hit the button for my floor and almost hit hers, but she stops me.

"I have to make sure you get to your desk." She gives me an apologetic smile. "I'm on your service until the end of the day, depending on your night plans," she finishes.

"Well, my night plans are going home since Oz has already annoyed me."

"I was told you agreed to have security on you, since you and Oz…" She trails off, clearly not wanting to talk about my banging her brother, and I don't want her to say it either.

"I did. I did. It seems weird, but I'd rather it be you." The elevator dings and we both exit. "Lunch?" I ask her, making my way to my desk.

"I'll text you, but I should be good for lunch unless something comes up. Either way, the cafeteria, right?"

"Yeah, that's fine," I tell her, dropping my bag at my desk. "I told Oz I wouldn't leave the building without letting you or him know." I'm tempted to call Paige "mom," but I can tell she's a little uneasy that this whole security thing might upset me. But really, when I think about it, it doesn't bother me. I'm just not used to it. A little security won't hurt if it makes Oz and Paige both feel better.

I have no idea if their talk about me being a target is really accurate, but I'll do this for them. Besides, it's not like I go anywhere without them, anyway. Paige and I used to be connected at the hip, but now it looks like Oz is trying to connect himself.

"Cool. I'll text you," she says, and heads back toward the elevator. I glance over at Skyler's desk, then to Eric's. My stomach does a flip. I totally forgot about what happened on Friday night. When I take a step closer, I look down over the cubicle wall and see his desk is completely cleared out.

"Shit." I hated that little weasel because he never did his share, but that doesn't mean he should get fired for hitting on me. Shuffling through my bag, I find my phone, pull it out and send a text to Oz.

Me: You fired Eric! That's so not staying out of my career.

Oz: I'd be more than willing to talk to you about this matter in my office right now if you'd like. I've been trying to guess all morning what color panties you have on. I want to see if my guess is correct.

Me: Oz, I'm being serious.

Oz: I was thinking blue.

Me: OMG! You better not have a camera in my bed-room!

I fire the text back because I do have blue panties on.

Oz: I wish, but if you'll let me, I'll have some installed today. Or you could move in upstairs and I could watch for myself each morning. That way I'll always know what color they are.

Me: I'm trying to yell at you and you're asking me to move in with you?! Focus. Eric.

Oz: Eric was drug tested and failed after he flipped out on Ryan. That's the last time I care to talk about the man who I caught trying to fuck MY woman.

Me: Who the heck is Ryan?

Oz: The security guard who's with you when Paige and I aren't.

Me: Oh, Captain!

I laugh a little at not knowing Captain's real name.

Oz: Captain?

Me: Oh...there's something you don't know? You don't know all about Captain?

I can't help myself from teasing him. Maybe he's right. I do like when he goes a little caveman possessive because I seem to find myself poking at him when I get the opportunity.

Oz: I'll come down there and find out.

Me: No! Paige and I call Ryan Captain because he kind of looks like Captain America. Don't come down here.

I try to inject as much emotion into the last line as possible. I know it's only a matter of time before people find out about us, but I need a few more days to get my bearings.

Oz: Do you find Captain America attractive?

Yeah, like I'm answering that loaded question.

Me: No one is hotter than you.

I avoid that question, but it's true. Captain America can be hot, but he's got nothing on Oz.

Me: Promise you're not coming down.

Oz: Promise. Promise me you'll stay in for lunch but have dinner with me tonight.

I already planned on staying in for lunch, hopefully with Paige so I can get some gossip about Eric losing it on Captain and failing a drug test.

Me: I'll stay in, but let's see how the rest of the day goes before I agree to dinner. You have this thing where you like to make me mad. I want to make sure that doesn't happen.

Oz: I spent all weekend making you unmad. I remember you rather enjoying it.

He did spend the whole weekend make me unmad. On every surface of his home. The reminder makes me tingle. I've gone from virgin to sex fiend. It's crazy how fast life can change.

Me: I'll think about it.

I drop my phone onto the desk. I have a feeling I'm going to crack. Even more so if he shows up at my door doing his whole caveman act. I smile and get back to work.

TWENTY-EIGHT

Mallory

THE PAST TWO DAYS have been pure bliss. Every day I walk to work with Paige, and Oz follows behind us, always keeping watch but still giving me space when I ask for it, even if he doesn't want to. Then every night, Oz takes me out to dinner and then back to his place to make love to me all night until I'm too exhausted to climb from his bed back to my own.

My days are filled with lots of work, and Linda has been praising Skyler and me for keeping up with the workload, even though Eric is gone. Skyler rolled her eyes after Linda walked away, saying we'd been doing his work from the beginning. But it's nice to know that our hard work has been recognized.

Wednesday morning, I sit down at my desk to find a hot coffee waiting on me, a note beside it. Oz had to come in early for a meeting, so it was Paige, Captain and me walking into work today.

Picking up the note, I recognize his impeccable handwriting and a stupid grin spreads across my face.

This is almost as sweet as you, and almost as hot.
I can still smell you on my fingers.
Love, Oz

My face burns so brightly I think I might set off the smoke alarms. Jesus. How can a few words send me into a state of molten need? He's too good at melting me. Grabbing my phone, I shoot him a quick text.

Me: Thank you for my coffee, and for making me blush.

His response is immediate, making my goofy grin even bigger.

Oz: It's my life's goal. To worship you and make you smile.

Me: Success!

Oz: I've mentioned this before, but every Wednesday I have lunch with my mother. I'd like for you to join me today, Mallory. Please.

I pause with my fingers over the letters, unable to come up with a response. He'd asked me once before all the drama happened, and I thought it was a joke. This is a big step. Meeting his mother? Am I ready for that?

Oz: You're my life forever, baby. I'd like for her to meet the woman I've been telling her about.

That snaps me out of my haze.

Me: You've been telling her about me? What did you say?

Oz: How incredibly smart you are, and how stunningly beautiful. And how we promise to give her 10 grandchildren.

Me: 10?! You did not say that!

Oz: You should probably come to lunch and correct me then.

I shake my head smiling, and then give in. I know what I feel for Oz, and I know what he feels for me, even if we haven't said the exact words out loud. He's it for me, so I know it's going to happen at some point.

Me: Okay.

Oz: You continue to make me the happiest man alive.

I send a kiss emoji and place my phone on my desk. I smooth my hands down my light blue linen dress. Summertime in New York is hell on heat, so I wore something that was cooler, but now I'm wondering if it's appropriate for meeting Oz's mother. An off-white ribbon ties around the waist and I absentmindedly adjust it. I'm wearing cream wedges and my hair is pinned up, now that the freaking hickey has faded on my neck. Thank God, I never would have agreed if that thing was still there.

Taking a breath, I try to relax. It's going to happen at some point, so it might as well be today. And I'm wondering if Oz didn't mention it until now so that I didn't have enough time to change my mind. He knows me far too well.

Skyler comes in wearing a royal blue blouse and white, high-waisted slacks that cling to her slim legs. She's got her stick-straight dark hair pulled back in a severe ponytail and greets me as she hangs her bag up.

Leaning over our cubicle wall, she looks at me. "Who died now?"

I laugh because I swear she's said that to me every day before Oz and I finally settled all our drama.

"No one yet." She cocks her head to the side and I continue. "I'm meeting the mother."

Skyler makes a sound only dogs can hear and does a kind of happy-clap jump. I don't know how she does it in her shiny black stilettos, but I roll my eyes and try to bite back a laugh.

"I don't usually go all girlie, but this is exciting news." She walks around the wall and sits on the edge of my desk, putting her fists under her chin like an expectant child waiting on a story, and that makes me burst out laughing.

"Shut up! You're supposed to be the friend that doesn't care." I playfully knock her arms out from under her.

"I'm trying to be supportive," she says on a fake huff, and walks back to her side of the cubicle. "Hey."

I look up and see her watching me.

"That's really a big deal, and also really cool that he's asking you to." She shrugs a shoulder like it's hard for her to get serious about our personal lives. "I think if he's good enough for you, then you should give it your all." With that, she moves back away from the wall.

I take a sip of my coffee. Unsurprisingly, it's exactly how I like it. A lot of cream, a lot of sugar and a dash of cinnamon.

It's perfect. And so is Oz, in his own way.

Pushing my fears aside, I get to work, knowing that dwelling on it doesn't change a thing.

TWENTY-NINE

Mallory

Oz ARRIVES AT my desk before noon, and I hear Skyler on the other side of the wall humming the *Jaws* theme music.

"Dun dun. Dun dun. Duh duh duh duh."

Oz raises an eyebrow at me, and I shrug. I put my hand in his and he leads me out of our department and onto the elevator.

"You're nervous?" he asks, lifting our joined hands and kissing my wrist.

My pulse is fluttering there, and that's how he knows.

"A little," I confess, giving him a smile. "I've never done this before."

He rubs my knuckles against his short stubble and looks at me with those beautiful sapphires of his. "Me either, baby."

It's then that it occurs to me he might be nervous, too. I know his mother is important to him, and he probably wants us to get along. He's never felt this way about anyone but me before, so he's obviously never brought another woman to lunch to meet her. Having this knowledge is kind of empowering, and it's as if my focus has turned from myself to Oz. I can do this for him. I can make this first meeting as hard or as easy as I want it to be, and for Oz I will put his own fears to rest.

"I hope she likes me," I say, and this time I put some determination into my voice. Thinking about this being a big moment for the both of us goes a long way to calm my nerves.

"She'll love you."

His words are final as the elevator goes to the bottom floor and the doors open. Oz leads me through the lobby, but instead of exiting the building, he turns me by the security desk and I realize we're headed to the garden. My garden.

Oz opens the door for me and I walk through, remembering my first time in this space. The weather is beautiful today, and the shade from the wisteria flowers helps to keep the garden cool. Oz takes my hand and leads me down the stone path until we wind around to the open grassy area.

I look up to see a beautiful older woman sitting on the bench. A table, like the one laid out when I was here before, is placed in front of her with two chairs opposite.

She stands as soon as she sees us and takes a step around the table. She's wearing a soft yellow pantsuit with brown wedges. I can even see the tips of her pink toenail polish peeking out of the peep toes. Her hair is to her shoulders and a beautiful salt-and-pepper. Her smile is easy, and she has the most beautiful dark green eyes.

She walks toward us, opening her arms, and I'm shocked when she comes straight to me and takes me in her arms.

"Mallory, it's so wonderful to finally meet you."

Her mothering embrace seeps into me, and for half a

second I feel like I could burst into tears. All of my emotions are on the surface, and it's as if I've been thrown back into my childhood and I need someone to hold me.

Her arms are strong, but her hold is gentle. After a moment, I embrace her back. It's a little like the first time I met Oz. Like I've been waiting my whole life to get to this moment.

"Mom, this is Mallory. Mallory, this is my mother, Vivien Osbourne."

She pulls back and extends her arms while still holding on to me. She looks me up and down, and I swear I see something like a tear in her eyes.

"Well, aren't you beautiful," she says, making my stomach warm.

"Thank you, Mrs. Osbourne."

"Vivien," she corrects me, and then leans in a little to whisper. "Or Mom." She gives me a wink and then one last squeeze on my arms before she releases me and gives Oz a kiss on the cheek.

"Shall we?" Oz motions to the table.

We all sit down, Vivien taking a seat on the bench, and Oz and I across from her. He takes my hand right away and suddenly I feel completely relaxed.

There's a spread of food before us; each of us has a salad, then there's a small tray of sandwiches and a plate of fruit and cheeses. Vivien goes about serving me a plate of food, and then makes Oz one before filling her own.

I take a drink of my tea and brace myself for the questions.

"Mallory," Vivien says, "I know everything there

is to know about you, except why in God's good name you'd choose to stay with my son."

The laugh bursts from my lips before I can hold it back, and Oz stiffens beside me. Vivien rolls her eyes at her son.

"Excuse me?" I say, trying to buy some time.

She eats one of the small sandwiches and gives Oz a wink. When she's finished chewing, she waves a hand around the garden.

"He built this three years ago. At the time, I knew about you, but I didn't realize his obsession. Then as time went on, I began to understand, and I tried to get more and more out of him about you. Could see what you meant to him. It started to change him. I had hoped that one day you would see this place and fall in love with it." She takes a drink of her tea, and then continues. "I think any mother would worry about her son if they were given this situation, but I knew a long time ago that Miles was different. When he made his mind up about something that was that. There was never any changing it. And I knew the day he told me about you, that you were it for him. I hoped that when you knew the truth that you would stay. And here you are." She gestures to where I'm sitting. "So I guess I want to know why."

"It's a fair question." I begin to answer and sit up a little. "I think anyone who would look at Oz's—"

"Oz?" she asks, smiling and looking at the two of us.

"A nickname," Miles answers, and I continue.

"Yes." I laugh, trying to hide my blush. "I think, on paper, what he's done without my knowledge could be seen as strange, but when I met him and began to see what I meant to him, how could I turn him away? So

many women go their entire lives without feeling a frac-
tion of the attention and devotion Miles has shown me."

A somber look crosses her eyes and she nods in
agreement.

"I'm sure our relationship sounds crazy, and it may
very well be. But to have a man so consumed with my
happiness and with giving me the best in all aspects of
my life, why would I not give in to him? Sure, at first
I was upset, because I felt deceived, but as I've grown
to care for Miles—" I turn, looking into his deep blue
eyes "—as I've grown to love him, I know that it came
from the best and brightest part of his heart. He's given
me something I've never had before."

Oz lets go of my hand and reaches up, grabbing my
face with both of his. He places his warm lips on mine,
and with them he's telling me everything he feels. I
know Oz loves me. I've known it since the beginning.
But speaking it out loud locks something into place for
us. A final commitment to each other.

He doesn't deepen the kiss, pulls back a little and
rests his forehead against mine.

After a moment, he moves away and grabs on to my
hand again. Vivien sits with a gigantic smile on her face,
and I let out a laugh, a little embarrassed at the intimate
moment in front of his mother. This is all surreal, but it
warms everything inside me, like this is the beginning
of the family I've always wanted.

I rest my hand on my lower belly, thinking of how
true that thought might be. This could very well be the
beginning of my family. And instead of scaring me, the
idea makes my heart grow with love. To have a baby

with Oz, to have Vivien as a mother…it's almost too good to be true.

We spend the next hour talking about me, which is embarrassing, but Vivien goes easy on me, asking about my job with Osbourne Corporation and school. When I mention Paige, she gets a soft look in her eyes, and then she glances over at Oz.

"I met Paige a few years ago when Miles found her. She didn't like me at first, and I understood why. The two of them share a father, but he was very different in their lives."

Vivien looks away to the small waterfall and lets out a sigh.

"Paige's story is not mine to tell. But I can tell you about Alexander Owens."

Oz sits forward a little as if he's uncomfortable, and then stands. Vivien watches him as he walks over to the waterfall, looking at the little pond below and watching the koi fish swim.

"I was eighteen when I met Alexander. I came from a middle-class Midwest home that was very religious. I was an only child and my parents were extremely strict with me. The only time I was allowed to go to social functions was when it involved the church. That summer our church had a weeklong festival fund-raiser, so I was expected to participate. I was in charge of selling pies, and before closing one night, he walked up. I was smitten with his good looks and charm right away. Alexander was the kind of man I'd never seen before. Smart, wealthy, and said all the right things. He was older than me at twenty-five, and to an eighteen-year-old girl who'd been sheltered most of her life, he looked like a movie star. He knew exactly what to say to my father to get him to agree to let him see me.

"The first few times we were allowed to be together we were chaperoned. It sounds old-fashioned, but my mother thought since he was so much older than me, that it would be for my own benefit. I think maybe deep down, she knew what Alexander was after."

Vivien has a faraway look in her eyes, but continues.

"I made a promise to sneak out one night and meet him at the park. He picked me up in a brand-new car, and I felt like Cinderella. But there was something different in him that night and as soon as the door shut behind me, I knew I'd made a mistake."

Vivien looks down at her hands and lets out a sigh.

"I was too ashamed to tell anyone what he'd done. I'd said no, and tried to stop him, but he was so much stronger than me. I knew no one would believe me. I was a young girl that had sneaked out, and he was so charming and knew how to make people believe him. I'd hoped after that night he got what he wanted, and would leave me alone. I avoided seeing him, and tried to forget the rape. When I found out I was pregnant, I didn't have any options. I sat down and told my parents, and I explained what happened. But they didn't believe me, just as I had assumed. They contacted Alexander and said he had to marry me, and he agreed. I didn't want to, because I knew what kind of man he was, but they said if I didn't that they'd kick me out. I had no real education and no money, but I still refused. I would have rather lived on the streets than go to him willingly. I was surprised that he agreed to the marriage, but I think he liked the idea of control. So when I said no, all it did was whet his appetite."

My heart breaks for her, knowing there are so many women who have gone through terrible things like her, and have no choice.

"When I held my ground, he threatened to take the baby. It was his only bargaining chip, and he used it. So I thought that if I went along, that maybe it wouldn't be so bad. He had money, so I knew our baby would be provided for, and I told myself that I would make it work. I knew there was something about his business dealings that wasn't honest, but I ignored it. Looking back, I wish I'd fought harder."

"You did what you could," Oz says from the fountain, still not looking over at us.

"He started hitting me after I gave birth. And that's when the real monster came out. He would be gone all hours of the night and come home smelling like alcohol or other women, and find something to yell at me about. I tried to leave so many times, but he always threatened to take my son from me and never let me see him again. And I knew that if Miles was left alone with Alexander he would fill his head with lies about me. I couldn't bear the thought of never seeing my child, and thinking that he might hate me one day if I did leave. Alexander never laid a hand on our son, and I made sure I never gave him another baby. The day Miles turned eighteen I told him everything and we left together. I walked out with only the clothes on my back and went to stay with a friend. Miles had a scholarship to Yale, and the trust fund that was in his name Alexander couldn't touch. When Miles turned eighteen, Alexander didn't have anything to hold over my head anymore, and by that time I think he was bored of me. There wasn't anything else he could do to hurt me, and he knew it."

"I never knew," Oz says through gritted teeth.

"He kept it away from you, from everyone as much as possible. He had an image to uphold. He was grooming Miles to do his dirty work, but I wasn't going to stand by and let that happen. We found out later what he was truly capable of. I didn't want Miles to become like his father, but I never meant to send him down a path of revenge."

"Revenge?" I ask, looking between the two of them. Wondering what Oz had planned.

"Miles wants to make him pay for what he did to me, but that's not why I told him. I told him the whole story so Miles wouldn't follow in his footsteps, not so he would hate him."

Vivien looks between us, and Oz walks over to sit down beside me.

"I went back to my maiden name of Osbourne after I left Alexander, and Miles changed his name, too. He went to college, and I was able to get a job making my own money. Miles went looking into Alexander's past further and dug up some things that made me realize that I'd walked away lucky."

I can't help but think Paige wasn't that lucky.

"I told him to leave it alone, but you know Miles. When he's got his mind set on something, there's no stopping him. He found out that Alexander was involved in human trafficking, prostitution, money laundering, illegal gambling and selling stolen guns. I think I may have been the only piece of his life that kept him somewhat human, because from what Miles uncovered, he's truly a monster. I don't know how he's managed to avoid the inside of a jail cell for this long, but the amount of money he has keeps him clean. He's got a lot of businesses around the city that funnel the money. He thinks I was ignorant to all that went on, because if I had dirt I would have used it by now. Or maybe it's the twenty-four-hour security Miles keeps on me, or the overprotective measures he uses to keep me safe."

I nod, because I understand all too well.

He turns to me then, his eyes soft and warm. I squeeze his hand, letting him know I'm here and I'm real.

"There's so much about Alexander that's horrible, and the things he's done…?" She breaks off and lets out a breath. "There are so many things I wish I could change, but I can't. We just have to move forward and try to live our lives the best way we know how."

I can't imagine living through what she has, and possibly the guilt she carries. But looking into her soft eyes, and seeing her still able to smile shows her true strength. She looks to Oz and then to me.

"Two beautiful women have found their way to us, and for that I'm thankful," Vivien says, looking at me. "Paige is very special to me, though I know it's harder for her to see it that way. I hope that one day she understands how much I care for her. And maybe one day you and I can have that, too."

Warmth spreads in my chest, thinking about having a mother in my life. What I've always wanted.

"And maybe then you can get on those ten grandbabies Miles promised me."

"Mom," Miles warns, and Vivien laughs.

She wiggles her eyebrows at me and points between us. "Don't wait too long. I'm not getting any younger."

The cloud of sadness passes, and all talk of Oz's father is pushed aside.

"Mallory, I think it's time I get you back to work," Oz says, standing up and holding out his hand for me.

I take it and stand up, then we say our goodbyes to Vivien.

She wraps me in a soft embrace, and I melt into her. I never knew how much I needed a hug like hers until I got it. She pulls back, squeezing my arms again and giving me a big smile.

"Lunch next week, Mallory?"

I nod happily, unable to hide my excitement.

"Good, we'll leave Miles at home then."

She gives me a wink as she turns to him, giving him a hug and shushing his protests.

I walk out of the garden holding Oz's hand, feeling light and cheerful. "She's an amazing woman with an amazing son," I say as Oz holds open the door for me.

"Flattery will get you everywhere, my sweet Mallory."

We walk through the lobby and onto the elevator. Before I can push the button for the accounting floor, Oz takes my hand and hits the button for his.

"Oz, I need to get back to work." I lean into him playfully, but the look on his face is serious. He runs his knuckles along my jaw and the look in his sapphire-blue eyes is so intense, I reach up and grab his wrist. "What's wrong?"

"My mom told you her story about my father, and now I want to tell you mine."

The elevator dings, and the doors open revealing his secretary seated at her desk. She stands when she sees us, and they exchange a look, and she nods. It makes me anxious. He grips my hand a little tighter as we walk toward his office and to the double doors.

I'm hesitant, but then he moves his hand to the small of my back and opens the door in front of me. When I step inside I see a blonde woman facing away from us, and a big man in a suit next to her, his hand on her waist. She turns when she hears the door open and gives a soft smile.

I'm shocked when I recognize her as Ivy Lennox. My mind churns as she stands there, her hands twisting in front of her. She's wearing a cream summer dress with a matching cream blazer, the sleeves pushed up. Her peach-colored sandals look expensive, like the rest of her, and I remember thinking when I saw her in the picture in the article with Oz that she appeared wealthy. I don't know why that irritates me, but it does. But maybe it's her presence that's doing it. The large man beside her is in a dark suit, and he stands in such a way that's protective. And my annoyance turns to curiosity.

Oz closes the doors behind us, and when I hear the click I snap back to reality. Turning to face him, I get right to the point.

"What's going on?"

"Mallory, I'd like you to meet Ivy and her husband, Brian. Ivy, this is my Mallory."

His hand presses against the small of my back again, and it comforts me, even if I'm still confused. And I'd be lying if I said I didn't love the way he says "my Mallory." But more questions are filling my head. This is the one woman I've ever seen him photographed with, and he's never mentioned her. Oz leads us forward, and Ivy holds her hand out to shake mine. I automatically take it and feel how soft and delicate it is. A little insecurity runs through me, but Oz's large palm moves up and down my back as if petting me and reassuring me that everything is going to be okay. Brian doesn't move to shake my hand, though he greets Oz with a stern nod. He steps possessively next to Ivy and I can't help but think he's probably feeling the same way I am right now.

"It's so nice to finally meet you." Her voice is as delicate as her touch.

"Let's have a seat. There are some things I'd like to discuss." Oz indicates the small couch and chairs over to the side, and we all walk over. Ivy sits on the chair, Brian silently moving next to her. Oz and I sit on the couch opposite them, and he scoots close to me. He takes my hands in his, gently squeezing them and letting me feel his strength. It's like he knows what I need in this moment and isn't hesitating to give it to me. I see Brian rest his hand on the top of Ivy's crossed legs, while he stares at us, not speaking.

"I asked my assistant to set up a meeting with Ivy, and I wanted you to be here for it. Ivy and I went to Yale together and had some of the same classes. We were working on a group project one afternoon, and we happened to walk out of the coffee shop together."

I glance from Oz to Ivy, and she tucks a lock of blond hair behind her ear nervously and picks up the story.

"My family is from old money in Connecticut and they have political ties to the White House. I was considered an up-and-coming socialite, so I was photo-

graphed every now and then when I was in college.
Miles was obviously someone to watch because of his
father's business, and Miles's growing reputation at
Yale." She puts her hand on top of Brian's and continues. "We were photographed one day after a study
group. I couldn't even remember leaving together, and I
never saw the person taking the photos. When my mom
called me the next day and asked if I was dating Miles,
I brushed it off. Neither of us had any romantic feelings for one another." She lets out an exhausted laugh,
one that indicates she still doesn't understand. "Miles
and I weren't even friends. We were in a study group
together, so we were hardly acquaintances. But knowing the way paparazzi make things out to be, I told my
mom there was nothing going on and to brush it off."

Oz nods, agreeing with Ivy, and he continues the
story. "I'd had a couple of run-ins with my father when I
was in college because he was disgusted I wasn't going
to follow in his footsteps. I'd started digging into his
past and figured out where the dirty money from my
trust fund came from, and the truth about some of his
black market dealings. I found out that the source of it
may have been made from the blood he'd shed. The trafficking, the guns, the drugs. All of it made me sick. I
made a mistake then, and tipped my hand too soon. I'd
told him that I was going to ruin him and take everything away from him. I didn't want him dead, because
that would have been too easy. I wanted him broke, ruined and worthless." He shakes his head as if he's remembering something he doesn't want to. "I was young
and angry and instead of making plans and carrying
them out, I told him how I was going to get my revenge.

I made a costly mistake that day. I showed my hand too early and I swore it would never happen again."

Ivy smiles softly, picking up where Oz left off. "I was driving back home for a long weekend, and the only thing I remember is going around a curve and being run off the road by a black SUV. I woke up two months later in a hospital bed, not knowing what had happened. And with Brian at my bedside." She turns to him and smiles so sweetly, you can see the love in her eyes.

"My father reached out to me not even hours after Ivy's accident, letting me know he was behind it. That if I didn't back off he'd do more to the people I cared about. Assuming Ivy and I were together. We weren't but it still hurt that I'd gotten Ivy into this because of my anger and running my mouth."

Ivy shrugs like it was no big deal what happened to her.

"That day gave me Brian back. He was the head of security for my family and I'd always had the biggest crush on him. We'd fallen in love, but never said the words. He refused to be with me, saying I had to go away for college for the experience. I think he thought I'd get over him if I wasn't with him all the time. After the accident, he never left my side once in the two months I was in a coma, and when I woke up, he said we'd never be apart again." He leans over, nuzzling her neck and giving her a kiss on the cheek.

She smiles at Oz and I. "I know I shouldn't say this, but I don't regret what happened. It brought us together, and for that I'm forever thankful. I don't blame you for what happened that day, and I've made Brian swear to not seek his own revenge on your father."

She glances over to him and then back to us. "To be honest, his need for payback almost broke us. It was only when I explained to him that his desire for vengeance felt more important than me and our future. There comes a point in your life where you have to decide what's most important. I didn't want the anger and hate to consume him, or come in the middle of our relationship anymore. Being with Brian and being in love was the most important thing. Letting that go, and living our lives, is the only thing that matters now."

I examine Oz, who has his brow furrowed and a concerned thought in his eyes. Seeing our joined hands, I think about what it would mean if he continued to seek his own revenge. Would it always be a cloud between us? Would only the death of his father fix everything? Somehow I don't think the answer is yes. And Oz doesn't want him dead, he wants him ruined. Eventually will that be enough? Will this be a constant worry?

"I never meant for any of this to touch you, Ivy. And it's the reason I kept Mallory at arm's length for so long. I wanted to be sure all of my plans were in place before I let it be known what she meant to me." He turns to me and brushes a loose strand of hair from my eyes. "I wanted you to understand the danger you were in by being seen with me, but the time's come for all that to be over. I promise to watch over you, and to take care of you. Always."

We sit for a moment in silence before a deep voice breaks it.

"If you need anything, you know where to find us."

With Brian's words, we all stand, and he and Ivy make their way out of the office. After the double doors close, Oz comes over to me and we sit down on the couch again.

"Are you okay, baby?"

His eyes that have held a part of my soul for so long, give me a sense of being more connected to him. To know that all of this has been to protect me, makes my love for him even deeper than before. Oz doesn't do anything lightly, and to know that he calculated all of this so that none of his darkness touched me, could only make me cling to him more.

"Yeah, I think I understand now."

"It's the reason I had Paige on you from the beginning. It's the reason I've always had eyes on you, and I've panicked every second you haven't been completely protected, or by my side." He grabs my face with both hands, and the intense, almost-dark shadow in his eyes shows me all of his emotions. "I can't lose you. And I won't allow a situation where that's a possibility. Ever."

His words are hard and final, and I know there's no stopping his plan that's in place. I can only hope that at the end of this, we both come out safe.

He kisses me so passionately and so thoroughly that there is no room for argument. I belong to him now, and as much as I should be fighting it, I won't. I'm his, and he's mine. I would do whatever it took to protect our love, and our possible family in the making.

THIRTY

Mallory

THE NEXT DAY, I walk through the lobby with Oz. Paige
had to be in early for some training exercise, and when
we get on the elevator, I'm about to hit the button for
the accounting department but Oz halts me and presses
the button for his floor.

"I don't know what you're up to, Oz, but I'm going
to be late." I turn to him, and his face is sheepish. He
already tried to make me late by pouncing on me this
morning when I was getting dressed. Then he insisted
on dragging me back up to his home to pick out a tie
for him to wear, all while mumbling we wouldn't have
to do this if I moved my stuff in already.

"Oz?" I say hesitantly when he won't look at me.
"What's going on? What did you do?" He tenses a little, making me worry more.

The elevator shoots to the top floor and the doors
slide open. His administrative assistant, Jay, is at her
desk, and stops writing furiously when she hears us
arrive.

"Mr. Osbourne, Ms. Sullivan," she says in greeting,
standing and nodding to us. "The offices have been
moved and are in place."

"Thanks, Mrs. Rose."

The admin smiles brightly and sits down, going back to scribbling away once again.

Oz takes my hand and leads me to the right, away from the double doors of his office.

"Oz, where are we going?" I ask as he pulls me down the hallway, making me wonder if anyone will see. People have got to be noticing that we seem to be together a lot, but I haven't heard any whispers yet. I'm guessing no one would say anything to me. And his administrative assistant seems to know.

At the end of the short hall is another set of double doors, and Oz opens them wide. There are two desks facing one another in the middle of a large, window-lined room. Sitting at one of the desks is Skyler, tapping away on her computer.

"What the…" I say, and Skyler turns to look at us.

"I like the view a lot better up here, so don't get all sassy yet," she says, cutting me off, clearly enjoying the office change.

I turn to Oz, who shrugs, and I give him a death stare.

"Perhaps you can give us a moment of privacy, Skyler?" I ask, not taking my eyes off Oz.

"Sure, I'll go grab a Diet Coke from the cold Keurig in the break room." As she's about to exit the room, she throws over her shoulder, "Cold Keurig, Mallory. Don't ruin this for me."

I roll my eyes, and then the door shuts. I cross my arms over my chest, waiting for an explanation.

"I actually need some help with a special project, and I talked to Linda about borrowing you and Skyler."

"And you didn't stop to think about what I want? Oz,

I've told you I need you to respect my space when it comes to my career. I know you're the one who gave me the scholarship, but I worked my ass off for my grades. I know what I earned, and I don't want that taken from me so you can give me some fluffed-up desk job so that I'm closer to you. This is bullshit."

I actually stomp my foot on the last word, but I don't care. I may sound like an ungrateful brat, but he can't push me around like this. He told me he wouldn't do the very thing he's doing.

Oz puts his hands in his pockets like he's trying very hard not to grab me, probably knowing I'll pull back from him. He hates it when I do that.

"I understand how this might look, but I promise you, I've got a plan and I need your help with it. I had the office up here converted months ago, but I've been unable to hire the right person for the job. Then I saw the production rate that you and Skyler were working at and I think you'd be perfect for this position."

He's taken some of the wind out of my sails at his statement. Now I'm interested, but I don't want to give up my stance.

"Couldn't we have done this job from the floor we were already on?" I snap, a little sharper than I intend to.

"Actually, no." His voice is smug, and he's acting as if he's won this round. "The project will require you both to work with me and my admin closely. Whoever I hire for the position will have this office, no matter if it's you and Skyler or someone else. I think you both could do this project a lot of good. I want someone I can trust."

I let my arms fall down to my sides, interested in where this is going, even if I'm still a little pissed. Oz is like a steamroller, and way too good at making me give in to what he wants. But if there's a real chance for a real job and not an internship, then I'm very interested.

He reaches out, grabbing my hand and pulling me from the office and back toward him. Jay jumps up from her chair as we approach.

"Coffee, sir?" she asks, and Oz shakes his head.

"No one in," he tells her as he pulls me into his office, sealing us in. The sound of the lock turning echoes in the room.

"What are you doing?" I try to pull my hand from his, but he grips me by the hips, lifting me up and carrying me over to the sofa next to his desk. He sits down with me straddling him. I try to move, but he tightens his hold. The action both turns me on and pisses me off. My body reacts to him like it always does when he becomes controlling.

"As was discussed at our private lunch yesterday, I found out that my inheritance came at a price. And though I've made that money back a hundredfold, I don't like knowing that it began from something..." He pauses as if trying to think of the best word. "Unsavory."

I nod, understanding. I wouldn't want to have anything of mine tied to someone I despised. But I can't help but wonder how ill-gotten the money was. What horrible things had to take place to earn it?

"For a long time I sought revenge, and though a part of me still hates him, I think my energy is better spent taking care of those I love."

My stomach does a little flip at his words. The idea that maybe I've made him want to put his focus somewhere else warms me.

"I've decided to invest a large portion of my money in philanthropic projects. I need two people I can trust to sort out who's in need of money and where it should go. I've seen what you and Skyler can do with numbers, and I trust you with everything I have, Mallory. I'd like for you to head this project and help me do some good with everything that I've been given."

"You want us to run your company's charities?" My mind suddenly races with ideas.

"Yes. I think between you and Skyler, you could do a lot of good and make sure the money goes to all the right places. I want to really make a difference in children's lives. Ones who maybe don't have a support system to help them along the way."

"Like me," I say, looking into his eyes.

"Like you," he confirms. "I hate my father, but I wonder if I would've found you without him. And that's something I can't hate him for. So instead of investing all my energy in revenge, I want to invest some of it in something good. Giving back what was given to me."

His words are sweet, and I want this. Badly. I look away from him, not sure what to say. He eases his grip on my hips and turns my face to make me look at him.

"Oz." I lean into his hand as he cups my cheek, his thumb brushing back and forth. "You have to talk to me. Not run me over with what you want."

"I know," he says. I can hear a trace of guilt in the two simple words. "I'm trying. I want what's best for you, and I'd be lying if that also didn't include you being as close to me as possible. But I promise I'm trying." His hand slips around to my back and he pushes me closer to him. "I could have moved your apartment stuff like I did the office." He half smiles, but I roll my eyes, biting the inside of my cheek. "See? I'm trying."

I have an inner battle going on inside me. Part of me wants to stand on my own two feet, and the other part wants to fall into Oz. I want to enjoy being taken care of for once in my life. I don't even know why I'm fighting for control with him, when deep down I like the idea of letting him take over. That really the struggle isn't for control, it's the fear of losing him. I'm afraid to enjoy something that could be taken away from me. I should know better than anyone how possible that is. I might not remember my parents, but I've seen pictures and have photo albums tucked away in my closet at home. We look happy in them. Like a normal family. Then *poof*, they were gone. Knowing how perfect things could be with Oz makes me so happy and so scared at the same time.

"I'm being serious," I scold, but find myself wiggling against him.

"I am, too, sweetheart. I'll work better with you close. The security on this floor is the best in the building." His hand moves to my belly and slides along it. I know what he's thinking. He's been doing this since we spoke about the possibility of my being pregnant. "I need you close."

Then his fingers find the edge of my loose dress, sliding up my thighs and around to my ass. "When I know you're near, I can breathe better. As crazy as that sounds."

His sweet and powerful words are my undoing. I only move in a little and he's on me, flipping me over onto my back and coming down over me. His mouth covers mine in a devouring, intense kiss as he works his hand between us. It only takes him a moment before he's sliding my panties to the side and filling me with himself.

I moan into his mouth as he thrusts into me hard. Each plunge jerks me against him. His strokes are deep and long, and he takes me as if he hasn't had me in days. As if we didn't make love an hour ago.

"Fuck, I get so hard when I make you mine," he grunts, pulling away from my mouth. "When I know you're sinking into me a little more. Day by day. Bit by bit. Letting me have you." His mouth goes to my neck, and I lean to the side to give him what he wants.

He uses one hand to brace himself over me, the other holding my hip to keep me in place for his hard thrusts.

"I can't seem to get enough of you. Get close enough. I keep thinking if I have more, some of this obsession will cool. But I think it's only growing," he rasps in my ear. I clench around him at his words, getting off on being his obsession.

"You like it, don't you? Knowing how fucking crazy I am for you. That I can't breathe without you."

"Yes," I admit. The word falls past my lips before I realize it. I didn't mean to say it out loud.

"I love you." He says the words, and it sparks my orgasm, sending me over. I feel his release deep inside me, and the warmth of him and his love fills me.

"I love you, too," I say, not trying to hold back anymore. I don't want to fight this. I don't care how crazy everything is. I'm only complete when I'm with him.

Like I'm finally whole. If Oz wants to consume me, I think I might let him.

He jerks against me. "Say it again."

"I love you." It comes so easily from my lips because it feels right. Perfect.

He nuzzles against me, and I don't know how long we lie there, but he gets hard again.

"Oz." I wiggle beneath him, knowing I should get back to my desk and figure out what I need to be doing.

He slips free from me, moaning as he does. The mixture of our passion coats my thighs as my panties slide back into place. His hand runs along them, then cups my pussy before pulling my dress back down to cover me.

I watch him as he rights his own clothes, tucking his still-hard cock back into his slacks, then straightening his shirt and tie. The sight has me wanting to pull him back on top of me. He looks like he had hard, rough sex in a hurry, which I guess he did. I like the idea that it was me who gave him that look.

"You keep looking at me like that and you're never getting out of here." He stares down at me with that familiar hungry expression. I giggle and jump up, looking down to make sure my dress is in place and I don't look like I had sex in his office.

I move toward the door, but he grabs me by the wrist, pulling me back to him. Then he plants a kiss on my mouth that knocks the wind out of me. I don't know how he does it, but with each kiss it's like he's devouring me, but doing so with infinitely soft sweetness.

All too soon he's pulling away.

"Go, or we'll be back on the couch." I hear the locks click on the door, and I make my escape, heading back to my new office, where Skyler is once again typing away on the computer at her desk. Her head pops up when she hears me enter.

"I've got so many ideas!" she says, popping up from her chair as I make my way over to my new desk and sit down. I have to admit it's nice not being in a cubicle anymore. The first thing I notice is a picture of Oz and me on my desk. It's from the weekend. I'm lying in bed, half-asleep on his chest. I don't even remember him taking it. It makes me smile that he thought to do something so adorable, and I wonder if he has one on his desk, too.

I open my top drawer to see if I have a notepad, but slam it shut when Skyler leans up against my desk. Oh, God, I hope she didn't see what was inside—a freaking copy of *What to Expect When You're Expecting*! She cocks her head to the side, clearly knowing I was trying to hide something.

Then she glances at my desk and picks up the framed picture. She studies it for a moment.

"People are whispering," she says, putting the picture back down. "I think it's better we're up here, even without the kick-ass project."

I groan, thinking about the office gossip, but it is what it is. Our relationship was bound to come out sooner or later.

"How bad is it?" I ask, unable to help myself.

"The gossip's not really about you. More about Miles," she admits, piquing my interest. "Guess the word is Mr. Osbourne doesn't date. Like, ever."

I think back to all the times Oz has whispered to me how long he's waited for me. That there has never been anyone since the moment he saw me. If that were the case, then I could see people saying that.

"And how he is with you. Or what people have caught anyway." She drops her eyes, like she doesn't want to say the next part too loud. "He's always been kind of cold and never even cracked a smile. Now he's walking around dreamy-eyed."

"He is not." I laugh. I'm not sure I'd call Oz's eyes dreamy. Intense, sure. Okay, maybe they're soft and sweet a lot, but I like the idea that I'm the one getting that from him. That I'm the only one who can do it. The thought makes my stomach flutter for the millionth time today.

Skyler shrugs. "Yeah, he seems more caveman to me, but I've also seen him punch a guy over you, so my view may be skewed." She glances around the office. "An awesome caveman, though." She whispers the last part like Oz might hear her. She really wants to keep this office.

"What do you have?" I nod toward the papers in her hands.

"I'm thinking bigger than donations and events. With the budget we've got, we can afford to." She drops the papers in front of me. "We can make a big difference, Mallory." I look down at them.

"Now I see why the White House wanted you."

THIRTY-ONE

Mallory

"I'M HAVING SOME THINGS delivered to your office today."

I turn around to see Oz standing behind me in my bedroom while I pick out clothes for work.

"More singing telegrams?" I ask over my shoulder, then turn back to my closet.

His warm hands cup my ass. I've got on a gray lacy thong and matching bra, which Oz is feeling up appreciatively.

He laughs a little and gives me a playful smack before sitting down on my bed. "Sadly, not this time. We've got an event tomorrow, and I know you won't have time to shop, so I'm having some dresses brought up for you to look at."

Turning around, I put my hands on my hips. "Tomorrow? And you're just now telling me? What the hell, Miles?"

"I know when you say my real name you're angry." He knows I'm mad, but that stupid grin is still on his face. "Besides, you promised me you'd go. So I'm being helpful."

He takes a sip of his coffee and I stand there in my underwear, trying to think back to when I said I would go to anything like an event. Then suddenly a small memory of a text from him saying that I had to go with him flutters through my mind. He's right, but it seems like a lifetime ago that he said it.

"Oz." I stomp my foot, knowing he's right. "You could have given me some notice. What's the event for?"

"Baby, I've got it all taken care of. You only have to show up and stay glued to my side. You always look stunning, so that won't be a problem."

I roll my eyes, trying to ignore his sweet words. "Oz," I say, this time with a warning edge to it.

"There's a silent auction that benefits The New York Foundling. It's a charity dedicated to helping provide families with safe housing and educational support."

My heart warms at his words. "Okay," I say quietly, and turn to grab a dress.

"Okay?" he repeats.

I slip on a navy blue shift, and Oz comes to stand behind me. He gives me a kiss between my shoulder blades before zipping my dress up.

"Yes. I'll go with you. I wish I had more notice so I could get prettied up."

He turns me around so I'm facing him and wraps me in his arms. "You, my love, are going to be the most gorgeous woman in the room, no matter if you try or not." He leans down, giving my neck a kiss, and tells me he loves me.

"I love you, too," I say, unable to stop my smile.

His warm amber and honey scent surrounds me, and I lean into his suit. The dark navy is nearly identical to mine, and it makes me smile. We're both way too crazy about one another, but I roll with it. It makes me feel cherished and I don't ever want to let it go.

"Now let's get to work before I take this pretty dress off you and rip another pair of your panties."

"HERE WE GO," Skyler says, sitting back in her chair.

I'd told her when I got to work today that there would be a delivery. I didn't expect it to come two seconds after I walked in the door.

I shoot a rubber band at her, and she dodges, giving me a smug face.

Jay holds the double doors open as a young woman with dark hair and dark skin comes in wheeling a huge rack of clothes. She's wearing a bright yellow wrap dress that accentuates all her curves and looks so pretty against her flawless skin. I immediately like her look and hope she's got something on that rack that will look half as nice on me.

Standing up, I greet her, extending my hand. I'm nervous but excited.

"Hi, I'm Mallory."

"Nice to meet you. I'm Kimmi Ford."

Skyler peeks over my shoulder practically clawing to get at the clothes and waves at Kimmi. "I'm Skyler, and I'm a size four."

"Ignore her," I say, elbowing her in the ribs.

Kimmi laughs and waves to the dresses. "I've got nothing but twelves on this one. Sorry, babe." She winks at Skyler, and then looks me up and down. "You're going to be fun to dress. Great cleavage, nice hips. Yep. Let's get rolling."

I look over at Skyler, who rubs her hands together like this is the greatest day ever.

"Are you shy?" Kimmi asks, looking around for a private section of our office.

I laugh. "No. I lived in an all-girls dorm for four years. I'm good." Then I think for a second and look over at Skyler. "I'll change on the other side of the racks. Jamie looks like she could snap my neck without even trying."

Skyler laughs and picks up her phone, no doubt to tell Jamie exactly what I said. But I don't want to be disrespectful to their relationship, and I know Jamie is very protective of her.

Kimmi wheels the rack over to a sitting area, and I stand on the other side, blocking my view of the two of them. I strip off my dress, and Kimmi points to where I should start.

The whole rack is nothing but long gowns that look as if they're meant for something really fancy. Am I meeting the president or going to a silent auction? I guess I have to trust that Miles and Kimmi know what they're doing.

I try on three dresses, and every time I walk around the rack, Kimmi shakes her head. It's like I don't even have an opinion, but again I'm going to trust her. The fourth dress I grab is gold and looks metallic. I have to take off my bra and panties to put it on, but when I do, the cool material feels so nice against me. And it fits me like a second skin.

As I walk out from behind the rack, Kimmi looks up from her phone and beams at me. "That's the one."

"Whoa," Skyler says, giving me the once-over. "He's going to kill you." Then she smiles like the Grinch, and I can't help but laugh.

Kimmi pulls a full-length mirror from inside the rack and I stand in front of it. The dress is gorgeous and accentuates all my best features. It has tiny strings that crisscross in the back and it dips low at my waist. The gold mesh isn't see-through, but gives the illusion it is. The dress is cut low in the front as well, revealing my ample cleavage. The way the dress catches the light makes it looks like my skin is dusted with shimmer. It curves around my hips, and then goes straight to the floor, where it pools at my feet. It looks like I'm wearing liquid gold, and I've never felt sexier.

"He's going to kill the both of us," Kimmi says, but she's got the biggest smile on her face. "I'll make sure it's wrapped up when it's delivered. It will be our secret until it's too late."

"I like her." Skyler nods in approval.

I look myself up and down, still not believing what I'm seeing. I've never worn anything like this in my life, but I look good. Even I can't find a hidden flaw, and that's saying something.

"It's a shame, really," I say, running my hands up and down the material.

"What?" Kimmi says, looking at me in the mirror.

I turn around and shrug a shoulder. "When he rips it off me, I won't be able to wear it again."

THIRTY-TWO

Mallory

AFTER WORK, Oz and I walk out holding hands, and it gives me warm fuzzy feelings floating in my belly. I'm over the moon in love with him; it's like nothing can touch us.

"Dinner?" I ask, as my stomach growls.

"I've got something planned."

Oz winks at me, pulling me closer, and we get into the back of his limo parked out front. When we get inside he hands me a small duffel bag. I look at it skeptically, but he smiles and tells me to unzip it. Inside, I see a change of clothes, and my suspicions are up.

"Are you wanting to watch me undress?" I ask, giving him a rueful smile.

He takes his tie off, pulling out his own bag. He opens it and takes out a gray T-shirt. He unbuttons his dress shirt, removing it, and my eyes trail down his chest and hard abs. There has to be some kind of law against looking this good, but I ogle him as he tugs on the fitted shirt. It hugs his body in all the right places and he winks at me because he knows I'm getting distracted.

"We're having a date night, baby. Keep your hands to yourself."

I roll my eyes at his cocky, yet accurate request, and watch as he pulls out a blue baseball cap. It's then I see the Yankees logo on it, and on his shirt. Taking out my own clothes, I see we have matching hats and shirts.

"A Yankees game?" The excitement is clear in my voice.

"Hope you like baseball." Oz slips off his slacks and puts on a pair of jeans and tennis shoes.

I look down in my bag and pull out a pair of jean shorts and blue cork wedges. The man thinks of everything. I turn my back to him so he can unzip my dress, and he places a soft kiss on my spine as I slip it off. When I look back at him he pulls his cap down low, making him look even sexier. He stretches back in the limo seat and gives me that earth-shattering smile of his.

I take off my dress and put on the shirt and shorts. "Not really a fan, but I love hot dogs and beer. I went to a couple of games in college, but never to a professional one. I'm not sure I get what all the initials mean, but I understand the basics. More importantly, I hear the Yankees put on a spread."

He laughs at me, and then proceeds to tell me everything he knows about the team. His favorite players growing up, and about the few times he was able to go. As he talks, his face lights up with excitement, and I can picture him as a young man and it melts my heart. It makes me happy to know that even through all the shit with his father and growing up, that there were good times for him to look back on and be able to share with me. By the time the car pulls up in front of the stadium Oz is happily grabbing my hand and tugging me behind him. His own enthusiasm is driving mine, and I'm nearly giggling as we reach the gate.

As is usually the case when we go somewhere, the security guard at the gate looks at him and smiles, opens the rope and allows us unobstructed access. Oz gets the VIP treatment everywhere we go, and it's still a little dizzying to get used to. I've never had the best of everything, and sometimes on this kind of scale it's overwhelming, but at the same time, kind of badass.

We make our way to the concessions stand first, grabbing beer, hot dogs and soft pretzels. After that we walk to our seats, right behind home plate. The view of the stadium is incredible, and my simple college experience can't compare to something on this grand scale. Even if you're not into baseball, or the Yankees, there's something to be said about the magic of it all. Being surrounded by this many fans of a sport they love, and seeing top athletes compete is a thrill. But the best part is being with Oz. I think he could take me to clean toilets and we'd still end up having the best time together. He's become my other half, and as long as he's with me, I'm good to go.

We sit and chat for a few minutes and he points out players and coaches as they warm up. To my surprise one of the pitchers he pointed out earlier sees him and calls him out by his last name.

"Osbourne! Who's your girl?"

The player looks over at me and throws his hand up, waving. I begin to wave back, but Oz grabs my wrist and puts my hand back on my thigh, gripping it possessively.

"Mind your business, Rodriguez."

I have to bite my bottom lip to keep from laughing as Oz practically shoves over in front of me to block me from view. Sitting back in my seat, I rub his broad shoulders, hoping that helps the jealous streak pass.

After the national anthem, Oz gives me a kiss on the cheek and whispers in my ear.

"Sit tight, baby. I'll be right back."

He walks over to the side of the dugout, where there's a small door, and security opens it for him. My jaw nearly hits the ground as I see him walk onto the field and the Rodriguez guy gives him the baseball. There's a second of teasing between the two of them before they do a man hug of slaps on the back. After that, Oz takes the pitcher's mound and the arena claps and cheers.

"Holy shit." I cup both hands over my mouth. Suddenly I'm so nervous and excited all at once. I can't believe he's about to throw out the first pitch at a Yankees game and he never told me.

I watch as he stretches his long muscular arms and the catcher moves into place. The crowd starts to cheer, and Oz looks to me and winks before taking his stance. I hold my breath as he winds up and releases the ball. It's like time stands still as I watch the ball slowly leave his hand and make its way across home plate and into the catcher's glove.

My man is good at everything. And throwing out the first pitch at a baseball game is no exception. His form is worthy of any major league team, and the speed and precision are perfect. I could say I'm shocked, but I'm not.

I jump up and down, throwing my arms in the air and cheer the loudest I can. If I'm not mistaken, I see a blush on his cheeks as he leaves the pitcher's mound, and the Yankees take the field. He stops and poses for a few pictures with some staff, and then makes his way back up to the arena and over to where I'm sitting.

I leap into his arms and wrap myself around him in pure excitement, like he won the World Series, instead of throwing a single pitch. He kisses my neck and hugs me back before putting me in my seat and taking his beside me.

"You were incredible. How could you not tell me?" I playfully slap his arm and he reaches over, squeezing my thigh.

"Didn't want to jinx it." He kisses my neck and I catch his warm amber scent. It makes my toes curl, and my heart flutter, but all too soon he's moving back. "Besides, I like surprising you."

"So it seems."

We watch the game for several innings, ordering beers and having a great time. I never thought I could have so much fun at a baseball game, but being with Oz does that to me.

"Okay, where's the bathroom?" I ask, looking around.

"At the top of the stairs on the left." Oz points. "Hang on a second and I'll go with you."

Just then a reporter comes over and asks for a quick interview with Oz. I see the look on his face and he begins to tell them no, but I squeeze his arm and let him know it's okay. He looks longingly at me for a moment, and I laugh, leaving him talking to the reporter, while I slip off to the restroom.

Once at the top of the stairs I see Captain. It's like he pops out of nowhere. I give him a small wave, then

spot the restroom right away. I take a step without looking and run straight into someone.

"Oh, sorry—" I stop suddenly when I look to see it's
Joel. I haven't seen him since the night of the club when
Oz came in and punched him in the face. It takes him
a second to recognize me, but when he does he throws
his hands up and takes a step back.

I want to explain about that night, and apologize.
"Hey, Joel. I didn't get a chance to—"

"Mallory. You're a nice person, but I'm not getting
in the middle of you and your boyfriend." He takes another step back. "I don't need your drama."

"My drama?" I take offense at his insinuation. Like
his trying to grope me without my permission was totally okay.

"Yeah, I don't need your man chasing me down"

He turns, walking away, and I think about yelling
something to his retreating back, but then I think about
how it's probably best to let it go. Oz will always protect me and keep me safe, and as much as I liked Joel
as a professor, I never had any feelings beyond professional for him. Walking to the bathroom, I decide that
I have no guilt about what went down that night, and
I'm glad to be done with him.

After I finish, I walk out and see Oz leaning against
the wall. He looks so hot in his low-hanging jeans, tight
shirt and down-turned baseball cap. Something about
the way he's leaning makes him look cocky, and I can't
help but like it a little more.

Walking over, I wrap my arms around him, and he
bends down to kiss me sweetly.

"Funnel cake?" he mumbles against my lips, and I immediately perk up.

"Oh, you really do know the way to a woman's heart."

"There's only one woman's heart I want."

God, the things he says are like something out of a romance book. How could I have gotten so lucky?

"Keep buttering me up like that and I might share some of my funnel cake with you."

I wink at him, but I'm a little bit serious, too. I grab his hand, pulling him behind me as I lead us over to where they're selling them.

By the end of the game, the Yankees have won and I'm nearly hoarse from singing and cheering. I never thought going to a baseball game could be so much fun, but I should have known with Oz, everything is better than I imagined.

When we walk toward the exit, Oz pulls me in the other direction. "This way, baby. One more stop before we go home."

He leads me down a hallway, and to a set of elevators, after a second the doors open and I'm surprised to see his mom.

"There's my guy!" Vivien beams, and reaches out, giving him a warm hug. "Excellent pitch. I'm sure you could hear my instructions from the box." She lets go of him and turns, pulling me in the same embrace. "Mallory, you two looked adorable cuddled up down there. So sweet of you two to walk me out."

"I didn't know you were here." I smile back at her.

She looks adorable in her navy slacks and Yankees cardigan.

"Oh, Oz got me season box seats. What can I say, my blood bleeds Yankee blue." She gives me a little smirk, and it's then I can see such a resemblance between mother and son.

"Just thought I'd walk you to the car and listen to you tell me how amazing my pitch was," Oz says, holding his arm out for his mom.

"Always searching for a compliment." Vivien rolls her eyes. I really do love this woman.

We walk out front to where her driver is waiting and she reaches up to give Oz a kiss on the cheek. She gives me one too, but before she pulls away she whispers in my ear.

"I've never seen him smile so much. Thank you, Mallory."

With that, she steps back and Oz helps her into the back of the car. Once the door is closed the driver takes off, and we walk a little farther down to where Oz's limo is waiting.

"What did she say to you?" he asks, squeezing my hand affectionately.

"She said I looked good in Yankee blue, too."

He laughs, and the sound tickles my ears. His smile is big, and his dimples are full-on showing, and I realize that there's not much I wouldn't do to keep this sight before me.

THIRTY-THREE

Mallory

I STRETCH LAZILY in the bed, loving the smell of Oz wrapped around me. I'm on my back in his bed, with his head between my breasts and a leg thrown over the both of mine. I've gotten used to sleeping with his weight on me now, to the point that I don't know if I could sleep without him.

Hearing a faint knock, I stop stretching to listen. After a moment, the knock comes again.

"Oz, I think someone is at the door."

"Mmm?" he hums, burying his face farther into my cleavage.

His hips thrust forward, and his heavy length is against my thigh. My pussy automatically clenches, wanting to accommodate his insatiable need.

This time when the knock comes, it's louder. Oz looks at the bedside table and checks the time.

"It's nine-thirty. They can wait," he grumbles, then stuffs his face directly back into my breasts.

I laugh and push at him but don't move him an inch.

"Who's here?"

"Someone who's cock blocking," he says, moving his big body over mine.

Without taking his face away from where he's nuzzling, he knees my thighs apart and pushes his cock against my opening. He's not even fully awake and he's demanding entrance. I wrap my legs around him, opening up for what he wants, and he plunges inside me all the way to the root.

"Good morning, baby." His words are muffled by my nipple, which he's now sucked into his mouth.

His thick cock spreads me wide as he begins to thrust in and out. There's another knock, but now I've stopped caring because he's inside me and nothing else in the world matters when we are connected like this.

Suddenly, the landline beside the bed rings, and Oz lets out a growl. He thrusts hard into me one time before reaching out and grabbing it.

"What?" he shouts, still buried balls deep inside me.

I hear someone speaking into the phone but can't make out what they're saying. After a second, Oz puts his hand over my mouth and moves again. My eyes grow wide with shock that he's fucking me while he's on the phone. But for another, darker reason, I'm soaking wet because of it.

"I heard," he says, licking his lips and looking down my body. I know he wants his mouth on me. He can hardly keep it off every inch of me when we're making love.

I spread my legs wider, and my slickness coats his cock as it slides in and out of me.

There's more talking coming from the phone, and I decide to play along with this.

I open my mouth under his hand and lick his palm. When I look into his beautiful sapphires, I see them darken, and he grips the phone tighter.

"Five minutes," he growls into the phone and then he slams it down beside the bed.

He removes his hand and kneels, taking me with him. He growls as I sit up, and he takes hold of me, thrusting angrily into my body. The fierce look in his eyes and the aggressive possession flowing from him make me climax instantly.

I cry out into the room as he thrusts one last time, emptying his own orgasm into me. We cling together, trying to catch our breath as we both come back down from the crazy, hot sex.

"Where did that come from?" I ask, smiling against his chest. I kiss the tattoo that bears my name, and then press my cheek to it.

"There's a team of people here to help you and Paige get ready for tonight, and I wasn't ready to give you up yet."

As I look up into his soft blue eyes, he gives me the sweetest kiss.

When he pulls back, I smile at him and climb off the bed. "Let me rinse off then, and you can greet our guests."

I hear him grunt behind me, and I look over my shoulder to see him watching me walk away. He's insatiable.

I pile my hair up and take a quick shower, not knowing what to expect today. Oz told me last night that he had Kimmi arrange for someone to come do my hair today, but this is kind of early. I guess she wanted to make sure she had enough time, because the event isn't until six tonight.

When I get out of the shower, I wrap a towel around

me and go into Oz's closet. I plan on grabbing a button-up shirt and some of his shorts to wear while I'm getting my hair done today. I flip on the light and then stop, looking around the space.

"Miles!" I shout, not moving from where I'm standing.

After a second he comes up behind me, wrapping his arms around my waist. He kisses my bare shoulder and I wave my hands around the room.

"What the hell is this?"

Over half of the closet has been filled with clothes I know damn well aren't mine but will fit me like a glove.

"I don't see the problem, Mallory. You don't want me to push and do things without talking to you. So I didn't move your things from the third floor up here. I got you new things."

"Oz." I drop my head in my hands in exasperation.

"Loophole, baby," he says, and smacks me on the butt. "Now put something on. They're setting up in the dining room."

He walks out of the closet before I can ask him what he means by that. I shake my head, having no time to fight with him. I walk over to the first rack of clothes. I thumb through a few pieces and check for something comfortable. But as I push the hangers, I notice something on all the tags.

Maternity.

My stomach does a flip, and I think about my period, which is supposed to arrive any day now. Oz must really want this if he's already planning for it. After a moment, I come up with a plan.

I go over to another rack and see they're normal

clothes, so I grab a tank top with a built-in bra and a pair of yoga pants so I don't have to worry about underwear. Though God knows if he bought me a closet full of clothes, he probably bought those, too.

Walking out of the closet, I stop and listen for Oz. I hear him talking down the hall so grab my purse from the dresser. I pull out the burner phone Paige got me the night we sneaked out and turn it on.

I send her a quick text, hoping she has it turned on, and wait. After a second she texts back, and I'm both relieved and nervous at the same time.

THIRTY-FOUR

Mallory

TWO HOURS LATER, I'm being buffed and polished to within an inch of my life.

Kimmi was here briefly to drop off the secret gown, now hanging next to my new wardrobe. She left already, but gave me a mischievous smile on her way out.

There are two people here to do my nails and toes and a third to do my makeup and hair. I've been plucked and scrubbed, and as the gel finishes setting, Paige walks into the dining room. She's got her purse over her arm, and I stare at it.

"Hey," she says, looking me up and down, then glances around the room. "Where's Oz?"

"He wanted to get some work done while I was getting pampered." I look at the women working on me and smile. "Do you ladies mind if I take a break? It's almost lunchtime. Maybe we all should."

Oz had a few platters of food brought in, and Paige is already halfway to finishing a sandwich.

They all agree, and I get up from my chair and walk to the bedroom with Paige following me. When we get there, I drag her into the master bathroom and lock the door behind us.

"Don't you think this is a bit suspicious?" she says in a hushed voice.

"Just give it to me." I hold out my hand and wait.

Paige unzips her purse and pulls out the pregnancy test, slapping it into my hand.

"You wouldn't believe what I had to go through to get that, Mal. I think Captain popped a blood vessel when he saw what I was buying." She gives me a smile that looks a little evil, and I would laugh if I wasn't so scared.

"I threw away all the packaging so you wouldn't get busted with the trash lying around. But I read it all. One line, not pregnant. Two lines, you're knocked up. It seems pretty easy to use."

I nod and look at the stick, walk over to the toilet, and sit down. I hold the stick and try not to pee on my hand as I do what Paige tells me to. After I'm finished, I set it on the counter, and then get up, washing my hands.

"You okay?" Paige asks, and looks at me nervously.

"Yeah. I'm scared, but I don't know why. I love Oz, and he loves me. Having a baby with him would be wonderful, but I'm antsy about it. I'm probably pregnant with all the sex we have and all the protection we *don't* use."

Paige laughs and nudges my shoulder. "Do you feel pregnant? Have you been sick?"

"No, not at all. But I've never been pregnant before, so what do I know?"

"This is a big deal, Mal. But I know you, and you wouldn't have done any of this if you weren't sure. Maybe even if it's in the back of your mind, I think you knew from day one with Miles that he was it."

I nod and a warmth spreads over me. She's right. I knew deep down he's it for me. And if our love made a child, then I'll be the happiest woman in the world.

Paige checks her watch, and then nods at me. I walk over to the test and pick it up, my fingers nearly shaking. When I look at it, my heart falls when I see there's only one line on it.

"Negative." Paige confirms what I see.

"Mallory? Paige?" Oz says, knocking on the bathroom door.

Panicked, I open the bottom cabinet and hide the test under a roll of toilet paper. I stand up and look at Paige, who has her arms out like she doesn't know what to do.

"Be right out, Oz," I say, and try not to sound like I'm up to something. "Paige, um, Paige had to help me go to the bathroom so I wouldn't mess my nails up," I rush, trying to cover my fumble.

Paige gives me two thumbs-up, and I put my hands to my mouth so I don't panic.

"Okay," Oz says, but doesn't sound convinced. "I'll be in the dining room when you guys are finished."

We wait another minute or two before we take a breath and exit the bathroom.

"Damn, that was close," Paige says, and for some reason her words sting.

I'm not pregnant, and I'm surprised at how sad that thought makes me.

THIRTY-FIVE
Mallory

"I CAN'T BELIEVE I agreed to this." Oz runs his finger
down between my breasts. The simple touch sends
goose bumps up my arms. I lick my lips and look up
at him. We've only been here twenty minutes and Oz
hasn't released me from his hold. I've been pressed up
against him since I walked out of our building. In fact,
I think he's even avoiding people by keeping us hostage
in a little corner of the ballroom.

"See, you're cold. You should take my jacket." He
goes to take off his jacket, making me laugh.

"I'm fine." I smile up at him and he scowls.

"I'm going to have a talk with Ms. Ford about the
things she picks out for you," he mumbles, more to himself than to me as he looks around the room. He moves
himself a little, blocking me from view, and I have to
fight a smile.

"Are we going to hide in this corner all night?" I
mold myself into him more, trying to cool some of his
caveman tendencies. Tension rolls though his body
under his jacket. He's wearing an onyx-black tux and
a matching dress shirt. But he's not wearing a tie tonight. Instead, he's got the top button of his shirt un-
done, and his sexy neck is on display. Every time his

Adam's apple moves, I want to run my tongue across its ridge. He looks dark tonight dressed in all black, and I'm having a hard time controlling my dark desires.

Reaching up, I wrap my arms around his neck, and it makes him look back down at me. I lift up on my tiptoes, and he meets me halfway, putting a soft kiss on my lips. "I'm only yours. I promise," I tell him when I pull back.

"I know. But I don't like fuckers looking." His hand rests on my back, then slides down to my ass, giving it a small squeeze. I kiss his exposed neck before dropping back down.

"Oh, sorry, I got some lipstick on you." I swipe at the shimmer on his neck, but he stops me.

"Leave it." He squeezes my ass one more time, then pulls me into his erection. It digs into my stomach, and he makes a grunting noise. "I like your mark on me. You should have let me leave one of my own."

Bending down, he kisses my neck, but I pull back before he can deepen it. "No more hickeys. At least where anyone can see them." He smiles against my neck, and I'm happy that his inner caveman is appeased. For now.

"Not the kind of mark I was talking about. I meant between your legs. I think I would have felt a hell of a lot better about you in this dress if I knew that right now you had me coating your thighs." He takes a little bite of my neck, and I shiver with desire. "And your pussy."

My core clenches at his words, but I only tilt my head more for him. I wish we'd done what he's saying, but that would've been hard with security waiting for us in the living room when I'd come out ready to go. Which is probably why he didn't mark me to begin with.

"Miles," a man says. Oz tenses a little at the sound of his name, and he reluctantly lets me go. He turns around, and I redden even more at being caught having a little make-out session.

"Tom." Oz pulls me close to his side with one hand. With his other, he reaches out to shake the speaker's hand. He looks to be in his midfifties with salt-and-pepper hair, and I get the sense I've seen him before, but I can't place where. Like everyone else here, he's dressed in a tux that probably cost more than I make in a year.

Tom looks at me with curiosity. I saw a few of those looks from others when we walked in together. Oz said people aren't used to seeing him with a date, unless his mom comes with him.

"Mallory, this is Tom Sanders. He works in real estate." Tom reaches out to shake my hand. It's then I realize where I've seen him before. His face is plastered on buildings and buses around the city.

He takes my hand and bends to kiss it, but Oz grabs my wrist, pulling my hand back and kissing it himself. The other man laughs.

"Never thought I'd see the day," he says, and for some reason, I feel a sense of pride. Oz has only ever wanted me.

I look around the room and see others looking at us, but they turn away when my eyes meet theirs. There might have been some buzz about Oz and me possibly dating, but everyone will know now that it's much more than that.

"The day was long ago. She's been mine for years, just not here in the city for me to be able to bring her along," Oz corrects, making me smile up at him. Every time I tell him we might be moving too fast, he always corrects me, too. He says we've been together since the day he laid eyes on me, and I roll my eyes. But inside, I always melt. It's still hard to wrap my mind around the fact that this man waited years to be with me. Which makes me understand even more why Oz is so stingy with sharing me. He's waited all this time, and he's self-ish when it comes to me. How could I not adore that?

"No more Vivien then?" I can see the disappointment in the man's face, and it sparks my interest. I'd never even thought about Oz's mom dating, but clearly Tom's interested if the look on his face is anything to go by.

"Not tonight," is all Oz offers, and even I'm a little disappointed at that.

"I've seen your face around on buildings, haven't I?" I ask, drawing Tom's eyes back to me.

"God, those things are haunting me." He laughs. "My marketing team's idea. Suffice it to say, I will not be doing that again."

"Why? I think you look handsome on them." Oz's hand on my hips flexes, and I elbow him. "I remember I saw one when I was with Vivien and she said the same thing." I can't stop the little white lie from slipping free.

"Really?"

"Don't you remember, Oz? It was last week." I look up at him, encouraging him with my eyes, but apparently he doesn't read my body language like Paige does. So I elbow him again because that seemed to work last time.

"I don't recall," he says drily.

I see Paige rush by out of the corner of my eye. She

and Captain both came to the event tonight but dressed inconspicuously so as not to look like bodyguards. Oz offered the two of them, along with a few others, for security tonight—what with there being high-priced auction items up for bid they wanted all the security they could get.

Paige got her makeup and hair done at Oz's with me, but she went home to get dressed. I look her up and down as she approaches wearing a tight strapless dress that goes all the way to the floor. It looks conservative until she takes a step, and then I see that a slit runs all the way up to the top of her hip. I'm pretty sure underwear isn't an option when wearing a dress like that, and it makes me smile. She looks incredible, and Captain looks like he's chewing on glass.

"Excuse me," I say, but Oz doesn't let me go. "Ladies' room." He looks over my head and must see Paige, because he releases his death grip on me.

"Come back to me."

"Always," I tell him, getting another quick kiss before I turn to follow Paige. I can tell by the look on her face that she's pissed.

I catch her outside the ladies' room and grab her by her arm. "Listen," she snaps, but stops short when she sees it's me. It's then I get a good look at her face. Her lipstick is all kinds of smeared.

"Who'd you suck face with?"

"Grr," she growls, reminding me of her brother. I still forget they're related, but every now and then something like this makes me remember. She grabs my hand, pulling me away from the bathroom and down a little hallway into what looks like some fancy sitting room.

"Captain kissed me!" she finally says, using the back of her hand to wipe at her mouth. "Or maybe I kissed him. I don't know. I wanted him to stop talking. Then, well…" She throws her hands up in the air like she doesn't really know what happened at all.

"Was it good?"

"Mal, I'm serious here."

I want to tell her I am, too, but I decide against it. I don't know why this is such a big deal. Haven't they been dancing around this since they met?

"What happened?" I decide to ask instead.

"He kind of cornered me about the pregnancy test."

"Oh, God, you didn't tell, did you?" I haven't even told Oz yet, and I have a feeling he's going to be disappointed when he finds out I'm not pregnant.

"Of course not." Her faces scrunches like she can't believe I asked her that.

"I'm sorry. I know. Just panicked a little."

"Ryan thinks it's mine, and he's been on my case about it."

"So he thinks you're pregnant? You didn't tell him you weren't?"

A sheepish look crosses her face "When I dropped the bag in front of him and I saw how pissed he was about it, I might have let it hang out there."

Of course she did.

"Then tonight he cornered me. Said I should be on desk duty if I was in fact pregnant. Then I went ahead and told him to mind his own fucking business."

That isn't shocking either. "And that led to a kiss?"

She shakes her head. "He started pushing, asking who the father was. He was pissed, Mal. Like, seriously pissed. Then he said there couldn't be anyone, and I asked him how he knew."

"They know everything," I say, confirming what she already knows.

"Yeah, but then…" She shakes her head again like she can't believe what she's about to say. "Then he said that if there was someone else, then he must not be around and that Captain'd be around if I wanted him to be." She takes a step toward me. "Even put his fucking hand on my stomach, Mal." I'm not sure if she's pissed about this or in awe.

I'm definitely melting at how sweet that is, because I see the way Captain watches her. He wants her, but to step in on something like that—her possibly being pregnant with another man's baby—and he wants to be involved. That's big. That's saying a lot about how he feels if you ask me.

"Then we kind of started going at it. Like full-on. He picked me up and pushed me against the wall, like this is a fucking movie or some shit."

"I'm not following why we're mad about this, because you look pissed."

She brings her hand to her mouth again, like she's still feeling the kiss. "I don't know. All I can seem to feel is mad, and I'm not even sure who I'm mad at. Fuck, Mal, I could really fall for him."

"What's wrong with that?" I take a step toward her.

"He's not right for me. And if he knew the real me, he'd be gone. Think about it. He's like Mr. Perfect, does everything by the rules, and well—" she looks down at the floor "—I'm not, and I don't have any plans to be. In fact, I've got plans that…" She trails off, and my heart clenches for her.

I want to tell her to let whatever plans she has go, but I know that will get me nowhere fast. In fact, it might get me pushed away from her in areas of her life I've been trying to push in on lately. Ones she's been keeping hidden. The part that makes Paige, well, Paige.

The door suddenly opens, making us both turn to see Oz and Captain standing in the doorway. Paige freezes. I walk over to Oz. "Sorry. Needed help fixing something on my dress," I say, making my way toward the men. I take Oz's hand.

"Will you show me the auction now, or are you going to keep me in the corner all night?"

He pulls me toward him once again, gluing me to his side.

"As long as you don't leave my side again."

"Deal."

We walk past Captain, who steps out of the way for us.

"Got a little something." I point to my mouth, and he reaches up, wiping it away. I have to bite back a smile as he removes the lipstick. Paige follows us out, then pushes out in front of us, putting as much space as she can between her and Captain.

As we make our way over to the auction tables, Oz has to stop a few times to talk to various people as we look at the different items. He seems so much colder and more clinical with others. I hadn't really noticed it before. Probably because it's usually him and me, and we can be ourselves. It's amazing to me to see the difference in him. I'd be lying if I said I didn't like that only I get the sweeter side of Oz. As we move down, we get to an antique ring, and I can't seem to pull my eyes away from it. The center stone is square and deep blue. There are small diamonds surrounding it, and it sparkles under the light. The blue is the exact same color as Oz's eyes. It's got to be the most beautiful sapphire I've ever seen.

"You like it?" he asks.

"It's beautiful." I almost choke when I pick up the information card about it. The bid starts at four million dollars.

The card proclaims it to be the Devotion Stone, and I flip it over to look at the other side. There's a note about the history of the ring.

> This ring was given to Abigail Richmond by her beloved, Baron Frederick de Mandeville. They were married in secret in 1885 because she was the daughter of a farmer, and his family didn't approve. Frederick gave Abigail the two-carat sapphire before renouncing his title and choosing to live a modest life in the country with his wife. After 44 years of marriage, Abigail passed away on October 2nd, 1929, and Frederick de Mandeville is said to have died the next day of a broken heart. The ring has been donated by the surviving estate.

"Oh, that's so sad," I say, putting the card back.

Oz runs his nose along the column of my neck. "Why is that sad? Sounds sweet to me."

"I don't know. He loved her so much. The ring should find the same kind of love again. Not be up in some auction. But I guess the money will do a lot of good though." I turn, looking up at him. He brings me more into his body, and I wish we were home. Alone. Not so many eyes on us. They all seem to be lingering.

"Everyone is staring at you," I tell him.

"No, they're staring at you," he corrects, and I can hear his underlying irritation.

"Take me home then? Where only you can look at me."

"Fuck yes." He grabs my hand, pulling us through the ballroom, and I can't help but laugh. He uses his other hand to pull out his cell phone, telling his driver to pull around. I've wanted to leave almost from the moment we got here, and not because I felt a little out of place. But because Oz's whole territorial act seems to get me worked up. In every way. I really can't let him know that little piece of information, but I think he might already suspect it.

We come to a dead stop, and I nearly run into Oz's back when we enter the lobby of the ballroom. Oz's hand clasps mine tighter, and I follow his line of sight to see Paige talking to an older man with short dark hair. As if stopping in the middle of his sentence, he turns a little and his eyes land on us. The same eyes I'd recognize anywhere now. Sapphire blue.

My stomach tightens. The man walks toward us, leaving Paige standing alone. She stares at his back, her face pale and unreadable.

"Look at our little family reunion," the man says.

Paige takes a few more steps toward us, but still hangs back. Watching everything. Her eyes look a little wild.

"I was wondering if I'd see you tonight." Oz's voice is cold and calculated.

"Not even going to introduce me?" The man, who I assume is Alexander, Oz's dad, ignores Oz to stare at me. Oz pulls my arm back and steps in front of me, blocking me from the man's view making it clear he won't be doing that. I have to poke my head out to even see what's going on.

"I assume you received the paperwork today. How does it feel to have everything bought out from under you and taken apart?"

Alexander takes a step closer to Oz, until they're only inches apart. "I warned you, Miles, don't fuck with me. I'll make sure this one doesn't wake up."

A chill runs down my spine at his insinuation, and before I can process what this all means, Oz is on him. He's got Alexander by the throat, pinned up against the wall with his feet dangling inches off the ground. Alexander's hands are trying to pull at his wrist, but Oz only squeezes tighter. His face is turning a deep red, and he's gasping for air as he struggles to breathe.

"You threaten what's mine, and I'll fucking end you. Do you hear me?" Alexander's feet kicking against the wall are the only sound in the room. "We're done. I've taken all your businesses and put them under. I've got piles of dirt on you a mile high, and if you so much as step foot in my town again, I'll do more than fuck with your money. Do. You. Understand. Me."

Oz clips out each word at the end, but all Alexander can do is nod. His breath is coming out in choking gasps, and he's turned from red to purple.

Walking over, I place my hands on Oz's back. "I

want to go home," I tell him, and I feel him release a deep breath. It takes a solid minute before he relaxes, but he finally releases him, letting Alexander crumple to the ground.

Oz turns to look down at me, grabbing my hand once again. I look over at Paige, who's looking at her father like he's a pile of trash on the floor. After a beat she turns to us, and I see something flash in her eyes, but it's gone so quickly I'm not sure if I even saw it.

"Your driver's out front, sir." Captain's words break the silence that's fallen over us.

I glance around, not knowing what to do, but Captain walks over to Paige and takes her hand. He looks back to us and he and Oz share a look, and I feel that there's so much passing between them that I still don't know. But there's not time to explain, because Oz wants to get me as far from here, and as far from Alexander as possible.

He wraps his arm around my waist and we walk out to the street and quickly climb into the back of the limo. I don't fight him, wanting to put distance between that situation as much as he does. Oz wastes no time in pulling me into his lap.

"You okay?" I ask, worried about what the confrontation might have done to him.

"I've been after revenge for my mother all these years, and she doesn't even seem to give the man two thoughts." He lets out a deep breath. "But I knew when you came into my life that it needed to end. I couldn't live a life where I was worried about you around every corner."

"I'm not scared of him, if that's what you're thinking.

I'll keep my security and do as you guys ask if you're worried about him coming after me," I offer.

"You don't want me to let it go?" he asks, a hand coming up to cup my cheek.

"I want you to do whatever it is you think you should do, but I don't think Paige is going to let it go."

He's still for a few seconds, as if he's thinking about what he should do.

"I wouldn't stand in the way of Paige," he tells me. He wouldn't but I also can't stand aside and let her walk alone. I don't tell Oz that. Maybe with time I can bring Paige and Oz together. Make us all a family.

"Did it scare you when I grabbed him in there? Threatened to kill him?" he asks, and I can see the worry in his eyes.

"I've never been scared of you, Oz. You were protecting the people you love. That doesn't scare me. It's another reason I love you."

"I told myself I'd never be like him but I can't help but compare some of our similarities."

"Oz, you are nothing like that man! How can you even think that?"

"How can you not?" he returns, his words sounding sad.

I cup his face. "You'd never hurt me. Ever. Think about it, Oz. Everything you have ever done when it came to us is for me."

"Is it? Or is it for me?" He takes my hands and places them on his chest, letting them rest there. "I stalked you when I knew I wanted you, did everything to make sure I could have you. I mapped out your whole life to lead to me, so that you would need me. I've even been trying to get you pregnant. Each time I took you that thought flooded my mind. That if we had a baby you could never leave me. We'd have something that linked us together forever. The worst part is knowing that I'll never let you go. Can't you see how selfish I've been?"

I smile at that because he's put himself in the corner. "Oz, am I like your father?" He tries to cut me off but I keep going. "Because I would never let you go either, and if anyone ever threatened you or tried to take you from me I'd kill them, too."

His eyes search mine. The longing to believe that what I'm saying is true is written all over his face. Has he done crazy things to get me? Yes. I could see myself doing those things, too. He's watched me for years, and I can see why he's gone a little crazy. I haven't known him long either, and I'm starting to have those thoughts already.

"I love when you take me bare." I drop my voice and try my own seduction. I have the same need to tie us together as he does.

I watch all the fear and worry drain from his face and body, realizing how much I care about him. His actions tonight don't make him like his father. He kisses me softly. "I think I should make love to you for the rest of the night." His hands roam my body. "I don't know if this dress is going to make it home." He growls the last part as my back hits the limo floor.

THIRTY-SIX

Miles

I HEAR THE soft tones of my alarm, and I reach over to quietly turn it off.

Mallory is on her stomach, her hand tucked under her pillow. Her lips are slightly parted as she sleeps, and I ache to lie there and look at her. I could watch her every second of every day and only fall deeper in love with her.

I tuck the blanket around her and slip out of the bed silently. I pull on a pair of jogging pants and a T-shirt and make my way out of the bedroom and into the kitchen.

When I get there, I call down to the front desk and make sure the arrangements are in place. Then I get to work on making my woman breakfast in bed.

We stayed up late last night, and my cock twitches with the memory of getting her home and ripping that scrap of a dress off her body. Her curves were driving me insane all night. I took her until she passed out, and then I watched her sleep. I'd made some calls after that, and put things into motion. I couldn't wait any longer. I'd waited years, and I was done.

Seeing my father last night put a damper on things, but coming home with Mallory made all of that fall away. I've been getting away from wanting my revenge for some time, focusing only on Mallory. Each moment with her seems to lessen the anger that had built inside me over the years. She makes me want something else. Something not filled with hate.

I was young when I began on the journey to make him pay, but as I've gotten older, I want to let it go. Why hold on to something so hateful? I'd rather spend my energy loving Mallory and making a life with her. Everyone is asking me to let it go, and Mallory showed me last night that I'm nothing like him. That I've done what I set out to do. My mother is happy and I am the man I want to be.

The only thing that worries me now is Paige. She doesn't seem ready to let her vendetta go, and I can't say I blame her. She's got her own story with him, and I'm not sure she's going to move on anytime soon. Alexander was a different kind of man with her, and I don't think there's anyone out there who would deny her revenge. I still don't even know all the details of what she went through with him. It's one way Paige and I are alike. We're both good at keeping secrets.

But the time has come for me to let that part of my past go. I'm done chasing after hate, and I'm done wasting a single thought on him when I could be thinking about the woman I love. Whatever happens next with him is up to Paige, and if she needs my help I'll be there. He's got a lot to answer for when it comes to her, and she'll make him pay. But otherwise, I'm shutting my book on Alexander Owens. I got the closure I was looking for last night, and I know that my family will be safe from him. There's nothing left he can do to hurt us, and if he tried, there would be no second chance.

I'm starting new with Mallory. I don't want this in our lives together. For it to ever touch our children. And Ivy was right, that the cloud of revenge hanging between us isn't as important as living in the love and making a future with Mallory. I recognize that a large part of me was scared I would end up like him, but after hearing Mallory last night I know I won't. I would never do anything to hurt her, and I would die to protect her.

It's as if a weight has been lifted off my shoulders, and I can finally let go. I never knew I was holding on to so much, until I released it last night. I had my company acquire what was left of his assets and I dismantled them. His world is going to crumble. Now I feel like that part of my life is finally finished, and I can concentrate on more important things in my life. Like my love asleep in the other room.

When I've finished breakfast, I decide to run to the bathroom and clean up. I sneak past Mallory, checking that she's still asleep, and smile down at her. In the bathroom, I brush my teeth, but when I'm finished, I notice there's no hand towel around. The cleaning lady must have taken it for laundry, so I reach under the cabinet to get a new one. When I grab one in the back, I pull it out, knocking over toilet paper rolls as I do. Reaching down to stack them back up, I see a white piece of plastic sticking out from under one. I push the rolls aside and pull it out, seeing it's a pregnancy test. My heart hammers in my chest as I look down at it, and then suddenly the doorbell rings.

Putting the test in my pocket, I sneak back through

the room. Mallory hasn't moved an inch. I make my way through the house, then to Chuck the doorman arriving with my delivery. I takc it from him and close the door and lock it.

I take a moment, unsure of what to do, and then decide to go with my original plan I'd begun this morning.

From the kitchen, I take the tray of homemade waffles and berries and carry it into the bedroom. I set the tray on the bedside table and sit on the edge of the mattress.

Leaning down, I kiss Mallory's shoulder until she turns on her side to look up at me.

"Hey," she says in the sexiest sleepy voice. The sun is shining through the windows and it glows behind her like a halo.

I run my fingers through her hair, and then trail them down her naked back, soaking in having her in my bed, wanting her there every morning.

"Mmm," she hums, stretching into my touch like a cat.

I kneel beside the bed and nuzzle against her. My words are caught in my throat, and I don't know how to get them out.

"Oz?" she says, but I can't answer. I keep my face in her neck. "Oz, what's wrong? Are you okay?"

Sitting back on my heels, I look at her and she sits up, pulling the sheet across her breasts. There's a look of worry in her eyes now, and I rush to explain.

"I'm sorry. I've done this in my head a thousand times. Everywhere we go, I look for the right spot, and every time I hold you, I try to find the right words, but I can't seem to make it sound perfect in my head."

"Oz," she says, a nervous sound in her voice. "What are you doing?"

I pull out a small box and place it on the bed in front of her.

"Mallory, I've loved you from the very second I saw you. The very second. There was no hesitation from my heart that day, and I knew I had to make you mine. I may have gone about it differently than some men would have, but I wouldn't change anything since it led me to you."

I reach out and take her hand, placing the box in her palm.

"I realize that this is soon for you, but it's been years for me. Years in the making, baby." I smile at her, and then I see a tear fall from her eyes. I reach up, swiping it away with my thumb, and she bites her lower lip. "I've waited for you to see me, for you to love me and for you to marry me. Please, baby. Don't make me wait another day."

I open the box in her hand and show her the ring. She gasps and puts a hand over her mouth, looking from me to the ring and then back to me again. It's the Devotion Stone.

"When you saw this last night, I was so relieved you loved it. I found out about it from an antiques dealer and got in touch with the estate. They agreed to sell it to me after I told them about you. And that I planned to put it up at an auction at a price I knew no one could touch. This way, the foundation would benefit from the love I have for you, and this ring would find a new home on your hand. I want it to carry our love story for the next one hundred years."

Tears are streaming down her cheeks, but I stay on my knees in front of her.

"Mallory Ann Sullivan, will you marry me?"

She nods once, then throws herself at me, and I barely catch the ring in time before she tackles me to the floor. Mallory peppers kisses all over my face, and I feel my own eyes water. Relief and love wash over me, and I roll us over, pinning her under me.

I take her hand and slip the ring on, kissing it and then kissing her palm. Looking into her gray-blue eyes, I see nothing but happiness, and that's all I've ever wanted to see there.

"I love you so much," she says, reaching up with her other hand and rubbing my stubble. "Yes, I'll marry you. Even though you're crazy obsessed and a border-line stalker."

"Don't act like you don't like it." My smile feels as if it could crack my face in half. And the moment could not be any more perfect. Because I know she does. I see it in her eyes when sometimes I go a little too far, unable to help myself. It's why we fit.

Mallory laughs, and I reach into my pocket, pulling out the test and holding it up for her. "And when were you planning on telling me about this?"

Mallory's smile dips for a second, and then she gives me a small shrug. "Just a false alarm."

I look at her in confusion, look at the test, and then look back to her.

"Baby, how is being pregnant a false alarm?"

Her eyes grow wide, and she snatches the test out of my hand, sitting up so fast, she nearly knocks me off her lap.

"What?" she shouts.

She looks down at the two blue lines, and the test clearly says two lines means pregnant.

"How is this possible? There was only one yesterday."

She looks up into my eyes, and it's my turn to shrug. Like I know anything about how those tests work. "It's two lines. It says pregnant."

"I must not have waited long enough. Oh my God. Oz, we're going to have a baby." She pauses, like she's testing out the words. "We're going to have a baby."

She beams at me. She's so happy, and then she's crying again. I let out a small laugh, pulling her in my arms. She's all over the place this morning.

"Sorry, you proposed to me, and I found out I'm pregnant all in the same moment. It's kind of an emotional overload."

"For me, too, baby."

I pick her up and lay her back down on the bed. She pulls at my shirt, and I kick off my jogging pants. This moment calls for skin on skin. Holding her face with both hands, I kiss her, long and slow, trying to pour all of what I feel into it. All the years of waiting, all the years of longing have led to this. I've finally got my ring on her finger and my baby inside her. What more could a man need from the love of his life?

I enter her slowly, like the kiss, and take my time making love to her. Her legs wrap around me, and the cool band of the ring presses against my back, reminding me that she's all mine. Her body welcomes me, opening up and offering me all that she has to give.

When I find my release, she's right there with me

as we whisper words of tenderness to one another. The moment is so beautiful and so sacred it feels as if there's never been love like this before. We've created something so perfect that it can never be touched. Not by our pasts or by anything around us. Our intimacy has sealed our bond, and my soul is forever entwined with hers.

"I love you, Mallory. I will love you until my last breath."

"I love you, too, my beautiful man behind the curtain."

EPILOGUE

Miles

About nine months later...

I GROWL AS she slides her mouth down my cock, and I fist my hands into the sheets so I don't thrust up into her mouth or try to grab her. Even after months of having her in my bed—our bed—my control still isn't great. My need for her hasn't lessened over time.

"I'm going to come."

She had me ready to explode before I even knew it was happening. Waking up with her mouth on me is a sweet torture. But I knew what she was up to. She'd been pouting about it for the past five days now and I hadn't given in.

She takes her sweet mouth off my cock, making me groan at the loss. Fuck, she's trying to kill me. I finally open my eyes, something I don't do on purpose, because I know what I'm going to see. And I know that sight would send me over.

There she is. Her hair, messy from a night of sleep, falling all around her, her eyes hooded with arousal. She licks her full lips as she climbs up my body. The only thing she's wearing is the ring I put on her. I should tell her to stop, but I only dig my fingers into the sheets as she straddles me and slowly begins to sink down on my cock. There's nothing better in the world than being skin to skin with her.

I should have seen this coming. That baby book has finally blown up in my face. She hated the damn thing, but now here she is, using it against me as she slides down onto me, making me moan her name. I haven't felt her sweetness wrapped around me in over two weeks.

"See? I'm fine," she says as she moves on top of me with slow, sweet thrusts. I can't even move. I stare up at her. I thought she was perfect before, but now she's a fucking goddess. Finally, I let go of the sheets and bring my hands to her very pregnant belly in a purely possessive move. She's already a week overdue.

"I don't want to hurt you." I groan as her head falls back and she keeps moving over me. The book said sex could bring on labor, something Mallory has wanted for weeks. As for me, I was enjoying watching her waddle around, even if it was a little selfish on my part to want to keep her like this.

My hand moves over her belly, then up to her breasts as she slowly rides me. It's a bittersweet torture, and it takes everything in me not to thrust up into her. Not to grab her hips and make her move faster, and not to come because it's right there. Ready to release inside her, from the sight of her riding me like this. But I won't, not until she comes first. Not until I feel her sweetness grip my cock.

"Oz, trust me, this isn't hurting anything."

She moves a little faster, and I slide my hand from her breast, over her belly to where we're joined. I brush my thumb across her clit, making her jerk. Her pussy grips me even tighter, and I don't know how much longer I can last.

"Baby, I would have eaten you all morning if that's what you wanted."

Her head falls forward and she glares at me.

"I love you, Oz, but I'm over your mouth. I want you inside me."

Her hands fall to my chest, her nails digging into me. Every time she tried to get sex, I'd have my mouth between her legs, giving her all the orgasms she could take until she passed out. Then I'd go to the bathroom and take care of myself because I didn't even trust myself to jerk off while I ate her sweet pussy. Fuck, a few times I didn't have to touch myself and I came with her. Just the sight of her naked, pregnant body sent me over the edge. I was scared I'd take her too hard.

"Take what you want then, Mallory. You know everything I have is yours." I mean every word of it. It's been hell denying her, and I can't do it any longer. Not that she's going to let me. I might be able to push my way into getting something, but when it comes down to it, she always gets what she wants. I can't tell her no as long as whatever she wants has me beside her. I need to be near her.

I stroke her clit fast and her breathing picks up. My name falls from her mouth over and over again, and then she finally lets go. She squeezes hard around my cock, taking me with her into orgasm, her nails digging into my chest, and I hope they leave little marks on me.

I grip her hips, holding her in place as I release deep inside of her. I keep her still until we both recover from the intensity.

"See? Nothing bad happened." She smiles down at me and traces my tattoo of her name on my chest. I grunt because it's all I've got in me. I poured two weeks of pent-up lust inside her, and I'll be lucky if I can move in the next hour.

She slowly climbs off me, my cock slipping free and already coming back to life. Fuck. Neither of us can ever seem to get enough of her. Thank God she's mine forever.

Getting up from the bed, she turns, leaning down to kiss me. I push my hands into her hair, deepening the kiss before she pulls away.

"Bathroom," she whispers against my lips, and I release my hold on her hair as I watch her get up from the side of the bed.

"Do you think we can get those cream cheese bagels?" she asks over her shoulder.

"They're already set to be delivered." I glance over at the clock next to the bed. "In thirty minutes."

"God, you're good at this," she says as she makes her way to the bathroom.

I'm watching her pert ass wiggle with each step she takes when she suddenly stops.

"Oh, shit," I hear her whisper, making me spring from the bed. She turns to look at me, and a smile crosses her face. "It worked!"

I look down between her legs, and that's when I see that her water has clearly broken.

"Damn that book."

EPILOGUE

Miles

Three years later...

"I LOVE YOU this much," I say, spreading my arms as far as they can go.

Henry sits up and looks at the span, his eyes growing wide. "That's big," he whispers, and snuggles back down beside me. I turn the page and keep reading the book about the bear dad telling his bear cub how much he loves him.

This is one of the best parts of my day, putting him to bed and reading him a story. He's all over the place at this age, but he loves being read to. Mallory is soaking in the tub, and I'm trying not to think about all her curvy bits covered in bubbles. I'll get to her bedtime story soon enough.

When I get to the end of the book, Henry looks up at me pleadingly and says, "One more."

"Okay, buddy. But this is the last one." Tucking him in, I look down at his eyes that are so much like his mother's and begin.

"Once upon a time, there was a very beautiful princess. The most beautiful princess in all the land."

"Mommy?" Henry asks, his eyes big and bright.

"Of course. So the beautiful princess didn't know, but a very handsome prince was watching her."

"Daddy?"

"You know it, buddy," I answer, smiling at him and watching him yawn. "So, this ruggedly handsome prince was protecting the princess from all the dark things around her. He kept his distance while she grew up, and then one day, she wandered onto his land."

Henry's eyes are getting heavy, but he's not quite there yet.

"After many years of watching the princess from a distance, finally she was within reach. So the prince knew it was time to reveal himself. But once the princess found out about all he'd done behind her back, she was very angry."

"What happened?" Henry asks, his eyes closing and taking a moment to open again.

"Like any good prince, he fought the dragons and witches and climbed the biggest tower in all the kingdoms to rescue the princess and make her see that he did it all for love."

I brush a dark wave of hair out of his eyes, which are now closed, heavy with sleep. His breathing is even now, and he's out cold, but I still sit there looking at him.

"Lucky for the prince, he was so good-looking, the princess couldn't resist."

Mallory comes up behind me and wraps her warm arms around my waist. I smell the rose scent of her bubble bath and smile.

"Lucky for the princess she got out of the bath. Her knight in shining armor was about to storm the tub."

Turning off the lamp, we leave Henry to his dreams and make our way to the bedroom. The king needs a night with his queen.

EPILOGUE

Mallory

Six years later...

I LOOK DOWN at Henry as he studies the ice-cream cart outside his father's office building. Our office building. Things like that still feel strange to think about, even after all these years together.

I picked our son up from his first day of kindergarten, and we're celebrating. It was bittersweet watching him go in this morning. Oz had to hold my hand to keep me from crying all over the place.

Even Henry cupped my face and told me, "I got this, Mom." Which made me want to cry more. I'd barely hung on to the tears until Oz had gotten me into the back of the car, where I sobbed all the way to work while he whispered sweet things into my ear. Still, it was hard seeing our only child go off to school.

His birth was rough, and I ended up needing an emergency C-section after ten hours of labor. I'd lost a lot of blood, and it scared the hell out of Oz. After that, we both decided that one healthy baby was all we needed. We were lucky, and it felt like that worked best for us. I love Oz and Henry so much, I'm not sure I could have more room in my heart for anything else.

Sometimes it feels like I could burst from how much love and joy is inside me.

Oz could see how much this affected me today. He popped into my office thirty times throughout the afternoon to check on me and make sure I was doing all right.

I'd kept my job after having Henry. I worked from home sometimes, and not always full weeks, but we'd made it work so I could have both my career and my family. It also helped that Oz set up a day care on the floor below ours. While I might have been stepping into my career, Oz had taken some steps back in his own, freeing up a lot of his time. Heck, I thought it was hard having Henry a floor down for a few hours. Now he's blocks and blocks away.

Oz finally came into my office this afternoon and told me to go already. That he had a car waiting to take me. I jumped up, rushing over to the school to get our little man. I was thirty minutes early and the first parent outside waiting for the school day to finally end.

Now we're back at our office building, and I'm letting Henry get an ice cream from the vendor outside while we wait for Oz to come down.

"It's always a tough decision," the man next to me says. I look over at him and give a friendly smile. He looks like he just got off work, briefcase in hand, and his suit looks like it's been worn all day with a few wrinkles in it.

"Oh, to be five and for this to be the toughest decision of the day." I laugh, placing my hand on top of Henry's head. I run my fingers through his wavy hair, like his father's. Almost everything about him is, except he got my gray-blue eyes.

"How about you?" The man's eyes run over me. "I'm guessing you want strawberry." He cocks a smile at me, like he's got me pegged. I want to roll my eyes, but I glance over to where one of my security guards is standing about ten feet back from me. Like always, they're blending in.

"She likes chocolate," Henry says, pulling my eyes back to him as he looks up at the man. "And stop talking to *my* mom."

"Manners," I remind him.

"Yeah, manners," Henry says to the man. He's still glaring up at him. It's a face I've seen on his father many times. I have to bite the inside of my cheek to keep from smiling.

"Just being polite, little dude," the man says, holding his hands up, but he narrows his eyes on Henry.

"I'm not your little dude," Henry practically growls back.

I feel Oz's presence come up behind me. He wraps an arm around me, then turns me to him. Before I can even say a word, his mouth lands on mine in a possessive, claiming kiss right in the middle of the street. When he finally pulls back, I stare at him then roll my eyes. The man is long gone.

"I had it, Dad," Henry says, making Oz laugh.

"I know you did."

Henry nods, looking back at the ice-cream board. I gape at both of them before I shake my head. I should be shocked, but I'm not in the least.

"I'll take vanilla," I hear him tell the vendor as Oz

leans in, taking a nip of my neck before bringing his mouth to my ear.

"I'm going to fuck you so good you won't even be able to talk to another person for the next week," he whispers, then licks the shell of my ear.

"And my wife will take a chocolate," he says, and I smile.

EPILOGUE

Mallory

---

20 years later...

THE SMELL OF rum and sunshine rolls around me, and I smile. I'm lying on my stomach with a cool breeze across my skin, and I feel his lips at the base of my spine.

I feel something ice-cold trail a little lower, and I realize it's Oz's tongue.

One of his big hands comes up and palms my ass cheek, squeezing it, and I let out a laugh.

"You're acting like this is our honeymoon," I say, rolling over and feeling Oz move over me.

I reach up, running my fingers through dark waves scattered with gray. He's smiling, and the crinkles around his eyes show all the years of it. He's ruggedly handsome at almost fifty and can still melt the panties off me. He's shirtless, letting the tropical sun turn his olive skin a deep brown. His swim trunks are wet but feel good against my hot body.

"Every time is like the first time, baby," he says, leaning down and burying his face in my cleavage.

We decided to take a trip to Hawaii, celebrating our anniversary and my retirement. We rented a house with a private beach, and Oz has been taking advantage of it in every way possible.

"I'm starting to think you like having sex outside."

I laugh as his mouth moves lower, pushing up the tankini top of my bathing suit and kissing my belly. I'm not as trim as I once was, and this is as close as I can get to a two-piece bathing suit, but Oz can't ever seem to keep his mouth off me.

"I'm thinking I like making love to my wife in the sunshine."

Our house is secluded, with security on a perimeter far away from sight. The lava rocks surrounding the beach make a cave for us, and it seems like we're on a private island.

I feel his mouth on my breast, and then his cool tongue. He's been making us strawberry daiquiris all day, and I'm feeling a little buzz running through my veins. And not because of his teasing tongue.

I run my fingers through his hair, gripping the locks and holding him to me. His mouth moves lower, and my legs instinctively fall open for him. He manages to wiggle down the large sun bed we're lying on, getting between my thighs.

This is exactly what I've been wanting since I decided to give up working. I ran the philanthropic division of Osbourne Corp for nearly twenty years, and it was time to let it go. Our son, Henry, had shown an interest in stepping in, and Oz finally convinced me he was ready. I said that if I wasn't working, he needed to keep me occupied, and he jumped at that chance all too quickly.

Oz's fingers slip inside my bathing suit bottoms, and soon those are pulled from my body.

"If you'd quit putting these damn things on, I wouldn't have to keep removing them," he says, nipping the inside of my thigh.

"Don't act like unwrapping your present isn't half the fun." I smirk, but then I moan as his mouth finds my center.

Out here in the sunshine with the rum making me tingly, I have zero inhibitions, and I let him have his way with me. The cool sheet of the sun bed under me and the warmth of his body between my legs has my orgasm flowing through me faster than I saw coming.

A burst of pleasure runs up and down my arms and legs, and I cry out Oz's name.

"Fuck, I'll never get enough of hearing you scream my name," Oz says next to my ear, and I smile. He must have crawled back up my body while I was recovering.

He unties his board shorts and frees his thick cock. In one swift motion, he's fully seated inside me and I'm too spent to move. My legs lie open, and my arms are spread above my head as he thrusts in and out of me.

His lips find mine, and the flavor of my desire passes to me. He bites my bottom lip, and all I can do in response is moan. I'm boneless, yet somehow, I'm building to another orgasm.

Oz's hands pin down my wrists, but the move is unnecessary. There's no way I'm moving, and no way I'm fighting against him. His powerful body thrusting on top of mine is the only thing I need to keep me in place.

"Oz," I moan, and he leans down, taking one of my hard nipples in his mouth. The little bite of pain is exactly what I need to send me over the edge, and he knows it.

Tensing up, I try to arch my back, but his hips keep me in place. I pull against the tight hold of his hands, but the grip is solid. My body fights against the new pleasure, but as always, Oz wins. I give over to his demands, and I skyrocket into a million fragments of sparkling light that I see around us when I open my eyes.

"So beautiful," I hear him say as he thrusts a final time and finds his ending inside my body.

He rolls us over so that I'm on top of him, my head cradled against his chest. His warm amber and honey scent embraces me as I breathe him in. It's the scent of home and safety, and also of love. His strong arms stroke my back as we listen to the waves crash.

I don't know how long we lie there, with the warm breeze blanketing us and the rhythm of his heartbeat soothing me. But after some time, Oz rolls me over and begins to love my body all over again.

"The first time I saw you, I thought I'd woken up in the land of Oz," he says, trailing kisses down my wrist. "It was like seeing color for the first time."

"I always liked picturing you as the wizard who saved me." I smile up at him, pressing my palm to his stubble.

"Oh no, Mallory. Don't you remember? She's the one who saved the wizard." He pauses, smiling back at me so big I can see his dimples.

"Anything for you, Miles."

"And *everything* for you, baby."

* * * * *

BONUS MATERIAL:

First time Miles and Mallory Meet

"PAIGE'S NOT EVEN responding to my text messages,"
I tell Ryan as I get out of the car. He shrugs as if to
say *what else is new?* He looks down both sides of the
street before motioning to one of his guys. Paige has
been giving me resistance for the past few months, and
now that she's actually here in the city, I feel like she's
stonewalling me.

Ryan may shrug, but I can see the tension in his body.
I chalk it up to us making an unplanned stop somewhere
that he hasn't scoped out in advance. Normally he'd
have fought me on something like this, but he's grown
to realize that when it comes to her, there is no stopping me. I should be stopping myself, but I can't seem
to keep my feet from closing the distance to the front
of the club. I tell myself I'm only going to have a look,
make sure she's okay. It's something I could easily ask
my security to do, but now she's too close. Too easy for
me to get to. It's as if I can't fight my own body.

Ryan motions to the bouncer, who lifts the rope as
we bypass the line. The club is crammed full of people, the music pumping, but as if I'm drawn to her, can
feel her, my eyes go right to where she's standing next
to the bar and everything else in the club fades away.

I'm once again moving, pushing myself through the crowd toward her.

I should stop, I really should. This isn't part of the plan, but I've waited so long, wanted for so long. I need a taste. Maybe it will cool all the emotions pumping through my body.

I watch Mallory's eyes move across the room and find myself following them to where Paige is standing. Ryan looms over Paige, most likely giving her an earful. Maybe he can talk some sense into her. Unlikely.

I look back at her and see that Mallory has her head tilted back, eyes closed as if listening to the music and feeling the beat. I stalk over to where she is, moving in behind her, wanting a smell. I lean in and inhale her scent, her sweetness filling my lungs.

The bartender glances over at me, and I take a step back, knowing I've been caught. Before he places her drink in front of her, I reach into my back pocket, grab my credit card and hand it over.

She turns slightly, looking over at me, and her eyes travel up my body until they land on my face. I smile at her, wanting to mask the other things I'm feeling right now. The things running through my mind. That she's mine. That soon I will know every part of her. Not what I read in my daily reports. Reports I haven't been getting lately. Likely part of the reason I've snapped and I'm breaking all those plans I've been making for us.

"You didn't ask," she says as the bartender brings my card over and hands it to me. I slip it back into my pocket.

"What would you have said?" I tease her as I sign the receipt and push it toward the bartender.

She examines me, running her eyes over my suit. This time she wants me to know what she's doing. Her eyes make my cock impossibly harder. It's been hard since I knew her little ass landed in New York. I can't help but run my eyes over her, too, enjoying what's finally in front of me.

She's got on tight black pants that mold to her curves, and heels that don't hold up against my height. I wonder if she likes what she sees as her eyes run over me. It's something I've never wondered before. Normally I don't care what others think of me, but with her I do.

"So?" I ask, finding myself closing the distance between us a little more, wanting her answer. Needing it.

"Definitely not," she says, smiling, before taking a sip of her whiskey, her full lips hitting the rim of the glass. I instantly become jealous of it. I want her lips on me. I want to know what they taste like. I've been wondering for years.

I both hate and love her words. I want her to want me, but I like that she doesn't easily give in. I can't help but laugh.

Her light eyes stare at me over the tumbler, and I find myself smiling at her again.

"Good thing I didn't ask," I tell her. I don't typically ask for anything. Ever. I take and tell. She moves in a little toward me, and I'm not even sure if she knows she's doing it. Her sweet scent hits me, and I ache to have more. I can't wait for that smell to coat me, my sheets and everything else I can get it on.

Patience, I remind myself. With great effort and restraint, I reach for her tumbler instead of her. I turn the glass to put my lips where hers were. I'll take whatever I can get tonight, and if this is all I can get, I'll still count it as a win.

I take a sip and am disappointed I can only taste the

whiskey, but I watch as her eyes light up with a flash of desire.

"I thought since I paid for it, I should at least get a taste." I smirk, turning the glass back to where I'd placed my mouth, and hand it to her. She takes a sip again from the same spot, and I have to fight a groan. She's playing with me. The sweet burn I feel isn't from the whiskey.

"Tell me your name." I move in a little closer, pushing her for more.

She eyes me like an inner battle is going on inside her.

"Let's not, shall we?" she says before turning back to the bar. She looks up and down, probably looking for the bartender. I want her eyes back on me. Finally, she turns a little. "Let's pretend this is the Emerald City and you're the wizard behind the curtain."

I can't stop from reaching out and touching her. Grabbing her full hip, letting my fingers sink into her, looking into her eyes. I don't like her pulling away from me. Not even a little. It burns deep. I've wanted this for so long.

"Please," I say as she stares up at me. A word I'm not used to saying.

She takes a step toward me, my fingers sink more into her hip in a possessive hold. "Mallory," she says. Then I watch as pink hits her cheeks. Her eyes move past me, and I follow them once again to Paige, who's still with Ryan. She taps her watch at Mallory, making me clench my jaw because I know what's coming. She's leaving. First I didn't want her in this place, and now I don't want her to leave. I want a little more, but I remind myself this is only the beginning.

"Are you leaving?"

She looks back up at me and gives me a disappointed smile. "It appears so."

"Give me your number," I say in a rush. I already have it. Hell, I have fucking tracking on her phone, but I want the go-ahead from her to finally text her.

She looks around hesitantly, like she's trying to come up with a good excuse why she shouldn't.

"If I ask your friend over there, will she give it to me?" I test her, wanting to know what she'd say. I know Paige made sure men didn't bother her, but for some reason I find myself wanting to test it. To know for sure.

She glances over at Paige and back to me with a smug smile on her perfect face, her little button nose scrunching a little. God, she's fucking perfect. "Not a chance."

I reach into my pocket, pulling my phone out anyway. I'm getting her number before I walk out of here. I have to have it now. There's no way I can go another day without talking to her. Or at least knowing that I can.

She lets out a cute little huff, before rattling off her number as I pretend to put it into my phone. Paige comes up next to us as I put it away. She looks between the two of us before dismissing me like she doesn't know who I am.

"You ready?" she says.

"Yeah. I'm right behind you," Mallory tells her, and Paige walks toward the entrance. Mallory turns to me, and I reach out, needing to touch her one more time tonight, because I'm not sure when I'll get to again. I run the edge of my knuckles along her jaw. I never knew skin could feel so soft. I'd bet everything I have that all of her feels this way.

"I wanted more," I whisper to myself.

Mallory stands there, staring up at me like she can't pull herself away either, and I wonder if she feels it, too. What I felt the first time I laid eyes on her. That I'd found what I'd been looking for my whole life. Something I didn't even know I was looking for to begin with.

"She's waiting," I finally say, nodding toward Paige, who's got one shoulder propped against the wall watching us, her eyes narrowed on me.

I reluctantly drop my hand and take a step back. I have to make myself, or I'll never let her go. *Slow*, I remind myself. We'll have her soon. I force a smile as I watch her turn and disappear.

I pull out my phone and text Ryan.

Me: Follow them home.

Ryan: Already on it.

When I slide into the back of my car, I can't stop myself from texting her.

Me: You tasted sweeter than I ever imagined.

IT FEELS LIKE FOREVER before she finally texts me back, but in reality it was only a second.

Mine: What do I call the man behind the curtain?

I feel myself smile.

OZ.

ACKNOWLEDGMENTS

WE'D LIKE TO thank Carina Press for taking on the two of us. We know it was like herding cats, but we tried to make our video chats extra special with our pajamas and demands for more glitter. We hope you enjoyed the show!

To our agent Laura Bradford, you cuss a lot, and we love you for it.

To our editor Angela James, your comments were a pain in the ass, but we still want to be friends. (Sorry for all the mom jokes.)

To our beta readers, Jessica Rupp, Lisa aka Belle, Rochelle Paige, Nicole Hart, Polly Matthews, Gi Paar and Angela Pullen. You guys were honest and insightful, and we swear we only said hateful things about you for seven whole minutes.

To Eagle, the most special bird in all the land. Thank you for being with us from day one, for telling us we could do this, and for not trying to escape from our basement. You're so pretty, and kind, and you smell good.

To Jen Frederick (Wands Up) thank you for being the best at everything and then showing us how to do it. You're not only an amazing mentor, but a solid shopping buddy. We love you more than your purse.

To Jeanette Mancine, our beloved panda, thank you

for being with us through all the hardest parts of this job. You made all the bad times brighter and were the rock we could rely on. Your encouragement and honesty brought this book to a whole new level. You're one in a million and we're so incredibly thankful to have you in our lives. We love you!

To all the readers who begged us for a longer book, and wouldn't stop asking until we did…thank you. You pushed us to reach a word count we never thought possible, and we cursed you the whole time!

And last, but always first: to our husbands. You love us despite all the early morning and late night voice texts we have to play out loud. You've supported us through trips across the country so we could edit together in one room and left you with the kids. You've forgiven us when we forgot to make dinner or bathe, and that's really what true love is, isn't it? Without the two of you, we'd still be thinking that writing was a nice idea. But because of you, it's a reality. Thank you both for making every one of our dreams come true.

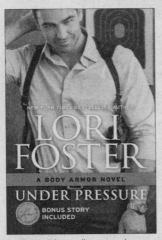

Private security gets a whole lot more personal and provocative in *The Protectors*, a sexy new series by *New York Times* bestselling author

BRENDA JACKSON

Strong enough to protect her.
Bold enough to love her.

When good girl Margo Connelly becomes Lamar "Striker" Jennings's latest assignment, she knows she's in trouble. And not just because he's been hired to protect her from an underworld criminal. The reformed bad boy's appeal is breaching all her defenses, and as the threats against her increase, Margo isn't sure which is more dangerous: the gangster targeting her, or the far too alluring protector tempting her to let loose.

Though Striker's now living on the right side of the law, he's convinced his troubled past keeps Margo out of his league. But physical chemistry explodes into full-blown passion when they go on the run together. Surrendering to desire could be a deadly distraction—or finally prove that he's the only man qualified to keep her safe, and win her love.

Available January 31!

Order your copy today.

Be sure to connect with us at:

Harlequin.com/Newsletters
Facebook.com/HarlequinBooks
Twitter.com/HQNBooks

www.HQNBooks.com

PHBRJ000